Born in the beautiful Georgian town of Whitehaven in Cumbria, J Lou McCartney has completed her second novel for all those readers who are eager to follow her on this incredible journey. J Lou said:

'There is no doubt that sex trafficking is global and a constant in today's media. The frightening thing is that for every sex trafficking ring that's closed down a dozen others will spring up in its place and so the vicious cycle goes on. As an author I was inspired and drawn to this topic and I hope as the dramatic storyline unfolds it will touch everyone who dares to read it.'

By the same author

De Marco Empire (Vanguard Press) 2008
ISBN 978184386 439 4

DANTE'S WAY

With much thanks once again to Pegasus Publishers, Vanguard Press, Mercy Kaggwa, the Editorial team and the Illustration department who have been professional throughout the publication process.

J Lou McCartney

DANTE'S WAY

Vanguard Press

VANGUARD PAPERBACK

© Copyright 2011
J Lou MacCartney

The right of J Lou McCartney to be identified as author of this work has been asserted by her in accordance with the Copyright, Designs and Patents Act 1988.

All Rights Reserved

No reproduction, copy or transmission of this publication may be made without written permission.
No paragraph of this publication may be reproduced, copied or transmitted save with the written permission of the publisher, or in accordance with the provisions of the Copyright Act 1956 (as amended).

Any person who commits any unauthorised act in relation to this publication may be liable to criminal prosecution and civil claims for damages.

A CIP catalogue record for this title is available from the British Library.

ISBN 978 184386 698 5

Vanguard Press is an imprint of
Pegasus Elliot MacKenzie Publishers Ltd.
www.pegasuspublishers.com

First Published in 2011

Vanguard Press
Sheraton House Castle Park
Cambridge England

Printed & Bound in Great Britain

Disclaimer

All the characters portrayed in this book are fictitious and any resemblance to actual persons living or dead is purely coincidental.

*In loving memory of the late Mona McCartney
and
Midnight*

Prologue

Present day
Lake Garda, Italy

Ella's nerves were in shreds as she contemplated the last couple of months, so much had happened in such a short space of time. She didn't think it was physically possible to cope with any more heartache. Sighing with frustration she tapped the rim of her wine glass.
"For goodness' sake, don't do that, it's driving me insane!" Yelena snapped at her.
"Oh, sorry I didn't realise I was doing it." Ella glanced at the state of her fingernails and shook her head. Once they were beautifully manicured and always well presented, but she had bitten them down to the quick.
"Where do you think Grazia is? It's so unlike her, she's usually so prompt." Yelena was becoming increasingly worried.
"What is it? Do you think something may have happened to her?" Ella knew that if it had then she would finally crack up; feeling emotionally drained she realised that she wasn't strong enough to deal with anything else right now. As she clenched and unclenched her fists she tried her best to keep it together, she had to for everyone's sake.
"What did you find out?" Yelena demanded.
"I should ask you the same question!"
"So, you don't trust me?" Yelena drawled in her distinct Russian accent.
"It's not about trust Yelena, I just want the truth, don't you?"
Yelena tutted. "My God, what happened to you Ella, you've changed?"
"That's no surprise after everything we've been through is it!" Ella snapped back.
"Just pull yourself together for Christ's sake."
"Who do you think you are talking to me like that? I'm not one of your servants." She paused. "Don't underestimate me

Yelena; if you think you can walk all over me you are very much mistaken!"

"My, my Ella, I don't know whether to admire the new you or despise you," Yelena joked, trying her best to calm the situation.

"Look, we've all been through hell and back, you don't come through things like that totally unscathed."

"You're right of course, I'm sorry if I offended you." Yelena was genuinely sorry.

"You are entitled to your opinion of course."

"Of course darling, let me top up your glass." Yelena proceeded to refill Ella's glass; a couple of drinks should diffuse the tension.

"It's such a beautiful day, isn't it?" Ella walked out onto the veranda. "The view is just stunning don't you think?" It should have been an ordinary day relaxing in the Italian sunshine, celebrating her second wedding anniversary with her beloved husband. She couldn't hold back any longer and the tears flowed; she hadn't cried when he was viciously murdered and now she didn't think that she was ever going to stop.

"Ella, please don't fall apart on me, not now, you are the strong one, the wisest of all of us." She put a soothing arm around her shoulder. "Nothing any of us can do will ever bring them back."

Nodding her head she knew Yelena was right. "It's about justice now. I won't rest until we get justice," she sobbed.

Yelena handed her a tissue. "Why don't you go and get cleaned up? You don't want Grazia to see you like this."

"Fine." Ella picked up her Gucci handbag and headed for the bathroom. Grazia had excellent taste, the bathroom was all white marble and the taps were eighteen carat gold, even the toilet seat was gold. Ella smiled remembering Nico insisting that he wouldn't put his backside on anything worth less than him.

*****

Grazia was trembling, what she had uncovered was going to shake them to the very core of their beings. She could scarcely believe that any of their husbands were actually involved in any of this. What would Yelena and Ella make of it? They were not fools; surely once they had seen the evidence it would be damning. She reached down for her mobile phone and pressed in the number.

"Ella, it's me Grazia."

"Oh thank God, where are you, I thought something awful had happened to you?"

"Listen to me, we have to go to the police, I have found something quite disturbing, something so shocking that it will change our lives forever."

"What, what is it?" Ella didn't understand what she was saying.

"I'll be there in a few minutes, just make sure you pour me a stiff drink, I'm going to need it." Grazia snapped the phone shut. Her heart was racing, they were all in extreme danger. She had to get them out of the villa before it was too late. Grazia's car screeched up the driveway, her heart was pounding so hard it felt like it was going to explode. Noticing a helicopter hovering close by she looked up at it for a few seconds. *That's unusual*, she thought. *Very unusual.* This was a quiet area and there were definitely no helipads nearby. Jumping out of the car she locked the door and glanced back up, it was getting nearer, something was wrong; she could feel it, very wrong indeed. It was them, it had to be, they were coming for her, for them, she thought she would have had more time. *Dear God, these people weren't messing around.* Panicking she threw off her stilettos and raced towards the villa to warn the others. But it was too late, there was a deafening hail of gunfire, Grazia didn't stand a chance, her body must have taken at least a dozen bullets. It was all over in seconds.

*****

Yelena had been watching the helicopter from the veranda when she saw Grazia screech up the drive. When she realised what was happening she made a dash into the villa just as the windows were being blasted out, the shrapnels of glass flew in every direction. Trying desperately to take cover she threw herself to the ground holding her arms in front of her face to protect herself. Feeling the red-hot pricks shoot into the back of her arms she looked at the damage: pieces of glass had pierced her skin and the blood was seeping out.

Hearing some kind of commotion Ella ran out of the bathroom. "Jesus Christ, what the hell was that?"

Yelena was slumped on the floor, the sight of her own blood made her feel nauseous. "Help me."

Ella could feel the hairs on the back of her neck stand on end, she was shaking with fright. "What... what happened?"

"I think Grazia is dead," was all she could say as she tried to get to her feet.

"No, no, what are you talking about, it can't be true!" she yelled.

"We must get out of here before they come back to finish the job." Yelena ripped open the sleeve of her white silk blouse which had turned crimson with blood.

"Come on." Watching her struggle Ella helped her stand up. "It's not as bad as it looks, honestly," she sighed.

"You never could lie." Yelena felt queasier as she surveyed the wound.

"It's going to be all right. I'll take you to the hospital."

"No, no, it's not safe, if they found Grazia here then they can find us anywhere." She paused. "How can we be sure that they are not going to come back?"

"We can't. I just want to know who these people are and what it is they want from us."

"I wish we knew. Now, you'd better go and check Grazia's car, she must have found something out and we need to know what that is."

"Okay." Ella's voice was surprisingly quiet and calm. She took a sharp intake of breath as she walked out onto the drive. Grazia was face down on the ground, her body was still. Bracing herself for the worst Ella checked her pulse. Nothing. She was definitely dead. Poor, beautiful Grazia, she didn't deserve to die in this way and what for? Who could do such a terrible, terrible thing? Ella felt the bile rise up in her throat, for she had to search Grazia, see what they were after. Gently she pulled Grazia's handbag from underneath her. "I'm sorry," she whispered to the lifeless body in front of her. What the hell was she supposed to be looking for? She emptied the contents onto the driveway and looked through Grazia's personal items. There was a picture of her husband Nico, they had been a handsome couple, some would even say perfect. They certainly complemented each other and they had been so in love. What a shame that they were both dead. *At least they're with each other now*, she told herself. *Not like me and Marcus.* He had worshipped the ground she walked on; it was several years before he won her heart and thank God he had persisted in pursuing her. She threw everything back into the bag and picked up Grazia's car keys. Opening the driver's door she frantically searched the interior, there was nothing to be found. Picking up Grazia's jacket she looked in the pockets, still nothing. She checked the glove box and the boot, but it was to no avail, *whatever Grazia knew had died with her*, she thought. Walking back towards the body she gently placed the jacket over her. "Rest in peace." Knowing Grazia was religious she did the sign of the cross. "Bless you, you were a good friend to me and I'll miss you," she whispered softly.

*****

Yelena grabbed the bottle of vodka and slugged it down, for the pain she told herself as she prised a rather large piece of glass out of her arm. The blood seeped out. Gritting her teeth she held her arm out in front of her and poured neat vodka over it. "Jesus Christ!" she yelled, "that really fucking hurt."

"Yelena what on earth are you doing?" Ella was watching the spectacle from the doorway.

"Just see if you can find a bandage or something to tie around this," Yelena said through gritted teeth as she gulped down the rest of the vodka.

"I don't think this is the time for drinking, do you?" Ella grimaced as she looked at her arm. "I think you may need stitches."

Yelena pulled a silk scarf out of her holdall. "Here, this will do –" She thrust it into her hand "– and be quick."

Ella wrapped her arm as best she could. "There, it's not ideal, but it should be ok until we get to the hospital."

"I told you that we are not going to any damn hospital." Yelena was like a woman possessed as she shoved her clothes and toiletries into her holdall.

"What are you doing?" Ella demanded.

"What does it look like... well is Grazia dead?"

Ella nodded as she watched Yelena in a total frenzy. "Stop, you're scaring me."

Yelena froze. "We need to leave, right now!" Her voice was on the verge of hysteria.

"But nobody knows that we are here, we came in a taxi remember, don't you think if they knew we would be dead by now too!"

"Yes, yes but it's only a matter of time before they realise we are here and then they will come back for us."

"I'm afraid we can't go anywhere in Grazia's car, the tyres were shot out, what are we going to do?"

"The boat, yes the boat! That's how we will make our escape," Yelena exclaimed. "Get your things, we're out of here!"

Ella wasn't too sure, what did either of them know about boats. Yes they had been on many and occasionally steered but they had no real experience of sailing. "We're fucked aren't we?"

"We'll learn as we go, come on!"

"We need help."

"No, not until we find out who's behind this... we can't risk trusting anyone and I mean anyone, do you understand?"

"Yes, I'm not a bloody idiot Yelena!"

"I'm sorry I didn't mean to snap at you."

"There is one person I could go to, we can trust him implicitly," Ella muttered to herself, not meaning to speak out loud.

"Who is it?"

"It doesn't matter who it is, let's discuss it on the boat."

The two women hugged. "We'll be fine," Ella told her. "You'll see."

As they made their way down to the jetty, Grazia's mobile began ringing. Yelena grabbed Ella's arm. "Don't answer it!"

"It could be important." She looked at the handset: *number not recognised.* "Hello, who is this?"

"You know what we are looking for and if you don't give it to us you're a dead woman!"

The voice sent shivers down Ella's spine. "I... I don't know what you are talking about." she gasped.

"Give it to me." Yelena snatched the phone from her hands. "You don't scare us. You have murdered our husbands and now Grazia." She paused. "You see we have nothing to lose anymore, so do your worst!" she said defiantly.

"Make no mistake, I want the disk or I will take out your fucking mother, father, sister and her two children!" the man threatened her. "I will do it!"

Seeing the grim look on Yelena's face, Ella quickly retrieved the phone. "This is Ella Treymayne, truly we do not know what you want, you have to believe me."

"The disk sweetheart and there'll be no more murders!"

"What disk?"

"Enough chat, Grazia had it, so you'd better search her things, I'll be in touch."

The call ended.

"Jesus, who the hell was that man and what is this disk that they want, I don't understand!"

"I think you had better contact this person you say we can trust. You are right. We do need help."

"Are you sure?"

"It looks like we have no choice now Ella." Yelena looked pale and drawn. "Whatever they are after they are prepared to kill for it and I for one don't want to die like Grazia."

Ella nodded her head as they stepped onto the boat. "See if you can get this thing started and I'll make the call." Her heart pounded as she punched in Dante's private number.

"Yes?"

She recognised his voice immediately. "It... it's me Ella."

"Ella, my God, Ella it's such a pleasure to hear from you, how have you been?"

"Dante, I need your help."

"My darling Ella, you know I will do anything I can." He paused. "What's wrong?"

"I can't get into that right now, I just need your protection, there's somebody after me, it's a matter of life or death," she babbled, saying more than she had intended to.

"Ella, I never thought I would hear from you ever again, not after what happened between us."

"Will you help me or not?" Ella snapped.

"Of course, where are you?"

"I'm on Nico de Luca's boat in Lake Garda."

"Does anybody else know where you are?"

"I don't think so."

"Good."

"Dante, we can't trust anyone, you are our last hope and believe me when I say how difficult it was to make this call."

"Just stay where you are and I'll send someone for you, don't call anyone, anyone at all," he told her.

"How will I know who it is?"

"He'll have a code word, '*Bella* Ella'." He waited for her reaction.

Ella's mind flashed back as she remembered how deeply she had once loved him, in fact if she was truthful to herself part of her still loved him and she hadn't expected that. "Very well," she murmured, the son of a bitch was reminding her of what they once had, but it was such a long time ago.

"And Ella, I can't wait to see you, you know I have never stopped loving you."

Ella snapped the phone shut, her head was spinning. Why did he have to say that to her now, now when she was feeling so lost, so vulnerable? He was stirring up all those old suppressed feelings she still had for him, ones she had buried or thought she had years ago. Half of her was excited about the prospect of seeing him again and yet the other half was wary, very wary indeed.

Chapter One

Ten years earlier
London, England

Ella was enjoying a pleasant evening with four of her girlfriends when she felt someone staring at her. Looking up she saw a smartly dressed young man, tall and lean with dark hair, his blue eyes and tanned skin making him look foreign. He smiled at her, unable to resist she smiled back and lowered her eyelids. He was gorgeous, she thought, and that dimple in the middle of his chin was so sexy.

"Are you listening Ella?" Her girlfriend nudged her.

"Er, sorry what were you saying, I was miles away."

"Just saying that it won't be the same without Tara, we'll miss her," Carolyn said.

"I know, we'll miss all the gossip and of course your shining personality," Ella told her.

"Oh, please don't you'll have me in floods of tears and I don't want to ruin my make-up!" Tara blurted.

They were interrupted by a dashing young waiter who presented them with a bottle of champagne and five glasses. "These are with the compliments of the gentleman over there." He pointed towards the striking man with the dimpled chin at the bar.

Ella blushed as he raised his glass and winked at her. She had never believed in love at first sight but now she wasn't so sure, there was something about this young handsome man that made her heart race.

"Methinks he has the hots for you Ella," Carolyn giggled. "You've gone all pink!"

"Me? You think he has the hots for me?" Ella's voice was incredulous.

"Of course he has, it's obvious."

The waiter popped the cork on the champagne and dutifully filled their glasses. "Enjoy."

Ella lifted her glass and looked back over to the bar. He was still looking at her, smiling, it was as if they were the only two people in the room. Without realising it she had given him the cue to come over and he wasn't wasting any time in doing so. He headed straight towards her.

"I hope you don't mind me taking the liberty of buying you beautiful young ladies some champagne." His voice was warm and rich and definitely foreign.

"Not at all, it was very kind of you," Tara told him.

"Ah, but where are my manners, please allow me to introduce myself, I am Dante Moretti." He bowed.

"I'm Ella Reynolds; this is Carolyn, Tara, Becky and Siobhan."

"Charmed I'm sure." He kissed Ella's hand.

It was like an electric shock surging through her entire body. God, what was it about him that made her react like this, for once in her life she was lost for words.

"So, Dante, where are you from then?" Becky asked him.

"Ah, so you noticed the accent and here I am thinking that I had mastered the English accent." He laughed. "I am from Milan."

"Wow, Milan is so beautiful," Becky gushed. "I have been several times you know," she bragged.

But Dante only had eyes for Ella. "Now, tell me why there are no men here?" It was his way of finding out if Ella was available.

"It's a girly evening." Becky was totally smitten and it showed, she was desperate to get his attention. "Why don't you sit down, Dante?"

It was embarrassing watching Becky practically throwing herself at him and Ella was cringing.

Dante smiled. "You don't mind if I sit next to you Ella." He didn't wait for her response, just pulled up his chair and squashed between her and Carolyn. "So, you have boyfriends?" he persisted.

"I'm engaged to a lovely man," sighed Siobhan as she showed Dante her ring.

"That looks very expensive, he must really adore you."

"Oh yes he does." Siobhan giggled.

"And you?" he asked Tara.

"My boyfriend is French and very, very rich!"

It was Carolyn's turn. "I've been seeing a guy called Charlie for a couple of months but it's nothing serious, he's packing his bags as we speak and off on a world tour."

"Perhaps you should consider going with him?" Dante asked.

"As I said it's not serious."

Becky was all breathless as she spoke. "I'm not currently dating anyone, but I am open to offers right now."

Carolyn kicked her underneath the table. Boy, she was making a total fool of herself and becoming progressively worse. She was an idiot if she didn't realise he only had eyes for Ella.

Becky scowled at her and continued to try and get Dante's attention. "So, Dante what are you doing in the UK?"

"Ah, now that would be telling." He turned his back on her and took Ella's hand. "So, are you single?" he whispered in her ear.

His warm breath on her neck made her shiver. "Yes, I was recently dumped by my playboy boyfriend."

"Oh, I find that very hard to believe." He studied her appearance: she was stunning, a beautiful blonde with green eyes. She was very slim, but shapely in all the right places, he thought, as his eyes swept over her body.

"It's true," Becky interrupted. "Rupert was an arsehole; he didn't know a good thing when he had it, always playing the field."

"So, why did he, as you say, dump you?" Dante ignored Becky; the damn girl was beginning to grate on his nerves.

"He... how can I put this?" Ella was struggling to put it into words.

Once more to Ella's annoyance Becky jumped in. "He basically wanted her to have a threesome with another girl he was also seeing and when she refused he dumped her."

"What?" Dante was furious. "He dared to treat you in that way, who is this person? I will have words with him!"

"It doesn't matter, to tell the truth I'm pleased to be rid of him, he was quite controlling."

"Rupert Giles is his name, he's due to inherit his daddy's construction business, Giles Incorporations Ltd." Becky was loving the look on Ella's face and she knew talking about Rupert still made her feel uncomfortable.

Due to inherit his daddy's business, hmm we'll see about that thought Dante. He hated disrespect to women, especially to a woman like Ella.

"So, do you mind me asking if you are a natural blonde?" Dante changed the subject.

"A lady never tells," Ella laughed. "No, I'm really a mousy brown colour, quite boring really."

"I would totally disagree, you would look breathtaking whatever your hair colour, I can assure you."

Ella blushed once more. "You're too kind."

"Don't be embarrassed, you are one of the most beautiful women I have ever met, has anyone ever told you?"

"Er, no."

"Well they should."

Ella nearly choked on her champagne; she had never been flattered like this before and she didn't know how to react.

"So, I never asked what you young ladies were celebrating."

"Tara is going to live in France with her family and of course to be nearer Jacques, so I guess this is her farewell party," Siobhan told him.

"But you will all keep in touch, yes?"

"But of course, we will visit as soon as she settles in," Carolyn promised.

"Well, I'm afraid I must leave you to it, I have a prior engagement." He leaned over and whispered into Ella's ear. "I would really love to see you again, what do you say?"

Ella was lost for words, his hot breath in her ear had totally distracted her and all she could do was smile at him like a blithering idiot.

"I'll take your silence as a yes then." He pressed his business card into her hand. "Please call me tomorrow and we will meet up, do you promise?"

"Yes," Ella said in a quiet voice.

"Good, that's settled then."

She watched as he left the bar, he was something else that was for sure.

"So, what did he say?" Carolyn asked.

"He... he wants to meet me tomorrow."

"And, are you?"

"I'm not sure, there's something about him, something that scares me a little."

"It's just one date Ella," Becky reminded her. "If you don't want him, I can always go," she half joked. "Jesus, I would have jumped at the chance."

"We know you would have!" Carolyn laughed.

"Well, he was hot, wasn't he?" Becky blurted.

The girls all agreed as they raised their glasses to Tara. "Here's to you and a wonderful new life in France."

Chapter Two

Ella shared a flat with Carolyn in Kensington. They had grown up together and attended the same boarding school; they both came from wealthy families and hadn't worked a day in their lives, in fact they were extremely privileged. The two young women were totally grounded with well rounded personalities and knew that they were indeed very fortunate. The flat was totally luxurious and they had enjoyed splashing out decorating it.

Ella took the business card from her purse and studied it: *Dante Moretti, Computer Programmer, Moretti Corporation, Milan, Italy.*

Carolyn playfully grabbed the card from out of her hands. "Oh my God, another wealthy playboy, you seem to attract them these days!" she teased. "Lucky you."

"You know money doesn't matter to me, I'm set up for life, what with the trust fund and father's thriving business!"

"Yes, but Milan is the fashion capital of the world – wow, fashion, fashion, fashion girl! I'm thinking shopping and having an absolute blast, it will be wonderful!"

"True." Ella giggled. "Do you think someone like him could be single, because I for one find that very hard to believe."

"That's a good point," Carolyn agreed. "But the fact remains that you are very attracted to him, as he is to you."

"I guess so, but still I have to wonder what I am getting myself into. I mean, he was very smooth wasn't he?"

"You're so cynical at times Ella, just take it one step at a time, you deserve some fun, especially after that rat Rupert, he was one sick pig!"

"Thanks for that Carolyn."

"For what, honey?"

"You just make a lot of sense. Maybe you should have been a counsellor."

"*Moi*, sensible? Never!"

Ella braced herself as she picked up the phone and dialled Dante's number. "No, I can't do it!" she exclaimed as she replaced the receiver.

"Don't be silly." Carolyn picked up the card and dialled the number. She put her finger to her lips, indicating for Ella to be quiet. "Oh, hello this is Ella Reynolds' personal assistant; I would like to speak with Mr Moretti, Dante Moretti please if he is available."

Ella had to put her hand over her mouth to stop herself from laughing out loud. Carolyn sounded so ridiculous with that put-on posh accent, she was such a hoot at times.

"Is this Mr Moretti?"

Dante was impatient to know why Ella hadn't called him herself. "Yes," he barked down the phone, he didn't have time for games.

"Miss Reynolds would very much like to meet with you for dinner and suggests that you make the necessary arrangements and, of course, collect her on the way."

"Oh, she does, does she?"

"If it is a problem Mr Moretti, I can assure you Miss Reynolds has plenty more options, after all her company is well sought after."

Ella had a look of horror spread across her face as she tried unsuccessfully to prise the phone out of her friend's hand.

Carolyn slapped her hand out of the way. "Yes eight o'clock will be fine. I'll just give you the address."

"So, what did he say?" Ella demanded.

"He would be delighted to take you out for dinner, his treat of course."

"Did he say where he was taking me?"

"Sorry, honey, he didn't elaborate, but you can bet it will be somewhere exclusive!"

Chapter Three

Dante was desperate to meet Ella but he had some pressing business to take care of first and he was hoping everything ran according to plan.

The meeting took place in a recently renovated café bar, which wasn't open to the public yet. Alessandro Esposito was not a happy man and it showed. "So, tell me Moretti, what the fuck is this all about? Some of us have real jobs to be getting on with."

Without warning Dante launched himself across the table and had Esposito by the throat squeezing it tight. Two of Esposito's men grabbed Dante's arms, but he was like a man possessed, his strength was amazing for someone so lithe. Slowly he released his grip, turning around he punched one of the men full in the gut and kicked the other in the groin. Both men dropped to the ground in agony.

"That wasn't a very nice welcome, Signor Esposito, are you going to hear me out or do you want some more violence?" Dante didn't wait for his response. "Signor Mancini has noticed, shall we say, some minor discrepancies; do you see where I am coming from with this?"

Still unable to breathe properly Esposito nodded.

"As a gesture of goodwill Signor Mancini will forget about what has happened, which is very generous of him, don't you think?"

"Really?" Esposito spluttered.

"Yes, really, on the condition that you agree to sixty-forty split."

"You're having a fucking laugh aren't you?"

"I'm deadly serious." Dante stared at him with those intense blue eyes, which were totally void of any emotion.

"That won't go down well with Franco and Ritchie."

"That's the deal, take it or suffer the consequences, either way I don't really give a shit, it's your choice."

"It isn't much of a fucking choice, Moretti."

"So, you know who I am then?" Dante laughed.

"You little punk, who the fuck do you think you are? I'll tell you who you are, a fucking nobody. Up and coming are you? You'll get yours mark my words!" he vehemently spat out the words.

"Oh, I know exactly who I am and that's exactly what you should be worrying about and don't threaten me, Esposito," he snarled at him. "You wouldn't win!"

Esposito couldn't believe the audacity of the two-bit punk. Moretti's reputation as a hard man preceded him; he was nothing short of a vicious thug. Still Esposito took comfort in the fact that Moretti hadn't killed anyone and that meant he was safe at least for now.

"Do we have a deal?"

Against his better judgment and with great reluctance Esposito stood up and shook his hand. Dante shocked him by giving him a big fat hug and insolently planted a kiss on both his cheeks. "Nice doing business with you, Signor Esposito." Dante straightened his tie in the mirror and admired his reflection grinning back at him, hmm. *Not bad*, he thought. *I scrubbed up pretty well.*

After he left Esposito went berserk and smashed the place up in sheer frustration. One day that smug little bastard would pay for insulting him like this and he hoped it would be sooner rather than later. Just because the cocksucker was on Mancini's payroll and happened to be his nephew didn't give him automatic rights to treat him in this fashion. The little prick thought he was some kind of God or something. Esposito sat on the floor and wiped the beads of sweat from his forehead, breathing deeply.

"What do you want me to do boss?" A voice interrupted his thoughts.

Esposito glared at his minder. "Nothing for now, if we take that bastard out it could have serious repercussions, a turf war between the families and at this moment in time we are not in a position to deal with that."

*****

Vitelli had witnessed the violent display between his boss and Moretti and decided to personally take the matter into his own hands.

No one disrespected Esposito.

Chapter Four

Dante wasted no time in contacting his uncle. "Yes, he agreed, everything ran smoothly."

"Good, you have passed the first test; I will let you know in due course what I require you to do next."

"Ok." He abruptly ended the call, silly old fool, what did he take him for some kind of idiot? He knew he wasn't in the UK purely to rough someone up.

He drove up to the luxury apartment block as per Ella's personal assistant's instructions. He had to laugh at her audacity though, PA my backside! It was a shame that he was probably going to have to take out her father; he'd been paying unusual interest in their business this side of the ocean and the Mancini family didn't like meddlers, especially one as powerful as Mr Reynolds. *What a shame this fling with Ella will be short-lived. There could never be a future between them. Oh well, such is life*, Dante thought. He rang Ella's apartment from reception and, when he heard the delight in her voice about the dozen red roses and a diamond bracelet he had especially couriered over, he felt really pleased with himself.

Ella descended from the lift wearing a red strapless top, complete with a short black skirt and black stilettos. Her golden hair flowing in the breeze made her look almost angelic, he enthused. Coolly he walked over to her and kissed her hand. "The bracelet looks good on you, no?"

"Oh Dante, you shouldn't have really, it's so beautiful." The diamonds shimmered in the light.

"I think you are the kind of woman who should be showered with many such gifts."

Ella smiled adoringly at the handsome young man in front of her, he was one of the most generous and thoughtful men she had ever encountered.

"Come, I have taken the liberty of booking us into a very delicious Italian restaurant." He paused. "Tell me, you do like Italian don't you?" He turned to her, his rich voice was verging on suggestive.

Ella knew exactly what he meant. "I am partial to a nice bit of pasta from time to time," she flirted with him.

Dante chortled, she had skirted around that brilliantly. "That is just what I wanted to hear."

Ella somehow doubted it, there was something powerfully sexy about him and he knew it. She felt herself inexplicably drawn to him, he was so charming.

The food was excellent and the company even better; Ella found herself intrigued by this drop-dead gorgeous Italian.

"So, my beautiful one, what would you like to do next?" Once more he was coaxing her, daring her to give in to him and her own desires.

"I really don't mind, honestly."

Dante's mobile went off. "Hold that thought, please excuse me *uno momento*."

He was talking in Italian and Ella couldn't understand a word of it. She studied his facial expressions and tried to work out what was going on. Whatever the exchange was about, Dante didn't look very happy.

"I'm so sorry, Ella, that was business."

"Oh?"

"I'm afraid that I must cut the evening short, one of my major client's computer systems has just crashed and I have to go and fix it, it's my job." He noted the disappointment on her face. "I'll make it up to you, I promise."

Ella couldn't believe her ears. "But we haven't even had dessert yet," she protested, gutted that he had to go.

"Here." Dante threw a wad of notes on the table and summoned the waiter. "Please get the lady whatever she wants, this should cover it."

"But…"

Dante took her hand and gently kissed it. "I'm truly sorry, Ella, really I am, but it is an emergency."

"What kind of emergency?" Her words fell on deaf ears as he had almost cleared the room. She flipped open her mobile and dialled Carolyn. "Hi, it's me. You'll never guess what happened!"

"Oh, no what?" Carolyn's heart sank, poor Ella, she was stunning but yet for some strange reason she never seemed to have any luck with dating men.

"It's Dante, he just threw a load of money on the table and I mean a lot of money and then left me on my own, he just took off, something to do with work. Oh Carolyn it's so embarrassing people are looking at me!"

"Where are you and I'll come and get you? It's going to be all right."

Ella gave her the address of the restaurant and sat tight as she glanced around the room.

Vitelli was sitting at the bar wondering what to do, this woman obviously didn't mean much to Moretti by the way he dashed off. No, he thought, there was no point in taking her out, Moretti wouldn't even bat an eyelid. He would just have to find another way to make him pay and pay he would.

If only Ella knew the real danger she may have been in, if she had been more involved with Dante her future would have been snuffed out there and then.

Chapter Five

"What is the urgency, I was just enjoying some leisure time?" Dante was really mad.

"I really don't give a damn, the orders are to take out Esposito and take him out now," Victor told him.

"I thought I was only supposed to rough him up for fuck's sake, why didn't Zio Mancini tell me this before?"

"Things have changed dramatically. He was taking more than the piss and now he must be silenced, permanently."

"That doesn't give us much time to arrange alibis does it?" Dante remarked, in his game alibis were essential. "How does he want it done?"

"That's entirely up to you, I know his movements and I'll fill you in on the way," Victor told him.

"But what has happened since I saw Esposito?" Dante persisted.

"Look, you know Mancini, he has eyes and ears everywhere and I mean everywhere."

"Meaning?"

"Esposito is planning retaliation. We have a couple of guys on the inside, fair enough he isn't going to do something right away, but we can't afford for him to come up with a plan, he is very clever, Dante. We need to show him who is the boss and silence him now!" Victor exclaimed.

Dante's brain went into overdrive, they knew Esposito's every move it shouldn't be difficult to eradicate him. He would wait until the small hours when Esposito was leaving his mistress's house, when he was alone in the dark.

*****

"I can't understand why he just rushed off like that, it was so romantic and then it was over in an instant!" Ella was totally dismayed. "You know what? I think I am just meant to remain single for the rest of my life."

"Oh, Ella, just forget about him, he's a complete idiot to abandon you like that. There's plenty more fish in the sea, you know."

"I don't think I'll ever fall in love, I can honestly say that I will never give my heart one hundred per cent to anybody."

"Come on, honey, it was just one date, his loss." Carolyn was trying her best to lift her friend's spirits.

"I just feel so foolish."

"Don't, you did nothing wrong."

"What if he hated my company and staged that call to get away from me?"

"Now you are being completely ridiculous Ella."

"Why do I always scare men away?"

"It's not you, it's them. Why don't we have a cocktail now that I'm here?" Carolyn suggested as she glanced around the restaurant.

Vitelli observed the two young women as he sipped his brandy. Moretti obviously meant something to the blonde woman. What a shame and what a waste, she certainly was a pretty little thing.

"No, let's have one back home. I just want to get out of here."

"Ok, honey, whatever you want."

They walked past Vitelli who shot Carolyn an admiring look, but Carolyn was oblivious to his interest in her. It appeared that her only concern was for the welfare of her friend.

They sat on the balcony of the apartment and sipped a tequila sunrise. "It's such a beautiful evening isn't it?" Carolyn asked Ella.

Ella sighed. "What do I do wrong, Carolyn? I just can't seem to keep a man." She resigned herself to the fact that she would end up an old spinster.

"Here, have another tequila, it's your favourite, I made it extra strong."

"Oh, you know how I like them," Ella giggled. Already she was feeling slightly tipsy.

"That's better, Ella, forget about him, he's nothing."

Maybe nothing to you Carolyn, Ella thought but he was something to me.

*****

Dante bided his time; he was good at that and getting better every day. He watched Esposito swagger into his girlfriend's house and laughed when he took out a breath spray. "I think we'll let him have his fun first and then finish him off, it's only fair. I mean, it's his last day on the planet after all."

Victor nodded, so Moretti wasn't totally heartless after all he thought. That indeed made a change from the rest of his family who didn't give a damn about humanity unless they personally profited from it.

Esposito was busy pleasuring his mistress, enjoying her screams for more. His big fat belly bounced onto her slender frame, but Rita didn't mind, after all he was well endowed and she enjoyed him taking her. The apartment was all courtesy of his money, and that gave her every reason to keep him happy. She thought about the massive pay-off she was just about to receive and licked her lips in delight. What a shame this would be the last fuck she would ever have off him but she wanted him to remember it vividly. His sweaty body was dripping all over her and his huge belly was like a lead weight squashing down on her. She thanked God that she was a superb actress as she arched her back and writhed underneath him, it was nearly over, just a few more seconds now. Once he was out of the way she would target an even wealthier version, after all sex was just sex to her whoever it was with.

After Esposito was spent Rita casually jumped off the bed. Esposito pulled her roughly by the arm. "Did I say I was finished?"

Rita shook free from his grasp and smiled sweetly. "I'm just getting us a nice ice-cold glass of that fabulous champagne you brought, just how you like it and then we can begin round two." She winked seductively at him.

Esposito nodded, Rita was so thoughtful. He was knackered anyway, getting too old to keep a mistress and a wife. He dozed off.

Rita mixed the drug into his glass just as instructed by the nice young Italian who was going to pay her a handsome wedge. Coming back into the bedroom she switched the lights on and off three times.

"Er ... what's going on?" Esposito blinked.

"Just trying to get your attention, stud." She blew him a kiss.

"You're insatiable, do you know that?"

"It's all because of you!" Rita giggled in her childlike voice.

Esposito laughed too, Rita just knew the right things to say to him and it turned him on. She was scantily clad in a red love heart thong, complete with red tassels dangling from the tips of her nipples. "Do you like it?" she laughed as she rubbed her breasts.

"Oh yes, very much, come here!" he demanded.

"First drink your champagne," she insisted as she turned up the music and began to dance seductively around the room.

Esposito was beginning to get a second wind. *God how he wanted her* he mused as he sipped on his champagne. What a woman! She would do whatever he wanted, whenever he wanted, he was one lucky son of a bitch. Still he was under no illusions, this busty young redhead would never look at him under normal circumstances, but his money spoke volumes. Esposito started to feel relaxed, too relaxed, he tried to speak but no words came out. He tried to move his body but nothing happened, he was paralysed. *Fucking bitch! Fucking whore! What had she done to him?* the words screamed in his brain. *She's betrayed me! The slut has betrayed me* were his final thoughts as he slipped into unconsciousness.

Dante and his two sidekicks arrived, he handed a large holdall to Rita. "You did real good."

Rita's eyes lit up as she placed the bag on the table and unzipped it, this man was as good as his word, she was delighted. Thank God, she thought, they could have so easily have disposed of her too. Her greedy little eyes darted over the money.

Esposito was one heavy fucker and it took all three men to haul him into the laundry basket. Dante nodded to Rita, no words were needed, it had been easy, a win-win situation all round.

They made his demise look like a suicide as they placed him into his car and started the engine. Dante took out the hose pipe and connected it from the exhaust into the car. Esposito had a very easy death in his book, they could have tortured and mutilated him, but that wasn't really his style.

Everyone would think that he had just had enough, especially when his wife had just found out about his indiscretions with a prostitute. And the delectable Rita would never be found. She would be on a plane out of the country with a new life waiting for her in Spain where she originated from. With Esposito's wife finding out about the other woman, the humiliation would have been too much for him to bear.

Dante was proud of himself; there was no trace of any foul play, only poor pathetic Esposito taking himself out of the picture for good.

Chapter Six

Philip Reynolds was in his mid-fifties, happily married to Helen with a grown-up twenty-four-year-old daughter, called Ella. He was ready to retire after making his millions in the car industry. He was tying up some loose ends when he discovered something that disturbed him. Money had been systematically siphoned out of his business accounts at an alarming rate. One day the amount would come in and then go straight back out again. Somebody was cooking the books and he was livid, what the devil was going on? His business was being used for some underhand dealing of that he was absolutely certain, but who or what was behind it?

He called an urgent board meeting, he had to get to the bottom of it and quickly. These men he had employed were faithful to the company and he trusted them implicitly. But one of them had to be involved in laundering this dirty money through his accounts and he damn well wanted to know who that person was.

Philip was an old-fashioned man of honour and he was determined to keep the sorry state of affairs under wraps. By keeping the matter confidential he hoped that someone would confess, otherwise he would have no alternative but to bring in the police. The last thing he wanted was a long drawn-out police investigation in the public spotlight. All he had was two weeks to put in until he was due to retire, what awful bad timing to discover something like this! He had already approached Marcus Treymayne from his Sussex branch and the paperwork was all drawn up and duly signed by both parties. Treymayne would be a good, decent honest boss; he had passion and drive which would be required to sustain the already established business. It was in excellent shape, the market was widening all the time and Marcus would be ideal to seize each and every opportunity that came his way.

The secret meeting was scheduled to take place in a private suite in The Albert Hotel. The key people were already waiting for him wondering what all the commotion was about. It was unusual for Philip to call any kind of meeting outside the office.

Philip checked his briefcase; he had prepared six reports, one for each key player on the board detailing what he had discovered. He was careful to leave one in his safety deposit box just in case something happened to him. These were dangerous times and he knew he was potentially in deep trouble. As he got into his Rolls Royce and headed for the hotel he sighed – this wasn't supposed to happen, not now, not ever, he was a good businessman, a straight one who worked within the law. He could only imagine who was capable of such a thing. How could one of his most trusted employees do this to him, now of all times when he was on the verge of taking early retirement?

He had told his wife nothing of his discovery, it was best she was kept in the dark. Helen was such a worrier and would have insisted on involving the police, but the problem was that his business would become tainted and nobody would touch it ever again. Everything he had built up from scratch all his life would disintegrate, it would certainly be a scandal and then the business would be in ruins.

Helen was cooking his favourite meal that night, a nice beef roast dinner he was already looking forward to. She excelled in the kitchen. He patted his well-rounded stomach and smiled to himself; yes this was a result of his wife's excellent cuisine over the years. The day had turned out to be long and rather worrying, but hopefully someone would confess and he would be able to sort it out with no police presence. The meeting should shed some light on what exactly was going on.

Philip put his favourite CD on to help him relax, classical music always relaxed him. His nerves were really frazzled and he needed to calm himself down. He had heart problems in the past and he certainly didn't need any more stress right now.

He noticed a young lady on the side of the road who appeared to have broken down; he drove past her and then felt guilty. Reversing back he noted the look of distress on the lady's face, he was a sucker for a pretty face. Looking at his watch he sighed, damn it he was definitely going to be late for his own board meeting. Being a perfect gentleman he just couldn't leave the young woman stranded, it could have been his own daughter and he hoped that if this ever happened to her then some kind person would stop and help her out.

He got out of the car and approached her. "What seems to be the problem?"

"Oh, thank God you stopped. I have been here for over thirty minutes and not one person stopped to help me."

"I'm sorry to say that it's today's society unfortunately."

"I appear to have a flat tyre but no jack to change it."

Philip smiled, this was his domain and it had been many years since he last had to change a tyre but he was always prepared. "Allow me; I have a jack in the boot."

"Oh thank you, you are so kind."

"It's my pleasure young lady."

As Philip opened the boot of his car he noticed another vehicle pulling onto the hard shoulder. While he was searching the boot a man walked up behind him and without warning stabbed him in his lower back. Philip slumped to the ground in a pool of blood, his life ebbing away before him. There was so much more living he wanted to do, so many things to sort out but there was no time now. He thought of his beautiful wife Helen and his wonderful daughter Ella. As he took his last breath he imagined Helen in his arms, until we meet again my love.

The young man ransacked the car and retrieved the desperately sought briefcase complete with all the evidence. Just for the fun of it he went back to Philip's limp body and searched his pockets. He removed his wallet, gold chain, rolex watch and even the rings from his fingers.

It had all been over in a flash and Philip Reynolds died alone at the side of the road.

Chapter Seven

As Dante was already preoccupied disposing of Esposito he sent some of his associates to finish Philip Reynolds once and for all and in a way he was glad not to be involved in his demise especially after he had just met Ella. It was a bizarre coincidence that they had met, purely by chance. He didn't feel bad about her father's murder, it had to be done, he was going to blow their cover and he couldn't allow that to happen. He was one hundred per cent faithful to his uncle and family came first he reassured himself, although if Ella ever found out he would deny everything; it was best she knew nothing of the man he was fast becoming.

Feeling frustrated he wandered the streets; he went into a wine bar and sank a couple of drinks. Once again fate intervened when he overheard a conversation.

"Come on, Rhianna, you know you want it baby and I know I want you," the young man bragged.

"Oh, Rupert, if you weren't so good looking I would slap you."

"So, how about it?"

"No way you freak!"

"Hey, do you know who I am?"

"Yes, Rupert Giles, a complete prick if I may say so!" The young buxom brunette walked away in disgust.

Dante's ears pricked up, so this was the little shit that humiliated Ella? He would pay for that with his life.

"What are you looking at?" Rupert was aggressive.

"Nothing mate, just admiring your pick-up technique. Are you like that with all the girls or is there someone special?"

Rupert sniggered as he sat down beside him. "Well there was this one chick that was kind of special but a bit straight-laced, if you know what I mean."

"Tell me more," Dante humoured him.

"She was drop-dead gorgeous but not nearly sexy enough for me."

"How's that mate?"

"Well, come on women are just for sex, don't you agree, not got the know-how for anything else, know what I mean?"

Dante nodded with disgust. He would love shutting this arsehole up, permanently.

"This Ella chick, well she thought I wanted to marry her and that's how I got into her knickers. She was a looker but a complete dense blonde bimbo." Rupert supped his drink off.

"Here let me get you another," Dante offered.

"Cheers pal. I'll have a Bloody Mary, make it a large one."

Dante summoned the barman and plied Rupert with drink. "Carry on."

"Well she was as hot as fuck and I was the envy of many a guy, but she was –" he paused "– bit boring in the bedroom department so I thought I would spice things up a tad."

"Oh, yeah?" Dante encouraged him.

"I was seeing another girl at the same time, Loretta, huge tits and up for anything."

"Sounds like fun." Dante was seething but didn't show it.

"Yeah, so one night when I was fucking Ella I asked her if she truly loved me then she would have a threesome, you know, me watch them and then fuck 'em man!"

It was all Dante could do to contain his contempt for this little pervert.

"Well, she burst into tears and asked me if I was joking, which of course I wasn't. The daft bitch told me I had to make a choice between her and Loretta. Not being funny mate but Ella hasn't exactly got the biggest tits in town and she wasn't dirty like Loretta, so of course Loretta won." Rupert was pleased with himself. "She had the looks and the figure but, Christ was she boring in bed."

"I see!" Dante spoke through gritted teeth. All he wanted to do was smash Giles' head straight onto the bar – the uncouth bastard sickened him.

"Hey, I'm having a sex party tonight man if you want to come."

"Some other time maybe, next time I'm in London."

Rupert gave him his business card. "The ladies would adore you. Do anything you ask if you get my drift."

"I'll bear that in mind." And with that Dante left the bar. He leaned against the wall as he lit a cigarette. That bastard had to die, poor Ella, how could he treat her like that? She was beautiful, innocent and didn't deserve to be cast aside like a cheap piece of meat.

He inhaled deeply while he decided what to do; it would have to be quick. He dialled Rupert's card. "Hey, we just met at the bar, I've changed my mind but I would like to invite two Romanian girls who do each other while we watch, you fancy it?"

"Sure man, where are you?"

"Look this is not for the faint-hearted, come alone and don't tell anyone where you are going."

Rupert was excited and promised not to say a word; he slipped out the back of the bar.

Dante was waiting for him.

"So, where are the girls then?"

"On the way my friend, don't worry." Dante reached into his back pocket and pulled out his silencer.

"Hey man, what do you want?"

"I want you to apologise for what you did to Ella."

"Ella, you mean Ella Reynolds, what do you know about her?"

"Enough." Dante put the gun to his head.

Rupert proceeded to urinate in his trousers.

"Not such a big man now eh?"

"Please, I'll do whatever you want, man," Rupert pleaded.

"Say sorry to Ella!"

"I… I'm sorry Ella."

"Please forgive me Ella, I was a complete wanker."

"Eh?"

"Say it you tosser."

"I'm sorry man, I'm truly sorry."

"Not to me to Ella."

Rupert was quaking in his boots; this man was mental, completely off his trolley. "Ella…" he sobbed, "I'm so sorry please forgive me."

"I was a complete wanker." Dante held the gun to his bollocks.

"I... I was a complete wanker. Please mister don't shoot me, I've got money."

"I don't really give a rat's arse." Dante shot him in the privates and then in the head. "Little fucker, rest in peace scumbag." He got what he deserved, disrespect to women was one of his pet hates and he wasn't having this son of a bitch treat Ella in that way. Flipping open his mobile he rang the cleaners to eradicate any trace of a murder having taken place.

Once back at his hotel he rang Mancini. "It's done." He was of course referring to Philip Reynolds' murder.

"Good, now I wish you to return to Milan directly."

"Very well." Dante wanted to see Ella before he left, but thought better about it. It was definitely not one of his best ideas. Instead he decided to send her a huge bouquet of flowers with a note providing his contact details. If she wanted to phone him then that was up to her, if not, well that was her loss. All in all it had been a very successful trip, a piece of cake he laughed to himself as he packed.

Chapter Eight

Mrs Reynolds rang her husband's mobile; she wanted him to pick up some nice red wine to go with his roast beef dinner on the way home. After several attempts she finally got through.

"This is Philip Reynolds' phone," said a male voice that she didn't recognise.

"Oh, this is his wife, may I speak to him please?"

"I'm PC Broadbent and I'm afraid that I have some bad news concerning your husband, madam."

"What... what is it?" she exclaimed gripping the breakfast bar so hard that her knuckles turned white.

"Your husband was involved in a fatal road traffic accident less than twenty minutes ago."

Helen Reynolds dropped the phone. Accident, accident, how could that be? Her husband was an excellent driver, he never even had a scratch over the years. This can't be happening, she thought.

PC Broadbent shouted down the phone. "Are you still there, madam? I'll send someone right over."

But Helen never heard the words as she slumped to the kitchen floor in the darkness. She was numb, void of all emotion, her wonderful, dynamic husband dead. *No, it's a mistake. It has to be. The police must have got it wrong.* Bizarrely some part of her brain seemed to shut down, unable to register the awful news. It was as if the phone call had never taken place. Picking herself up off the floor she switched on the kitchen light and continued cooking Philip's favourite meal. She looked at the clock, he would be home in less than an hour, she'd better get her skates on if it was to be ready on time.

*****

Ella was sitting chatting with Carolyn when the intercom buzzer rang.

"You expecting anyone?" Carolyn asked.

"No, are you?"

Carolyn shook her head as she went to answer it. "Yes?"

"Ella Reynolds?"

"No, this is her flatmate Carolyn Reid."
"Is she at home?"
"Yes, who wants her?"
"It's the police can you buzz us in?"
"Sure." Carolyn pressed the button. "What's going on?" She turned to Ella.
"I have no idea; what would the police want with me?" Ella paused. "Damn, I'm always parking illegally!" She jumped when there was a loud knock. As she opened the door she was greeted by two sombre-looking policemen.
"Ella Reynolds?"
Ella shook her head. "Yes." She hesitated. "Has something happened?" Her voice was quiet.
"May we come in? I'd rather do this inside the flat."
Ella opened the door fully and signalled for them to enter the apartment. Once inside the officers introduced themselves.
"I'm PC Taylor and this is WPC Harman."
"Please, just tell me what the hell is going on?" Ella demanded.
"It's about your father. Your father is Philip Reynolds?"
"Yes." All of a sudden she felt faint.
"I'm sorry to have to tell you, but he has been involved in a fatal road accident and was pronounced dead at the scene."
"Oh, my God." Carolyn went to hug her.
Ella was in total shock. "You are sure it was him?"
"Positive miss."
"What about my mother, does she know?"
"Yes."
"Then I must go to her, see if she is ok."
"Would you like a lift?" PC Taylor asked her.
"No, I'm perfectly fine."
Carolyn gently reminded Ella of the fact that she had had several cocktails.
"Fine, fine, I'll just get my handbag and you can give me a damn lift," Ella snapped as she went to get her overnight bag.
"I'm sorry officers. She obviously isn't herself at the moment."
The officers nodded sympathetically.
Ella reappeared. "Carolyn, I... I don't know how long I will need to stay with her for, I'll call you."
"Take as long as you need, honey."

Chapter Nine

Ella let herself into her parents' lavish house which was set back off the road in its own grounds, complete with electronic gates for security and completely private.

Her mother was busy setting the table. "Oh, Ella, I didn't know you were coming dear, I'll set another place. Heaven knows where your father has got to; it's not like him to be late," she tutted.

"Mum, please, you're freaking me out, please stop it!"

The two officers looked on helplessly. Mrs Reynolds was acting as if nothing had happened.

"Would you and your friends like a glass of wine dear? It will have to be white though, your father should be on his way with the red." Her mum proceeded to pour wine into the tall crystal flute glasses.

"Mum, this is the police, they are here about Dad," she said gently.

"No, no, no, send them away I must get on!" her mum shrieked.

Ella ushered the police into the other room. "I'm sorry, as you can see she is in no fit state to go and identify my...my Dad, I'll have to phone Dr Shaw..." she broke off.

"We understand. However it is imperative that someone identifies your father's body."

Ella nodded. "I'll phone my dad's brother, he will be the best one to go." She had never seen a dead body before and she certainly couldn't bear the thought of seeing a shell of what was once her father.

After they left she rang her uncle who was completely dumbstruck to hear the dreadful news. "Its fine, I'll go to the mortuary and call on you tomorrow, how is your mother taking it?"

"She's not. She thinks he's on his way home now. I've called Dr Shaw, he should be here soon."

"If there's anything I can do you only need to ask."

"Thanks, Uncle Desmond." Ella ended the call and sat on the sofa. She had been a daddy's girl and now he was gone she didn't know what she would do without him. But what she did know was that, right now, her mother was having some kind of breakdown and she had to stay strong for them both.

*****

Dr Shaw wasted no time in sedating Mrs Reynolds. It was the only thing he could do. "I'm afraid your mother is in total denial."

"How long will she be like this?"

"It's hard to say, her brain can't cope with the news, so she is acting as though your father were still alive."

Ella sighed. "What can I do?"

"It's difficult Ella, if you keep pushing her to accept your father's death it could tip her over the edge."

Just then the doorbell rang. "That will be Esther, my mum's best friend."

"Just ring me anytime day or night. If she doesn't improve perhaps we can talk about a short spell in a clinic."

"She's not crazy you know!" Ella was mortified at the thought. She wasn't about to pack her mother off to some kind of weird clinic where she would be drugged up to the eyeballs and left sitting in a chair in a zombie-like state, staring into space.

"That's not what I meant; there are experts who could help her. Make sure she takes the medication I have prescribed for her."

"Ok, thanks, Dr Shaw."

"Ella, I am so sorry about your father, he was a wonderful man and also a close friend."

As she let him out Esther pushed her way in. "Where is she?"

"She's been sedated."

"And how are you? You look positively dreadful."

"I feel pretty dreadful too."

"Come here, poppet." Esther put her arms around her and stroked her hair. "There, there, let it all out dear."

Ella sobbed quietly in her arms. "I... don't know a thing about making funeral arrangements, Mum's in no fit state."

"Don't worry dear, perhaps Desmond and I can sort it all out. I'll speak with him tomorrow."

"Oh thank you, Esther."

Chapter Ten

Dante was going through Philip Reynolds' belongings and he spotted the key. Picking it up he wondered where the safety deposit box was and what exactly was in it. Time was of the essence so he pocketed it. He would have to deal with that at a later date. Opening the laptop he set about trying to crack Reynolds' password. He typed in Helen: nothing. He tried Philip's date of birth: nothing. He tapped in Ella and he was in. It amazed him why people still used names of their nearest and dearest for passwords. He proceeded to delete all the files. Once he was finished he instructed one of his men to dump the laptop.

As Dante boarded his flight he thought about beautiful Ella, she would get his flowers and card about now. He hoped it would encourage her to visit him in Milan.

Mancini was impressed with Dante and now knew that he was prepared to do anything for him. Now he had proved his loyalty he wanted to bring him into the human trafficking side of the business, which was turning out to be very lucrative indeed. Orders were coming in thick and fast and he had to find new ways of smuggling in his cargo. Perhaps Dante would come up with a plan. Yes it would be the final test, if he managed to open up new routes then he would be his successor. He didn't know what the world was coming to; it seemed the perverts were increasing in numbers all the time. And the younger the cargo the better, it was big money. But Mancini did have some standards and the ages ranged from seventeen to twenty-five years, any older and they were considered to be past it.

He had two children, a boy of ten and a girl of fourteen, if anyone laid a hand on them he would be up for fucking murder. He would tear the bastards limb from limb.

The clientele list amused him, some of them were very successful businessmen and women, politicians, chief superintendents, lawyers, you name it they were on his list. He always kept the list up to date; no one knew of its existence, it was his get out of jail free card if he ever needed it. If it fell into the wrong hands then God knows what they would do with it. It would be a blackmailer's heaven.

Mancini was ready for retiring, he would train up Dante to run the business until his son was old enough to take over, or at least run it side by side as partners and equals. He sat back in his reclining leather chair and lit one of his favourite Cuban cigars. He was going to enjoy his retirement, travel a bit more and buy himself a bigger luxury yacht. As he puffed on his cigar he decided Dante had become invaluable to him and he wanted to show his gratitude. Perhaps a huge party, yes that would be good and he would invite some nice young Italian women see if he could find a suitable partner for him. Dante needed to learn family values; it's what kept Mancini going over the years, his family kept him grounded. He laughed at the thought, Dante was one wild son of a bitch and he wasn't the type to settle for one woman. No, Dante was uncontrollable, a bit like he was at his age and he admired him for that.

Chapter Eleven

Ella didn't sleep much that night, she was frightened to close her eyes in case she saw her father and she would be unable to bear it. Burying her face into her pillow she sobbed. Her father had been her rock and there would never again be anyone like him. It was such a dark, cruel world, one that would be worse without her father in it.

As she was finally drifting in and out of strange dreams she was startled by the security gate bell. Rubbing her eyes she went into the office, it was eight in the morning. Checking the security camera she saw the police, what the hell did they want? Reluctantly she buzzed them through the main gates. Looking at herself in the mirror she couldn't believe how ghastly she looked, pale and exhausted with dark circles under her eyes. Grabbing a brush she ran it through her hair and slipped on her tracksuit bottoms and T-shirt. *There that will have to do* she thought.

"What is it?" Ella asked as she opened the door. The detective flashed a badge in her face.

"I'm DCI Lewis, this is DC Harvey, we need to speak with Mrs Reynolds."

"I'm sorry she's indisposed, I'm Ella Reynolds, her daughter, can I help you?"

"I would prefer to speak to your mother."

"Well you can't she's drugged up to the eyeballs, anything you want to say to her you can say to me!" Ella was frustrated; she couldn't understand what this was all about.

"May we come in?"

"Yes, please follow me." She showed them into the conservatory. Maria, the housekeeper hadn't arrived yet so it was up to her to make them coffee. "Please take a seat and I'll put some fresh coffee on." As she left the room she heard them chattering.

"Wow, Mr Reynolds must have been worth a bob or two to have a beautiful house like this."

"It's splendid, absolutely splendid, I'll never own anything like this on my paltry salary."

"Yep, that young lady is extremely lucky."

Lucky, Ella thought, what, lucky that her father was dead? Lucky that he would never enjoy his retirement, lucky that she would never, ever see his face again? She was far from lucky, she thought bitterly.

Five minutes later Ella returned complete with a tray of hot coffee and biscuits. "Please, help yourself."

As DCI Lewis poured the coffee he spoke directly to her. "I'm sorry to have to tell you this, but your father was stabbed to death and then robbed."

Ella dropped her cup. "What... what are you talking about? The police said it was a road traffic accident," she spluttered.

"No, it was a road traffic incident, not uncommon in this day and age I'm sorry to say."

"Wait, wait, I don't understand, why are you telling me this now?"

"Look, Miss Reynolds, there was no senior person available to talk to you last night, that's why we are here now."

Ella's brain ached. A car accident she could just about handle, but murder? Who would want to murder her lovely father? She banged her fists on the table. "Murdered!" she screamed.

Maria the housekeeper stuck her head around the door. "Ella, what on earth is going on?"

"Oh, Maria, thank God you're here!" she exclaimed. "It's father he... he's been murdered!"

"Oh my goodness." Maria was shocked, but she knew that it must be true if the police were here. "I will make some strong sweet tea to steady your nerves." She scurried off to the kitchen; if she kept busy then she would be fine. The tears welled up in her eyes, she could scarcely believe it. Mr Reynolds murdered!

"I'm afraid it looks like your father stopped to help a young woman with a flat tyre. It seems she was merely a decoy for a ruthless gang of thugs. Your father had the boot open, we assume to find a jack to help the woman." The DCI took a deep breath. "It was then that the thieves came up behind him and stabbed him in the back."

"My God!" Ella gasped. "Have you arrested anyone?"

"Not yet, but we will. We think it was a professional gang." He paused, weighing whether the poor girl had too much to take in already. "I know this probably won't help but it was quick, I mean he wouldn't have suffered."

"Yes, you're right it doesn't help at all. You see he was all alone in his final moments on this earth, I can't think of anything worse, can you?"

"No."

"So, what are you doing to get this evil, murdering scum?"

"We have got our best team of investigators on the case; it's only a matter of time before we bring these people to justice."

Ella looked blank, her head was spinning and she felt sick to the pit of her stomach. Putting her hand to her mouth she rushed from the room and just made it to the toilet in time. She retched for so long that her stomach hurt. Throwing cold water onto her face and brushing her teeth she returned to the conservatory.

"I'm sorry about that."

Just then Maria knocked on the door. "I made some tea." She plonked the steaming pot on the table.

"Thanks, Maria."

"Can I get you anything else?"

"No, thank you."

"I'll be in the kitchen if you need me for anything." And with that she left the room.

"So, what did these murderers kill him for?" Ella spat out the words.

"The main thing appeared to be his wallet, jewellery and laptop."

"And what about his motor, that was worth a fortune, did they take that?"

"No, we think they were disturbed before they had a chance, panicked and left the scene."

"I see," was all Ella could say. She dare not tell her mother, it would kill her.

"We'll keep you informed at all times of any developments."

"I appreciate that, thank you."

Maria showed the police to the door and tutted to herself, what a sorry state of affairs.

"My Mother is not taking this very well as you can imagine, she still thinks my father will walk through that door at any minute."

"Oh dear. If there's anything I can do Ella you only need to ask me."

"I'm expecting Uncle Desmond and Aunt Alice some time this morning. I'm just going to take a shower."

"This is such terrible, terrible news," Maria said in a hushed voice.

"What is it?" Helen Reynolds stood in the doorway in her dressing gown all bleary-eyed.

"I'm sorry about Mr Reynolds," Maria told her.

"What do you mean? Philip is away on business, he just called me."

"Mother!" Ella exclaimed.

"Oh Ella, don't be so loud. I need to get a shower, waken myself up, I so hate it when Philip is away it is so lonely without him."

Maria looked at Ella in total disbelief. Ella shrugged.

"I told you she was in denial and now you've seen it for yourself, I just don't know what to do, no matter what I say to her she is determined that Father is very much alive."

"Don't take this the wrong way love but I think she would benefit from some professional help."

Reluctantly Ella was inclined to agree with her, it was a goddamn awful business. She had lost her father and now she felt like she was losing her mother too. It just wasn't fair, why was this happening to her family? They were all good citizens and certainly didn't deserve this.

Chapter Twelve

Dante was greeted at the airport by his very own personal chauffeur and he was delighted to see the stretch limousine waiting just for him. So Mancini was pleased with him he thought, that was a good start. He would look after him just as he promised the silly old fool. He would soon take over the business and become very powerful, he grinned to himself. All he ever cared about was rising through the ranks and one day becoming the boss of all bosses.

As he got into the limo he saw a message on the leather seat, it was from his uncle. *Welcome home. Change into this suit and be prepared for a royal reception.*

Dante lifted the lid off the box, inside was a black silk suit, complete with a cream silk shirt and black tie. Dante wondered what his uncle had in store for him; the suit was rather formal so he was expecting something quite lavish.

When the car drove up the winding driveway to the manor house Mancini was standing on the veranda smoking a cigar. Dante despised cigars, they choked him. He wanted to get it and ram it down the fat bastard's mouth. Gritting his teeth he stepped out of the limo and smiled.

"Welcome, welcome, it's good to see you." Mancini gave him a huge hug and kissed him on both cheeks.

"Hey man, I've only been away for a couple of days, no need for all this fuss!"

"Don't be silly, Dante, you have sorted out a few minor hiccups and I am very grateful. Now come inside, there are some people I want you to meet."

The house was full of Mancini's business associates and they were all falling over themselves to speak to him. He was loving the attention, he felt like a king.

"Come, let's go into my office I have a few special people I want you to meet."

Dante was intrigued, what was his uncle up to? Mancini sat in his recliner chair and lit up his cigar. "Pour the brandy Dante," he ordered.

Dante willingly obliged, anything to keep the fat bastard happy made him happy. It was a means to an end he told himself.

There was a knock on the door. "Enter!" Mancini shouted.

Two men came in and shook hands with Mancini.

"I want you to meet my nephew, Dante Moretti; he's going to oversee the business. Dante this is Nico de Luca and Aleksei Petrov."

"Oh?" Nico wasn't sure about this new arrangement.

"Do you have a problem with that Nico?" Mancini boomed.

"I'm just concerned with his lack of knowledge in this field."

"That's where you and Aleksei come into it; he will shadow you, not at the same time of course!" Mancini laughed at his wittiness. "He will learn from you both and then he will oversee the cargo going into the UK."

"You sure about this?" Aleksei wasn't convinced. He had heard about Dante and he had a funny feeling that if he became involved then it was only a matter of time before it all came crashing down.

"You are not being very polite," Mancini told him.

"I apologise, I don't mean any disrespect."

"Let's have a drink to seal the deal." Mancini poured the brandy. "You will make a great team, to Nico, Aleksei and Dante."

The four men raised their glasses. "Nico, Aleksei and Dante."

Mancini was a happy man, a very happy man. Dante was going to be an asset to the team and he had a plan, an audacious plan. They couldn't use their usual transport anymore it was becoming way too dangerous and that's where Ella Reynolds would come into it. She had caught Dante's eye and he could work it to his advantage. It wouldn't take much to arrange. Her father was dead, her mother was having some kind of breakdown and she needed a shoulder to cry on. Dante had already sent her flowers asking her to come to Milan. He would tell him to invite her over after her father's funeral.

Chapter Thirteen

Ella's mother still hadn't accepted the death of her husband and didn't even attend his funeral. Instead she became reclusive, shutting herself off from the entire world. Dr Shaw had again advised Ella to seriously think about getting her mother some treatment. He had given her a list of clinics to choose from telling her that it was for the best. But she still wasn't convinced. After the funeral she had slipped away to contemplate her mother's future. Carolyn had been a tower of strength to her and she was grateful to have such a friend especially now. She discussed the possibility of having her mother temporarily admitted inside one of those clinics and she was ashamed to even be considering it. Finally she convinced her aunt to take her mother on holiday, see if a trip to a retreat would help her move on. She had been pleasantly surprised when her mother agreed. Her mother had busied herself preparing for the trip and it stopped her from thinking too much. She was leaving the following day and Ella felt relieved, it was a terrible thing to feel relieved, palming her mother off onto someone else, making her someone else's problem. It was for the best she told herself and deep down she knew that it was the only thing she could do.

She rang Carolyn. "Hey, I was wondering if you could do me a favour?"

"Anything, Ella."

"I need some company, it's the reading of Father's will today and as my mother won't be coming, I could really do with some support."

"Sure thing, honey, where's the reading?"

"It's at Henshaws on Harmond Street at ten thirty."

"Should I just meet you there?"

"No, I'll collect you on the way."

"Ok, I'll be ready."

"Oh, and Carolyn."

"Yes?"

"Thanks."

"I'm your friend silly don't thank me." Carolyn put the phone down, she felt slightly guilty about not telling her about the flowers, but she still had the unopened card. She popped it into her bag; she would give her it later, she decided.

They arrived at the solicitor's office an hour later for the reading of her father's last will and testament. As she sat nervously in the waiting room Carolyn put her arm around her.

"Do you want me to come in with you?"

"I don't think that you will be allowed but I am grateful for your support."

Carolyn didn't know what to say, she was amazed at her friend's strength, if she was in her position right now she would be in bits.

Ella recognised a few faces from her father's business and supposed that they must have been left something in the will. A man was watching her intently and it made her nervous.

"I'm sorry, allow me to introduce myself, I'm Marcus Treymayne." He extended his hand to her.

"Yes, my Father mentioned you. I didn't see you at the funeral," she remarked.

"I was there but didn't attend the wake I'm afraid due to business commitments."

"I see."

Mr Pomfret's secretary interrupted. "Can you all make your way into the office please?"

Ella got to her feet, she felt a little shaky.

"Are you ok, Miss Reynolds?" Marcus asked her, concerned that she may faint at any moment.

"Yes, I'm fine. I think I just got up too fast."

"Here, take my arm."

Ella put her arm through his and let him guide her into the vast office. Mr Pomfret was a small dumpy man with a receding hairline and fat, chubby little hands. Ella stifled a laugh, all of a sudden she wanted to laugh out loud. His suit was very questionable, an old-fashioned outfit that was too tight for him. His belly strained at the material and Ella had visions of it bursting out at any second. She put her hand over her mouth as she tried to stop herself from giggling.

"Is something funny Miss Reynolds?" Mr Pomfret asked her.

"I just told her a joke that's all," Marcus Treymayne told him.

"Well I don't think that is appropriate in these circumstances do you?"

"My Father always loved a good joke, so I would say it was most appropriate, what do you say Mr Treymayne?"

"I concur."

Mr Pomfret was not amused. "Please, sit, sit, let's get on with it." He opened the document in front of him and cleared his throat. "This is the last will and testament of I, Philip Trent Reynolds. I hereby revoke all wills and testamentary dispositions of every nature and kind whatsoever by me hereto before made."

Ella yawned, this was so boring.

Mr Pomfret glared at her; he took his job very seriously. "Shall I continue?"

"Please, do we really have to listen to all this jargon; can you not just cut to the chase?"

"I have to read the document in its entirety, my dear," he told her.

She sighed and sat back into her chair, this was going to take an age. As she listened to him mutter on his words seem to run into each other and she couldn't understand a word of what he was saying. "I need to get out of here." And with that she scraped back her chair.

"Miss Reynolds, I really must insist that you stay for the entirety of the reading."

"Mr Treymayne can relay the information back to me." She turned to him. "Is that ok with you?"

"Of course, but please call me Marcus."

"Here's my mobile number, just call me when it's over."

"I will."

"I'm so sorry everybody, Uncle, Aunty." She nodded at them as she left the room.

"That was quick," Carolyn commented.

"Oh, let's just get out of here, that pompous buffoon was doing my head in. I don't know what he looked like, he looked like a penguin stuffed into that suit," Ella giggled.

"I think we need a drink."

"I agree, where's the nearest wine bar?" Ella asked the secretary.

"There's a nice one called Parry's, it's just around the corner."

"Thank you, perhaps you would be so kind as to tell Mr Treymayne that's where I'll be?"

"Very well."

It was over an hour before Marcus turned up. Ella waved to him as she saw him come through the door.

He wished he had met her under different circumstances, he liked and admired her father so much. He'd been a great boss, he thought.

"Here, have a seat." Ella patted the chair beside her. "What happened then?"

"Your Mother was named as the sole executor and trustee of the will as you probably expected."

"So, what did I get then for my Father's murder?" she asked bitterly.

"A nice inheritance of ten million pounds and control of the motor businesses."

"What... Phew, I didn't realise he was so rich."

"There was a stipulation though."

"Oh yes?"

"Yes, I am to have the day-to-day running of the London business and you are to be my trainee."

"What? But I don't know a thing about prestige motors."

"Well, you'll have to learn."

"And if I refuse?"

"Then I'm afraid the money will remain in trust until you are thirty years old."

"What, you're having a laugh aren't you?" Ella gasped.

"No, I'm afraid that it's true." He handed her a copy of the will and pointed it out.

"So, all I am to get is an allowance of a thousand pound per week if I don't agree to being trained up." Ella shook her head, with her expensive lifestyle she would be unable to survive.

"But, I can authorise releasing funds to you if I think it necessary."

"You... but I don't even know you!" Ella exclaimed.

Carolyn was looking on at the exchange between her friend and Mr Treymayne, Ella was about to blow a gasket.

"It's what your father wanted."

"Just how well did you actually know my father?" Ella demanded.

"Look, I can't change what the will says, I'm sorry that it's not what you wanted to hear." Marcus was trying to stay calm.

"You, you're not even a relative, why do you get all the power!"

"Please, Ella, I don't think you should have any more to drink, it's not helping." He turned to Carolyn. "Perhaps you should take her home."

"How dare you tell me what to do!" Ella jumped up and threw her wine right in Marcus' face.

Marcus pulled a handkerchief out of his pocket and wiped his face and suit. By this time half the customers were watching with amusement. "I'll forgive you for that. I'm not the enemy, you know."

Ella looked horrified at what she had done. "Oh, I'm sorry; I don't know why I did that!" She burst out crying.

Marcus was embarrassed; he wasn't used to dealing with emotional outbursts. "Come on, I'll give you both a lift home." He escorted them to his car. "Where to?"

Carolyn gave him directions to the apartment. Nobody spoke during the short drive.

"Call me tomorrow, honey." Carolyn patted her arm as she got out of Marcus' car.

Once Carolyn had entered the building Marcus looked at Ella. "Do you fancy a coffee or something before you go to your mum's?"

"I suppose, I can't go home in this state."

"I just need to get out of this wet suit," he laughed.

Ella never spoke, she just closed her eyes. She must have dozed off and woke up with a start when Marcus gently shook her. "What…. where am I?" she exclaimed, rubbing her eyes.

"I didn't like to disturb you, you looked so peaceful."

They were parked next to a burger van. "Fancy one?"

Ella nodded, her stomach was rumbling and she suddenly realised that she hadn't eaten anything all day.

Five minutes later he returned with two cheeseburgers and fries and two steaming mugs of tea. "Sorry, they didn't have coffee."

Ella shrugged. "That's fine with me."

After they had finished Ella got out of the car to stretch her legs. "Your car will stink something rotten now."

"It's ok I'll just get it valetted."

"Yes, courtesy of Reynolds Prestige Motors." She sighed.

"Do you fancy a walk, blow the cobwebs away?"

"Ok." Ella felt a bit chilly as she pulled her short jacket around her.

"Wait a minute."

He went back to the car and produced a jacket. "Here, it may be a bit big for you but it will keep the draught out."

"Thank you." Ella put the jacket over her shoulders.

Marcus put his arm around her and she flinched.

"Don't worry my intentions are strictly honourable."

Ella leaned her head on his chest, she felt strangely relaxed, safe in his company.

There was something vulnerable about her, Marcus thought; she put on false bravado to cope with losing her father. He would make it his business to get to know her and he was in no hurry, after all, they would be working together. He couldn't help but think that they looked like any other courting couple, and smiled to himself. One day they would be, he thought, when the time was right…

Chapter Fourteen

Milan, Italy

Mancini summoned Dante, he had plans he wanted to instigate. Dante was late, he was always late, not a very good timekeeper and he didn't like to be kept waiting.

Dante straightened his tie before he got out of the car. He always liked to be well presented, that was one thing about him. He had style and he had class, not like some of the others, namely his big fat uncle who knew nothing about fashion. He was loaded and didn't have a clue how to dress himself, even with his own personal tailor at his beck and call.

He was greeted by Giancarlo one of Mancini's bodyguards. "Dante, you look very well." He shook his hand.

"What's all the urgency Gi?"

"Oh, you know your uncle, he just likes to click his fingers and have everything happen in an instant."

"Just slightly impatient then."

"Exactly, just go right on in he's expecting you."

"Sure." Dante sauntered slowly through the mansion taking in the luxurious surroundings. Yes, one day all this would be his, he thought.

"Dante, where the hell have you been?"

"Sorry Uncle, you know how it is, that broad was too demanding."

Mancini chortled. "Just like me when I was your age, women couldn't get enough of me." He patted his rounded belly. "I wasn't always like this, all that rich pasta Mama Isabella has fed me over the years."

Mancini waddled out onto the balcony and surveyed his land. "I'm thinking of retiring."

"Oh, yes." Dante tried to play it cool; this is what he had been waiting for.

"But there's something I need you to do for me first, it will ensure a wealthy retirement."

Dante was all ears. "Yes?"

"The girl you met, Ella Reynolds, I heard that you were quite taken with her."

Nothing seemed to get past his uncle. "What about her?"

"You plan on seeing her again?"

"I'm leaving it up to destiny."

Mancini rang a little bell. He had had it specially made so that when he wanted one of his staff they would be there in an instant. A petite middle-aged woman appeared.

"Yes, Signor Mancini?"

"Just bring the decanter of my favourite brandy and a couple of cigars."

The maid quickly scurried out of sight and was back in a flash. She placed the tray on the table and was just about to pour it when Mancini shooed her away.

"Take a seat, Dante, this may take a while."

He was wondering what the old bastard was up to now and why he was intent in some way involving Ella.

"Don't look so worried Dante; I have every confidence in you. First I want you to go to Russia, see how it's done over there and then replicate it in the UK. The market is expanding all the time and we need to be in it."

Dante accepted the glass of brandy and uneasily sipped on it. "Go on."

"Patience Dante, just enjoy the view, wonderful isn't it? All this land, all these staff and I still strive for more."

"I've been thinking about Vasiliev and he's not going to like us muscling in on his action."

"Fuck that Russian idiot, there's plenty for all, you'll see to that Dante."

"We don't want a war with the Russians man," Dante told him.

"You are going to meet with Petrov in Moscow. He will set up a meeting with Vasiliev try to get him to see sense. He already knows that we have been testing the water so to speak and he has not approached us yet."

"Wait a minute what has all this got to do with Ella Reynolds?"

"The car business ring any bells?"

"So?"

"Come on, I thought that you were smarter than that."

"So, you want her to get into the import export business, to make it easier to smuggle the cargo?"

"I knew you were smart Dante."

"I'll need to take a couple of my own men to Moscow."

"Whatever you wish." Mancini rang the little bell again and this time one of his bodyguards came and he handed over a package. Mancini gave it to Dante. "Tickets to Moscow for tomorrow, Aleksei will meet you."

Dante looked in the package; there was a serious amount of cash in there too.

"Just in case you need to pay anyone off." He paused. "And Dante, if they won't be bought off just kill them!" Mancini laughed, he wished he was still young enough to be in the middle of all of this action.

"And when you come back I need you to tempt Miss Reynolds over here. Take her shopping in Milan, romance her at La Scala Opera House, hell, fuck her if you like but just make sure you persuade her to pay a special interest in de Luca's motors."

Dante had to hold himself back; he didn't like his uncle talking about Ella as if she were some kind of tart. He was surprised at how strong his feelings were for her and he had only met her twice.

Picking up the package he nodded and left. As he zoomed off in his gleaming silver Maserati Spyder Cambiocorsa he felt honoured to be given such a dangerous task and was looking forward to the challenge.

Chapter Fifteen

London, England

Ella was chatting with her aunt. "So, where is this retreat then?"
"It's in the south of France, very peaceful and relaxing, here take a look at the brochure." She pulled it out of her bag.
Ella studied the glossy brochure as it looked impressive. By tasteful photography of a secluded property set in majestic surroundings she read: *"Revitalise your body, open your heart and expand your soul while becoming one with nature. Enjoy a healing programme designed specifically for your own personal well-being. Our practitioners are at your beck and call any time day or night."*
"What are you thinking, Ella?"
"Do you think this will work, make her realise the truth about my father once and for all?"
"I think it's worth a shot."
"Well, I'm willing to give anything a go right now. If this retreat is as good as it sounds then go for it."
"I've already taken the liberty of booking us in for a week of tranquillity, see how we get on."
"I can't thank you enough for this."
"I am her sister-in-law; it's the least I can do."
Ella continued reading. "A swimming pool, jacuzzi, steam room, horse riding, walking."
"Yes, but you are missing one thing, Ella."
"What's that?"
"It's very secluded; there are no towns nearby, nothing to distract your mother."
"Good."
Just then Helen appeared, looking picture perfect with full make-up and designer suit. "I thought we would pop to my favourite clothes department before we leave," she announced.
"I don't think it's that kind of place Mum, it looks very casual."
"Don't be silly darling; you know I how like to look my best."

Chapter Sixteen

Moscow, Russia

Dante was greeted at the airport by Aleksei Petrov who had a car waiting for him. Dante pulled his coat tightly around him, it was fucking freezing. It beggared belief how anyone could even dream of living in a place like this.
"I'm glad to see that you made it." Petrov shook his hand.
Dante cupped his hands and blew into them. "Jesus, how the fuck do you survive in a place like this!"
Petrov shrugged. "I'm used to it."
"So, when do we meet?"
"We are meeting Vasiliev later this evening," Petrov told him as he started the engine.
Dante glanced in the rear view mirror and noticed that they were being closely followed.
"Don't worry it's just a little protection, one never knows when we may need it."
"So, this Vasiliev, tell me what is he like?"
"He is one mean motherfucker; I heard a tale that he sold his own wife into the business just because some guy was showing her some attention. There was nothing in it of course because she would never have gotten involved with anyone, she wouldn't have dared. Vasiliev wanted to make an example out of her. He was showing everyone just how ruthless he could be. Believe me when I tell you he is not the kind of man to be crossed." Petrov shook his head. "Family means nothing to him; he has no heart this man."
"What happened to her?"
"After she was repeatedly raped and beaten for many months she could no longer stand it and one day, when the opportunity presented itself, she threw herself out of a sixth floor window, but she didn't die straight away."
"What do you mean?"
"A truck was coming quite fast, the driver didn't have a chance to stop and he hit her head on. Apparently pieces of her body were still being washed off the streets days later, it was

such a bloody mess. The talk is that Vasiliev bribed the street cleaners to take their time with it, it turned him on!"

"What a sick fuck!" Dante spat his disgust. "And what of the rest of his wife's family?"

"They are under police protection somewhere in the world with new identities. If Vasiliev ever finds out where they are, well they are dead meat!" Petrov flattened his hand and made a slashing sound as he quickly ran it under his chin for effect. "Do you get my drift?"

"Fuck me, he sounds one fucking dangerous individual," Dante commented as he watched the snow begin to fall. It was quite hypnotic and he was feeling tired after the flight.

Petrov turned up the heating. "Make no mistake he is extremely dangerous so we must tread very, very, carefully."

"Have you met him?"

"I've only had the pleasure once and that was enough."

"Oh?"

"I won't spoil it, you'll find out soon enough."

"Whatever, Aleksei, but I need to know what he knows about me." Dante was acting like the hard man again.

"Only that you have very interesting connections in Italy and the UK and a very special business opportunity you wished to talk to him about."

This was heavy stuff, even for Dante, this guy sounded like a complete psychopath. To do that to his own wife was sick.

"Did I say that Vasiliev's in-laws have his son, the one that he had with his wife?" Petrov paused. "Now if you were to find out where he was and return him safely, then he would owe you one massive favour, would he not?"

The cogs were going around in Dante's head. It was a good solid idea that Petrov had come up with, if anyone could pull it off he could. Dante didn't like to be beaten by anyone and he had just been offered a challenge he was unable to resist.

Dante patted Petrov's shoulder. "I think you and I are going to make a great team. Now, where the fuck are we staying so that I can get some shut-eye before this meet?"

"Nearly there." Petrov was pleased with himself, he liked masterminding the ideas and getting someone else to execute them, he was very good at that.

Chapter Seventeen

The meeting was arranged for eleven o'clock that evening. Dante couldn't help but feel a little apprehensive; he was worried that Petrov would pick up on it so he sat on the edge of his bed willing himself to be cool. He stared into the freestanding mirror opposite him and stood up. No one would mess with him and he didn't give a fuck who they were, least of all this Vasiliev. Before the night was over he would have him eating out of the palm of his hand. It wouldn't be easy, this was definitely a tough challenge but he could do it, he had to. Mancini expected nothing less of him and he was not about to let him down no matter what.

The problem was if it all went pear-shaped, he had two of his own men with him and that was all. Vasiliev would be surrounded by his; he was slightly freaked about that. Both he and Petrov would be sitting ducks if they upset this Vasiliev. Dante would have to improvise, play him at his own game. Yes, yes it would be a piece of cake he told himself. Positive thinking, positive thinking he repeated in his head. If he wanted this badly enough then he would have to make it happen and make it happen he would. He clenched his fists and stared at his reflection, he made punching sounds as he cracked his knuckles in the air. He moved his head from left to right and rotated his shoulders. Reaching to the bedside table he grabbed his whisky and glugged it right back in one go. It took his breath away but it seemed to do the trick, he felt calm, remarkably calm.

Dante called Carmine. "Hey it's me, everything sorted?"

Carmine cursed in Italian. "Do you know how difficult it was planting that bomb in his fucking warehouse? The place was crawling with his men."

"Just remember the fucking code, only do it if I give the signal, do you understand?"

"Of course." Carmine knew that they were in dangerous territory and if discovered they would be mutilated beyond recognition.

Dante snapped his mobile shut; he knew Carmine along with Flavio would have everything in place just in case. He jumped when there was a knock on the apartment door. "Yes?" He called out.

"It's me Petrov."

Dante checked his spyhole and opened the door.

"Are you feeling more refreshed?"

Dante nodded. "What's that?"

Petrov laughed as he threw him a long thick woollen overcoat and Russian fur hat.

"You don't fucking seriously expect me to wear this clobber do you?"

"It's cold out, but if you want to freeze your bollocks off then that's up to you."

Reluctantly Dante put them on and looked at himself in the mirror; he looked like a fucking idiot.

"You would pass for a Russian now my friend." Petrov passed him some black leather gloves. "Here."

Dante was quietly pleased that Petrov saw fit to help him blend in, nobody would be any the wiser, unless of course he opened his mouth. But Petrov would do all the talking if they got into any difficulties.

"Are you ready to go, see what Vasiliev's work entails?"

"You bet I am."

In a way Petrov admired him, if he was in the least bit frightened it didn't show. Either he was a complete fool or a superb actor, whichever one it was he didn't mind, he was beginning to admire him more and more. "Then let's go."

*****

Somewhere on the outskirts of Moscow

The drive took almost an hour; they had reached some kind of exchange point with lorries of all descriptions pulling up. Petrov drove up onto the top of the hill out of the way. "Here." He passed Dante some night vision binoculars.

"I don't know what the fuck you want me to see."

"You will see what you will be getting into, if you don't have the stomach for it then now is the time to say so."

Dante glared at him and put the binoculars to his eyes, even he was shocked at what he was seeing. It seemed that some of the local police had turned a blind eye to what was occurring, some of them even getting in on a bit of the action.

He paid particular interest to a greasy-haired little man barking orders. Although he couldn't make out what he was saying he could imagine by the events unfolding in front of his eyes. One of the lorries had been unloaded and a line of young women stood at the side of the lorry. They were all huddled together and looked petrified, not daring to look up.

He zoomed in on the man who seemed to be giving the orders. Dante shuddered when he saw the patch over his eye and a scar which ran around his neck making him look very sinister. Dante watched as he walked over to one of the women and grabbed her by the hair. He threw her to the ground and shouted something to her. The young woman shook her head. The man pulled out a pistol and shot her in the back of the head. Dante dropped the binoculars.

"Seen enough?" Petrov laughed.

Dante shook his head and bent down to retrieve the binoculars off the ground. "Not nearly enough!" He cringed as he watched what happened next.

The girls started to remove their clothes; it was minus fucking fifteen degrees and this filth were enjoying humiliating these girls.

It was that freaky-looking man who took control once more. He grabbed one of the girls by the hair and dragged her kicking and screaming across the snowy terrain. Unzipping his trousers he put a gun to the girls head. Dante zoomed in on the girl's petrified face, those eyes, big and wide filled with terror made him shudder. The girl's mouth was eventually forced open by the gun and the man shoved his erection in as hard as he could laughing all the time while he was pushing her face into it. The girl gagged and struggled to get free, eventually vomiting over the sick fuck's shoes. The man hit her with the back of his hand as hard as he could. She sprawled helplessly in a pool of blood just in front of the other girls. As she tried to crawl away a shot was fired into her startled face. Dante would never forget the look in the girl's eyes; it would be one that would haunt him for years.

Then it seemed to turn into some kind of orgy, the men all taking turns with the girls, knocking back vodka and laughing. Dante wanted to be sick. "But, I don't understand!"

"You will my friend watch carefully."

He watched as other lorries pulled up and other girls were taken out. They all stripped without any further incidents and then it seemed they were split into groups and taken into different vehicles.

"You see, the first lorry was to set an example of how these girls could end up if they disobeyed."

"And the other vehicles?"

"Split into different categories my friend: age, hair, big breasts, small breasts, skinny, meaty. Vasiliev has a client list. He wants to make sure he is sending the right cargo to the right people and this is his way of fulfilling his order."

Dante couldn't believe the manner in which this happened, surely there was a more humane way.

"I know what you think, Dante, believe me it is best not to think too deeply about this."

"He is one formidable cunt this Vasiliev."

"Now, you know as much about him as I do." But Petrov had deliberately missed out one vital piece of information.

Chapter Eighteen

Moscow city

Petrov was disappointed to learn that the meet had been cancelled until the following day; apparently Vasiliev had some urgent situation he had to sort out.

Dante was trying to work out whether to stay or get out of this goddamn hell hole; he had really bad vibes about the place even more so now. He had psyched himself up for the meeting and now he was going to have to do it all over again.

"How about coming over to my house, meet my wife Yelena? She's an excellent cook, I'm sure she wouldn't mind rustling something up at this time of night."

"No thanks, I'm not hungry."

Petrov summoned one of his men. "Go and get me a bottle of vodka and a take away of some sort."

Dante was looking out of his hotel window wondering what the fuck was going on. He managed to text Carmine to put off the plan until the following evening; it wouldn't do if someone discovered the bombs before the meet.

"You surprise me, Dante. I thought you were one tough son of a bitch."

"Don't underestimate me, Petrov." Dante's voice was hard and emotionless.

There was something about this man that got to Petrov; at times he was almost normal and yet other times he was void of all emotion. He wished he knew what was going on in his head.

Dante was thinking back to when his elder sister had run away from home with her Russian boyfriend. She had vanished into thin air; Rosa was only seventeen, what a foolish young girl she had been. Dante had only been fourteen at the time, but he was at an impressionable age. He remembered wanting to help his father in the search, but his father had sent him away to Sicily to stay with his family. It was for his own good, he was told.

It was almost five years later when he returned to Milan. And what he discovered were some shocking family secrets. He had managed to break into his father's safe and found some documents on Rosa's boyfriend. Yakov Garshin had been in the Russian military, he had been disgraced and thrown out after serving two years in military prison. There was a photograph of Rosa looking absolutely petrified. Dante couldn't make sense of what it all meant so he had no alternative but to confront his father.

"So, what the fuck is all this about?" He threw the papers at his father.

"I am still the man of the house Dante and it is none of your business!"

"You never talk about her, why is that?"

"All you need to know is that she is never coming back!"

His father refused to elaborate. Dante was only nineteen years old but even then he was strong as an ox; he jumped on his father and grappled him to the floor placing his knee tight across his throat. "You're going to fucking tell me the truth or I'm going to fucking kill you I swear on Rosa's life," he spat as he released him.

Dante's father held his throat as he tried to gasp in air, his son had made a good job of trying to kill him.

"I'm waiting."

His father put up his hand. "Just... just let me catch my breath."

Dante sat on the big brown leather sofa opposite him; he couldn't believe this man was actually his father, this big shithouse lying on the floor cowering in front of him.

"She was sold."

"What do you mean fucking sold?"

"Yakov had a talent for making young girls fall for him and then he would sell them on." He coughed up phlegm.

"What are you saying?"

"Come on, Dante, you're fucking old enough to work it out!"

Dante's stomach turned. "Where... where is my sister?"

"I don't fucking know, probably dead somewhere. It's been five years, no one could survive that life for so long."

Dante was enraged. "Did you find this Yakov?"

"Yes, but he was too well connected to get at!"

"And what of Rosa?"

His father shrugged.

Dante proceeded to knock shit out of him until his body was still and lifeless. "You're not fit to be a Moretti you fucker!" And with that Dante left his home and swore never to return.

It was sometime later when he heard his father had made a full recovery but then hit the bottle; he died several months later of a heart attack. Dante was pleased.

He had made it one of his lifetime ambitions to find his sister and seek out the fucker that did this to her. When he found him he would make him pay.

Petrov interrupted his thoughts. "Here, drink this it's good Russian vodka, it will put hairs on your chest."

Dante downed the drink in one and held out his glass for more.

"Whoa, slow down this is one hundred per cent proof."

"I don't give a fuck, just leave the bottle and get out!"

Petrov knew that he was being deadly serious. "Ok, ok I'll check in with you tomorrow morning."

After he left Dante's mind wandered back to his sister. He poured another drink; he was just about to drink it when he caught his image in the mirror. No, no, what was he doing, he needed his wits about him. Grabbing the bottle he hurled it at the mirror and lay on the bed laughing, 'seven years' bad luck, yeah right. Dante was invincible and he knew it. He had a score to settle and one day it would happen, he would avenge his sister's death because there was no doubt in his mind that she had died a long time ago, at least he hoped that she had. It pained him to think that his big sister had had to endure that sordid world; he just hoped that the end had been relatively quick.

Chapter Nineteen

London, England

Ella was relieved to see her mum off to the airport. As she kissed her goodbye she sighed. Her mum's behaviour was bizarre to say the very least. Now, she prayed that perhaps this trip would do her the world of good.

She met up with Carolyn at the local bistro.

"Hey how are you?" Carolyn threw her arms around her. "You've lost weight, honey."

Ella shrugged. "I haven't had time to eat."

"Let's order something nice, what do you fancy?"

"Just a salad will be fine thanks."

Carolyn was worried about her best friend. She was slim to start with but the weight was dropping off her and she was starting to look like skin and bone. "Should we sit outside, it's such a nice day?"

"Sure." Ella's voice was flat and unemotional.

"So, your mum got off ok then?"

"Yes."

"Ella, I'm your friend, honey, please talk to me."

"I'm sorry, Carolyn, I guess I'm not much company right now."

Carolyn leaned over the table and rubbed Ella's arm. "If you don't want to talk about it, it's fine with me."

Ella looked sad. "Everything's been such a blur since Father died – no since he was murdered," she corrected herself.

"Have the police been in touch?"

"They had a couple of leads but they amounted to nothing, it looks like the scum who did this will get off scot free."

"Oh Ella, I… I don't know what to say."

"I just hope that, one day, whoever did it suffers a cruel and horrific death!"

Carolyn was shocked by Ella's outburst, this was so unlike her. "I do have something to tell you though, it may cheer you up."

"I doubt that very much."

"Dante Moretti sent you flowers." There she had finally told her.

"Dante… what, when?"

"It was the day after you heard about your father."

"Why didn't you tell me?"

"There just didn't seem to be a right moment." Carolyn opened her bag. "Here, there was a card with them too."

Ella snatched it out of her hands. "I can't believe that you didn't tell me." She tore open the envelope. *My dear Ella*, he had written, *I wish I had gotten to know you better, there's something so special about you. I want you to come to Milan. I'll be in touch, yours Dante.*

"What does it say?"

"Here." Ella passed her the card.

"Wow, he seems really keen after just one date, what are you going to do?"

"Nothing of course." Ella's heart skipped a beat. She so wanted to get away and maybe this was the answer, escape for a while, have a good time and see what happened.

"I know that look." Carolyn smiled; she knew Ella was seriously thinking about it. "But you don't know anything about him," she warned.

"He's so good looking, immense fun and a total gentleman."

"So are you going to ring him?"

"If he really means it he'll contact me again, then I'll see."

They ordered two chicken salads and a nice bottle of Italian wine to go with it.

Carolyn was delighted to see Ella nearly eat the whole thing; it must have been the news about Dante that had suddenly made her appetite reappear.

"You haven't told me what happened with Marcus Treymayne."

"Oh, nothing, he's quite sweet really, I suppose."

"Oh?" Carolyn raised an eyebrow. "Could there be romance on the cards?" she joked.

"No, I mean he's lovely and everything but way too nice for me. The only guys I fall for are bad boys!" she laughed.

"So, do you think Dante is a bad boy?"

"I don't think so, but there is definitely something exciting about him." She had a dreamy look in her eyes.

"You know that hostel I was helping out at, the one in Harper Street?" Carolyn changed the subject.

"It amazes me that you give up your free time to do that."

"Well, the police did a raid on this block of flats and found four prostitutes."

"And?"

"They were from Slovenia, sex slaves!"

"What, do things like that really happen?" Ella's voice was incredulous.

"Yes, I'm afraid so, the poor things were made to work around the clock. God knows what diseases they have."

"Jesus!"

"Mum is part of the team of counsellors so if she can help them in any way, then she will."

"What will happen to them, will they be deported?"

"No, if they are sent back home they will be killed or trafficked right away."

"My God, what kind of people do things like that?"

"Ella, believe me you don't want to know!"

"Did they get the people who did that to them?"

"They got the monkeys, not the organ grinder!"

"Do the girls know who was behind it then?"

"If any of them do they are not saying, too scared of the repercussions I suppose. They all have families back home and if they speak out they are afraid of what the gang will do!"

"That's awful, so awful." Ella shook her head. "And here I am being miserable and feeling sorry for myself. There are people in the world that are much worse off than me."

"Do you want to come to the centre, help out, it may take your mind off things?"

"What would I do?"

"Just talk to the girls, take them some magazines, whatever, it doesn't really matter."

"Oh, I don't think that I could, it would just upset me too much."

"Well if you change your mind just let me know, honey."

"I will." But Ella doubted that would happen any time soon.

Chapter Twenty

Moscow, Russia

Vasiliev was livid, he wanted revenge and he wanted it now. Somebody must have tipped the police off, the raid in London should never have happened. Thank God he was top of the chain, nobody could get to him and nobody would give him up. He had many gangs all over the world and only they knew of his existence. "So, what the fuck happened?" he yelled.

"I... I don't know!" Tavrovsky was nervous, really nervous.

"You better fucking find out and do it fast." He glared at him. "Do you know what I am saying Tav?"

"Yes." Tavrovsky gulped, he knew only too well. Vasiliev wanted someone's head for this and it wasn't going to be his that was for sure.

"I expect results in twenty-four hours, after that if you come up with nothing then it is you who will pay!"

"I understand." Tavrovsky was a hard man but Vasiliev was one mean fucker and it didn't pay to cross him.

"Go! Get out of my fucking sight." The veins in his neck were standing out; his temper was rushing to the surface.

Just then one of his men came into the room. "Sorry to interrupt, there is a phone call for you sir."

"Take a fucking message, can't you see that I'm busy!"

Fearing for his life the young man quickly left the room.

"Are you still fucking here? The clock is ticking Tav, tick tock." His voice was menacing.

Tavrovsky nodded and left the room. Once outside of the building he leaned against the wall, what the fuck was he going to do now? The raid was down to him, but he had to find a scapegoat. He didn't care who it was, someone had to take the rap.

Vasiliev poured himself a large vodka; he didn't trust Tav and ordered some of his men to follow him just in case he tried anything. He worried about how much the police knew about the girls and how much they knew about the trafficking ring. True it was only a small part of his empire but if any of it crumbled now it could potentially ruin everything he had worked for.

When Tavrovsky was out of sight he got on his phone. "It's me. Vasiliev is not a happy man, and someone will have to give their life for this so I suggest you find a suitable scapegoat, one that is believable!" He snapped his phone shut. His whole body was trembling; he had never felt so scared in his life. It was all he could do to stop himself from being sick. What had he been thinking trying to help out one of the Italian gangs; no money was enough if he had to pay for it with his life. They had offered a fair wack to oust the Russians out of their territory. Gambling was his downfall, he had creditors on his back and he needed money fast. Out of the woods for now he knew he had to change his lifestyle, he had a family to think of. It was coming up to his fortieth birthday and he wanted to be around to celebrate it.

Vasiliev's men watched with interest wondering what Tav was up to and, more importantly, who he had been talking to. Their boss definitely had a sixth sense about people and he was usually right, this man was a traitor they just had to find a way to prove it!

Chapter Twenty-One

Petrov hadn't been able to get in touch with Vasiliev and hoped that the meeting was still on. He banged on Dante's door.

Dante appeared looking immaculate as ever. "Come in."

"Did you get a good night's sleep then?" The first thing Petrov noticed was the shattered mirror.

"Fine thanks." Dante noticed him looking at the mirror. "I had a slight accident."

"I'll say!"

"No big deal, the maid will clear it up." Dante looked impatiently at his watch. "What's happening then?"

"I haven't heard anything different from yesterday so assume it must be on."

"Listen Petrov. I haven't came all this fucking way for nothing!"

"Calm down Moretti, everything is under control."

"It better fucking had be."

"You got your story sorted?"

"Of course I have, what do you take me for a fucking idiot!" Dante spat.

Petrov didn't know who he was most afraid of Moretti or Vasiliev. They were both strong characters and he had a funny feeling neither of them would give an inch. It was going to be interesting watching them together. "Let's go then."

Dante grabbed his coat and hat; he felt like an idiot wearing them, it just wasn't his style. Still it was better than freezing his bollocks off in this artic weather. The sooner the deal was struck and he was out of Russia the better he would feel. He just hoped that this Vasiliev was a reasonable man, he would find out in about an hour.

*****

The drive took approximately forty-five minutes, neither men spoke; they were concentrating on the forthcoming events. It was a make or break situation and they both knew it.

Dante knew that he had to prove himself once more. He kept thinking that if he pulled this off then he would be the number one to inherit Mancini's throne, and as far as he was concerned that couldn't come fast enough. After everything he had done he deserved this chance.

They arrived at the warehouse and were frisked by Vasiliev's men. Dante had back-up if he needed it, his two close bodyguards were already in the vicinity and the bomb was set to go off. If he had to give his life then he would. His mind briefly flicked to his sister and then to his mother and finally to Ella Reynolds. He hoped that he would come out of this completely unscathed determined to find the bastard that did that to his sister and to marry Ella and have many children. If he lived long enough to father children, he would be an extremely happy man.

There were men everywhere all armed with Kalashnikovs. Dante knew that he had to play it safe; there was no way he wanted to die here today. They were led to the middle of the warehouse which was bare apart from a table and three chairs.

"You sit!" the man barked at them.

Dante nodded as he pulled out the chair and sat down. He looked around; it was a funny kind of place to do business, he thought.

"I am Vasiliev."

Dante turned around and was shocked to be greeted by the man with the eye patch and a pink scar, the very same man who had shot the girl in the head the day before. The expression on his face was one of total disbelief.

Petrov smiled to himself, that had shocked him, not so cocky now he thought.

"I am Dante Moretti and I'm here on behalf of Mancini."

"Yes, I know who you are. Tell me, what do you think of my country?"

"Fucking freezing!"

Vasiliev stared at him for several seconds before laughing and patting him on the back. "You fucking Italian wimp!"

Dante laughed with him, but what he really wanted to do was torture the fucker to death. He didn't like his sort, an evil bastard who didn't give a damn about human life. He treated those girls like something he had just stepped on just because he knew that he could.

Vasiliev wore a long leather coat which he flicked up to enable him to sit down. He was only about five foot three, but oozed confidence and his manner was commanding. There was something frightening about him and Dante knew he would have to tread very carefully.

"So Mancini wants us to join forces." Vasiliev lit a cigarette and blew the smoke straight into Petrov's face.

Petrov started coughing he hated cigarettes.

Vasiliev jumped to his feet and leaned across the table. "Are you fucking disrespecting me?" he boomed.

"No, he just has allergies." Dante was quick to diffuse the situation and Petrov was very grateful.

Vasiliev sat back down. "Why would I want to work with Mancini, I am doing perfectly adequate as it is."

"It makes good business sense, you help us, we help you. You see we all win."

"If you get the route sorted out come back to me and I may be interested."

"I'm working on it as we speak."

"Was there something else?"

Dante needed to stay in favour with this man, gain his trust. "I may be able to help you in locating your son."

"Impossible, I have ears and eyes everywhere and nobody knows a goddamn thing, it's like he fell off the face of the planet."

"I have contacts. If you like I could look into the matter further for you."

"Why would you do that?"

"To prove to you that I am one hundred per cent trustworthy."

Vasiliev shook his hand and stared into his eyes. "If you do this for me then I will be indebted to you."

"All I ask is that you seriously consider Mancini's offer."

"Very well." He stubbed out his cigarette. "Now I must go I have a shipment coming in and I like to personally oversee it."

Dante gritted his teeth. This fucker got some kind of sick enjoyment humiliating and killing these innocent women, it made him sick to the pit of his stomach.

"It was a pleasure meeting you." Vasiliev liked this Moretti, he had spunk that was for sure.

"Likewise, I'll be in touch." Dante got up and started walking away. Petrov followed him.

Just then they saw a man being dragged in, he had a bag over his head. Dante stopped, he looked at Vasiliev and then back to the man who was desperately trying to shake free.

"A fucking traitor I need to take care of," Vasiliev told him.

Petrov knew how brutal he could be but did not wish to witness it first hand – he started walking faster. As they neared the exit they were blocked by two armed men who signalled for them to go back in. "What's going on?" he whispered to Dante.

"Just do what they want, it will be all right trust me."

Petrov had a weak stomach and just wanted to throw his insides up. It was all he could to do to stop himself from shaking.

Vasiliev had the man forced into the chair, his arms and feet were tied and the bag was still over his head. "Come, you need to see with your own eyes what happens to anyone who betrays me. Tell me, have you ever seen a man tortured before?" He smiled, a cruel little smile that curled maliciously at the ends. His face was all contorted as if he was getting some kind of sick kick out of it.

The victim was having problems breathing, he was panting, gasping for breath. "Perhaps we should make Tavrovsky a little more comfortable; we don't want him to suffocate now do we!" Vasiliev was enjoying taunting him.

One of his men removed the bag. Tavrovsky blinked and tried to adjust his eyes; he knew that this was the end of the road for him.

"Bring in his wife!" Vasiliev ordered.

Katalina Tavrovsky was petrified; it was obvious that she had been roughed up. Her face was battered and bloody, as was her dress.

"You... you fucking monster, I... I'll kill you." Tavrovsky tried to kick out at Vasiliev but all he succeeded in doing was overturning his chair and landing on the concrete floor.

"She was good, very good if you know what I mean, great body." Vasiliev paused. "You would never think that she had children."

Tavrovsky threw up. This was his worst nightmare come true.

One of the men hauled his chair upright.

"Please just let her go, do what you want to me but please do not kill her."

Vasiliev removed his overcoat and took something silver out of the pocket. He tutted. "It is a great shame that it has come to this." He walked over to his wife and hit her full in the face. The blood spurted everywhere as the woman screamed in agony, her eyeball was ripped out of its socket. Vasiliev looked at it for a second and then pulled it off throwing it onto the ground and stamping on it for effect. "For fuck's sake shut that fucking woman up." He put his hands in his ears and made screaming noises. His men just stood and watched.

Dante lurched forward and grabbed one of the Kalashnikov rifles and shot her in the head. Before he knew it six guns were on him.

Vasiliev laughed a blood-curdling laugh that sent shockwaves through Dante's body. "So, my own men did not even have the guts to kill her. I salute you, Moretti." He nodded to his men to lower their rifles.

Tavrovsky was making low wailing sounds like an animal being tortured. Vasiliev took out his hand gun. "Open your fucking mouth." He tried to force it in as his saliva sprayed all over his face.

Tav shook his head, he was sweating profusely. Vasiliev started to walk away from him, then without warning he turned around and shot him in the foot.

All his men could do was join in the laughter as Tav screamed. "P... p... p... please," was the only word his victim could say.

Vasiliev taunted him. "Do you hear that? He is begging for his life, p... p... p... please don't kill me." He put on a pathetic voice.

Dante caught full sight of the knuckleduster which had two-inch spikes protruding from it; he had never quite seen anything like it in his life. The poor woman hadn't stood a chance and he was glad to have put her out of her misery.

Vasiliev took off the knuckleduster and threw it to Petrov. "I am giving you a chance to show me what a man you are."

All eyes were on Petrov. "I... don't wish to offend you but I am not a violent man."

"And you fucking think I am!" Vasiliev walked up to him and put his face close to his in a threatening pose.

"Here, allow me." Dante had saved Petrov once more from Vasiliev's wrath. He held out his hand.

Petrov's trembling hand passed him the implement. He had no idea what Moretti was about to do, he just wished this madness was over.

Dante walked up to Tavrovsky and punched him in the heart, hoping his agony would soon be over.

Vasiliev watched this young man in awe, he was so like him when he was his age. He would be a good ally to have. He went to him and patted him on the back. "Very good, Dante, now please I must be the one to finish this."

Dante went to pass him back the knuckleduster.

"No, you must keep that as a memento," he insisted.

All the while Tav continued to bleed all over the warehouse. He was on the floor now trying to focus on his wife.

"Yes, yes you will be with her soon enough." Vasiliev walked over to one of his men and grabbed a six-inch blade from him. He took it out of the pouch and stared at it. "It is a beauty is it not!"

Tav just wanted it to end, the pain was searing through his body and all he wanted was to be with his wife.

Vasiliev grabbed Tav by the hair and held the knife to his throat. "Oh, by the way, you will also be meeting up with your children!" And with that he slashed his throat and dropped him to the ground. "Get these fuckers out of here, burn them!" he ordered.

Noticing the blood on his boots Vasiliev cursed. "Fucking cunt." He spat on Tav's body and wiped the blood off the knife onto his jacket.

As his men hastily wrapped up the bodies Vasiliev spoke. "I trust that you will not let me down Dante, it would be such a shame if something were to happen to you."

"You can trust me implicitly."

"I hope that you are right." He nodded to the men to let them leave.

They carried on walking. Once they were safely in the car Petrov sighed with relief. "I thought we were dead men and if it wasn't for your quick action then we probably would have been."

"I had back-up just in case." Dante sent the text and called it off.

"You…? What, are you insane!" Petrov yelled at him.

"Just taking precautions, it is the sensible think to do; if we had been taken out then the whole of those fuckers would have been too. So, you see, we would not have died alone!"

Petrov couldn't believe the words coming out of Moretti's mouth. "If he had any inclination about what you were up to we could have ended up like that poor son of a bitch!"

"Ever thought that you were in the wrong line of work!"

"Never, ever have I seen anything like that, it was too twisted for words, and the fucker actually enjoyed it!" Petrov was still in shock.

"Why the fuck didn't you tell me the other night who Vasiliev was!" Dante snapped at him.

"Just having a bit of fun, your face was a picture man."

"Idiot." Dante laughed, he could kind of see the funny side.

"So, do you think he will go for it then?"

"I proved myself to him today and if I manage to find his son, then that will be the icing on the cake."

Petrov had to admit he was impressed with Dante's calmness and quick action. He was definitely a man to be around if the shit ever hit the fan.

Chapter Twenty-Two

London, England

Ella drove to the car showroom and headed straight for her father's office. She was stunned to find a plaque on the door saying *Marcus Treymayne, Managing Director*. Pity he hadn't jumped into her father's grave as well, she thought.

"Miss Reynolds, I'm so sorry about Mr Reynolds, I mean your father." Hannah offered her sympathy. "I'm afraid Mr Treymayne is in a meeting and he asked not to be disturbed."

"Oh, did he now?" Ella was annoyed at how quickly Marcus had slipped into her father's shoes.

"Come on, let me make you a cup of tea, dear."

Ella sighed, she couldn't be bothered with a fight right now. Perhaps Hannah was right, a cup of tea would calm her nerves.

"Tell me how is Mr Treymayne doing?" Ella enquired.

"Yes, very well he seems to have a natural talent," she chattered. "I mean he sold four of our most expensive cars yesterday and all to footballers, would you believe it!" Hannah's voice was full of admiration. "He's got the customers eating out of the palms of his hands."

Ella daintily sipped her tea; she kicked off her stiletto heels and rubbed her feet. "God my feet are killing me. Things we do for fashion eh?" She smiled.

"Ooh yes, dear, I see what you mean," Hannah giggled.

They were interrupted by the intercom buzzing. "Yes, Mr Treymayne?"

"I'll have that tray of coffee now please."

"Certainly, Mr Treymayne."

Just as Hannah was about to carry the tray in Ella spoke up. "Allow me."

"Oh no, I can't let you do that, what would it look like?"

"I don't know and I don't really care. Don't look so worried I'll tell him that I insisted." She brushed Hannah aside and knocked on the office door. Marcus opened it.

"Er… what are you doing?"

"Bringing the coffee in of course, what else?"

Marcus didn't need a scene right now, not when he was in the middle of such an important meeting. Reluctantly he stepped aside and let her in.

There were two gentlemen looking through documents and chatting to each other. Ella banged the tray down startling the two men. "Whoops, sorry did I disturb you, let me introduce myself, I'm the owner Ella Reynolds, and you are?"

"Owner, but I thought you were the owner, Mr Treymayne?"

"Well I'm not the owner as such but do have full control in all aspects of the business."

Ella sat on the edge of the desk and crossed her long legs. Marcus cringed; she wasn't even wearing any shoes.

"Heels, they're such a pain in the backside, I mean my feet are killing me," Ella giggled enjoying making Marcus uncomfortable.

"Er... perhaps we should take these away with us and get back to you." The men stood up.

"Oh, please don't go on my account," Ella smiled sweetly.

Marcus showed the gentlemen to the door. "Mr Grant, Mr Miller." He shook their hands.

"We'll be in touch." And with that the men made a hasty exit.

"What on earth are you playing at?" Marcus demanded.

"I don't know what you mean."

"Ella, I know that you've had a lot to deal with lately but that's no excuse to sabotage my meeting."

"I thought you wanted me to get involved."

"Not like this I don't, you could have lost me the deal!" Marcus was angry.

"Don't be silly."

Marcus grabbed her arms. "You've got to stop acting like a child. Grow up, Ella."

"How dare you, get your hands off me!" Ella shook free from his grasp.

"Seriously, Ella, this is your father's business. One that he built from the ground up, for you and for your mother. Do you want it to go down the pan, does it mean that little to you?"

Ella knew that he was right she had behaved foolishly. "It means everything to me," she said in a hushed voice.

"Is there a reason that you came here?"

"Yes, I'm thinking of taking a trip and, well, I need some funds."

"How much?"

"Fifty thousand should do it," she said matter of factly.

"Where the hell are you going, around the world trip?"

"Never you mind, now can I have the money or not?"

"I'll sort it out, it'll be in your bank account by tomorrow, is that ok?"

"Fine." She kissed him on the cheek. "See that wasn't too difficult was it?"

Marcus watched as she left the room. He put his hand on his face. It was all he could do to stop himself from taking her in his arms and kissing her. One day he hoped that she would feel the same way, too.

Chapter Twenty-Three

Milan, Italy

Dante explained the situation to Mancini. They had to find Vasiliev's son and sooner rather than later.

"I'll give you whatever you need to find him," Mancini told him. "Tell me, what was your impression of Vasiliev?"

"He is evil, totally evil. If we pull this off we'll have to be very careful. He does not suffer fools gladly; you wouldn't believe the things he is capable of."

"This is your baby Dante, I expect you will nurture it, do what you have to do."

"Very well Uncle, but I want to go and see Ella first."

"Ella… you do sound a bit taken with her, it would not be a good idea to fall for her. Just get her to do what I ask of you and then forget about her."

"Very well."

"You must marry a nice Italian girl, make the bond with the other families. I was thinking Concetta, she is a nice decent young woman."

One that puts it about, so Dante had heard, there was no way he was marrying that slut; God knows what diseases she had.

"Now, go and do what you have to, to seal the deal." Mancini opened his safe and passed Dante a package. "Just a little something to show my appreciation."

Dante gratefully accepted the token offer and put it in his inside pocket.

"I'll get someone on Pavel Junior's case, when there's any news I will contact you."

"Ok, Uncle." Dante left the room. He had a bad feeling about all of this and he really didn't want to involve Ella more than he already had. But life had a funny way of turning out and whatever was meant to happen would. For now Dante would go with the flow, see where it took him.

He reminded himself once more about his sister. He was only in this to find out what happened to her. All he wanted to do was bring these fuckers down once and for all. It wouldn't be easy, he would have to be very clever and appear whiter than white.

Chapter Twenty-Four

London, England

Ella picked her mother and aunt up from the airport. "Mother I'm so happy to see you, how was the trip?"

"Ella, darling, please take me to the cemetery."

Her aunt nodded her head. "It's ok."

Ella was shocked; her mother was finally acknowledging her father's death. She felt relief sweep over her entire body. "Oh, Mother!" Ella hugged her.

"I'm fine, Ella, I just have to go to your father."

Whatever had happened in France must have been for the best, it had certainly changed her mother's outlook and that could only be good.

As they got out of the car Ella's aunt held her back. "No, she needs to do this on her own."

They watched as her mother walked to the grave. Ella had arranged for a headstone to be erected. It was white marble etched with gold writing and outlined in black to make it stand out.

Her mother took a handkerchief out of her bag and began to gently wipe the headstone. Helen knelt down and picked up a handful of soil. No, no, Philip was in here, it wasn't true. She started digging with her bare hands.

Ella and her aunt ran over. "Please Mum, stop it, stop it!" she yelled.

Her mother was hysterical and sobbing. "Why... why?" she screamed.

The caretaker saw the commotion and ran over to help. "Is there anything I can do?" he asked.

"Oh, please help me get her to the car," Ella pleaded, she couldn't bear to see her mother like this, it was soul destroying.

Once they got home Ella wasted no time in calling Dr Shaw. "I need your help," she told him. "Mother seems to have accepted father's death but she is hysterical, please hurry." She returned to the kitchen, where her aunt was making a pot of tea.

"I don't want tea, I want my husband back!" she screamed. "What's happening to me, Ella?"

"Oh, Mum." Ella held her shaking hands. "It's true he's gone and he is never coming back."

"My poor, poor Philip, I don't know what I'll do without him, how will I cope, what about the business?"

"Don't worry about the business it is being well looked after." She paused. "I miss Father too." They held each other, mother and daughter sharing in their grief for the man they both loved.

Maria let in Dr Shaw. "Follow me, it's not good Doctor," she warned him. The screaming had been heart wrenching, but at least Mrs Reynolds knew the truth now.

"Helen, my dear, how are you?"

"How do you think I am? My husband is dead!"

The doctor opened his bag and pulled out a large bottle of tablets. "I want you to take two of these twice a day; they will help calm you down."

"I don't want to be drugged up." She snatched the bottle off him and threw it to the other side of the room.

"Helen, I promise they will just calm your nerves, you do trust me don't you?" he gently asked.

"Yes, of course I do."

The doctor picked up the pills and opened the bottle, he passed her two tablets. "Just take them."

Ella poured a glass of water and gave it to her mother.

Helen took them and sat down. She looked thinner Ella thought, she can't have been looking after herself properly.

Dr Shaw picked up his bag. "If you need me please don't hesitate." He told Ella on the way out. "It is good that your mother has finally acknowledged what happened, she will get better, I promise. Right now she is grieving, be patient."

Ella closed the door and leaned against it, the whole situation was tearing her apart, she had to get away.

She rang Carolyn. "I'm coming over later. My aunt is going to stay with Mum for the next few weeks."

"Oh, I was just about to go out, honey, I've got a date."

"That's fine, Carolyn, I just need some space, some time alone away from here."

"I don't mind cancelling if you want some company."

"No, don't do that, I'll be there in about an hour."

After Ella's mum went for a lie down she spoke to her aunt. "What happened in France?"

"She was having energy healing, it's a hands-on treatment that traces emotional and physical symptoms. I guess this must have triggered something inside her." Her aunt continued, "She had another couple of sessions, they told her that she had emotions blocked away because they were too painful to deal with."

"I guess it was good therapy for her then."

"Yes, she was a lot calmer and relaxed if that's possible."

"The question is, what happens now?"

"She'll deal with it in her own way. It's just a matter of time."

"Do you mind if I stay at the apartment tonight? I just need some breathing space."

"It's fine, I'm here, you go and I'll see you in the morning."

"Thanks."

Chapter Twenty-Five

Ella was just getting out of the bath when the phone started ringing. Throwing a towel around herself she dashed to the phone. "Hello?"

"Ella, it's so good to hear your voice."

She recognised that smooth Italian accent immediately. "Dante?"

"Of course the very same, who else would it be? Tell me, did you consider my offer?"

"I haven't really had a chance to think about it."

"Well, if you don't come to me I'll guess I'll just have to come to you."

They were interrupted by the doorbell. Damn, Carolyn must have forgotten her key again, she thought. "Hang on, there's someone at the door." Ella was astounded to see Dante on the doorstep.

"Pleased to see me?" Dante grinned as he presented her with a bouquet of flowers. "For you, aren't you going to invite me in?"

"Oh, sorry, yes please come in." Ella felt slightly embarrassed, her hair was dripping wet and she was conscious of the minute towel that only just covered her modesty. "Make yourself at home; I'm just going to make myself decent."

Dante grabbed her arm. "No need to on my account, you look ravishing as ever."

Ella blushed. "Just give me five minutes." She hurried off; there was something that drew her to him like a magnet. She didn't know if she could trust herself being alone with him, especially when she was virtually naked.

Dante picked up the photograph on the cabinet and studied it. Philip Reynolds, his wife and daughter all smiling and looking very happy. He felt a pang of guilt, but only for a split second.

"That's my mum and dad," Ella told him.

Dante looked at her. She was wearing a tracksuit now and her long blonde hair flowed around her, she was absolutely stunning even without make-up.

"My father was murdered."

"I'm so sorry, what happened?"

"He was mugged, but I don't really want to talk about it," she told him.

Dante put the picture back down and expertly skirted around her father's death. "So, how have you been?"

"I've had better days, would you like a glass of wine or something?" Ella asked as she put the flowers into a vase.

"Sure, whatever you're having."

"Have you eaten?" Ella asked as her stomach began to rumble.

"No, do you want to go out for something?"

"I'm not really in the mood, why don't I rustle something up?"

"Why don't you go and relax and I'll see what I can come up with, I am quite a whiz in the kitchen." He gently steered her towards the living area.

"I… but," Ella tried to protest.

"I will not take no for an answer." Dante took off his jacket and threw it onto the settee. "I won't be a second." He reappeared with a glass of wine. "Here, relax, I insist."

Ella gratefully accepted the wine. "Well thank you, kind sir, one could really get used to this treatment."

"It's my pleasure." Dante busied himself in the kitchen. He was glad to see she had pasta, herbs, Parmesan and some ham and mushrooms in the fridge. Twenty minutes later he was putting it on the plates.

Ella appeared in the doorway. "Mmm, something smells nice." She surveyed his toned body, he definitely took care of himself, she noted.

Dante placed the plates onto the table. Ella giggled as she noticed the apron he was wearing. He quickly removed it. "No jokes please."

"It's just that I've never seen a man in an apron before."

Ella tasted the pasta. "Wow, you really can cook! I thought that you were joking!"

"I take my food very seriously indeed."

"I can tell." Ella couldn't eat it all; her appetite wasn't quite back to normal.

"You look like you have lost weight; you really should look after yourself."

"Thanks for the concern Dante, but really I'm fine."

"So, how about Milan?" he persisted.

"My mother needs me right now," Ella told him as she looked sad.

Dante extended his arm across the table. "She would want you to have some fun." He held her hand and then gently kissed it.

Ella felt shock waves shoot threw her entire body; she quickly pulled her hand back.

"What are you afraid of, Ella?" His voice was soothing. "The last thing I want to do is hurt you, believe me I will treat you like a princess."

Ella started clearing the table; she had to do something to get away from him.

Dante wanted her so badly but he knew that he would have to be very gentle with her. "I'll be here for a few days."

"Fine."

"I promise you that you will love Milan."

"I've heard that it is very beautiful."

"You'll find out soon enough."

"I hope you don't mind but I feel really tired."

Dante brushed her hair back from her face and looked into her eyes. "Very well, but please call me." And with that he left.

Ella's head was spinning, she wanted to run after him, throw herself into his arms. She imagined what it would be like to be with him. God, what was she thinking? She had never felt this way about anyone before, it was insane, she barely knew him. But she was seriously tempted to take him up on his offer.

Chapter Twenty-Six

Marcus was pleasantly surprised to hear from Mr Miller and Mr Grant; they had received a phone call from Ella who had apologised for her behaviour. She had explained that Marcus was indeed responsible for all the decision making and hoped that they would be able to do business together.

Ella never ceased to amaze him; she was quite a woman he thought. The two men were agents for two international footballers who were keen to purchase a Ferrari F430 Scuderia and a Porsche 911 GT2. He pressed the intercom button. "Hannah, get me Ella Reynolds on the line please."

Two minutes later Hannah put Ella through. "Ella I wanted to personally thank you for sorting that deal out."

"It's my pleasure Marcus. I just wanted to make it up to you."

"How about coming out for lunch to celebrate?"

"That sounds good."

"I'll meet you at Harry's."

"What? Are you treating me to fish and chips then?"

"Yes." Marcus laughed. "Let's say noon?"

"Ok, I'll see you then."

"Who was that?" Carolyn asked her.

"That was the lovely Marcus Treymayne inviting me for lunch."

"I thought you couldn't stand his nice manners?"

"I don't mind if it's in small doses." Ella laughed. "Oh and guess who turned up last night, totally out of the blue?"

"Who?"

"Only Dante Moretti!" she exclaimed.

"What, you mean he came to the apartment?"

"Yes, he cooked me a meal and we talked. He wants me to go back to Milan with him."

"And?"

"I'm thinking about it, he gave me a couple of days to make my mind up."

Carolyn was confused she was meeting Marcus for lunch but fantasising about Dante. "Hang on a minute, are you interested in Dante or Marcus or both?"

"I enjoy Marcus' company but Dante is much more exciting don't you think?"

"You lucky girl, spoilt for choice!"

"I know it's great to be in demand."

"How's your mum doing?"

"She's on antidepressants now. Doctor Shaw thinks that she should see a counsellor to help her come to terms with father's death."

"Does she know how he died?"

"No, I haven't been able to tell her yet; she's in no fit state."

"I promised the girls I would go and see Tara with them. I hoped that you would come too."

"Some other time. Now I need to get ready so you'll have to excuse me."

Carolyn was worried about her friend, worried that she was rushing into this trip to Milan, her involvement with Dante. He was very good looking and a perfect gentleman but she somehow knew that he was too good to be true.

"How do I look then?"

"Gorgeous."

Ella was wearing a knee-length white skirt and black and white top with matching black and white shoes. Her long hair was swept up into a ponytail and she wore her designer sunglasses on her head. "Do you think it's a bit fancy for the chippie then?"

"Not at all honey, Marcus is in for a treat. Anyway it's a beautiful sunny day, you'll be able to sit outside."

"See you later then." Ella was fashionably late.

Marcus thought he'd been stood up when he looked up and saw her standing there. "You look amazing." He gently kissed her on the cheek.

"You too!"

"So, what will it be, cod and chips?"

"Of course, oh and some of those lovely mushy peas."

Marcus placed the order. "Thanks for sorting the deal, I really appreciate it."

"It's the least I could do after making such a fool of myself. Gosh, I'll never be able to eat all of this." The cod was huge and the plate was loaded with chips and a big mound of mushy peas. "Can I get a glass of water please?" Ella asked the waitress.

"Certainly and what about you, sir?"

"A mug of tea would be nice."

Ella tucked into her meal, it was really good.

"So, are you going to tell me where you are going?"

Ella looked up. "Milan."

"Sounds like a wonderful idea, is Carolyn going with you?"

"Er... no."

"So, you are going alone then?"

Just then Ella's phone rang. "Hello?"

"Have you made up your mind yet?"

Ella put her hand over the phone. "I won't be a minute." She left Marcus sitting at the table while she walked over to the patio area.

"Yes."

"*Yes*, you've decided or *yes* you are coming with me?"

"Both." Ella giggled, "I'm coming with you."

"That's fantastic news, I'll pick you up tomorrow morning, seven a.m. sharp, be ready!" Dante put the phone down.

Ella walked back grinning like the Cheshire cat. Just the break she needed!

"Something happened?"

"No, sorry I'm going to have to leave you to it."

"Oh?" Marcus was disappointed. "Was it something I said?"

"Don't be silly."

"Can I ask how long you are going to Milan for?"

"I'm not sure, I'll be in touch." And with that Ella left.

Marcus noticed the admiring glances she got. She should have been a model; she certainly had the perfect figure, envied by women and lusted after by men. Ella didn't realise how beautiful she really was and he was glad that she wasn't in the least bit vain and that's what he loved about her. It was true he admitted to himself, he was falling for her in a big way, but unfortunately for him she wasn't in the least bit interested.

Chapter Twenty-Seven

Milan, Italy

The flight had been wonderful. Dante had booked them into first class and they didn't have to queue to get on the plane. They were greeted with a glass of champagne and a stack of daily newspapers. Dante held Ella's hand. "You don't know how happy you have made me," he told her in a serious voice.

Ella held her breath as Dante leaned over and kissed her gently on the lips. "What... what was that for?" she gasped.

"To show my appreciation."

Ella blushed, it was like he had awakened something in her and it felt marvellous. She settled back in her leather recliner seat and closed her eyes.

She must have dozed off because the next thing she remembered was someone gently shaking her. "Ella, wake up we're here. We've started the descent into Linate."

Ella yawned and stretched out her arms. She picked up her handbag and applied her lipstick and checked her appearance in her compact.

"You look beautiful, I am one lucky man."

"I could get used to this lifestyle." Ella smiled up into his handsome face.

"This is the start of something special and I intend to spoil you completely," Dante told her.

"I'll look forward to it!" Ella teased him.

As they waited for their luggage Dante put his arms around her. She gazed up into his eyes and he planted a kiss on her forehead. She felt that she had finally found her soul mate and it thrilled her.

Dante quickly grabbed their luggage off the conveyor belt. "Come on then, let's get out of here." He whisked her out into arrivals.

There was a chauffeur waiting for them. "Welcome home Signor Moretti."

"It's good to be back."

"Here, let me take your luggage."

Dante opened the car door. "After you."

He must be somebody really important she thought, his business must be doing really well.

"My house is situated in the centre of Lake Como. The views are out of this world, it overlooks Menaggio village and the beautiful Bellagio Peninsula."

"Sounds awesome!"

"But first we'll have a few days in Milan itself, so we can sightsee, shop and we must go to La Scala Opera Theatre."

"I think I can handle that, where are we staying?"

"I don't have an apartment here but I have taken the liberty of booking us into the Caruso Hotel et de Milan, it's very beautiful."

Ella's mobile started to ring, she looked at the handset it was Carolyn. "Hi!"

"I take it you've landed then!"

"Of course, I'm on my way to the hotel as we speak."

"I do hope that it's separate rooms!" Carolyn teased her.

"Me too," Ella joked. "Give my love to Tara when you see her."

"I will, take care, honey."

"You too, speak soon." Ella smiled as she shut her phone.

"A friend?" Dante enquired.

"Yes, you remember Carolyn?"

"Ah yes, very nice young lady."

The drive took about twenty minutes, the roads were pretty busy, everyone seemed to be in a complete rush but thankfully the traffic flowed.

As they drove up to the building Ella's eyes lit up. It looked very old, sort of Gothic in appearance, she thought. The chauffeur opened the door for them and arranged for their luggage to be collected. The doorman tipped his cap. "*Buonasera Signor, Signora.*"

"Buonasera." Dante pressed some notes into his hand.

Ella smiled, wondering why he had done that, the man only opened the door for them after all.

"You never know when we may need his services," he told her as if reading her mind.

The reception area was bright and airy with a huge domed glass skylight in the centre of the ceiling. Most of the room was decorated in rich red and golds with many objects d'art displayed in cabinets.

"Why don't you take a seat and I'll check us in?"

Ella nodded, still taking in her surroundings. She sat on one of the high-backed chairs and watched the hustle and bustle around her. There were many people checking in and she was amazed to see Dante walk right to the front of the queue.

Less than ten minutes later he was back at her side. "After you signora." He showed her the key cards. "We are on the top floor, but it has marvellous views over Scala Square."

Ella's stomach began to rumble. "Oops sorry, guess I must be hungry."

"Why don't I order some lobster and have it delivered to our suite?"

"Our suite?"

"What I mean is, my delightful Ella, have it delivered to one of our suites once you have freshened up," he told her.

Ella smiled. "That sounds perfect, then perhaps we could have an evening stroll to walk off all that fabulous lobster."

"Certainly. Allow me." He proceeded to swipe the card and open the door for her.

"Wow, it's gorgeous." She almost ran into the room and threw herself onto the bed, it was huge and so comfortable.

Dante watched her from the doorway, she was like a child he thought. Perhaps this trip would help her move on from the heartache she had recently endured. "I'd better leave you to it. I'll give you a knock in about twenty minutes is that ok?"

"Yes, yes that's fine with me." Ella sank further into the bed and moved her arms back and forth over the soft Italian bed linen. The bed was so comfortable she just wanted to close her eyes and drift into a deep sleep. Thinking better of it she sat up and looked around. The suite had wonderfully high ceilings and large windows, which she supposed led out onto the balcony. First she went to survey the bathroom. It was all done out in marble and the floor was actually heated. Giggling she shook her head, how ridiculously insane was that! When she got home she was going to have a heated floor, Carolyn would positively adore it and, of course, so would she.

The doorbell interrupted her thoughts. She peeped through the spyhole to see who it was. It was the bellboy, presumably with her case. "Oh *grazie*, for your trouble." She gave him a substantial tip, thinking if Dante could tip like that then so could she. As she sat on the floor to unpack her case she wondered what the trip was going to be like. Dante seemed genuine enough and, anyway, she was enjoying his company.

She brushed her hair, touched up her make-up and put on some fresh clothes, there, she felt better already. Flinging open the patio doors she walked out onto the wrought-iron balcony.

"*Bella*?"

"Oh, Dante I didn't see you there!" Ella exclaimed. He was on the balcony next to hers of course.

"Shall I come to you or vice versa?" he asked.

Ella shrugged. "I don't really mind, you decide."

"Very well, I shall come to you." And with that Dante climbed over his balcony and made the two-foot jump onto hers.

"My God, are you insane?" Ella's heart skipped a beat, it was a long way down if he'd have missed.

"I couldn't be arsed going the long way around." He laughed.

"Don't ever frighten me like that again."

"Oh, so you were frightened for me then?"

"I would be frightened for anyone pulling a stupid stunt like that!" she insisted.

"Come here." He grabbed her by the waist. She tried to struggle, somewhat unsuccessfully, which Dante hoped was a good sign. Pulling her to him he kissed her softly at first and then more deeply, more passionately, their bodies entwined and Dante picked her up.

"No, Dante no," Ella whispered.

The doorbell rang for several seconds before he put her down. "Damn it, saved by the bell, at least for the time being." He winked at her.

Ella leaned over the balcony and watched the people below, what the hell was she doing? Dante had some kind of hold on her and she was scared of what that meant. Should she go with her instincts and give in to her desire or should she listen to her head and hold back. It was a tough choice, but after everything she had been through surely she deserved some happiness, even if it was only for a while.

Feeling guilty she phoned her aunt. "Hey it's me. How's Mum?"

"She's sleeping right now, dear. I'll tell her that you said hi though." She paused. "Sorry, darling, there's someone at the gates I'll have to go."

Ella thought the call was rather odd, abrupt even.

"Hey!" came Dante's call. I can't possibly eat all of this on my own."

"Coming, darling."

Putting her mother's troubles to the back of her mind, Ella settled down to enjoy her evening.

*****

Back home the ambulance arrived to take Mrs Reynolds to the nearby hospital. She had taken pills and vodka. It would be many more times before she finally succeeded in taking her own life.

*****

They finished off the lobster with a nice bottle of Chardonnay and decided to go for a walk around the square. Dante couldn't resist putting his arm around her and was delighted when she didn't object.

"So, Ella tell me, how old are you?"

"Twenty-four." She sighed. "Why do you ask?"

"Because sometimes it's hard to figure it out, one moment you are all woman and the next a shy little girl," he tried to explain.

"And you Dante Moretti, how old are you?"

"I am twenty-six."

"Now I thought you may be a little bit older than that but when you do crazy things like pretending to be Superman and jumping across balconies I think you are about twelve!" she teased.

He stopped in his tracks and looked into her eyes. "This evening has been perfect and I don't wish for it to end, do you know what I am saying Ella?"

Ella knew exactly what he was saying and she surprised herself by nodding.

Dante smiled as he kissed her. It was like he had been hit by a thunderbolt, this woman drove him mad with passion.

Ella gave in to her desire for him and kissed him back, she kissed him like she had never kissed anyone. She was astonished at the wildness in her, the way she yearned and ached for him.

While they were totally engrossed in each other they were being observed from the shadows. It was time, the moment was right. The two men ran across the square, one ran into Dante knocking him over and the other snatched Ella's handbag, but instinct made her hang on.

"Drop it, lady." The man produced a knife.

Ella obeyed, suddenly remembering Dante she turned around. There were people around him now, seeing if he was alright.

"Ella, Ella…!" he was shouting her name.

She ran over. "Oh my God, look at your head."

"I'm all right," he said as he staggered to his feet. "What happened?"

"I don't know it all happened so fast," she said as she held his hand. "Someone stole my handbag."

Dante checked his pockets, that was funny his wallet and cellphone were still there. Something about this didn't quite add up, he was certain of that. Somebody wanted to find out all about Ella, but why, what exactly was their intention?

Ella linked him. "We should go to the hospital and get you checked out."

"No, no, hospital."

"Ok, but we have to at least call the police, in case this happens to someone else."

"Did you see them?"

"Not really, no," Ella admitted.

"Then do we really want to spend the next few days being interviewed by the *Polizia*, looking at photofits?"

"I guess not, you're right. I'll cancel all my cards as soon as we get back to the hotel."

Dante was relieved, he couldn't afford to be seen anywhere near the *Polizia*, not now and certainly not any time soon.

Once safely back into Ella's suite she began to search for a first aid box.

"What are you doing? It's just a scratch, look." Dante dabbed a tissue onto his head and removed the blood.

Reluctantly Ella went to look. If it was a gaping wound she would probably pass out. Taking the tissue out of his hand she peered at the damage. "I think you'll live."

Dante laughed and pulled her into his arms once more. "Now, where were we before we were so rudely interrupted?"

Ella slipped out of his grasp with ease. "First thing, is first, I must call my bank before someone runs up a bill of thousands!"

"Very well, I'll see you in the morning then." Dante smiled politely and left the room.

Jesus she thought, if he hadn't left when he did they probably would have been in bed together; half of her had wanted that to happen but the other was glad that it hadn't. After all, she didn't want to appear as some kind of loose woman.

Dante got on the phone to one of his colleagues. "I want you and Flavio to watch me and my companion at all times, from a safe distance of course. And Carmine see what you can find out, this is my home town and I won't be disrespected like this!" He wondered just what he was doing, involving this beautiful young woman. But it was too late now, he was hooked and he was never letting her go, no matter what.

*****

The man paid off the two thieves and dismissed them. He emptied the contents of the bag onto the table and spread them out. Picking up one of the credit cards he read out her name 'Ella Reynolds'. That name rang a bell, there had been some incident in London. He racked his brains, what was it? Yes, that was it there was a Philip Reynolds something to do with a mugging. He had been left for dead by the roadside, but who was he to Ella Reynolds and what was Dante doing with her? What was the connection? He wasn't sure but he was going to do his damnedest to find out. That arrogant little prick was going to pay for his boss's supposed suicide, but first he wanted to play with him a little.

Chapter Twenty-Eight

Dante awoke with a throbbing headache. He looked out of his bedroom window and saw Flavio and Carmine sitting opposite the hotel having breakfast at a bistro.

He quickly got dressed and was dismayed to find Ella's room empty. Panicking he rang Flavio. "What the fuck are you doing? She is not in her suite, has she left the building?"

"No, definitely not, we have her description and nobody resembling her has come out boss!"

"I hope for your fucking sake that you're right, you dumb fuck!"

Dante ran to the lift and impatiently pressed the button. It seemed to be taking an age so he decided to take the stairs. He shoved open the door and took the stairs two by two, nearly losing his footing on the way. As he reached the bottom he took out his hanky and wiped his face, taking a deep breath he opened the door and scanned the room. Where the fuck was she?

"Can I help you Signor Moretti?" The manager noticed he seemed a little agitated.

"Have you seen Signora Reynolds?"

"Oh, *si, si*, Signor Moretti, she is taking breakfast out in the garden."

Dante was relieved. Jesus for one horrible moment he thought that she had been kidnapped, with the life he lived anything was possible. After regaining his composure he walked down the red-carpeted hallway and made his way onto the garden terrace.

Ella spotted him and waved. God, he thought, if only she knew what was going through his mind ten minutes earlier. Calmly he went over to her table. "*Buongiorno, Bella Ella,*" he chuckled as if nothing had happened.

"*Buongiorno*, Dante."

The waiter pulled out his chair. "What can I get you, Signor?"

"*Caffé con latte, grazie.*"

"So, how is your head this morning?" Ella was still a little concerned.

"Perfectly fine." Dante placed the linen napkin on his knee. "Now, how about a shopping trip this morning?"

"Ooh yes please, but won't you be bored?"

"Not at all, in fact it is my treat."

"You do know that I have very expensive taste."

"Naturally I wouldn't expect anything else."

"You may eat your words when you see how much the bill comes to!" she teased.

"I know this beautiful boutique that has exclusive handmade dresses. I thought you could perhaps choose one for the opera tomorrow evening."

Ella's eyes lit up. "Oh, yes that would be marvellous, what are we going to see?"

"A ballet, but you will see tomorrow."

"I do adore ballet, it's so fascinating, in fact I once had ballet lessons."

"You would have made a wonderful ballerina."

"I'm afraid my parents forked out a lot of money, bless them, and I completely lost interest."

"Ah, such is life, Ella."

Dante's mobile rang, it was Flavio. "Any sign?"

"No," came the response, "everything ok?"

"Yes, yes we are just having breakfast." Dante put the phone in his pocket.

"Who was that?"

"Just our driver, we may need him later to transport all those purchases back to the hotel!"

Chapter Twenty-Nine

Dante knew exactly where to take her to experience real designer heaven. Walking down Via Montenapoleone took her breath away. It was full of luxurious boutiques including Gucci, Giorgio Armani, Prada, Valentino amongst many other top Italian designers. She was absolutely spoilt for choice and Dante enjoyed watching her trying on various chic garments. He made suggestions not always listened to by the lovely Ella because she invariably had her own unique style.

Three hours later and laden full of shopping bags Dante and Ella collapsed onto the nearest bench.

"My God I didn't realise how much hard work that was!" Dante admitted.

"I told you, I bet this is the only time you ever shop with a lady again!"

"Perhaps." Dante phoned Flavio. "I have some bags which need to be taken to the hotel."

"Don't tell me, that was your driver?"

"Yes, now what do you want to do for the rest of the afternoon?"

"I know, why don't we get a camera and take some pictures, it's such a shame to be here and not take any don't you think?"

"Excellent idea."

Flavio and Carmine picked up the shopping. "Anything else we can do?"

"Just don't go too far away in case I need you again."

Both men knew exactly what their boss meant.

"So, let's find the nearest camera shop."

Ella wondered how the two men found them so easily; she didn't recall hearing Dante give them directions. Perhaps he did, she thought, and anyway she was having way too much fun to dwell on it.

Dante took her hand as they walked through the bustling, crowded street.

Ella giggled and pointed to the sign. "Is this named after you?"

"Via Dante, no I'm afraid not but it is a nice street, the shops are a bit more specialised and we should find what we are looking for very easily."

They made their way through the throng of the crowd and it wasn't long until they found the store they were looking for.

The shopkeeper was very friendly and, assuming that they were very much in love, asked when the big day was.

"Oh, we... er haven't really known each other that long." Ella blushed.

"I am surprised. You seem to be very relaxed in each other's company, like how you say in English, soul mates?"

Dante chuckled as he paid him. "Perhaps you are right."

"Wait, I will take your first picture together to remind you of this time," the shopkeeper offered.

Dante passed him the digital camera back. "You win."

They stepped outside the shop and stood so the name of the street could also be captured. "Perfect, here see?" He showed them the playback.

"Marvellous, *grazie*."

Ella and Dante looked well suited together, there wasn't too much height difference between them and their complexions complemented each other. Dante was tall, slim but muscly with dark skin and blue eyes. Ella on the other hand, was a few inches shorter with glowing bronze skin, thanks to an all-over St Tropez spray tan with long shining golden hair and emerald green eyes.

They posed by many of the city's historical sights asking anyone nearby to take a picture of them both. Included in the snaps were them posing by the Duomo Cathedral, a fantastic one with the imposing statue of Vittorio Emanuele II astride a gallant steed behind them, and finally finishing in front of the La Scala Theatre, by which time they were ready for a rest!

Without warning a young man was suddenly beside them strumming his guitar and singing some romantic Italian melody, determined not to go away until he was paid for his efforts.

Dante thrust some money into his hand.

"*Grazie*, Signor." The young man swiftly moved on to the next loved-up couple.

"I was just going to say how romantic it is to be serenaded in such a beautiful city," Ella remarked.

"They are a regular feature in the streets of Milan," Dante informed her.

Giggling they disappeared down a side street and went for brunch in a small café bar. They decided soup and a hot roll along with a nice medium dry bottle of wine would suffice.

"Let me see." Ella grabbed the camera and started flicking through them. "Some of these are crazy!"

"Would you like, I take your picture?" the waiter offered.

Dante nodded as he handed it to him, pulling his chair close to Ella he put his arm around her.

"Please kiss your Signora."

Dante obliged and planted a kiss on Ella's luscious pink lips.

"Very nice." The waiter told them as he handed the camera back.

"Mmm, yes very nice and the kiss wasn't bad either."

"Dante, behave we're in public," Ella laughed.

"So, you are having fun?"

"I'm having a wonderful time, yes, I'm so glad that I came, I wouldn't have missed it for the world." She sighed.

"Me too."

After brunch Dante suggested they go and get changed into some nightclub gear. He wanted to take her to one of the most famous discotheques in Italy and, perhaps, if they were lucky, they might see someone famous.

Chapter Thirty

London, England

Helen Reynolds had her stomach pumped. She had been very lucky that her sister-in-law had popped her head into her bedroom to check on her and had found a bottle of pills scattered on the floor.

She hadn't the heart to tell Ella, especially over the phone. It seemed all that Helen wanted was to join her husband.

Dr Shaw had arrived; he was totally dismayed to find that one of his patients had attempted to take her own life, especially Helen. He knew that he had to do something and called one of his counsellor friends. Helen was still unaware of the brutal murder of her husband; everybody had agreed that it was not the right time to tell her the whole truth.

As he went into Helen's hospital room he wondered what he was going to say to her. She was sitting up in bed and Alice was by her side. "My dear, Helen, how are you feeling?"

"I'm alright," she said in a croaky voice.

"I want to introduce you to a close friend of mine, Andrew Peterson."

A tall, thin, gaunt-looking man entered the room. "Mrs Reynolds, I am pleased to meet you." He lightly shook her hand.

"Who are you?"

"I want to help you work through your grief by a series of sessions."

"What are you some kind of shrink?"

"No, I am a counsellor."

"It's the same thing isn't it?"

"Not at all."

"No, I don't want to talk to a complete stranger about what I am going through!" Helen was becoming agitated.

Alice took control of the situation. "You heard the lady, please just leave. Can't you see that you are upsetting her?"

The two men made their apologies and left the room.

Helen turned to Alice. "I know what I did was extremely foolish but you must promise me that you won't tell Ella."

"I don't know, it's not wise to keep secrets." Alice felt like she was contradicting herself, if only Helen knew everything about Philip's last day on this earth.

"I don't want her to stop living her life to look after me. It's a cross only I have to bear, we don't need to burden her with this."

"If you promise me you will take better care of yourself from now on."

"Of course."

"Hello, it's only me can I come in?" said a chirpy voice.

"Esther, darling." Helen mustered up a smile.

"What have you been doing to yourself?" Esther tutted.

"It was an accidental overdose," Helen told her.

Withholding the truth was one thing, but blatantly lying to her close friend was stepping over the mark. Alice made an excuse to leave the room. "I'll go and see if I can rustle up some tea or something."

Chapter Thirty-One

Milan, Italy

Vitelli pondered his next move. He wanted to hurt Dante and hurt him badly. This Ella Reynolds was a new girlfriend and maybe it wouldn't last all of five minutes. He wanted to wait until he was sure Dante was in love with her and then he would strike.

Esposito had been good to him; he had taken him off the streets, put clothes on his back and a roof over his head. He didn't have children of his own and had raised him like the son he never had. He made sure that he had a good schooling and money in his pocket; in fact he wanted for nothing. The holidays he took him on where extravagant and wonderful. One thing about Esposito, though, was that his wish was that he didn't want Vitelli to follow in his footsteps. Vitelli admired him and longed to be involved in the business but Esposito was adamant it would never happen. So he had gone off to university to study Psychology, to him it was the next best thing to find out how the human mind ticked. He was no fool and knew that he would need to be very cunning if he was to succeed in making Dante pay.

It still angered him that Mancini had sent this thug to do his dirty work and that now their profits from the heroin business had been depleted by sixty per cent it was a disgrace. Vitelli had to accept that the only person who really cared for him in the world was gone, gone forever.

He picked up the bottle of perfume and smelled the aroma; it was in a fancy bottle with a silver bow on the lid. Ella Reynolds certainly had good taste, it was just a pity she didn't in men.

He remembered Dante's first date with her in London and he also remembered when he rushed out of the restaurant. It was a great shame that his colleague had lost him that night. Perhaps he would have been able to stop the assassination of Esposito, but alas fate had been against him. He swore that he would avenge his death, that one day he would be laughing in Moretti's face.

While he was in Milan he would keep tabs on Dante and see what opportunities came up.

Chapter Thirty-Two

As they settled into their private box at the La Scala Theatre Ella could barely contain her excitement. "Swan Lake, it's my absolute favourite," she gushed.

"Ah yes, Prince Siegfried and his love for Odette and of course the evil Rothbart who tricks the poor prince into dancing with his daughter Odile who he has cast in Odette's image."

"Oh…" Ella was astounded. "You know this story so well."

"Yes, I have seen it performed many times."

"You do surprise me Dante."

Dante took her hand as the curtain went up and the stage filled with acrobats and jugglers entertaining the Prince as he celebrated his birthday. He put his arm around Ella and she leaned into him. There was something special about his Ella, something that calmed him, made him feel like he never wanted this moment to end.

At the interval he opened a bottle of wine. "Here." He passed a glass to her.

Ella's eyes were all red and teary. "That bit always makes me cry when Odette is forced away from her love, it's so sad."

Dante smiled, this woman was so incredibly delicate in every sense of the word, yet she was also beautiful and intelligent. "I am glad that you are enjoying it so much."

"Oh, believe me I am totally loving it and I will love it even better when Rothbart is destroyed by the swans."

Dante laughed. "It is only a made-up story my darling."

"Yes but it is wonderfully entertaining."

The curtains went up and the show recommenced. Ella touched Dante's hand; he immediately brushed it with his lips. Lowering her eyelids she continued to watch the show, the finale was spectacular in every sense of the word. As it finished the whole auditorium rose to their feet in a rapturous applause.

Dante noticed the tears in Ella's eyes and gently brushed them away. "You are far too beautiful to look so sad," he murmured.

"I just enjoyed it so much I can't tell you how happy I am that you brought me to see this."

"I am so glad. Now what would you like to do?"

"I don't know about you but all that emotion has drained me of any energy."

"Shall we walk back to the hotel and sit on the balcony?"

"Sounds wonderful, thank you."

"Don't thank me *Bella*, if you are happy then so am I."

Once safely on the balcony Dante made an excuse to go to his suite. "I just need to make a business call, give me five minutes."

He made contact with one of his men. "Any news on Pavel Junior?"

"No, Signor not yet."

"Keep me posted." The last thing Dante wanted was for the situation to linger on any more than a few weeks, he had to impress Vasiliev and by doing so he would become his close ally.

Ella sat on the balcony taking in the view and watching the throng of people in the square. She knew that this was the night she was going to give herself to Dante, it felt right. Touching up her make-up she slipped on a silk nightie and pulled on her robe. When she heard the knock on her door her heart skipped a beat, taking a deep breath she walked over and opened it. Dante was standing there with a bottle of wine and two glasses.

"Oh, sorry were you about to go to bed?"

"Yes, no I mean…"

Dante closed the door and put the bottle and glasses onto the table. He turned to her. "Ella…"

There were no words needed as he let down her hair and pulled her gently to him. Their lips met and he felt a wave of emotion he had never experienced before. *So this was love,* he thought. It had to be. He carried her to the circular bed surrounded by silk drapes, and gently lay her down.

"Oh, Dante," she moaned hardly daring to breathe in case she somehow spoilt the moment.

Within seconds he was naked and quickly removing her garments. He was on top of her now and, as she arched her back towards him, he thrust deep inside of her. As they gasped and moaned, enjoying every single moment of pleasure, it was as if they were as one. They seemed to know it was a magical moment, one that they would never forget.

"Oh, Ella, you are so beautiful I never want to let you go." Dante couldn't hold back any longer and gasped as they both finally gave in to each other's bodies, spent and exhausted.

Ella giggled. "My God, Dante, I never thought sex could ever be like that, I just thought it was a myth."

"I can assure you that was no myth and we made love, Ella."

She nodded and smiled at him. Yes, making love, she thought. Not just sex, this was special.

They lay there breathing deeply in the afterthroes of lovemaking, their bodies still tingling with pure excitement.

Ella closed her eyes; she never wanted the night to end.

Dante whispered in her ear. "Don't even think about going to sleep on me." He stroked her body as she gasped with delight. "Something tells me that this is going to be a long evening."

"Oh, I think I can manage that but can you!" Ella teased him as she looked forward to a repeat performance.

Chapter Thirty-Three

The following morning Ella awakened to find Dante missing, cursing she feared the worst. Had she given herself to him for nothing, was that all he had wanted from her. It wouldn't be the first time someone had used her, her thoughts turned to Rupert Giles. She took a long hot shower while she debated what to do. What a rat, how could he have walked out on her just like that? He was too good to be true and she had foolishly expected more from him, much more.

Why did she always attract the wrong sort? It was as if she were cursed where men were concerned, perhaps she should just be celibate. Stifling a laugh she dried herself off and rubbed the condensation from the mirror. It was insane to be so completely hooked on someone that she barely knew, what had she been thinking!

Just then her hotel phone began to ring, rushing towards it she picked it up. "Yes?"

"Signora Reynolds, this is the front desk."

"Yes, this is Ella Reynolds."

"I have been asked to inform you that Signor Moretti has been called away on business and will be back in a couple of hours."

"I see, was there anything else?"

"No."

"Thank you." As Ella replaced the receiver she sighed with relief, thank God, he hadn't dumped her.

*****

Dante met up with Nico de Luca for the next stage of the plan.

"So, what did you make of Petrov?"

"I liked him better than Vasiliev that's for sure," Nico laughed, "I'm afraid that I haven't had the pleasure of personally meeting Mr Vasiliev, is he that frightening?"

It was Dante's turn to laugh. "Don't worry I'll have him eating out of the palm of my hand soon enough."

"So, when are you going up to Lake Garda?"

"This evening."

"Then, how about Grazia and I turning up unexpectedly tomorrow afternoon? I'll pretend that I have come to see you personally to see how you are getting on with the Maserati?"

"Good idea, perhaps you can bring a brochure of your new stock for me to view, then you can invite me to the showroom and I, of course will bring Ella Reynolds, see if I can get her interested."

"And, will she be?"

"Yes."

"How can you be so sure?"

"Trust me, she is besotted with me." As I am with her, he thought, but he wasn't about to tell Nico. It was better all around if everyone thought he was just using her, then she would be of no use to his enemies.

"What a dog you are Dante, is there no lengths you wouldn't stoop to?"

Dante laughed. "I don't think that warrants an answer."

*****

Vitelli was watching from the rooftop, what was the fucker up to now? There was something going down, he knew de Luca was another scumbag and this meeting had a purpose. Moretti was hatching a plan of some sort and he was becoming impatient, itching to finish it once and for all.

As he continued watching them laughing and joking together he never heard the footsteps closing in on him.

Carmine and Flavio grabbed his feet and pulled him to the ground knocking him unconscious. When he came around he was dangling head first over the edge of the roof.

"So, Vitelli, do you want to tell me why you want trouble for Dante?"

"I... I don't know what you mean!" he gasped. "Let me up."

Carmine signalled to Flavio to lower the rope which was fastened tightly around his ankles.

"P... please let me up!" Vitelli begged.

"What do you want from Dante?"

"He murdered Esposito!"

Carmine rang Dante. "We got him."

"Anyone I know?"

"Esposito's adopted son, he wants revenge."

Dante wasn't worried about the inexperienced little prick that had spent most of his life in a boarding school; he knew nothing of the real world and was definitely not a threat to him. "Rough him up a bit and then let him go."

"Are you serious boss?" Carmine didn't like to leave loose ends they always came back to bite you on the arse when you least expected it.

"He's not in my league and therefore he is insignificant." Dante picked up his conversation with Nico.

Carmine and Flavio dragged Vitelli back up onto the safety of the roof. "The boss has a message for you."

And with that Carmine picked up a chunk of wood and whacked him on the shins making him fall to his knees.

"You… you don't have to do this." Tears ran down his face.

"See the fucking baby, not such a big man now are you!" Flavio punched him in the guts.

As Vitelli lay gasping on the ground Carmine spat on him. "Here's something to remind you of how close to death you came today!"

Flavio took out a piece of cloth and proceeded to gag him, then he grabbed his arm and stretched it out across the ground. He placed his knee across his elbow joint and put his fist onto his wrist to prevent any movement.

Once Carmine was sure it was safe to continue he took out his penknife and proceeded to hack off Vitelli's little finger. It took longer than he thought to hack through the bone and he couldn't believe how much blood came out. He glanced at Vitelli's ashen face, his eyes were on stalks and he was gasping for breath.

"We ever set eyes on you again and you're dead, do you understand?" Flavio threatened him as he yanked the gag from his mouth.

Vitelli looked down at his hand and promptly threw up. No words would come to him, he was in so much pain, he thought that he was dying. As Moretti's two thugs walked off he swore to himself that this wasn't over. He didn't care what happened to him as long as he got his revenge. One thing he knew for certain was that next time he had to be better prepared. He may be an amateur now but one day he would have people trembling at his feet and then he would pick off Dante Moretti's people one by one starting with that animal Carmine Gambini.

Chapter Thirty-Four

London, England

Carolyn Reid had just returned from visiting Tara in France, it had been wonderful getting away from it all. She had spoken to Ella several times since she had gone to Milan, but she still had her doubts about her involvement with Dante Moretti.

On checking her answer machine in the flat she found several messages from her mother. 'Carolyn, darling, I could really do with your help down at the centre, some of these girls are around your age and maybe they could relate to you better.'

Carolyn smiled, her mother was intent in making her a part of these young girls' rehabilitation, but it was heavy stuff and she didn't know if she could handle it. She played the next message. 'Oh, darling, do contact me as soon as you get home. We have had a new influx of girls and now there are fifteen.'

Her mother was persistent and obviously determined for her to take a more active part in the project than she had already. 'Carolyn, we want to take two of the girls out for lunch, perhaps you could suggest somewhere? I'm waiting for your call; don't let me down, darling.'

Jesus, talk about putting out the sympathy vote! Her mother knew her only too well and she was a sucker for a sob story.

Picking up the phone she reluctantly dialled the number. "Mum, it's me, I've only just got your messages, I did tell you that I was due back today."

"I know, darling, but really I need you down here, how long will you be?"

"Give me an hour to unpack and sort myself out."

"Ok, I'll see you at twelve thirty sharp."

She adored her mother but sometimes she could be so demanding. Donating some of her old clothes and shoes was fine, making tea and coffee was fine too, but to actually get to know the poor girls was something else entirely. Carolyn just hoped that she had the stomach for it.

True to her word she arrived at the centre on time. She was wearing jeans and a T-shirt and not much make-up as per her mother's instructions. As she locked her car door she wondered what the new girls were like. The four they had brought in a few weeks ago could barely speak a word of English between them, so all she could do was smile politely and offer them some refreshments.

Barely having time to set foot inside the doorway her mother was there.

"Carolyn, thank goodness you are here, come on, come into the office."

"Ok Mum, what's this all about?"

"The two girls the vice squad picked up have been offered new identities and a British passport if they tell them everything they know!" she said excitedly. "Don't you know what this means? We'll help get that scum put away for good!"

"Hang on a minute, just what has that got to do with me?"

"One of them is keen to experience the life of a typical English girl and I immediately thought of you!"

"What?"

"Well, Ella's away isn't she, I thought that maybe you could have a flatmate for a couple of days, what do you say?"

"I'm sorry I don't understand what you want me to do. I mean, I know nothing of this girl you want me to take under my roof, she could be some kind of headcase!"

"Darling, don't be silly, I have spoken with her at great length and she is very grounded especially after what the poor girl has been through."

"Oh, I'm not sure. I would have to put my life on hold, be very careful where I take her, what I say, what I do, it's a big ask Mum." Carolyn wasn't convinced.

"Darling, I have every confidence in your skills, if you hadn't taken a year out of university you would be a qualified counsellor too."

"Mum, please, don't start all that again." Her mother always had a way of making her feel guilty, like she had let her down for not completing the course when she was supposed to. "I'm not the only one to take time out, you know."

"Of course, but you have a way with people, you must see that you have a special talent. You were born to help others, you should be proud of that."

Her mother knew exactly what strings to pull to coerce her into helping out. "Am I allowed to know anything about this girl then?"

"Data protection dear, but what I can tell you is that she is originally from Belarus, she is one of six children, aged nineteen and was forced into the business six months ago. So you see, it's early days, she is one that we will be able to help, I am convinced of that. It's up to you to help her believe she is worthy to be on this planet, worthy of starting again, putting this dreadful past behind her once and for all."

"Ok, you win. What's her name?"

"Petra Lukashenko, come on I'll introduce you."

"Hang on Mum, what about police protection?"

Her mother tutted. "Sandra Ennis will be staying with you and there will be undercover police presence in the background, so to speak."

"Are you crazy?"

"Don't worry nobody knows she is here, they brought her from somewhere in Scotland."

Her mother was excited and Carolyn knew that all she wanted was to prove that with counselling, and slowly introducing the girls into their culture, that it was possible to turn them around. If she succeeded then she was promised a huge grant to upgrade the centre and send the girls off to college to learn a trade of their choice and hopefully get into the work environment, ultimately leading to independence and a flat of their own once they were ready.

Petra was a petite brunette, she was painfully thin. "Hello, my name is Petra Lukashenko," she said politely.

"Hello Petra, I'm Carolyn Reid and I am very happy that you are going to stay with me for a couple of days."

Petra nodded her head and turned to Mrs Reid. "I thank you for this opportunity."

"Carolyn will take good care of you."

"Do you have any belongings?" Carolyn asked her.

"No, just what I am wearing."

"I may have a couple of things you could have."

"No, I can't do that!" Petra exclaimed.

Sensing that the poor girl probably thought that she would have to do something in return Carolyn told her, "Ok, you can borrow some things if you wish, just while you're with me of course."

Petra half smiled. "Of course."

They drove back to the apartment in silence. Petra was like a frightened rabbit. Her eyes were darting around all over the place as if she was expecting something to happen.

"It's ok, we're nearly there now." Carolyn glanced in her rear-view mirror to see if Sandra was still behind them.

As she let them into the building Petra stood in the foyer. "You live here."

"I have an apartment here that's all," she told her.

"You are so lucky," Petra sighed.

"Come on, we'll take the lift up."

Petra was astounded by everything and Carolyn wondered just exactly what kind of place she came from to gasp every time she touched something.

When she let her into the flat Petra just stood there not knowing what to do. "Please come in," Carolyn told her in a gentle voice. "I'll show you where you will be sleeping."

"No, I want to sleep in here it is so beautiful." Petra ran her hand over the sofa.

"It's no problem; really you can sleep in my flatmate's room."

"Oh, no I can't do that, in here will be good."

"Whatever you want." Carolyn felt humbled to be in this girl's company, she obviously had never had anything like this in her life before.

Sandra Ennis was standing outside of the apartment ringing the doorbell. She was used to babysitting these girls but this was an unusual situation, one that hopefully would benefit her career in the long run, providing the girl gave evidence of course.

Carolyn opened the door. "Hello, Sandra, do come in."

Sandra marched in and headed for the kitchen. "I'm so hungry, when are we going for lunch then?"

"Please." Petra grabbed Carolyn's hand. "I do not like that woman."

"Actually Sandra, Petra and I were going to have lunch together to get to know each other a bit better, so if you don't mind."

"Ok, ok I get the hint, but I won't be far away!" Sandra stormed out of the apartment.

As soon as she closed the door Petra burst into tears.

"Oh, what is it? She is on our side you know."

"Is she?" Petra had doubts about that woman, there was just something cold about her.

"She is one of the good guys, she only wants to help," Carolyn tried to reassure her.

"No, she only wishes to help herself; she does not care about me."

In her heart Carolyn knew that Petra was right, it was well known that Sandra was only interested in her progression up the career path and she didn't give a damn who she used to get there. She couldn't help but feel sorry for the poor girl, after the hell she must have endured and then to be protected by a ruthless career woman, life just wasn't fair.

"Do you want to go and have some lunch?"

"No, please can I just stay here, perhaps take a bath?" Her voice was pleading.

"Petra please try not to be scared, you are in Britain now and I promise everyone has your best interests at heart."

"I think maybe it would be better to just go back to them before anyone else gets hurt."

"Don't think like that, this is a country of opportunity if only you trust in it," Carolyn told her.

"But I am not brave."

"Are you kidding me after all that has happened to you?"

"What do you know about me?"

"Nothing really, but I know of other girls that have been in your situation."

Petra laughed. "Really? You are lucky to have a life like this, what I wouldn't give to be you."

Carolyn knew that she was extremely privileged and pitied the girl but she wasn't sure how to respond.

"Tell me, what would you do if you lived in a small cramped house and your family were starving to death? Would you go and look for work, try to help them, or stay and watch them starve?"

"Petra none of this is your fault."

"You are wrong, it is my fault. I went with him willingly, I'm not a stupid girl."

Carolyn sat down next to her on the sofa. "No, you didn't know that you were being sold into slavery."

"A slave? No, I told you I wanted to go, I had to go!" Petra exclaimed.

"You were a victim of circumstance, there's no way you were to know exactly what was going to happen to you."

"I knew that I had to be with men for money for my family, so you see it is my fault!" she exclaimed. "The man that took me said I would only have to do it for about one month and then I would be able to find a real job to help my family."

"But he lied. That was almost six months ago, if the place hadn't been raided by the police they could have moved you on to another country, worked you to death."

"You know nothing of what you speak!"

"Perhaps that is true, but all I want to do here is help you in any way I can."

"Then you must get me back to them before they kill my family."

"Your family are safe, Interpol have arranged for them to come into the country. They are on the way as we speak." Sandra Ennis appeared in the doorway.

Petra jumped. "No, no you are lying to me!"

"How did you get in here?" Carolyn demanded.

"You didn't shut the door properly."

"You're not helping. I would like you to leave now!" Carolyn was livid.

"It is true, your family is in Britain right now. They are going through special security checks, all you have to do is give me a name."

Petra was shaking uncontrollably. "If what you say is true then I see my family first."

"Very well, I'll arrange it." And with that Sandra finally left them alone.

Carolyn went over to the door and bolted it, putting the chain on.

"Do you believe her?" Petra asked.

"Yes, yes I do, why would she lie?"

"Then I am happy to help but I must see my family first."

"I'll talk to my mother later. Now how about I show you the bathroom so that you can have a long hot soak and perhaps I can make you a bite to eat?"

Petra nodded. There was something about this woman she liked, she seemed to be genuinely caring and that was very unusual in the world she was used to.

After she had disappeared into the bathroom Carolyn poured herself a strong cup of coffee. Jesus, what was she going to do about this Ennis woman? She was totally unemotional and also frightened the life out of Petra.

"Mum, it's only me, I need a favour."

"Is something wrong?"

"That Ennis woman, I have a feeling that if Petra is going to give any names it certainly won't be to her, she is too cold."

"How is Petra?"

"If truth be told, she is absolutely scared to death and I am worried that if Ennis is on the case then she could do a runner or something worse."

"I agree, Sandra is not exactly the caring type, I'll see what I can do."

"Mum, is it true that Petra's family are in Britain?"

"Who told you that, Sandra I suppose?"

"Yes, she did, why?"

"I found out an hour ago that her family were all shot dead in Belarus."

"Oh my God!"

"You can't tell her, Carolyn!"

"That poor girl, now she has nothing, the authorities can't make her testify against anyone she has nothing to lose anymore."

"Yes, I totally agree with you."

"Then we need to get her legal help to stay in the country."

"I'll do everything I can."

"And Mother?"

"Yes?"

"You have to tell her the truth, she deserves to know."

"I know, but I think it best if she checks into my friend's clinic as an inpatient, there is no easy way to tell her and it needs to be in a safe environment. Do you understand what I am saying?"

"Yes, but please let me have these couple of days to try and show her what her life could be like before you break the news."

"Very well, I'll call you later then."

Carolyn was relieved, she didn't think now was the time or the place to drop this awful bombshell on Petra. She would try to coax her to go out with her and hoped that, one day, she would realise that she deserved to have her life back.

Chapter Thirty-Five

After a lengthy conversation with Vasiliev, Mancini had told him that as the gang responsible for the raids were Italian he would clear up the mess. It was a pity Dante was in Milan right now, this would have been a perfect job for him. The Petrelli gang had been trying to put the Russians out of business by tipping off the police. Ultimately they had hoped to bring in their own girls, but they were not in the same league as Vasiliev's men. He made the call to the UK and ordered the hit.

Mrs Reid was in her office, busy trying to raise more funds to tide them over until the grant came in, which she was sure would happen once the girls told them who was behind it all. She was 100 per cent committed to the welfare of the girls under her care and felt like she was finally doing something worthwhile. After her bitter divorce from Carolyn's cheating father she thought that she would never regain her self-respect. But finally she realised this was her life, to help these unfortunate victims of sex trafficking, help bring these evil scum to justice. She hoped that one day Carolyn would run the centre side by side with her. After she had finished talking to her sponsors she set about tidying up. The place was a tip.

Angela knocked on the door. "Is there anything I can get you before I leave?"

"No, no that's fine, I'll just say goodnight to the girls, where's Tony Deveraux?"

"He's in his usual place, sitting in the main hall, feet up and drinking coffee," Angela laughed.

"Wait until I see him, he's supposed to be keeping an eye on the girls!"

"Whoops, hope I didn't get him into trouble!"

Mrs Reid laughed. "No, not at all I'm just kidding, I think I'll join him for a coffee before I go home."

"Valerie should be here soon."

"Ok thanks, Angela and all the best dear, I will be sorry to see you go."

"Don't worry about me Mrs Reid, I'll keep in touch, Ireland isn't that far away you know."

"I know dear." Sheila hugged her. "If ever you change your mind, you know where I am."

"I do and I appreciate all that you have done for me but I feel now is the right time for me to move on."

Angela had been sexually abused by her uncle and his friends for many years before finally having the strength to go to the police. Mrs Reid became her counsellor and they had became good friends. They had stayed in touch and when Mrs Reid opened the centre she had offered her a job. Angela had been extremely grateful and had jumped at the chance to help other girls who had been sexually abused too. "Good night, Tony."

"Good night Angela, and all the best love." Tony nodded, looking up as he saw Sheila Reid heading his way. She was a striking woman, with a flawless complexion and beautiful shiny chestnut hair.

"Hi, Tony."

"Good evening, Sheila, may I say how stunning you look tonight."

"You certainly do know how to flatter me and I appreciate it, but I am almost eight years older than you."

"You don't look a day over thirty," Tony said seriously.

"Just for that I'll make you a bacon butty and a cup of tea."

"That would be lovely." He paused. "When are you going to come out on a date with me?"

"Are you serious?"

"You bet I am, I would love to get to know you better."

Sheila felt good, she had not been interested in men for the six years she had been divorced. She had thrown herself into the centre and that was all she had focussed on. "Keep flattering me Tony and one day you can take me out."

Tony grinned at her. "I knew that one day I would finally melt the ice maiden!"

"Cheeky." She threw a coaster at him.

"Don't be long with my butty!"

Sheila shook her head at him and headed towards the kitchen.

Valerie Cooper had just parked up when she noticed a van pull up beside her. Before she had time to react she was dragged from her car.

"Just do as you're told and you won't get hurt," a burly man told her, he was dressed in black and wearing a balaclava.

"W... what do you want from me?"

"I need you to get us in that building," the man told her.

Valerie was shaking and gasping for breath. "P... please I'm an asthmatic, I... I need my inhaler." She pointed to her car.

The man nodded at one of his men. "Go find it!" he barked.

The inhaler was shoved into Valerie's shaking hands, she sucked deeply on it trying to calm down and catch her breath.

"Ready?"

Valerie nodded as the man snatched the inhaler off her. Bracing herself she walked over to the building.

"See this?" The man pointed the gun at her.

Valerie nodded her head. "I... I understand."

Tony waved at her and opened the door to let her in. Before he had time to say hello he was shoved to the floor. He reached for his gun.

The head of the gang shot him at point blank range. Valerie screamed.

Mrs Reid appeared with a tray in her hand startling one of the men who shot her dead on the spot.

Valerie continued screaming and one of the men hit her with such force that she ended up halfway across the room hitting her head on the coffee table.

"Upstairs, finish it. Let's get out of here fast before someone phones the cops."

The girls didn't stand a chance; all of them were brutally murdered in cold blood. Nobody knew if they had talked, but if they had there were no witnesses left to bring anyone to justice now.

They were in and out in ten minutes.

Mancini rang Vasiliev. "The girls are taken care of."

"Excellent news, now what about the others?"

"It's happening as we speak."

And sure enough the four leaders of the Petrelli gang were taken out. It had been simple, they hadn't expected it and the element of surprise had been in Mancini's men's favour. The gang had met up to discuss their next move in an illegal gambling den. They were laughing and joking, congratulating themselves on how clever they had been; now all they needed to do was start bringing in their own girls. As they were chatting Mancini's men stormed the building and killed them all, none of them had time to react. The police would find them all dead, still sitting in their chairs.

Mancini's men took the drugs and the cash that was lying around. It had been an eventful evening, and the stash was a lucky bonus.

Chapter Thirty-Six

Milan, Italy

Dante had his car delivered to the hotel. He hoped that it would impress Ella and when Nico arrived everything would be in place. He arranged for their luggage to be collected and escorted Ella to the foyer. "You are going to love Menaggio."

As they left the doorman tipped his hat. "Come back soon, Signor Moretti."

"I will." Dante shook his hand.

"Wow, is this your car?" Ella stroked the bonnet of the Maserati. "This is gorgeous."

"I must admit this is my all-time favourite."

"Excellent choice, it's a pity we don't have any in our showroom, I just know it would sell really well."

Good, she was definitely interested, thought Dante.

As they drove out of the bustling city into the peaceful countryside Ella smiled at him. "It's beautiful out here, but I would have thought it was too quiet for you."

"I need my peace and quiet sometimes and what better way than living out here," he said proudly, pointing to the surrounding landscape.

They drove past the lake which was lined with trees and flowers and in the distance were dramatic mountains overlooking the village, like giant hands protecting it.

"Is this your house? My God, Dante, it is so charming."

The house was on top of the hillside set back from the road. An imposing nineteenth century building which Dante had recently renovated to retain its original character.

"I'll take you up to the tower. The views are out of this world."

Stumbling out of the car Ella instantly fell in love with the huge, ornate building and the landscaped garden. She was like a child eager to see everything at once. "Can we go inside now?"

"Don't you want to see the rest of the gardens?"

"Later!" Ella had never seen anything like it before in her life and it made a lasting impression.

Dante waved to the gardener who was busy cutting back the hedgerow. "Now, who's behaving like an excited child?"

"Touché, Dante, touché."

The top half of the house was a pale pink colour and a beige brick colour at the bottom, the windows were all arch-shaped with green shutters around them. In front of the house was a huge archway with a balcony on top of it surrounded by climbing ivy.

Dante opened the door. "Welcome to my little house."

"Little, you're joking right? How many rooms do you have?"

"There are five en suite bedrooms, three reception rooms, six bathrooms, living room, dining room, billiard room, cinema room in the basement and an attic I don't know what to do with yet."

"It must be so lonely up here."

Dante laughed. "I have many friends, Ella, but when I am here I like to have at least a few days by myself and everyone respects my privacy."

Ella admired the marble hallway and majestic staircase that broke off in two directions spanning the entrance hall.

Dante held her hand and kissed it. "Let's go out onto the patio."

Ella didn't resist and happily walked with him through the kitchen and outside. "You have a pool, how fabulous!"

"A heated pool, Ella, do you fancy a dip?"

"I don't have my bikini."

"Then I'll get rid of the gardener and we can skinny dip."

"You can't be serious!" she exclaimed.

"Oh believe me I am!"

"Dante!"

"And I'll call the chef to come and cook us some real Italian food."

"I couldn't possibly!"

"Are you embarrassed my love, because you shouldn't be, you have the perfect body and you should not be ashamed to show it off."

Ella couldn't help but blush as she turned to look at the views. She felt his arms encircle her waist as he nuzzled into her neck. "You are one amazing woman, you know that right?"

"Am I?"

"Yes, you are and don't let anyone tell you any different, come let me show you the master bedroom," he said suggestively.

Ella was like putty in his hands as he gently led her up the stairway. "This way my darling."

Before she knew it he scooped her up and threw her onto the huge four-poster bed.

"Dante," she gasped, but there was no need for words as they both succumbed to each other, the want and the need was too much to resist.

The more time he spent with her the more he wanted her to be with him forever, have his children and live happily ever after. It was just a dream he thought, it would never happen, his life was too dangerous to bring her into it.

"What are you thinking?" Ella whispered.

"Just how happy you make me, now shush my *Bella* Ella."

Their lovemaking was passionate and all consuming as they gave into their desire for each other. It was as if they were one, knowing exactly how to pleasure each other.

Finally they fell into each other's arms happy and joyous. "Dante?"

"Yes?" Dante kissed her on the top of her head.

"Do you think it will always be like this?"

"I hope so my love, now come here." He wrapped his arms tightly around her; he never wanted to let her go. If there was any time he wished his life to be different now was that time. But he knew deep down that it wasn't going to last. If Ella ever knew what he was capable of that would be the end of any future together. For now he was going to dote on her, love her with all his heart as he knew she loved him. "I love you, Ella," he said as he held her close.

Ella was at a loss for words as she felt his steady heartbeat vibrate into her back. "Dante."

"It's ok you don't have to say it back," he reassured her.

"I feel like a different person when I am with you, it's like nothing else matters."

"That's good enough for me, just for now though," he joked.

"I just don't want this to end, me and you I mean."

"And it won't, trust me I will never leave you." But you may leave me one day and then what will I do without you, he thought.

*****

Two hours later they were happy and relaxed sitting out on the patio in the moonlight. The chef had prepared a sumptuous meal which was far better than anything Ella had ever tried before.

"How about that dip then?" Dante asked.

"What about the chef?"

"He's already gone, we are completely alone."

"Oh, I don't know!"

"Remember I have seen all of you before!"

"Dante, behave!"

"I can't help it if I'm in love with a beautiful woman who happens to have the most desirable body ever," he teased.

"How can I resist you when you say such things?" Ella giggled as she began to undress. "So, what are you waiting for?"

Dante hurriedly removed his clothes and jumped into the pool. "It's lovely and warm, come on in."

Ella removed her bra and panties and dived in, when she came up for air Dante was waiting for her. They kissed and Ella gently pushed him away. "You'll have to come and get me first!" Taking a breath she dived under the water.

Dante wasted no time in diving in after her, grabbing her by the legs he pulled her towards him. Turning to him she wrapped herself around him and they kissed. They held hands as they rose to the surface.

"Dante, how are you?"

Ella quickly moved behind him to hide her body and her embarrassment.

"Nico, what are you doing here?"

"I was in the area and thought I would call in on you."

"Errm... perhaps you would like to wait in the lounge."

"Why of course, I'll let you make yourself decent." Nico winked at him.

"Oh my God, how embarrassing, who the hell was that?"

"He's my car dealer, probably has something new and flash he is trying to sell me!"

"Oh, yes?" Ella's ears pricked up; maybe she would show Marcus Treymayne that she too was capable of drumming up business.

"Don't worry he never saw anything, you are for my eyes only, don't ever forget that."

"How am I going to get back into the house?"

"Just stay here my darling. I'll get you a robe."

Ella touched his face and kissed him. "Ok."

"Don't do that or else Nico will be in for a long wait," Dante said as he cupped her breasts and bent down to tease her nipple.

"Oh, stop it!" Ella cried, secretly wanting him to take her right then and there.

"You love it really."

"Later," she gasped.

"I'll be back in two seconds."

Ella watched as he jumped out of the pool, his taut, muscly body glistened in the moonlight as the water dripped off his perfectly toned buttocks. She wondered where he had been all her life and why she hadn't met him sooner. He was everything to her and even though she hadn't told him she had to admit to herself that she was totally in love with him, totally in love with his lifestyle, it was exactly what she needed right now.

True to his word Dante appeared with a towel and a robe. "Come on my love."

Ella walked up the steps out of the pool. She looked like a goddess, thought Dante, he was so lucky to have her. He promised himself that whatever happened between them he would always love her and hoped that she would love him too. Wrapping the towel around her, he rubbed her body and gently kissed her on the lips. "You are very special to me Ella, never forget that."

"You have showed me a different life Dante and it is impossible to describe how happy I am."

"I'm glad, now go and put something on and meet my friend."

Once Ella was safely out of earshot Dante grabbed Nico by the lapels. "I thought you were coming with Grazia tomorrow!"

"I was, but some shit has happened in London and Mancini wanted me to tell you in person."

"Oh?"

"The raids in London were down to the Petrelli gang. After Mancini spoke to Vasiliev he ordered their death and also the death of the sluts who were about to stitch him up."

"Stitch Vasiliev up?"

"Who else?"

Just then Ella reappeared. Dante went to her. "Ella allow me to introduce Nico de Luca, his motor business is very exceptional in this part of the world."

"How do you do." Ella shook his hand.

"I am so happy to meet you." Nico kissed her hand.

"I too am in the motor business."

"That is interesting to know."

"What kind of motors do you trade in?" asked Ella.

"We specialise in Ferrari, Maserati, Lamborghini, Alpha Romeo and of course the classic Lanzia, what about you?"

"I have a manager who oversees the running of the business; we mainly trade in Porsche, Mercedes, BMW the new Lamborghini Gallardo Superleggera and the Ferrari F430 Scuderia."

Nico was impressed. "You certainly know your motors."

Ella smiled at him. "Yes, yes I do. My father always talked to me about the new models he was getting in."

"Perhaps when I am next in London we can meet and discuss business."

"That would be nice," Ella told him as her thoughts turned to Marcus; she had an opportunity to show him that she wasn't just a dumb blonde after all.

"I will look forward to that."

"Now if you will excuse me I need to take a shower." Ella left the room.

"She is very beautiful, very beautiful indeed."

"Don't you get any fucking ideas!" Dante snarled at him.

"Hey, chill out man! I am in love with my wife Grazia, I only have eyes for her." Nico held his hands up.

"Fine, now I would like you to leave and we'll pick up tomorrow as planned."

"Very well, but you must call Mancini, he has the details of Vasiliev's son's exact whereabouts."

Chapter Thirty-Seven

London, England

Carolyn was sound asleep when she was awakened to constant banging on her door. Rubbing her eyes she looked at the clock it was two in the morning.

Petra ran into her bedroom. "I am scared. Someone has come for me haven't they?"

"Just wait in here, I'll go and see who it is." Carolyn's heart was thudding in her chest; she was scared that Petra was right. Peering through the spyhole she saw a policeman. Oh, my God somebody was seriously injured or dead, she thought. Slowly she opened the door, leaving the chain on. "Yes?"

"Carolyn Reid?"

"Yes, what is it?"

"Can we please come in?"

Carolyn took the chain off and stood back to let them in. "Please tell me what is going on?"

"I am very sorry to tell you that your mother Sheila Reid has been murdered."

"W… what, but I was only speaking to her earlier this evening, I don't understand."

"We think the sex trafficking ring slaughtered them all."

"W… what are you telling me that everyone is dead?"

"There was one survivor." The Inspector looked at his notepad. "A Valerie Cooper."

"How did my mother die?"

"She was shot."

"Shot?" Carolyn slumped onto the sofa. "My mother shot?"

"I'm so sorry."

"Where is Valerie?"

"She was knocked out during the attack and is in hospital for observation overnight, she has a concussion."

Petra was listening to everything and as she moved closer to the door she tripped over Carolyn's slippers.

"Who's in there?" The Inspector nodded towards the door.

"One of the girls from the centre."

"But we thought they were all dead."

"I was doing a favour for my mum."

"Go and get her, she is still a witness and we need her now more than ever."

"Petra, it's ok to come out."

Petra walked towards Carolyn. "Is it true, Mrs Reid is dead?"

"Yes," the Inspector told her. "Now you must come with us, it isn't safe here."

"Hang on, this gang must think they got everyone, nobody will be any the wiser, so as far as I am concerned she'll be safer with me."

"Perhaps but we can't take the chance."

Petra sat next to Carolyn. "Please, please don't let them take me, I beg you!"

Carolyn looked at the Inspector. "You can't make her go with you."

"I think you'll find that we can, we'll put her in a safe house, she will be well looked after. Trust me, she is very important to this investigation."

Petra grabbed Carolyn's hand. "Please, don't let them!" she pleaded.

"I'm so sorry Petra, there's nothing I can do."

"But there must be!"

"I will help you as much as I can I promise, on my mother's life it's what she would have wanted." Carolyn squeezed her hand.

"Do you mean it, you won't forget about me?"

"I promise, now you must go with the police."

Reluctantly Petra went to get dressed; she wished she too had been shot dead in the centre, now she had lost Mrs Reid and the other girls. Even in Britain she wasn't safe and she doubted that she ever would be again.

The Inspector sat down next to Carolyn. "I know that this is a lot to take in, your mother was admired by many for the work she did." He paused. "Do you have anyone that you can call?"

"Yes, yes I do, but I must call my father first."

"I understand, here's my card, I would like you to come down to the station sometime today."

"Ok."

Petra reappeared. "I'm ready."

After she left Carolyn burst into tears. She felt empty, her mother had meant everything to her and now she was gone.

Chapter Thirty-Eight

Milan, Italy

Dante rang Mancini. "I just had an update from Nico."

"Good. Then I need you to go to Scotland, get the boy and bring him back here."

"Here? Why not just take him direct to Vasiliev?"

"The boy is our bargaining chip. I want Vasiliev to come here for him while we sort the deal out."

"The boy is Russian, how will I understand him."

"Yelena Petrov will escort you."

"Very well."

"Oh, and Dante you must make sure you leave no one behind, do you understand?"

"Yes Uncle." The phone went dead. Christ, he had to eliminate the grandparents, he wasn't happy about that but there was no choice.

Ella was standing in the doorway. "Everything ok?"

"Yes, fine."

"Who was that on the phone?"

"It was just business, I have to fly back to the UK tomorrow."

"Oh? Well, I suggest that we make the most of tonight then," Ella said suggestively as she lowered her robe off her shoulders.

Dante went to her.

"Ah-ah! You'll have to catch me first!" Ella turned on her heels and ran up the stairs, but Dante was too quick for her.

"Oh, stop teasing me, Ella." He picked her up with ease and carried her up the remaining stairs.

"I will miss you and all this," Ella told him.

"It will be difficult getting to see each other but I promise to make every effort."

"You better had."

"I have enjoyed being with you these last few days."

Ella smiled at him, she was definitely falling for him in a big way, but she was afraid to admit it.

"Now, come here and show me just how much you will miss me!"

Chapter Thirty-Nine

London, England

As Ella collected her luggage and went through arrivals she sighed to herself, she was on cloud nine and felt wonderful. Spotting Carolyn she waved at her. "Hi, I wasn't sure if you would get my message. I thought our answer machine was playing up again! I've had the best time ever!"

Carolyn looked solemn. "I've had the worst time in my life."

"What do you mean?"

"My mother is dead."

"Oh my God, Carolyn, what on earth happened?"

"We'll talk later. Let's just get out of here."

Ella felt guilty; here she was going on about having the time of her life while her best friend was mourning the loss of her mother.

"So, are you in love then?"

"Never mind me, I want to know what happened."

Carolyn passed her the newspaper. "Here look, I can't really bear to talk about it again, I've been in the police station for three hours and I'm so exhausted."

Ella scanned the newspaper. "Jesus Christ, what is this world coming to? Your poor mother, it's so awful, I just can't believe it!"

"And do you know the worst thing about it all?"

"What?"

"They will never get who did it. This gang are too well connected to be caught!"

"Don't say that."

"It's true, all they have is one girl from Belarus who is in a safe house right now. She has been sex trafficked, her family have been murdered and now my mother isn't here to help her anymore!" Carolyn sobbed.

Ella put her arms around her, she didn't know what to say, it shocked her to the core. "Have you spoken to your father?"

Carolyn nodded. "Yes, he's been brilliant."

"Is there anything I can do?"

"I wish there was Ella, I really do." Carolyn sobbed into her arms.

"Are you going somewhere?" asked Ella, noticing her case behind the sofa.

"I'm going to stay with my dad for a while. I need to be with him. I mean, I know that he and mum were divorced but he is genuinely upset about her death."

"It's ok; you do what you need to, but remember I'm here for you if you want to talk."

"Thanks Ella, that means a lot to me. Can you give me a lift to the hospital?"

"Sure, who are you going to see?"

"Valerie Cooper, she was a close friend of my mother and I need to make sure she's ok before I leave."

"Shall I wait and take you to your father's house?"

"No, it's ok. I'll get him to pick me up from there."

Chapter Forty

Valerie was just being discharged when Carolyn arrived. "What are you doing here?"

"I was worried about you and Angela."

"Angela has already left for Ireland, she doesn't know what happened." Valerie gasped. "I am so sorry about your mother she was a special lady."

"Thank you. Have the police spoken to you yet?"

"Yes, but I'm afraid that I can't help them, you see they all wore masks, I was so afraid!" Valerie sobbed. "What will we do without her? She was the only one who really cared." She could hardly breathe and fumbled in her bag for her inhaler.

"What do you mean? Come and sit down."

They sat in the hospital reception area and Valerie made her confession. "Nobody knows that I too was trafficked, it all started twelve years ago. I was in love you see with a Russian boy; he was wonderful to me at first. My family were against him from the beginning as I was only seventeen and he was much older than me."

Carolyn was shocked. "I... I didn't know, mum never told me."

"I made her promise. This was to be a new life for me."

"So, Valerie isn't your real name?"

"No, my real name is Rosa and I am from Italy."

"What happened to you?"

"I was supposed to be going on a trip to Moscow to meet his family, but things went horribly wrong. As soon as I got there I was taken to a run-down factory and dumped with many other girls from all over the place. One of them told me what they were going to do us and I tried to escape. I was gang raped in front of the others so that no one would attempt to get away again. After that I was moved to many different places, I must have been with thousands of men. I was like a zombie, and my brain was void of all emotion, I was in shut down I guess. Five years later and I was a bag of bones. I barely ate anything, I just wanted it to end. Anyway I was in a massage parlour in the Ukraine when it was raided. I was brought to the UK and I moved from hostel to hostel. I heard about your mother's project and made it my aim to meet her."

"My God, I would never have thought something like that could have happened to you. I mean, you are so grounded and you sound like you are English."

"That was all thanks to your mother, she saw to it that I had various health tests and even paid a tutor to teach me the English language."

"But you don't really have much of an accent."

"That is good for me and what your mother wanted, she just wanted to protect me and that's why she kept it secret from you."

Carolyn could barely take it in. "So, you are all right aren't you?"

"I am HIV positive and probably won't live to see thirty. I will never marry, never have children but while I am here I so much wanted to help the other girls."

"Valerie, I am so sorry."

"Don't be, I have accepted my fate."

Carolyn put her hand on her shoulder. "You are so brave."

"No, not really, your mother was. You see in a way she saved me, made me realise I could make a difference with the time I had left."

"What will you do now?"

"It's what you will do that matters."

"What do you mean?"

"Your mother would want you to re-open the centre, help girls like me."

"But I don't know the first thing about running it!" Carolyn exclaimed.

"You will learn and with me by your side it will be possible, but we need more sponsorship."

"Oh, Valerie I don't know."

"Please, just think about it and when you have made a decision, call me." Valerie opened her bag and scribbled down her phone number. "Don't wait too long."

Carolyn sat there staring at the paper, when she looked up Valerie had gone.

Chapter Forty-One

Ella decided to pay Marcus Treymayne a visit just to make sure that the business was running smoothly.

"Good afternoon Hannah is Mr Treymayne around?"

Hannah looked up from her desk. "Oh, Miss Reynolds were we expecting you?"

"I didn't realise that I had to make an appointment."

"Oh, I'm sorry I didn't mean anything by that, I just wasn't expecting you."

"Never mind, is he in?"

"No, he's with a client on a test drive but I am expecting him back very soon."

"I see, thanks." Ella walked over to the window and looked down into the car park; so Marcus seemed to be looking after the business very well indeed.

"Can I get you something?"

"No, I'm fine thanks."

Hannah pretended to take some files into Marcus' office and quickly rang his mobile. "Mr Treymayne? I thought that I should warn you Miss Reynolds is here waiting for you."

"And is she in a good mood?"

"I can't really tell, although she seems to be a lot more relaxed than the last time she was here."

"Ok, I'll be back in ten minutes, try not to let her into the office." The calm before the storm, he thought, but still he didn't mind if it meant seeing her again.

Ella was sitting cross-legged, randomly flicking through a magazine. She looked up when she heard footsteps. "Marcus, about time, I hope you have been making money while I have been sitting here waiting?" she joked.

Marcus laughed. "Of course, what can I do for you?"

"I wanted to talk to you."

"You'd better come into my office then." Marcus held the door open for her. "After you. Hannah, can you bring in some tea please?"

"Certainly, sir." Hannah watched as they disappeared. Poor Mr Treymayne, it was obvious to any fool that he adored her, what a pity Miss Reynolds couldn't see it. Maybe one day they would be together, they were so very well suited if only they knew it. Sighing to herself, she switched on the kettle.

"Please, take a seat."

Ella sat down. "I would like to see this month's accounts if that's ok with you."

"Certainly." Marcus opened the filing cabinet drawer. "There you go, as you can see we are well over target and I'm increasing our revenue as we speak." He paused. "How was your trip?"

"Oh, wonderful, it is a beautiful place, all that history." Ella had a dreamy look in her eyes.

Marcus' heart flipped, he realised that it had to be a man who had made this effect on her. "So, who is the lucky man?"

"Hmm? Oh, Dante Moretti, but I'm just having fun that's all," Ella replied absently, half hoping that by speaking the words aloud she would believe then. She could never let her heart be broken ever again.

"So, it's not serious then?" Marcus persisted.

"Marcus, never mind about my love life I may have drummed up some business."

"Oh yes?"

"Yes, I met an Italian gentleman called Nico de Luca; he owns a similar business to ours in Milan. It just so happens that he is coming to the UK in a few days and I've invited him to meet you. I hope you don't mind," she added.

"Mind? I'm impressed, how did you happen to come across this Mr de Luca?"

"Oh, Dante buys his cars from him and you should see the latest one, it's a silver Maserati Spyder and it is out of this world."

"Sounds interesting."

"Interesting? It's more than that Marcus, just think of all those playboys out there who would love to own something like that. Anyway I'll contact you when he arrives, what do you say?"

"I suppose there's no harm in seeing what he has to offer."

"I thought, import, export, you could help each other out, you must admit there could be lots of money to be made." Ella sounded triumphant.

"I'll reserve judgement until I meet Mr de Luca."

"Naturally, it is of course your prerogative being the manager of RPM."

Hannah knocked on the door. "Shall I pour it?"

"That's fine, Hannah, I'll do it," Ella told her, shooing her out of the office.

"Is there something else?"

"Have you heard about Sheila Reid?"

"I've heard something about her on the news, bloody damn unfortunate incident."

"Unfortunate all right. That was my friend Carolyn's mother, she started that centre from scratch and has literally helped thousands of girls over the years."

"My God, how has your friend taken it?"

"Distraught and I know exactly how she feels." Ella sighed.

"Is there anything I can do?"

"Not at the moment, but if I think of anything I'll let you know."

Marcus handed her a cup of tea. "You have had a lot of turmoil in your life lately, Ella."

"Life goes on Marcus, it has to." Ella slowly sipped her tea.

Marcus was worried about her, she seemed to be rushing into a relationship with a man she barely knew and now there had been another murder, which possibly was pushing her even further into this man's arms.

"I'd better go, I need to see how mother is," she told him.

Shit, that was another unfolding drama that Ella knew nothing of. "Give her my love won't you?"

"Of course, thanks Marcus, I'll be in touch soon."

"I'll look forward to it."

Chapter Forty-Two

The Vasiliev residence, Moscow, Russia

Vasiliev was holding a party for his many comrades in his huge mansion and he had brought some of the fresher girls in so that they could have some fun with them.

Just as the party was getting into full swing Yakov Garshin turned up keen to speak with his boss.

"Pavel, how are you?"

"What the fuck are you doing here? I told you I don't want to be seen in public with you, now fuck off, go and have some fun upstairs and I'll meet you later," Vasiliev snarled into his ear.

After all the business he had brought his boss's way and that was the thanks he got for his trouble. There had been many times he had almost been caught bringing the girls from various parts of the country and he had evaded capture every time. Taking the stairs two at a time he looked across to Vabnik who was armed with an AK47 rifle guarding one of the bedrooms.

"Who's in there?"

"If I tell you that then I would have to kill you, Yakov," Vabnik laughed. "Some ambassador, that's all you need to know."

"Any chance of having a quick look?"

"You are one dirty bastard, did anyone ever tell you?" Vabnik said showing his rotten teeth as he spat on the floor. "You can have them when he's finished." He held the door slightly ajar.

Yakov sneaked a quick look, some fat old balding man had one of the girls spreadeagled across the bed and her limbs were tied tightly to the bedposts. He was slapping her hard across the face as he forced himself onto her. Grunting, he was oblivious to his audience as he came in about two seconds. He turned to the other girl who was sitting naked on the floor rocking herself while quietly crying. "You're next, now come here."

The girl just sat there staring at him and shaking her head.

"Vabnik," he shouted. "I've finished with this one, get rid of her."

"Wait here," Vabnik told Yakov. "I'll deal with this." He whistled for two of his men to come and help him.

Still watching the show from the doorway Yakov lit a cigarette. Stupid fucking whores, why did they not do what they were told and then they would not be hurt?

The two men cut the girl free and dragged her out of the room. She was covered in blood and her face was a mess. As they came out Yakov told them to stop. He held the girl's chin and looked at her. "She is no good to anyone now, get rid of her," he told them.

"What about Vasiliev?"

"He won't make any more money out of her for a while, she is surplus to requirements." He pulled out a knife and plunged it into the girl's chest as the men half held her. She gurgled as she took her last breath, it was over in an instant. "Take her out the back and dispose of the body, make sure nobody sees you and I suggest that you wrap her up in a fucking blanket or something first."

The two men did as they were told.

"And get some fucker to clean up this mess," he shouted after them.

He knocked on the bedroom door. "Do you need any assistance in here Vabnik?" he asked as he walked into the room.

"This fucking girl, where the fuck did you get her from?"

Yakov laughed, it was yet another one of his many girlfriends he had tricked into the business. Walking over to her, the young girl cowered in the corner. Yakov grabbed her by the hair and yanked her head towards him. "You do what he says or I will cut off your mother's head and chop off your brother's legs, do you understand!" His face was inches from hers.

The girl promptly threw up onto his shoes. "Go and fucking clean yourself up!" he yelled cursing as he grabbed a towel and wiped his designer leather shoes.

Svetlana ran into the bathroom and looked at herself in the mirror. She could not do this, she would rather die. Looking around for a weapon of some sort she found a pair of scissors and held them with two hands poised at her neck.

"What the fuck are you doing in there, hurry up!" Yakov yelled, enjoying his power over these weak pathetic girls.

His voice was enough to give Svetlana the courage she needed, closing her eyes she plunged the scissors deeply into her neck severing an artery as she did so.

Yakov was trying to open the bathroom door. "Open the door you stupid fucking whore!" he screamed as he tried to shove the door open.

"Vabnik, give me a hand here she is trying to block the door with something."

Vabnik ran over and nearly slipped on the blood seeping through the bottom of the door. "What the fuck?"

As they managed to force the door open they found the girl with the scissors embedded in her neck and her body still twitching on the floor. Vabnik checked her pulse. "Dead!"

"Fucking dead!" exclaimed the ambassador. "I must get out of here, if any of this comes out…"

"Do not worry, you are not to blame ambassador, we will sort this out, these things happen in this line of business."

The ambassador nodded as he quickly got dressed. "I must go and mingle with the guests, act as if nothing is wrong."

"This girl was nothing." Yakov spat on her lifeless body. "She will not be missed."

The ambassador tidied himself up and left the room, he would go and see how his wife was getting on.

"How will you explain this to Vasiliev?"

"I can handle Vasiliev, I bring him a lot of business, he understands that these little misadventures are bound to happen from time to time."

Vabnik shook his head, yet another body for his men to dispose of. He hated this fucker, he was a liability, one that if he continued on this path of destruction would eventually bring them all down. He would have to speak to Vasiliev, but he knew that they were tight and that if he said anything against him then he would end up in a shallow grave somewhere. This was his life now, the life he chose and he was stuck with it until the bitter end.

Chapter Forty-Three

Scotland, UK

Dante took a direct flight to Aberdeen. He was to meet up with Yelena Petrov and together they were to kidnap the boy. The unfortunate thing was that he was going to have to dispose of the grandparents first and he wasn't looking forward to that, especially if Pavel Jr witnessed it.

Yelena had taken a direct flight from Moscow and had arranged to meet Dante Moretti a few miles down the road so that they would not be seen together. Her husband Aleksei had told her all about him and she was strangely looking forward to meeting him, the nephew of Signor Mancini. Yelena felt honoured to be trusted to take on the task of retrieving Vasiliev's son. According to her husband she would have total respect and Vasiliev would be forever in her debt. As she picked up the hire car and checked the map for the rendezvous point she checked her appearance. Yes, she definitely looked like a gentle woman on the outside, but underneath she had burning ambitions to be a somebody. It excited her to be sent on such a vital mission to a foreign country and she had to prove that she was more than useful to Vasiliev, perhaps then he would take notice of her.

Dante was becoming impatient. He got out of his four-wheel drive and lit a cigarette. Where the fuck was she? They had a window of opportunity and if they missed it they were definitely screwed. Just then he heard a car horn tooting away, turning to look down the road he cursed as he watched the car screech towards him at an alarming rate. It didn't look like it was stopping any time soon! Diving into the ditch to avoid being mown down he watched as the driver slammed on the brakes just missing his vehicle. He got to his feet and dusted himself down.

Yelena opened the door and the first thing Dante saw was a black stiletto emerge followed by a long slender leg. "Allow me to introduce myself, I am Yelena Petrov at your service!" She did a little salute.

"Are you fucking nuts, you nearly killed me!"

"Oh, don't be so dramatic, Dante Moretti, it is these damn British cars they are impossible don't you think?"

Dante grabbed her roughly by the arm. "We are supposed to be discreet and you have just sped down the road honking your fucking horn!"

"Oh, do calm down, Dante, darling, I'm here now aren't I?"

"Fucking calm down, Jesus you are positively crazy!"

"So, are we ready to go now?" Yelena drawled.

"Did you hire that in a different name?" Dante couldn't afford to take any chances especially now with this crazy woman who could get them both caught by her erratic actions.

"What do you take me for some kind of idiot!" Yelena snapped at him.

"Give me the keys." Dante extended his arm towards her.

"They're in the ignition get them yourself!"

Dante just wanted to fucking shoot her right there and then, she irritated the hell out of him. It was a good job she was Aleksei's wife or he wouldn't have hesitated putting a bullet into her pretty little head. He drove the car off the road and into a nearby field and then headed back towards the Land Rover. Opening the boot he took out a can of petrol. "Get in the fucking car!" he ordered.

Yelena stared at him for a second. He was very good looking, she thought, but that temper was frightening. Not wishing to make him snap she quickly jumped into the passenger seat. She'd got the reaction she wanted from him and now she had seen for herself that he meant business.

Dante set about dousing the car in petrol and retreated to a safe distance. Lighting a match he threw it down onto the trail he had left. Running to the Land Rover he jumped in, revved it up and sped off just as the car exploded in a huge fireball which could be seen for miles. Now the mission really began, the local fire crew and police would soon be here hopefully giving them the necessary time to get to the boy.

*****

Ivan and Olga Babichenko were sitting in their spacious garden, surrounded by trees and set back off the road. It was in a picturesque setting several miles from the nearest village. Pavel was almost four now and he had stopped asking for his mother, as if he somehow knew that she was never coming back.

It saddened Olga that she would never see her daughter again and that her son would never really remember her. If Irena hadn't met and fallen in love with that psychotic madman then she would still be alive today. It was hard for her to understand what her only child had ever seen in this evil man, because he was the most evil person she'd ever had the misfortune to come across. She had tried to dissuade her daughter from marrying him but the more she tried, the more Irena dug her heels in. It was unfortunately to lead to her downfall in such a vicious and shocking way.

Olga was glad that Pavel Jr had been staying with them that weekend when they received a call from Irina's friend Boris. He had given them a name of a man who would help them out of the country, as far away from Vasiliev as possible. Boris had begged her to leave but Olga desperately wanted to see her daughter. He had insisted that if they didn't do as he said and pack their bags and leave then Vasiliev's men would come and kill them. Sensing the urgency and hearing it in his tone Olga did exactly what he said. Her husband on the other hand wanted to stay and wait for them. He had a shotgun and he was ready to blast anyone to death who set foot on his property. They had taken his daughter but there was no way he was letting them get his grandson.

Olga had begged him, tried to reason with him, he had finally broken down and sobbed. She had never seen a grown man sob like that before, especially not her own husband. They had packed very little, time was of the essence, they were to meet the man within the hour.

Ivan had driven like a maniac and they were relieved to be greeted by a man they assumed was some kind of secret agent. He helped get them out of the country and gave them new identities.

The sacrifice they made was great, never to be able to say goodbye to their daughter and never to see her in her final resting place. It was one thing Olga would never be able to forgive herself for. Her thoughts were interrupted by little Pavel running around the garden after the chickens. It was times like that this that brought tears to her eyes. She was sure Irina was looking down from heaven watching him, smiling at his energy.

Pavel was almost old enough to start school and Olga was dreading it. He had been sheltered these last eight months and it was going to be more of a shock for her than him. Some of the villagers popped by every now and then to see how they were doing and to invite them to the regular fetes and charity events they held. But Ivan made sure that they kept a low profile, for the sake of the boy, he'd told his wife.

Olga had thanked God for the little church a quarter of a mile down the road where she could go and light a candle beside the photo of her daughter. It comforted her to say a prayer for her all alone in heaven.

The vicar was such a sweet old gentleman and this one particular day he had noticed Olga's photograph. "A relative of yours?" he asked.

"Oh!" Olga had jumped and put it quickly into her pocket.

"It's ok. You can talk to me, I can take your confession if you wish."

Olga hadn't hesitated in unburdening herself. Afterwards she felt cleansed and free, freer than she had felt in all these months. The talk had helped her, although the vicar did not offer any advice, he listened and said a prayer for them. It was then that Olga realised that she could not offer Pavel Jr the life he should have. They were no spring chickens anymore and it was becoming increasingly difficult to keep up with the child.

Olga and Ivan had sat down and talked at great length and they had decided to have him adopted by a lovely young couple in the village who couldn't have children of their own. It was agreed that they would still remain his grandparents and visits would be a regular occurrence.

The vicar had arranged everything and today was finally here.

Ivan held her hand. "We are doing the right thing," he told her.

"Yes, yes I know." Olga brushed away a tear. "But how I will miss him."

"We will still see him," Ivan reassured her.

"Yes, I know but it will not be the same." Turning away Olga walked over to Pavel Jr and picked him up. He was so heavy these days, she didn't think her back would manage once he grew a bit more. Pavel rubbed his cheek on hers. "Nana."

Olga held him close and patted him. "Remember the lovely lady, she is coming with her husband today, you will be staying with them for a while."

Pavel Jr gurgled with excitement. It was breaking Olga's heart.

Ivan got out of his rocking chair and gently took the child from her. "Why don't you make some tea and I'll amuse the little one for a while."

Olga nodded and slowly walked towards the house rubbing her tear stained eyes.

*****

Dante and Yelena had been watching from behind the trees, now was a perfect time to grab the boy.

Ivan was sitting in his rocking chair still holding Pavel in his arms when he dozed off.

Yelena wasted no time in taking out the little handheld yellow windmill which she stuck into the ground and blew on.

Pavel Jr wriggled out of his grandfather's arms and ran towards her.

Just then Olga emerged from the house and spotted her. "What are you doing? Who are you?" she shouted.

Yelena panicked and pulled the boy's face to her as she pulled out her automatic and shot Olga dead.

Dante was sitting in the Land Rover with the engine running waiting for her. He couldn't believe what was unfolding before his very eyes, straight in and out, no need to kill them after all, that had been his plan. They weren't supposed to see anything and now the grandfather had awakened. Dante jumped out and ran towards her, but it was too late, she shot Ivan too.

Pulling a bottle out of her pocket she held it over the boy's face, the ether would keep him quiet for quite a while. Picking him up she headed to the car.

"You fucking stupid bitch!"

"I did my job, Dante, don't leave anyone alive, remember?"
"I told you if we did this right there was no need!"
"Vasiliev gave orders." Yelena smiled at him.

Dante wanted to kill her with his bare hands. She didn't give a damn about human life, she was too heartless.

"Then I'll clean up your fucking mess!" Dante smiled back through gritted teeth.

He carried the bodies into the house and switched on the gas, he had to make it look like an accident.

The explosion was seen for miles and the first people on the scene were the vicar and the young couple who were just about to give Pavel Jr a new life. Tragedy had struck and now they were all presumed dead, although the boy's body was never found.

Chapter Forty-Four

London, England

Ella was disappointed not to hear anything from Dante, she wondered if their long-distance romance was going to work. She put it to the back of her mind, whatever was meant to be was meant to be, she thought.

As she applied her lipstick and fixed her hair she noticed how happy she looked. It was the first time in a long time that she felt really happy. Was she in love with Dante? Yes, she supposed she was. Who would have thought it, Ella would actually meet the man of her dreams? It was crazy, the whole situation, but the timing had felt right, she needed the love of a good man and Dante was that man.

He had wanted to know all about her, but strangely when she tried to get him to open up about himself he always managed to change the subject. She wondered what it was he was hiding from her, something about his family perhaps? Maybe he was ashamed of his past. If he truly loved her then he would have to tell her everything sooner or later, the last thing she wanted was secrets between them.

Her thoughts turned to Carolyn. She really wanted to phone her to see how she was coping. But her best friend had insisted that she would contact her when she was ready.

She was tidying around when there was a knock on the door. Not expecting anyone she peered through the spyhole and saw a woman that she didn't recognise. As she opened it the woman more or less shoved her way inside. "I beg your pardon, who the hell are you?"

"I could ask you the same question," the woman snapped back.

"What do you want?"

"I need to speak to Carolyn Reid right now, where is she?"

"I'll ask you one more time, who the hell are you?" Ella didn't like the woman's attitude one little bit.

"I am Sandra Ennis, I work for the vice squad."

"Vice squad? What do you want with Carolyn?"
"I'm afraid that it's personal."
"I'm sorry then, I can't help you."
"Very well." Sandra Ennis walked back to the front door and signalled for two officers to come in. "You start in the bedroom and you the kitchen," she ordered. "I'll do in here."
"You can't do that!" Ella was dumbfounded.
"Oh yes I can, here." She handed her a piece of paper.
Ella couldn't get her head around it, search warrant for her flat, this had to be some kind of mistake surely she thought. "I... I don't understand."
"Your friend has been harbouring a witness and she was taken into protective custody less than twenty-four hours ago."
"So?"
"She has absconded, it may be that she left something here the other night which may help our enquiries."
"You've lost me, I have no idea what you are talking about!"
"This is very serious, make no mistake," Sandra said as she started flinging cushions off the sofa.
"Do you mind telling me what you are looking for?"
"Not sure, I'll know if I find anything."
"I am going to report you to your superior, you are behaving disgracefully."
"You do whatever you have to and so will I, this is my job."
"Couldn't you at least be a bit more sensitive, especially now after her mother's death."
"Whose mother, Petra Lukashenko's?"
"No, Carolyn's of course." She paused. "Who is this Petra person?"
"Your friend put her up last night, she is the only witness we have left and it's vital we get to her before anyone else does!"
"I don't believe this!"
"Where is Carolyn?"
"She is staying with her father for a while, can't you just leave her alone?"
"Impossible, you'd better give me the address."

Reluctantly Ella scribbled it down on a piece of paper. "Here, promise me you will be sensitive."

"I'll see what I can do."

The two men reappeared. "There's nothing here."

"So sorry for the intrusion, Miss…?"

"Ella Reynolds, you'll be hearing from my solicitor."

"Whatever." Sandra Ennis recognized her type: a spoilt bitch who probably had her daddy wrapped tightly around her little finger.

As she left Ella leaned on the door, her head was spinning, she didn't understand what was going on.

Her first instinct was to phone Carolyn, warn her that this Ennis woman was on her way to see her. "I'm sorry Carolyn, I had no choice."

"It's ok, it's not your fault."

"So, is there anywhere else Petra could go to?"

"She doesn't know anyone else." Carolyn suddenly stopped. "Wait, there is someone."

"Who?"

"Valerie Cooper, she worked for my mother."

"Where does she live?"

"About thirty minutes from the apartment. Oh, Ella I need a favour."

"Name it."

"Will you go and tell her what has happened?"

"Of course I will."

"And when you see her make sure if Petra is with her that you tell her you are a close friend of mine and we are going to help her."

"How?"

"My mother has, I mean had –" she corrected herself, "– she had connections, she helped Valerie and perhaps she will be able to tell you the name of the solicitor who was assigned to her case."

"Carolyn, I don't even know these people. Why would they trust me, let alone talk to me?"

"Take that picture of me, you and mum off my dresser, that should convince her."

"Then what?"

"I'll sort it out, nobody knows Valerie's real identity so they won't be looking for her any time soon."

"What if I take them to my mother's house, she's still away, it's standing empty."

"Are you sure?"

"Positive."

"You are one hell of a friend, Ella."

"So are you."

"I won't forget this." Carolyn replaced the receiver.

Ella was kind of excited to be involved in the drama; it was true to say that she had never truly helped anyone in her entire life.

As she alarmed the apartment and left the building, she braced herself, unsure what kind of reception she would get from this woman. One thing was for sure, she was about to find out.

Chapter Forty-Five

Moscow, Russia

Vasiliev was excited at the prospect of seeing his son once more. Dante had been true to his word and found him; it was incredible that he somehow had the connections to do that. He had to admit that he could be very useful to him. And of course the lovely Yelena had played a vital part and he intended to reward her.

As Dante drove up to the house he looked at the boy, he looked very scared. Yelena was speaking to him in his mother tongue and that seemed to settle him a little bit. He wondered if he was doing the right thing bringing Pavel Jr home. Right now he was completely innocent, but one day he would grow up and turn into another Vasiliev and quite frankly one of his kind was enough. Sighing he realised that, one day, he would probably have to dispose of him too.

They were met by a team of bodyguards who ushered them into the mansion.

Vasiliev had his back to them. "Do you have him?"

"Yes." Yelena held the boy's hand as she walked towards him. "Here is your son."

Vasiliev faced him, he had a tear in his eye. "Pavel, my son you are home." He picked him up and swung him around. "I have missed you."

Pavel Jr didn't speak, he was confused, he outstretched his arms to Yelena.

"Perhaps I should take him up to his room," Yelena offered.

"Yes, good idea, get him settled in."

After she left Vasiliev shook Dante's hand. "I can't tell you how much this means to me, I am a very happy man."

"I am glad."

"And what of the Babichenkos?"

"They are dead, it was a house fire."

"So, it looks like an accident." Vasiliev laughed. "You did well, now I will deliver my side of the bargain."

Dante was relieved. "I thank you."

"We will make much money you and I, let us have a toast." He poured them both a straight shot of vodka. "Here." He handed it to him.

"To business."

They chinked the glasses together and swallowed the burning liquid in one gulp.

"Another?" Vasiliev asked him.

"Just one then I must return to Milan and tell Mancini the good new," Dante told him.

Yelena reappeared. "I have left him with Lidiya, I think he will be fine now."

"I have a job for you," Vasiliev told her.

"Oh, yes?"

"Yes, I would like you to become more involved in the business. Perhaps you would like to stay and have lunch with me and then we can discuss it in more detail."

"I would be delighted to."

Dante somehow felt in the way. "I will be in touch."

"Yes, yes, thank you once again." Vasiliev grinned at him.

As Dante drove off he felt sick to the pit of his stomach. What had he just done to that little boy, leaving him with that sick fuck? It was a means to end, he told himself. Some things he didn't like to do, no he didn't want to do, but it was a necessity.

Chapter Forty-Six

London, England

Ella was full of trepidation as she pulled up outside the shabby council house. It was nearly nine o'clock in the evening and she hoped that Valerie was at home. Locking her car she walked carefully up the garden path which was lined with rose bushes. As she neared the door she noticed the welcome mat. Somehow it all seemed out of place on this council estate, wasted in this area perhaps, she thought.

She knocked lightly on the door and waited. The curtains twitched as someone looked out. It felt like an age before the door finally opened.

"Hello, you don't know me but..." Before she had a chance to finish the girl went to shut the door.

"Wait..."

"Whatever you are selling I don't want it lady, now please leave." And with that the door slammed tightly shut.

Ella steeled herself and once again knocked lightly on the door.

The young woman opened the door once again. "I told you, you are wasting your time here."

"Please, if you just let me explain." Ella opened her bag and passed the photograph to her.

Valerie once more shut the door. She stared at the picture, it was of Mrs Reid, Carolyn and this woman outside her door, but what did it mean?

Ella waited patiently; she would give it another five minutes and if there was still no response then she would have to leave.

"You'd better come in." Valerie looked suspiciously up and down the road.

"It's all right, I can assure you, I am quite alone."

"Hurry up and get inside," the young woman instructed her as she leaned against the wall and sucked on her inhaler.

The house was sparsely furnished but was neat and tidy, quite comforting in a strange sort of way. Ella noticed that there were no family snaps anywhere, unlike her own home which was covered with them.

"What do you want?"

"I'm a friend of Carolyn Reid's, she asked me to come and see you."

"Why, is she ok, has something happened to her?" Valerie exclaimed.

"No, no, nothing like that."

"Then, what are you doing here?"

"It's about Petra Lukashenko, have you seen her?"

"No, why would I?"

"Because there are only you and her left from the centre and since she has escaped custody Carolyn thinks she may have headed here."

"Are you crazy? I barely know the girl." She grabbed her inhaler once more.

Something about the woman's tone didn't ring true, Ella could just feel it and usually her instincts were quite good. "Please, you can trust me, I am here to help you."

"Why, why would you want to help someone like me? You don't even know me."

"That's true, but you see Carolyn is my best friend and best friends do anything for each other in times of need."

"Why did she not come herself?"

"She was afraid that someone would follow her, possibly that bitch Sandra Ennis!"

Just then Petra appeared in the doorway. "I am Petra, who are you?"

"I am Ella Reynolds."

"Yes, I have heard of you, Carolyn has spoken well of you."

"Right now I need to get you out of here, both of you."

"Where, where would we go to?"

"Leave that to me, it is all in hand."

"But why me?" Valerie asked.

"I know that you too were a victim in the past and that Mrs Reid helped you stay in the country."

"But no one is supposed to know that!" Her chest tightened.

"I swear to you that's all I know, I know nothing of the details. Carolyn is just worried that the vice squad will turn up here because you worked for her mother."

"I see, are we going far then?"

"No, it's not far and you will be perfectly safe."

"How long for?"

"As long as it takes for Carolyn to present a case to the court."

Petra looked at Valerie. "What should we do?"

"We will go with her, I trust her and so should you."

"Ok, let's make a move."

"I should pack a few things."

"I wouldn't worry too much about that, there are plenty of clothes where we are going," Ella told them as she thought about her wardrobes overflowing with garments she had barely worn.

Once they were safely inside her mother's house Ella collapsed into a huge wicker chair in the conservatory.

"My God, is this your house?" Petra asked.

"No, it is my mother's."

"And where is she?"

"She is abroad at the moment."

"This is so beautiful, did you grow up here?" Petra gushed.

"Yes, yes I did."

Valerie remained quiet, totally unimpressed with the grandeur around her. "So, can we eat?"

"Yes, of course, please excuse my manners." Ella made her way into the kitchen, the cupboards were always well stocked as was the fridge.

"What would you like?"

"Anything," Valerie told her.

Ella couldn't understand the woman in front of her, she was calm, aloof, almost too calm.

"I would like some water please."

Ella passed her a glass of water. "There you are." She watched as Valerie opened her bag and swallowed several tablets.

"Are you ok?"

"I am fine, thank you for asking."

Petra switched on the flatscreen TV attached to the wall in the kitchen. She was like a child flicking through the channels. "I never had a TV back home."

"Oh, where is home?"

"It is..." Before she had chance to finish Valerie jumped in.

"It is better that you do not know anything about us for your own protection."

"Protection, what do you mean?"

"There are dark forces at work, ones that you should never ask about it."

Ella's heart pounded. "The people who killed everyone in the centre you mean?"

"Them and others." Valerie told her with a blank expression on her face.

Ella wondered just what had happened to this pretty young woman. She was like a zombie, she thought. Whatever it was it had crushed her personality.

"I'll make us some omelettes if that's ok? I'm afraid that I'm not much of a cook."

Valerie nodded her head as she sat down on the barstool and tried in vain to erase Yakov Garshin's smiling face out of her head. Even after all this time it still haunted her and she shuddered.

"Is ham and mushroom ok?"

"Yes, fine," were the only words she could get out of Valerie. It was like she had turned in on herself, withdrawing herself from the situation around her.

"The house is perfectly secure, nobody can get in or out without me knowing about it. The electronic gates can only be activated on the outside by a few select people, the rest have to be buzzed in by someone already inside the house. Nobody can see the house from the road."

Valerie nodded and closed her eyes for a split second, wishing the nightmare would finally end.

"Are you all right, can I do anything?"

"I will feel better once I speak with Carolyn."

"She promised to phone the first opportunity she gets." Ella had a funny feeling that it was going to be an extremely long night, and it turned out that she was right.

Chapter Forty-Seven

Marcus Treymayne had been trying to get hold of Ella for several days but with no success, both her house phone and mobile went straight onto her answer machine. He so wanted her to be there when Nico de Luca signed the deal. If it had not been for her then none of it would have been possible. He wanted to encourage her, make her proud of what she had achieved, God knows Philip would have been well and truly impressed.

He made one last attempt to reach her, but this time he tried her mother's house. "It's me Marcus, if you can make it for ten a.m. I would like you to be a witness to the deal you so cleverly set up, please call me when you get this message."

Ella was listening and smiling to herself, she had been very clever, very clever indeed.

"Is that your man?" Petra asked.

"No, he works for me."

"Really? But you are not very old."

"I am just very fortunate that my father built up the entire business so that one day I would inherit it." Ella picked up her father's photograph.

"Is that him?" Petra asked peering over her shoulder.

"Yes."

"He looks like a very nice man."

"Yes, he was. Anyway, the solicitor is coming here and he will be moving you both to another location, he is very optimistic."

"What does that mean?" Petra asked.

"It means, you have a good chance," Valerie told her.

"Oh, thank you for everything you have done." Petra threw her arms around her.

"It is Carolyn that you must thank. She has done all of this because she genuinely cares about you, as did her mother, God bless her."

"God bless her," Valerie said as she kissed her rosary beads.

Chapter Forty-Eight

"Marcus, I'm so sorry that I missed the signing of the contracts," Ella said as she burst into his office.

"It's ok I managed to get another witness."

"Please Marcus, you know I would have made it if I could, it's just all this with Carolyn."

"All what?"

"Sit down and I'll tell you."

Marcus listened intently. Ella wanted to give away a small fortune to the 'Sheila Reid Centre' and also make a yearly donation to help pay for security. "You want how much?"

"Come on Marcus, the Milan business will make a huge profit and you know that father always liked to donate to various charities."

"But this? How do you know that these women aren't just trying to get into the country?"

"My God, Marcus, trust me, I have met two of these young women and I was shocked and appalled to hear details of how these girls were lured or dragged into this sordid industry."

"I see."

"No, you don't see."

"I'm sorry."

"I would like you to be the patron of the centre."

"What?"

"Yes, you must be the patron and donate on my behalf."

"I think we should stay anonymous."

"So, you admit that you may be frightened for your life if anyone found out?" Ella laughed. "Were you just testing me?"

"I suppose, but if your heart lies there then I will sanction it, but it must remain secret."

"Very well." Ella shook his hand. "It isn't all about profit you know, putting something back into the community is what it is all about." Ella's mobile started ringing, she looked at the set, it was Dante. "Just give me a minute."

"Ella, you have been impossible to get hold of lately are you ignoring me?"

"Don't be silly, I've been rather busy," she told him.

"I'm coming over tomorrow for a few days and I would like you to come back to Menaggio."

"Ok, ring me when you land and I'll pick you up at the airport."

"Very well *Bella*, I will see you very soon and Ella?"

"Yes, Dante?"

"I love you."

"Me too."

"What did you say?"

But Ella didn't answer she just flipped the phone shut. "Where were we?"

"I am having dinner with Nico and his wife Grazia and would love you to join us, what do you say?"

"Ok, what time?"

"I'll send a car for you, say seven thirty?"

"Ok." Ella went to leave the office. "Oh, Marcus, I forgot to say, congratulations on the deal. You are one hell of a businessman, now I know what my father saw in you."

Ella had been like a whirlwind, as quickly as she graced him with her presence off she went again. Marcus felt positively exhausted in her company, she never ceased to amaze him and he hoped that she always would.

*****

As soon as Ella got back to her apartment she rang Carolyn. "Hey, how are you?"

"I'll feel better once the funeral is over with tomorrow, are you still coming from my house?"

"Of course I am."

"It looks like Petra will get residency, so that is one positive step to come out of all this mess."

"Mother sends her condolences and is making a substantial contribution towards the upkeep of the centre."

"That's very generous of her."

"So, you have no doubts about taking over from your mum?" Ella wanted to double check with her friend. "I mean you don't have to be hands on, someone could run it for you."

"I'm certain that one day my mother wanted me to take over from her, although it has come sooner than any of us could have known."

"The things that your mother did over the years, looking after the plight of those poor girls she would be happy to leave it in such capable hands."

"Thanks, Ella, there's not many people who understand what this meant to her."

"Don't mention it."

"Have you thought about my job offer? You would be good for the girls."

"I have thought long and hard, but this is your dream and I'm sorry to say that it's not mine, I hope that I haven't offended you."

"Don't be silly, as long as I have your friendship that's all that matters."

"I am prepared to help out financially though, and I would like to talk to you about that whenever you're ready, but I want it to stay confidential."

"Ella, you are too much," Carolyn sobbed.

"It's the least I can do, I know that if the shoe was on the other foot you would do the same for me."

"I am so grateful for everything."

"Don't be grateful, just be happy that I believe in what you are doing, it is amazing."

"There's nothing amazing about helping another human being live a normal life, a life that they were robbed of."

"I'll see you in the morning, honey, try and get some rest."

"Thanks, Ella."

Ella sighed. The year had certainly been eventful for both of them, although in completely different ways, but somehow the bond between them had grown stronger. Both had lost a parent and both knew how devastating it was.

Now she had to put on a brave face and meet Nico de Luca and his wife Grazia, she wouldn't let Marcus down. She had to admit he was fantastic at his job and she couldn't knock him for that, his business acumen was second to none.

Chapter Forty-Nine

Marcus picked Ella up at seven fifteen. "I thought we should get to the restaurant before the de Lucas."

"What did you think of Nico?"

"He was very knowledgeable and I'm sure he will be an asset to our company."

"Good." Ella was miles away thinking about Carolyn's predicament.

"Are you ok? You don't seem yourself at the moment."

"I'm all right, it's just the funeral tomorrow and with it being so soon after father's I don't know if I can cope." Ella sighed.

"I understand." Marcus was genuinely sympathetic. "Anyway, did I tell you how wonderful you look tonight?" He was trying to lighten the mood.

"Thanks," was all Ella could say.

"No, really this Dante person is one lucky man." He paused. "When will I have the pleasure of meeting him?"

"It just so happens that he is flying in tomorrow evening for a few days."

"Oh yes?"

"Yes, I think that you will like him."

Marcus felt pangs of jealousy consuming him, why couldn't she see that he adored her?

The car stopped just outside the restaurant. Marcus got out of the car and like a true gentleman he opened the door for her. She looked amazing in her little black dress and long, blonde hair that flowed like a halo around her.

"I hope they like Figo's."

"It is one of the finest and I'm sure that they won't be disappointed."

As they took their seats and browsed the menu Ella's phone rang. "Oh, please excuse me." It was Dante.

"I can't wait to see you, Ella, all I want to do is take you in my arms and make love to you."

Ella went crimson with embarrassment. "Er... yes that's nice."

"Do you have company?"

"Yes."

"Until tomorrow then," Dante teased her.

"Until tomorrow." Ella put her mobile back into her bag.

"Was that him?"

"Dante? Yes, he was just confirming the details of his flight."

Marcus nodded, he couldn't wait to meet the man who had this effect on Ella. He wanted to see what he had that he hadn't.

Just then Nico de Luca entered the room with a stunning woman on his arm, which Ella presumed must be his wife.

Marcus stood up. "Nico, so glad that you made it, I take it this is Grazia? She is much more beautiful than you described."

"You flatter me Mr Treymayne."

"Please, call me Marcus."

"And is this your wife?" Grazia asked.

"Er… no, this is my boss Ella Reynolds."

"I am delighted to meet you."

"Likewise." Ella shook her hand.

"So, let's eat," Marcus said as they all sat down. "I'm starving."

Chapter Fifty

Milan, Italy

Dante had been summoned to Mancini's residence for a debrief. "Vasiliev is one happy man thanks to your good work."

"It was nothing."

"It was much more than nothing, believe me. Now that the Russians are on side we will make an absolute fortune and we will be a formidable force."

"I thought that we already were," Dante laughed.

"I totally agree with you." Mancini lit one of his favourite cigars.

"But you are quite right we will be an even greater formidable force."

"Now, you must make sure that the Reynolds girl is in."

"I believe Nico has it all in hand."

"You must go to London and make sure, this side of the deal is extremely important."

"I understand."

"Good, but it is a shame that we are no longer able to launder the drugs through the company. Do we still have someone on the inside, to keep an eye on things?"

"Yes, you only need to say the word."

"Did you clear up all of Philip Reynolds' so-called evidence?"

"Yes," Dante lied remembering the safe key. He hadn't been able to locate the whereabouts of the safe yet.

Mancini leaned back in his chair. "I feel like I can relax now, since you have played a more active part I do not have to stress anymore."

"And that is how it should be," Dante told him, knowing that he had to find the last piece of evidence and destroy it as soon as possible.

"Now, there is something I have to tell you, something that only I know about, it is very big."

Dante's ears pricked up. It had taken a long time but now Mancini finally trusted him enough to reveal something of major significance.

Opening the safe Mancini took out a disk and inserted it into the computer's disk drive. "Come," he beckoned.

"What is it?" Dante looked at the list of names, recognising some of them as mafia leaders, drug barons, murderers and God knows what.

"It is a list, a list of many people and growing all the time."

"And what do you intend to do with it?" Dante was intrigued.

"Right now, absolutely nothing, you see it is my insurance policy Dante, one day we may need their help."

"Some of these names I have never heard of."

"They are people from all walks of life, some involved in arms deals, drug trafficking, murder, prostitution, you name it!" Mancini chuckled at his own cleverness. "If ever we are in a jam then these people will help."

"What makes you so sure?"

"If this list fell into the wrong hands, then a lot of people will go down, it will be the biggest swoop on international crime that the world has ever seen."

"You are very clever."

"One day you will inherit this, but for now I need you to keep a list of anyone and everyone involved in our new venture, it is vital!"

"Of course."

"And Dante, I do not have to tell you that this is to be our closely guarded secret, you must not speak of this to anyone."

"Very well."

Mancini poured them both a double whisky. "Here, get this down you, we make a great team, don't we?"

"Yes." Great team, what the fuck was he talking about? He was the one doing all the dirty work while this fat pig revelled in all the glory.

Chapter Fifty-One

London, England

Carolyn was grateful to see Ella arrive and threw her arms around her. "Hey, come on, honey."

"I'm just so glad to see you, can I offer you a drink, a glass of wine perhaps?"

"No, nothing for me." Ella had to stop herself from saying that it was way too early in the morning for that.

"Just a small one then, to the memory of my wonderful mother."

Reluctantly Ella agreed. "What's the news on Petra?" she whispered.

"There is a private hearing tomorrow and if all goes according to plan my solicitor said that Petra will be free to come and go as she pleases, without any hassle from the police, the vice squad and that cow Sandra Ennis."

"That's great news."

"It is isn't it?" Carolyn's mind wandered. "I forgot to tell you I've asked for anyone wishing to make donations to support 'The Sheila Reid Centre', I think that's what my mother would have wanted."

"Does that mean what I think it does?"

"Yes, I owe it to my mother to get it back up and running, but I will need more security, nothing like this must ever happen again."

"I admire you Carolyn."

"Me? I haven't got the faintest clue what to do really, but with Valerie and Petra's help along with a couple of business partners it should be fine."

"I wanted to talk to you about that."

"Oh, yes?" Carolyn sat down on the huge leather settee. "Tell me more."

"I want to invest a substantial amount to get you up and running and then make a donation every year as long as you need it."

Carolyn nearly dropped her glass. "What, you would do that for me?"

"Yes, of course I would, but there is one condition."

"Yes?"

"It must remain strictly private and confidential and I will be a sleeping partner."

"Why?"

"I can't be bothered being hounded by the press, I just want a quiet life."

"I am grateful, but I would like you to be on the board, when I eventually set one up that is."

"I would prefer that my name is not mentioned, Carolyn."

"Are you frightened of the repercussions?"

"No, not really, I just want to blend into the background and the only way to do that is to remain completely anonymous."

"Have you spoken to Marcus about this?"

"Of course, we haven't ironed out the details yet, but he will do what I ask."

"Ella, you certainly have him wrapped around your little finger!"

Just then Carolyn's father appeared. "Hello, Ella, I'm so glad to see you, thank you for coming."

Ella stood up. "It's fine, Mr Reid."

He turned his attention to his daughter. "That was Angela Stratton on the phone. She wanted to pass on her condolences and apologise for being unable to attend in person, but says her prayers are with you."

"Thanks Dad, I didn't expect her to come, she has this phobia about funerals." She stifled a small laugh.

"Carolyn, we have six cars coming and everyone will be arriving in the next thirty minutes. Are you ready?" His voice was full of concern.

"Yes, ready as I'll ever be."

"It will be a very sad day today, your mother did not deserve to die like that."

"Dad, please I just want to get through today without dwelling on that awful day that took her away from me," Carolyn sobbed.

"Ssh, ssh, it will be a wonderful service, everything is as she would have wanted it," he soothed.

Ella wiped away a tear, she too wanted the day over with as quickly as possible but for her own personal reasons.

The rest of the day was a bit of a blur; she remembered the beautiful horse-drawn hearse led by four white horses down to the church. The sun shone and the birds tweeted, which was unusual for the few funerals Ella had attended, but she was glad for Carolyn. It somehow made the day more bearable, if that was possible.

The service was an hour long, full of Mrs Reid's favourite hymns and readings from the Bible. As they left the church for the burial *Ava Maria* played, echoing gently around the large monumental building.

Carolyn was holding her father's hand and leaning against him, she could barely keep it together. The priest said a few words as the mourners stood around the graveside watching the coffin being lowered.

The immediate family members all dropped a red rose on top of the coffin as they said their final farewell, it was an extremely sad day. The press had been asked to keep a respectful distance and, just for once, they obeyed.

After the internment everyone returned to Mr Reid's residence where he sent her off in style, with a sumptuous buffet and Pavarotti playing in the background.

Ella went out into the garden to see how her friend was doing. She was sitting with Becky, Siobhan and Tara who had flown in especially from France.

"Hey, everyone."

The girls smiled at Ella.

"It's such a sad day," Becky said.

"Yes, it is," Ella agreed.

"It was a perfect day, everything was wonderful," Carolyn said wistfully as she looked up into the blue sky. "She will be up there looking down, thinking what a wonderful send-off, I wish I was there to enjoy it." She giggled.

"I propose a toast," Ella announced. "To a wonderful and astonishing woman, your mother Sheila Reid."

"To Sheila Reid." The girls raised their glasses.

"Oh, thank you all I'm glad that I have such good friends."

"I think this calls for a group hug." Siobhan smiled.

Standing in a circle the girls hugged each other. "To always being there for each other in times of need."

It had been a very tiring day and all Carolyn wanted to do was sleep for a month, but she knew that she had to go and speak with each and every person who had came to pay their respects to her dear mother's memory. "Now ladies I must go and mingle."

"I have invited her to stay with me in France, once she gets this other thing sorted," Tara whispered in her ear as she led her down the garden path.

"She told you everything then?"

"Yes, I can't quite believe it!"

"I know what you mean, it was a complete shock to me too," Ella confessed.

"Now then, I want all the gossip, regarding you and this Dante chap, is he the one?"

Ella blushed. "Er... perhaps!"

"Then spill the beans!" Tara wanted all the juicy details.

As they walked Ella was glad to have a girly chat and it warmed her that Tara was excited for her.

"You are one lucky girl."

"Yes, I am." Ella looked at her watch, he would be just landing now and that meant she would be seeing him in a few hours and she could hardly wait.

Chapter Fifty-Two

Ella returned home and quickly got changed out of her funeral gear. She tucked it to the back of the wardrobe and sighed, hoping that it would be an extremely long time before she needed it again. She felt a little guilty leaving Carolyn, but Tara assured her that it was fine and that she would look after her.

As she brushed her long blonde hair she thumbed through the recently developed photographs of her trip to Milan. Smiling to herself she picked one out, it had to be her favourite. It was the one in the Square and they looked a picture of total bliss. Who would have thought she could end up with a man like that?

The doorbell rang and Ella jumped up with excitement, that must be him. She didn't want to seem too keen so she took her time opening the door. Dante was standing there grinning at her behind a huge bouquet of flowers.

"*Ciao, Bella.*"

"*Ciao,* Dante." Ella graciously accepted the offering. "These are beautiful."

"Bright and aromatic, just like my beautiful Ella."

"Do come in."

"You are alone tonight?" he asked mischievously.

"Yes, I am and probably will be for a few weeks."

"Oh, where is your flatmate?"

Ella didn't want to go into details. "She's off to France to visit a friend for a while."

"Lucky girl."

Lucky, Ella thought. If only he knew, but she didn't want to feel depressed so she kept quiet.

"Have you eaten yet?"

"Is that an offer?" Dante couldn't resist teasing her.

"Really, Signor Moretti, is that all you think about?" Ella said indignantly.

"That and other things!"

"You are terrible!"

"And you are wonderful. Now, put those damn flowers down and come here."

"No, no, I must put them in water," Ella teased him back; she was dying to run into his arms and feel his lips on hers once again.

Dante grabbed her arm. "Which is your bedroom?" he whispered into her ear, his voice all husky and oozing with need for her.

"This way!" Ella beckoned him as she started to peel off her blouse, dropping it to the floor in a tantalising way.

"Stop that!" Dante groaned as he too started to undress.

Before they knew it they were in the bedroom making mad passionate love to each other. Somehow it seemed more exciting than before if that was even possible, they both felt a magnetic pull towards each other and neither wanted the magic to end.

"Every time we are apart I miss you more and more," Dante told her as he stroked her face. "I want you to come to Lake Garda with me to a party the de Lucas are throwing."

"Sounds like fun, count me in."

Dante kissed her on the end of her nose. "Good, that's settled then."

Ella snuggled into his arms and fell into a deep sleep.

The only thing Dante could think of was how he was going to get an invite to her father's house to try and find what Reynolds had hidden in his safe, assuming the safe was indeed inside the residence.

Tomorrow was another day and he would broach the subject then. One thing he knew was that he couldn't leave any loose ends not now, not ever.

Chapter Fifty-Three

Moscow, Russia

Vasiliev was finding it increasingly difficult to bond with his son as all he seemed to do was ask for his grandparents and he didn't know how to react to that. Growing impatient he summoned one of the child's many nannies. "I don't know what the fuck you are doing with Pavel Jr but I want it sorted and sorted now." He banged his fist on the table making the young boy burst into tears. "Get him the fuck out of here, this fucking snivelling has to stop, do you hear me!" he screamed at her.

"Yes, sir. Come on Pavel, we will go and play upstairs," she told him as she picked him up.

"And you can fucking stop with all that shit, do you want to make him into a simpering little girl!"

"But he is only a child, sir."

As the nanny left the room Vasiliev picked up a glass ashtray and aimed it at the door just as Yakov Garshin was about to open it.

"Is it safe to come in?" he yelled.

"Enter at your peril!"

"I take it this is a bad time?" Yakov laughed.

"A fucking bad time, I have no idea what that bitch's family have done to him, brainwashed him or something, the sooner he is old enough, the sooner I can introduce him into my world the better!"

"He's only a child, there's plenty of time."

"Right now he is a snivelling little runt and I want that knocked out of him. No son of mine is going to grow up a fucking little sissy boy!"

"What did you want me for?"

"These fucking random killings have to stop, you are getting too carried away Garshin!"

"There's plenty more where they came from, I should know!"

"Perhaps that is true, but disposing of your little indiscretions is becoming increasingly boring!" Vasiliev was not amused. "I am sending you to Yugoslavia for a while!"

"What? Are you fucking kidding me, the men respect me here and everyone knows who I am!"

"You will do as I say!" Vasiliev was losing his patience. "I want you gone tonight."

"But I am one of your best men, look at all the girls I have brought into this business!" Yakov protested but it was useless, once his boss had made a decision it was impossible to change his mind. "How long for?"

"I will send for you when you have proved yourself to me!"

"Very well." Yakov was livid, the ungrateful bastard, how dare he brush him aside like this? One day he would seriously regret his actions towards him.

Vasiliev dismissed him with the wave of his hand. "Now, get out!"

As he left the residence he seethed.

"All right, Yakov." One of the men smiled at him.

Yakov wasted no time in flooring him with one single punch. "Fuck off!" And with that he got into his car and drove off in a rage.

Chapter Fifty-Four

London, England

"So, when do I meet your mother?" Dante asked as he watched Ella make scrambled eggs on toast.

"Oh, she's away on another one of her retreats." Ella sighed. "She hasn't been the same since Father passed away."

"And you?"

"I'm ok."

"I would still like to see where you were brought up at though, how about it?"

"Oh, I don't know." Ella remembered that Petra and Valerie were still residing there.

"I'm just going to take a shower," Dante told her, wondering how he was going to get into the house without her.

"Don't be long, breakfast is almost ready."

"Two minutes," he told her.

Ella took the opportunity to ring Carolyn. "Hey, how are you today?"

"Surviving as you do, life goes on as they say."

"Any news?"

"Yes, the solicitor just phoned. We're going to get the girls this afternoon, they are going to stay with Father until I get back from France, that is."

"What's going to happen to Petra?"

"It's sweet that you care, but leave that to me it's not your concern, but thanks for everything you've done."

"It's the least I can do, shall I come with you?"

"No, just ring and let them know that I'll be coming for them around two."

"Ok, you will keep in touch won't you?"

"Of course I will silly."

Ella quickly rang her mother's house. "Petra, Valerie, it's me Ella, can one of you pick up?"

Valerie picked up the phone. "Yes, Ella?"

"Carolyn will be coming for you at two, can you remember the instructions to open the security gates?"

"I am not an imbecile, Ella."

"I know, I'm sorry I didn't mean to imply that you were."

"I am sorry Ella, where are my manners you have been very kind to us."

"Please say good luck to Petra for me, I hope everything works out."

"Thank you, I will tell her."

"Who was that?" Dante asked.

"Oh, just a friend, now come on and get these eggs eaten up before they go cold."

"I'm starving, hope they taste as good as they look!"

"Even I can do scrambled eggs you know, in fact I can rustle anything up with eggs. Fried eggs, poached eggs, er…"

"Just give them here." He laughed as he scoffed them. "Pretty good, I have to say."

"See, don't knock it until you've tried it."

"I'm going to be tied up for most of the morning, how about we meet up for lunch, say around one?"

"Love to."

"And then perhaps you can give me a tour of your family's place?"

"I suppose." Ella said thinking if she made it later in the afternoon they would be long gone.

"Now, come here," Dante demanded as he patted his knee.

Ella sat on his lap as he put his arm around her waist. "I was thinking, perhaps we could split our time between Milan and London, what do you think?"

"How?"

"We'll spend a few months at a time here and a few over there, instead of a couple of days here and there!"

"I'm not sure, what about my mum?"

"I thought she was away at a retreat?"

"She is but I don't know when she intends to come back."

"Well then, what's to keep you here? It's a short flight, you can come back whenever you like."

He sounded so persuasive Ella thought. "We could try it out, see what happens."

"That's my girl." He kissed her on the cheek.

"We need to fly back the day after tomorrow, so that we can make Nico's party."

"You are a fast mover."

"You wouldn't have me any other way," he teased. "We will have a wonderful time together don't you agree?"

"I'm sure that we will, now I must go and get dressed and you must go to your business meeting."

"Yes, boss."

Ella wriggled off his knee. "Let yourself out and I'll meet you at Cathy's Bistro at one, now don't be late."

"It's a date."

Chapter Fifty-Five

Flavio and Carmine accompanied Dante to his meeting with the second in line to the Esposito business; he needed to make sure everything was back on track.

He was welcomed into the family-run café, his two men placed themselves in areas where they had clear views of the entire area and if anything suspicious was about to go down, they would notice it.

Vincenzo was distantly related to Esposito and was in fact quite glad that he had disappeared. Pulling the huge napkin from under his chin and wiping his jowls he shook Dante's hand. "Please, sit, sit, can I get you anything?"

"Just a coffee will be fine thanks."

Vincenzo signalled to the waitress. "Coffee over here for the young man."

"So, do you have the money?"

"No need to get right down to business is there Dante?"

"Signor Moretti to you."

Vincenzo didn't know whether to laugh, was Dante being serious? "Why so formal?"

"Well, I am your boss after all, so I need you to show me the respect that comes with the job."

Vincenzo nearly choked on his bacon sandwich. "I... I have no problem with respect, Signor Moretti." He passed the briefcase underneath the table. "You'll find it is all there."

Dante flicked it open and smiled. "Everything appears to be in order."

"And my shipment?"

"Being delivered separately, it is not wise that we exchange the powder at the same time as I receive the cash."

"But there was never any problem before."

"It's a new way of doing things Vincenzo, my way of doing things."

"I see."

"From now on one of my men will come in my place, although I may occasionally attend from time to time." He scraped back his chair and left the café.

As soon as he left Vitelli appeared, he'd been listening from the kitchen. "So, what do you think of him?" He spat.

"Basically an arrogant prick," Vincenzo told him as he stuffed his face with yet another bacon roll.

"And what are we going to do about him?"

"We... I'm not going to do a thing and I suggest you do nothing either if you know what is good for you. This Moretti is one smooth motherfucker with plenty of clout, let him have his profit margin, we've still got the gambling."

"For now maybe, but how long do you think it will take before he wants his cut of that too!"

"Calm down Vitelli, have a bacon roll."

"I don't want a fucking bacon roll, don't you give a damn about this shithead's next move?"

"Not really, he is opening up another business which we will play a big part in."

"Oh?"

"You would not understand my friend."

"Try me."

"A bit of human trafficking," Vincenzo said simply.

"What, are you crazy, as in people?"

"People usually are classed as humans, yes."

Vitelli sat down opposite him. "And what exactly do you have to do?"

"We, you mean?"

"So, you are including me in this too?"

"Of course, Esposito was always good to you and now that he's gone I don't see why that should not continue."

"So, what are you talking, slave labour and suchlike?"

"Yes, something like that, we play the game and we become very rich too, you do want to be rich don't you?"

"Of course, who doesn't?"

"Then we do what we are told, it is the only way in the line of work we have chosen."

"I did not choose this Vincenzo, it chose me," Vitelli reminded him.

"I understand. Now, are you in or are you out?"

"Count me in."

"Good, then you can oversee the first shipment, due in next weekend." He paused. "I heard about your half-hearted attempt to invade Moretti's life, I don't know what you were thinking."

"I was foolish," Vitelli agreed. "It won't happen again."

"Make no mistake, if you try anything in the future I will take you out myself."

Vitelli's eyes widened.

"It's just business that's all."

Business, just business, the words buzzed around in his head. He was beginning to realise that it was dog eat dog in his world and nobody took sides unless there was a huge wedge of money exchanging hands and right now he couldn't afford to do anything about it. "Very well."

"Now, fuck off and let me eat in peace."

Chapter Fifty-Six

As Ella was enjoying her lunch with Dante, Carolyn was in the process of organising Valerie and Petra's move out of the Reynolds' home.

Her solicitor Andrew Falkoner and two private bodyguards accompanied her as they neared the house.

"So, all Petra has to do is sign the papers and she is a resident, I mean the authorities can't make her talk can they?"

"I assure you Carolyn, they can't make her do anything she doesn't want to."

"What about her family? We'll have to tell her at some point," she fretted chewing on her nails.

"Do you think that mentally she will be able to cope?"

"No, I don't that's why I've called upon one of my mother's psychologist friends, he is superb at his job. Once he has assessed Petra, I suppose we'll take it from there."

Andrew sighed. "What a life these women have, it's incredibly sad."

"I hope Valerie is willing to come to France with me until we are sure it is safe for her to return."

"I think that you are perhaps being overly cautious, she's been here six years and nobody knows who she is."

"I know it's unlikely anyone would be looking for her now, they probably think that she is long dead, but this gang will have read in the press that there was more than one survivor."

"Thankfully they are unaware Petra is still alive and as far as they are concerned Valerie was just one of the employees about to begin her shift, so she is not a threat to anyone."

"You are probably quite right, I just want to make sure that nothing goes wrong."

Andrew patted her hand. "Rest assured, we will check Petra into the clinic under a false name, just as a precaution. Once she's in there no one can get to her, the place is like a fortress."

"Thanks for helping me set all this up Andrew, I don't know what I would have done without you."

"It's my pleasure."

The car pulled up to the wrought-iron gates and Carolyn pressed the intercom system. "It's me." She smiled and waved into the camera, two minutes later they were putting the girls into the vehicle.

"Where are we going?" Petra asked.

"I am taking you to a clinic for a couple of weeks."

"What kind of clinic?"

"My mother's friend is going to counsel you, just as he was going to counsel all of the girls that were in the centre, the only difference is that it is now going to be in his clinic."

"He is a nice man?" Petra's voice was shaky.

"I promise you, he is a good man and is only concerned about your well-being. It will do you the world of good to speak to someone outside of our circle, he is an expert in his field."

"Field? I do not understand."

"His profession, his job, he is well respected."

Petra turned to Valerie.

"I trust Carolyn," she reassured her.

"Then so do I."

As they were driving down the long stretch of road Ella was on her way to her parents' house. It was two twenty and there should be nobody there now, she thought.

Dante was in the passenger seat, he patted his pocket. The key was safely tucked away and he was moments from destroying whatever Philip Reynolds had stashed.

As they passed the black Saab he had to do a double take. "Stop the car, stop the car now."

"What is it?" Ella said as she braked sharply and pulled onto the hard shoulder. "You do know that it is illegal to stop here?" she informed him.

Dante held his chest, that face of the woman in the car, she was strikingly similar to his missing sister, Rosa. He felt like he had just seen a ghost.

"Are you all right?" Ella leaned over, he looked white as a sheet. "You're not having some kind of seizure are you?" Her voice was full of concern.

"Do you have any water?"

"Yes, in the glove box, I'm afraid it may be warm though."

Dante gulped back the warm liquid.

"Well, what is it?"

"It must have been something I ate, sorry I just felt sick all of a sudden."

"I had the same as you and I feel absolutely fine."

"Maybe it was your eggs this morning then," he joked.

"Seriously are you ok? You had me very worried."

"I'm sorry that I startled you." Dante shook thoughts of Rosa out of his head. She was dead, he reminded himself. No one could have survived the life she had to endure for this length of time. And anyway, apparently everyone had a double somewhere in the world and he supposed if Rosa was still alive today then maybe she would have looked a little bit similar to the young woman who'd just driven past them.

"Are you ready to go before the police come and fine me?"

"Sure."

Five minutes later and Ella was pulling up to the gates, she punched in the security code and drove up to the house.

"It is very splendid." Dante had composed himself. "Your family has great taste."

"I was one fortunate little girl growing up here," she told him, remembering her fabulously happy childhood and the many birthday parties her family had thrown for her. She had been the envy of many of her friends.

"Happy times then?"

"Yes, very happy." Ella parked the car and Dante was quick to run round and open the door for her.

"Allow me."

"Thank you, but really there's no need, I'm perfectly capable of getting myself out of my own car."

"I know that you're independent Ella and that's commendable, but there's nothing wrong with being treated like a lady."

Ella laughed at him. "You are funny at times."

"I hope you mean that in the nicest possible way. Now, please give me a tour of your childhood home."

"It's just a normal house Dante, just everything is a bit bigger. It isn't as elaborate as yours that's for sure."

"Where would you like to see first then?"

"The bedroom," he laughed.

"I don't think so, the housekeeper will be coming over soon and I wouldn't want her to stumble across us in bed together, that would be soo embarrassing!" Ella exclaimed.

"That's a shame!"

"Come on." Ella took his hand as she showed him around the house.

All Dante could think about was where her father would have a secret safe.

"This is my father's study, sometimes he liked to lock himself in here for hours. You know, to have a bit of peace and quiet."

Just then Ella's mobile rang. "Excuse me for a minute, what is it Marcus?"

Dante took the opportunity to suss out the room. He checked out the desk: nothing. He looked underneath it, still nothing. He walked over to the bookcase and browsed quickly through the literature. Scratching his head he headed for the filing cabinet, surely he wouldn't be dumb enough to leave the evidence in one of the drawers? The key wasn't in the cabinet, damn it. He jumped when he heard Ella's stilettos on the polished floor.

"Oh, that's me celebrating my twenty-first birthday. My dad hired a posh hotel and hired one of my favourite bands, it must have cost him a small fortune," she explained.

Dante put the photo back down on top of the filing cabinet. "He looked very proud of you."

"Bless him, he was very proud of me, not that I've done much with my life but he didn't seem to mind he just wanted me to be happy." The tears welled in her eyes. "I'm sorry."

"Hey, don't be, come here." He opened his arms.

Ella wiped a tear away. "It's ok, I'm fine." She was afraid that if she went to him she would cry and never stop and she didn't want him to see her like that. "I'm just going to freshen up and then I'll see you out in the garden."

"Do you mind if I look through your father's book collection?"

"Help yourself."

It was like looking for a needle in a haystack he thought as he picked up the books and shook them. He didn't have much time and he suspected Ella would be back at any moment. He went back to the desk and sat down, picking up one of the pens he started twiddling it between his fingers when he suddenly groaned. Jesus, the filing cabinet key was hanging from the stationary holder, he could have kicked himself wasting all this time. He supposed that it didn't help that the key was silver and surrounded by the same colour paper clips.

Opening the patio doors he walked out into the garden. He headed towards the gazebo and sat down on the wooden bench rubbing his chin. Somehow he had to make sure that he stayed overnight so that he could get into the cabinet and see if the box was, in fact, inside it.

"Did you find anything you liked?" Ella interrupted his thoughts.

"No, not really it is all a bit too intense for me, I like something a little more easy-going."

"He did like heavy reading I suppose, he was a very intelligent man."

"I suppose that's who you take after then."

"Not really, I never had a head for business."

"But you do now."

"It's just one little deal that's all."

"It will make your father's business more successful if that is possible."

Chapter Fifty-Seven

Moscow, Russia

Yelena's husband was away on business yet again and she was bored out of her mind. She had spent the whole day shopping and being pampered from head to toe, yet she was sick of the same routine and longed for excitement.

"Here." She tossed the keys to one of her minders. "Get my bags out of the boot." Kicking off her shoes where she stood she noticed a huge vase of flowers.

"From Mr Vasiliev," the maid told her.

"Oh, what time did they come?"

"About an hour ago."

"Was there a card?"

"Yes, Mrs Petrov." The maid handed it to her.

My car will pick you up at eleven thirty it read. Smiling to herself Yelena bounded up the stairs.

"What time do you want to eat?" the maid asked, but the words fell on deaf ideas. She had worked her behind off today in the hope of going home early to her children; fat chance of that with Yelena Petrov fast becoming a law unto herself, she tutted.

Yelena managed to grab a couple of hours' sleep. She knew that it was probably going to be a long night. Her phone rang. "Yes?"

"It's me Aleksei, I'm missing you," he told her.

"And I miss you too, when are you coming home?"

"There have been a couple of hitches, nothing to worry about but it's going to take a little longer than I first anticipated."

"Oh, not too much longer I hope, that Vasiliev works you too hard."

"What have you been up to today?" Aleksei asked changing the subject.

"Just the usual."

"Ok, Yelena, I'm sorry darling but I must go, I'll call you tomorrow."

"Goodnight, darling." Yelena replaced the receiver. Since her husband became involved with Vasiliev she barely saw him and it was seriously pissing her off. It was wonderful to have all this money to be able to do what she wanted but having no one to share it with was difficult at times. Sergei, her bodyguard, had been a distraction. He worshipped the ground she walked on and was crazy about her. Totally loyal and smitten was just what she wanted, so she had never taken their relationship further, but one day if she needed to then she wouldn't hesitate.

Pulling on her warm coat she skipped down the stairs, wondering what the night was going to bring.

As she got into the car Vasiliev leaned over. "I have recently lost one of my assistants and wanted to see if you were perhaps interested in the position."

Yelena felt honoured. "Of course I will consider your offer, you know that."

A couple of hours later they turned up at a strip club. "Now, don't be shocked by what you are about to see, just remember these girls are whores, probably born whores." He gave a sickening laugh that sent shudders through Yelena's body.

"I have seen this sort of thing before, it does not worry me."

Vasiliev was well protected, he had cars both ahead of his vehicle and behind, just in case of any attempted ambush. "We are here." He leaned across and Yelena jumped. "Don't worry." He pulled the handle and opened the door. "After you."

The door to the club was heavily protected with armed guards. On seeing their boss they immediately stepped out of his way. "Good evening."

"Any trouble tonight?"

"No," the huge bulky man told him as he held open the door.

The place was dimly lit and Yelena had to let her eyes adjust for a couple of seconds. Some of the girls were pole dancing naked, they were little more than skeletons. The crowd which was mainly male dominated were jeering and clapping as they tried to grope the gyrating bodies in front of them.

The bouncers ran over and hit a couple of them on the back of the legs with chunks of wood. "You touch, you pay!"

An altercation broke out and the bouncers wasted no time in beating the shit out of the men involved and bodily dragging them out into the street to finish the job off, after relieving them of all their cash of course. The zombie-like girls carried on as if nothing had happened.

Yelena noticed that the topless waitresses looked like scared little rabbits. "I thought they were all house broken," she whispered to Vasiliev.

"They are new, some of them beg for drugs to help them perform and then, trust me, they will do whatever is asked of them if they want their next hit that is." He laughed a cruel little laugh. "That is where you come in."

"Oh?"

"Come into the office and I will explain."

Once seated in the grimy little office which was more like a cupboard Vasiliev started to explain. "My last assistant decided to distribute the drugs to make a profit, outside of the business, so I had to dispose of her."

"So, just out of interest what made you think of me?"

"You have proved yourself trustworthy and I need people like you."

"What do you want me to do?"

"I want you to talk to the new girls, tell them you used to be just like them and although you were scared you realised that this was a means to an end." He paused. "Tell them that after a couple of years you paid your debt off and were set free and now you are married to a very wealthy man."

"Do you seriously think that these girls will believe me?"

"You are very plausible Yelena."

"And that is all I have to do?"

"Elaborate a bit, these fucking whores need pulled into line, once they accept what you say is true then perhaps there won't be as many – shall we say? – disappearances. Besides, some of the girls are that drugged up they're putting my customers off and, as you can appreciate, the ones I'm sending abroad must be drug free."

"So, if I tell them to put up with this lifestyle for a couple of years they'll be more inclined to obey and no doubt save you a small fortune in the drug industry, too? That is very clever of you Vasiliev," she applauded him.

"That is why I am the boss."

"And what do I get for my trouble?"

"You will be greatly rewarded, but now I need to test you."

"Yes?" Yelena's heart skipped a beat, the danger excited her. She always wanted to be an actress and could make anyone believe anything she told them, it was a talent that she had.

"A new batch of girls have arrived, they are in the cellar being processed. I think it is time you introduce yourself and tell them how it is going to work."

"Is that a challenge?"

"Perhaps, but one more thing Yelena."

"Yes?"

"I will be watching and listening through a secret panel."

"I won't let you down."

*****

Yelena was led into a back room which must have been filled with at least a dozen or so girls all huddled up together on dirty mattresses. "Don't be afraid," she told them. "I want to help you."

Nobody spoke. They were traumatised and still trying to get their heads around what was happening to them.

"I can guarantee that every single girl in this room has nothing to fear."

"You cannot know what they are going to do to us," one of the girls spoke up.

"What is your name?" Yelena said in a calming voice as she went over and sat down next to her.

"Natasha."

"Well Natasha, it wasn't so long ago that I too was in the same predicament and look at me now." She paused for effect. "I am happy, wealthy and most of all I am alive."

Some of the girls looked at each other in total disbelief.

"It is true, I promise you."

"But I cannot do this, I have never been with a man before," Natasha told her as she quietly sobbed.

"Shush, shush now, it will only be for a while, just think of the money that will be sent home to each and every one of your families."

"And what of the men who took us, how much will they get?" a dark-haired girl demanded.

She was going to be a liability, thought Yelena, as she tried to keep her voice warm and friendly. "Yes, it is true that the money will be shared out, but there will be enough to go around."

"And how many times will we have to have unprotected sex?" the girl continued.

How was she going to answer that Yelena pondered? "It does not matter how many times, you must always think of a better life for your families and one day your own freedom."

"Freedom!" a petite blonde spat.

If Yelena didn't do something fast then she was going to lose control of the situation. "I know it comes at a price but I do not regret getting my family out of the gutter and neither should you."

"I am scared." Natasha's voice was shaking slightly.

"Don't be it is just your body, not your mind. If you do exactly what is asked of you then you will be taken to parties in huge mansions and on luxury yachts, even having the opportunity to visit other countries. So you see, it is not so bad."

"You make it sound almost normal!" the dark-haired girl piped up yet again.

"It is only a state of mind."

"How long did you have to work?" another girl asked, thinking of her young baby son living in a tiny run-down flat along with her parents and grandparents.

"Two years," Yelena told her, hoping that the other girl wouldn't chip in.

"I suppose then that I do not mind to have sex, I would do anything for my family."

"Then it is a small sacrifice to pay, don't you think?" If only she knew the gritty reality, she would probably be working at least twelve hours a day sleeping with up to a hundred men or more until their pathetic, worn-out and broken bodies couldn't endure anymore. By the time they realised they were in it for life, it would be too late to do anything about it.

"Perhaps she is right, if we obey then they will pay our families and let us go, we must think of that," said the young mother as she held Natasha's hand.

"Ok," Natasha whispered.

"Just accept that this is to be your life for the next couple of years and everything will be ok, trust me I am a living example."

"So, how many men did you sleep with?" the dark-haired girl persisted.

"I did not count," Yelena said coolly.

"Does it matter?" another girl chipped in.

"Now, I am told that you are being moved to some very nice accommodation so that you can freshen up and get some rest."

"Will we be split up?" Natasha asked.

"I do not know that, it is up to the boss." You have all been chosen to order you idiot, Yelena wanted to scream at her naivety.

"And who exactly is the boss?" This came from the dark-haired girl.

"I have never met him, but what I do know is that he will look after you while you are in his care, you have to trust me."

The dark-haired girl shook her head. "But we have been locked up in here for hours with no food or anything to drink."

"Then I will make sure you are supplied with these things immediately." Yelena made to leave.

"How do we know that you are telling the truth?"

Yelena was sick of hearing that girl's voice. All she wanted to do was punch her in the face to stop that bleating, it was driving her insane. "You don't have to believe me, I lived it."

Vasiliev was waiting in the next room and as Yelena entered he applauded her. "I have to say that you were very impressive."

"So, am I in?"

"Do you think you can do a similar talk each time I need you?"

"How often are you talking?"

"Every two weeks or so, it depends."

"What's the destination of this package?"

"You don't need to know that."

"Very well, how much are you paying me?"

"You see Yelena that is what I like about you, a woman who thinks exactly the same way as I do."

Yelena laughed. This was going to be easy money. "You haven't answered my question."

"Plenty, I am a very generous man." He turned to one of the bodyguards. "Watch them closely."

They went back into the bar area, Yelena was afraid when she saw the Russian military police just coming in.

"It's ok," Vasiliev told her.

"Vito." He shook the man's hand. "I have a pretty little virgin for you to take off my hands, what do you say?"

"You know I prefer them already broken in." Vito's rancid breath emanated in Yelena's direction making her want to puke.

Vasiliev signalled for one of his men to come over. "Once the lorry comes for the girls make sure that you keep the dark-haired mouthy one, take her to one of the rooms."

"So, I can keep this one then?" Vito smiled. It was a sinister little smile as he thought of what he wanted to do to this new gift.

"She is a bit feisty and we need to calm her down a bit, do you know what I mean?"

"I will look forward to it." Vito turned his attention to the woman at Vasiliev's side. "And who is this?"

"She is a business associate of mine and therefore strictly off limits," he warned him.

"Ah, so you want her all for yourself then?"

"Perhaps, now fuck off and enjoy yourself."

"You have a great deal of power." Yelena was once more impressed.

"I know many people and I also know how to keep them on side, now come I will get my driver to take you home, you have done well tonight."

*****

Several hours later while Yelena was snuggled up in her luxury residence fast asleep, all hell had broken loose in the topless bar.

Vito had wasted no time in getting the mouthy girl into one of the rooms. "So, what is your name?"

"Fuck you."

Vito laughed. "I like a bit of rough, I'm looking forward to fucking you good and hard."

"Over my dead body."

"That can easily be arranged," Vito said in a deathly quiet voice. "Just play nice and everything will be ok."

The girl was sick of hearing those words. She had tried to convince the other girls that it was all bullshit but they were having none of it since that woman came and talked to them. It seemed that she was the only one who knew that it was all lies. Something about her didn't seem quite right; she was probably working for the big boss, whoever that was. "Ok, I will do what you say." She started to undress.

"That is much better." Vito rubbed his groin in anticipation watching as the girl stripped to her underwear. "Take off your bra," he ordered.

Obediently she did as she was told as she felt Vito's leering gaze on her. "And the rest," he said as he removed his top and unbuckled his trousers.

Biting her lip she slipped out of her panties, she felt self-loathing as she braced herself for what was about to happen.

"You are very beautiful, I am going to en... enjoy..." He started coughing and pointed to his throat.

"What is it?" The girl pretended not to notice that he was choking on his gum.

Vito's eyes bulged as he fell to the floor gasping; they looked as if they were going to burst out of his head at any moment.

She grabbed her clothes and quickly got dressed. Spitting on the disgusting fucker, she picked up his gun and listened to see if anyone was outside of the door. There was some kind of commotion going on. A woman was screaming and there were footsteps thudding past the door. Holding her breath and with the gun ready she held the door slightly ajar. This was the only opportunity she would ever get to escape, although if she got out of here alive she didn't have a clue what she was going to do next.

She said a prayer as she sneaked quietly out of the room. Whatever was going on was enough of a distraction for no one to notice her. Trying to remember which direction she had came from she tried to retrace her steps. Hearing voices, she panicked and opened the door next to her. There was a girl lying naked on the bed trying to inject herself with heroin.

"P... p... please h... help me... to die," she could barely get the words out.

"My God, what have this scum done to you?" Looking at the poor girl's bruised and battered bony body she shuddered; this was how she was going to end up if she stayed in this place.

"Garshin..." she spluttered. "Yakov... Garshin."

Zeta hesitated, standing there not knowing what to do. There was no way she could leave her like this and no way she could take her with her either.

"P... please." The girl didn't have the energy to find a vein, let alone inject herself.

Gritting her teeth the Zeta walked towards the bed and held the girl's hand. Looking into her eyes she saw nothing, no emotion, it was like looking into a deep chasm.

The girl blinked as if to tell her to do it. Picking up the syringe she emptied all the contents into her vein and watched as the girl's lip curled in a half-smile and then, in an instant, she was gone. Just like that. Poor bastard, Christ alone knew how long they'd been working this girl, but it was definitely more than two years that was for sure. Looking around she noticed a window. Pulling back the curtain she peered out, it overlooked the back of the building. Carefully she undid the latch and climbed out. Whoever got that girl in such a state must have realised that she was going nowhere and therefore it didn't matter whether there were windows in the room or not, for her, escape was definitely not an option.

Somehow she had to get out of here before someone noticed she was missing. Hiding behind some large rubbish bins she waited for her opportunity.

A large lorry pulled up to drop off some beer. She watched in silence as the lorry was emptied of its cargo. The driver was talking to one of the minders so she took a deep breath and crept towards the open doors. She hauled herself inside and hid behind the empty beer barrels, hoping and praying that she would make it out of this hell hole alive.

Chapter Fifty-Eight

London, England

"Would you mind if I used your father's computer I just need to check on my e-mails?" Dante asked.

"Errm, I'm not sure, I mean no one has used father's computer since he died." The words almost choked her.

"I'm sorry I didn't mean to upset you," he said in a sympathetic voice. "I didn't mean to be insensitive."

"Go ahead it's fine, I need to pop over to the gardener's cottage and see if everything is ok so help yourself."

"Are you sure?"

"Yes, but please don't touch anything else. My mother will have a fit if anything is out of place and trust me, she will notice."

Dante kissed her on the cheek. "Don't worry about a thing, she will never know that I was here."

"She'd better not," Ella joked. "I'll be about twenty minutes, his cottage is a ten-minute walk from here and I feel like some fresh air."

Dante went back into Philip Reynolds' office and opened the filing cabinet. He searched all of the drawers and finally found a huge strongbox. Taking it out and placing it on the table he took the key out of his pocket and opened it. There were various documents but he didn't have time to study them all, time was of the essence and he needed to find whatever it was Reynolds had in his possession, fast.

Finally he came across a buff folder containing a print out of the company's accounts, listing dates and times of all monies coming in and out of the bank account. Dante shook his head, the dumb fuck that set this up had left a serious pattern which any fool could suss out. Looking around the room once more he spotted an electric shredder, he was definitely in luck. One by one he proceeded to dispose of the final evidence. Feeling relieved, he locked the filing cabinet and replaced the key. He turned on the computer and felt slightly saddened when he saw the desktop photograph of Philip, Helen and Ella Reynolds all looking the perfect family, a picture of bliss. Quickly he turned it off.

"Did you manage?" Ella asked as she came in through the open patio door.

"Yes, thanks for that."

"You're welcome, anything to report?"

"Such as?" Dante looked a little confused.

"Work of course, what else?" Ella smiled at him.

"Nothing that can't wait."

"Ok, let's lock up and go."

Dante hated what he had done to her. Although he physically didn't kill her father, he had ultimately sealed his fate and that was something he was going to have to live with forever.

Chapter Fifty-Nine

Moscow, Russia

The girls were tightly packed into the back of the truck. Natasha noticed that Zeta had not returned and she was worried about her. She did not dare ask where she was in case she suffered the same fate as her. Although she was only seventeen she was not a fool and realised that because her friend had been so vocal, they had probably murdered her. That was more reason for her to remain quiet and do as she was told.

The journey seemed to last for hours, but nobody inside the truck knew exactly how long, as they had no watches and they could not see outside.

Finally the truck came to a sudden halt. "Where do you think we are?" asked one of the girls.

"Do you think that they are going to kill us?" another asked.

"We are worth nothing to them dead," Natasha said, remembering Zeta's words.

The canvas on the back of the truck was opened up and the bright sunlight blinded the girls. "No fucking talking, do you understand?" The man pointed the gun inside and aimed it at one of the girls. "You, come here, now!"

The frightened young girl scrambled over the others and went to meet her fate. Once she was outside the canvas was quickly dropped so that nobody could see what was going on.

"Take off your jacket," the girl was instructed.

She obediently did as she was told as she was surveyed by a group of men.

"Will she do?"

One of the men walked over to her and prised her mouth open. "She is clean, yes?"

"Yes."

He grabbed her by the blouse and in a split second ripped it off her. Yanking down her bra he stood back and looked at her ample breasts. "What do you think men?" Laughing he turned his attention to his men who were ready for their little reward. "Take her, she is yours."

Inside the truck the other girls could hear the screams and they shuddered.

When the men had finally finished gang raping the young girl she was thrown back into the truck. When they set off again Natasha went to hold the girl's hand. "What did they do to you?"

The poor girl was so traumatised that she could not speak. Instead she pushed the other girls out of her way and clawed at the canvas trying to get out. "I must get out, somebody help me," she begged. "I would rather die than live like this." Forcing the canvas loose she jumped out into the road rolling heavily into a cold, muddy puddle which seemed to momentarily bring her to her senses.

The truck stopped and the armed men raced towards the girl lying in the road. One of them bent down to see if she was still alive, not out of concern for her but because, if part of the 'cargo' were lost, Vasiliev would be enraged. The soldier grabbed her roughly by the arms and yanked her to her feet. She struggled fiercely sending them both reeling backwards as they slipped in the mud. Noticing the glinting steel the girl wasted no time and pulled the knife out of his boot and shoved it right into his crotch. The man howled like some kind of wild animal and dropped to the ground writhing in agony.

One of the other men took out his revolver and shot the girl in the head, he was covered in her blood. Turning to his severely injured comrade he shot him too. "Bury the fuckers," he yelled.

He walked back towards the truck. "If any of you even think of trying to escape this is what will happen to you, remember it is only two years of your life!"

Natasha remembered what the blonde woman had told them, the only way to survive was to do as they were told.

The truck passed through Estonia, Latvia and Lithuania picking up another dozen or so girls. When they finally stopped again it was pitch black and they could hear the noise of the ocean lapping at the shore.

"Out, everybody out!" the voice boomed.

As they all quietly exited the truck they were rounded up like animals and led down to the waiting boat. "Quickly, quickly."

"Where are we?" Natasha asked one of the girls.

"This must be the Baltic Sea," the girl whispered back.

"Where do you think they are taking us now?"

"No fucking talking!" the man yelled.

And nobody talked for the next few hours as the boat guided them through Kattegat and Skagerrak until finally they were in the North Sea. The sea was choppy and there was a torrential downpour. Exposed to the elements the girls huddled closer together, trying their best to keep warm. To add to their misery several girls were retching violently over the side, seasickness had gotten the better of them.

Just then the whole place lit up like it was Christmas, an armed cutter was nearing them. "This is the UK Border Agency, heave to," boomed a voice. "You are entering UK International waters!"

The captain was unsure of what to do, but there was no way he could allow any of them to be captured. "Let's keep going we will have to fight it out!" he told his crew.

The English captain had received information that drug smugglers were in the area and that they were most likely to be armed and extremely dangerous. His heart thudded in his chest as he tried to stop them. "I repeat, turn off your engines, now, or we will have no choice but to open fire."

There was nothing that anyone could do to diffuse the situation. In desperation the Russian crew opened fire, but they were no match for the cutter's deck gun.

One of the Russians grabbed the nearest girl and put a pistol to her head threatening to shoot her if the cutter did not stop attacking them.

"Let the girl go and throw your guns over the side!" the voice boomed as he realised they had stumbled upon some kind of human trafficking ring. Just to prove he was serious the Russian shot the girl in the head and tossed her body overboard.

There was only one way for the boarding party to react and that was to join in all guns blazing as they shot at anything that was moving. It was a complete disaster, some of the girls jumped over the side into the icy-cold water in a state of total panic. Not wishing to leave anyone alive in case they talked, the Russians opened fire on the vulnerable girls and managed to kill some of them before they were all finally taken out.

Climbing on board the officers checked to see if anyone was still alive. Natasha had taken a bullet to her leg which was bleeding profusely and she had passed out with the pain.

"Over here, there's someone still alive, hurry!"

Natasha was the only survivor and the officers knew that they had to look after her no matter what. She was the only witness to the entire event and maybe she could help them prosecute whoever it was that did this to those poor girls.

Yet Natasha did not remember anything. Traumatised from the whole experience it appeared that she did not even know her own name. It was a sad state of affairs and, no matter how many times she was questioned, she feigned memory loss. Deep inside Natasha knew exactly what had happened but there was no way that she was ever going to tell anyone what she really knew. Thanking God that she was still alive she continued to pretend to forget the entire episode. She even started to believe it herself, she had to for her own sanity. The thing that would keep her safe was to keep her mouth firmly shut, and she intended to do just that.

Chapter Sixty

London, England

Dante rang Mancini. "Stuart Masterson is a liability. He left a comprehensive trail through the Reynolds' bank accounts," he told his uncle.

"Then he must be snuffed out."

They were the words that Dante wanted to hear. "Consider it done." He put the phone down, now all he needed to do was dispose of him but make it look like an accident.

He rang Flavio. "I've got a job for you and Carmine."

"I'm listening."

"I'll give you the address, just make sure there's no reason to suspect anything sinister has gone down."

"I understand."

"Who was that?" Ella interrupted him.

"Just a work colleague, are you all packed?"

"Yes, just about, but I wasn't sure what outfits to bring."

"Don't worry about that we can always pick something up."

"I'm really excited, what's Lake Garda like?"

"Wait and see, the de Lucas know how to throw a party that's for sure."

"I could get used to this lifestyle." Ella smiled at him, her life was finally on the up and it was all down to meeting Dante.

"And so you should, it's fun all the way from now on," he told her, taking her into his arms. "And you are the icing on the cake." He kissed her on the tip of her nose.

"I've just got to give Carolyn a quick call, do you want to make some tea?"

"Yes, my lady." Dante obediently went into the kitchen. Everything was easy as long as he had Ella, so far she had been his good luck charm and he wanted it to stay that way.

"Carolyn, it's me."

"Hi, how long are you going for this time?"

"I'm not sure a few days, weeks I don't really know."

"You'd better keep in touch then."

"Don't worry I'll give you a blow-by-blow account. How are the girls?"

"Valerie is staying with me for now and Petra has settled into the clinic."

"Does she know about her family yet?"

"No, she keeps asking to see them and thanks to that Sandra Ennis, she thinks that they are in the country being processed, it's a bit of a nightmare to say the least."

"That poor girl," Ella murmured.

"She'll be told as soon as the doctors say she can cope with the news, but until then I am afraid I must keep lying to her."

"I know you'll do your best, I'm glad that these girls have someone like you looking out for them."

"It's going to be a long hard road, but we'll get there in the end."

"Take care, Carolyn."

"You too."

Ella had to admire her friend's newfound capabilities and hoped that it all worked out for everyone involved, especially Carolyn herself.

"Tea's brewed!" Dante shouted.

"Coming."

*****

"How are we going to do this?" Flavio asked.

"Not sure yet, but we need to make it snappy if we are to make the flight," Carmine told him as he looked at his watch.

Stuart Masterson was oblivious to the two men intently watching him as he was cleaning the swimming pool. His wife had just left to do the school run and he was totally alone.

"Perfect."

"So, you got an idea then?"

"Just follow the master." Carmine got out of the car.

Before Stuart Masterson knew what was happening his feet became tangled in the hosepipe and he went head first into the pool. Frantically he fought for breath as he struggled to get free. He could just make out two shadows as his lungs filled with water.

"Let's get out of here."

The two men wasted no time in making their escape, the headlines would read 'death by misadventure'.

Chapter Sixty-One

Lake Garda, Italy

Grazia de Luca had booked her favourite chef weeks ago and had spent ages going through the buffet menu with him. As she walked into the kitchen area she was delighted by the trays in front of her ready to be transferred into the dining room once she had approved everything. There were platters of garnished meats perfectly presented, her favourite chicken picatta pieces, one of which she couldn't resist popping into her mouth: succulent was the word that sprung to mind.

"Now, now, Mrs de Luca, please do not disturb the masterpieces," the chef teased her. He was a rotund man with a red complexion due to the fact that he drank rather a lot of wine, yet that didn't bother Grazia just so long as he was fit to do the job. "Let me show you the rest of the spread." He guided her along the vast kitchen area. "Mozzarella pinwheels, various stuffed mushrooms, ranging from pesto and pine nuts to the more adventurous escargot, filled local cherry tomatoes, Italian sausages, various pasta dishes, soups, seasonal vegetable dishes, marinated mushrooms in herbs and spice, mixed salads etc. Oh, and I know how your husband just adores carpaccio."

"You always do a fantastic job, Carlo. I don't know why I stress out so much."

"And for dessert a huge selection of fresh fruit and puddings galore as per your instructions."

"Good, now please ensure that the kitchen staff are not seen in the dining room, the only people I expect to see are the servers and bartenders."

"Of course."

"And don't worry, Carlo, once I am being told by everyone how fabulous the spread is I will bring you out for your congratulatory glass of champagne on a job well done."

"You are so kind." He kissed her hand, wondering where his event manager was, he was cutting things a bit fine to say the least.

"I'll leave you to it then, everything looks wonderful."

Good job she hadn't noticed the missing Federico, he would have to ring him as soon as she left. "Where the hell are you?"

"I'm coming up the drive now, you panic too much, Carlo."

There was nothing for it. Carlo would have to replace him, he thought, as he gulped down a glass of red wine to calm his nerves.

Grazia checked the flower arrangements and smiled, everything was just so. She thoroughly loved throwing parties and this one was no exception. They always reminded her of when she first met Nico; she had been an event manager and had overseen many of Nico's elaborate parties. Thinking it rather unusual for one person to throw so many parties she couldn't help but laugh when Nico had finally admitted that because he was so shy, having all these bashes was the only way he felt he could get to see her.

Nico watched her from the doorway. His wife had busied herself all day overseeing the preparations and organising where she wanted everything to be placed and now she was looking a little flushed. "Stop fussing woman, it's only a few friends."

"You know how I like everything to be just perfect."

"And it always is, now I don't want you tiring yourself out, not in your condition." Nico gently patted her tiny bump.

"Sssh, I thought we were going to make the announcement tonight," Grazia said as she looked around to see if anyone was listening, but they were all engrossed in their individual jobs.

"We should be shouting it from the rooftops, you have made me the happiest man in the whole world." He picked her up and swung her around.

"Nico, you fool put me down at once."

"I do love you when you are cross."

"Just go and do something please," Grazia ordered. "I need to find something to wear."

"We've got a couple of hours yet."

"I know, that's what I'm worrying about!" Grazia tutted as she gently pushed him out of her way. "Oh, and Nico, make sure the gazebo is set up for the Bellini brothers, they should be here any second to set up and practise."

"All in hand my darling, now you go and make yourself even more beautiful."

"And don't forget to get changed into your tuxedo I had especially cleaned for this evening," she said as she disappeared up the staircase.

"Women!" Nico exclaimed. They were a law unto themselves and he doubted that he or anyone else would ever fathom them out.

Thirty minutes later and the six-piece band arrived. Nico sighed with relief, he didn't want anything to upset his wife.

"Good evening, gentlemen, follow me please." Federico the event manager took control.

Feeling that it was a good opportunity to check on his wife Nico slipped away. He bounded up the stairs two at a time, sticking his head around the corner he asked if it was safe to come in.

"Of course, what do you think?" Grazia was wearing an elegant red evening dress which was fitted on the top half and came out at the waist ending just above the knee. The bustier had gold sequins hand-stitched on it which sparkled in the light, all teemed up with a pair of golden stilettos.

"Wow, you look beautiful." He walked towards her and rubbed her bare shoulders. "Pregnancy certainly suits you."

"You won't be saying that when I get grumpy and want to sleep on my own," Grazia told him.

"You, grumpy, never!" he said kissing her neck.

"You'll see, hormones are a funny thing you know."

"I'll do whatever you want my darling you know that," Nico told her. "The band's arrived so now I am off for my shower, I would ask you to join me but I see you have already done your hair."

"Later Nico, now don't be long." Grazia adored her husband and she couldn't wait to have many more bambinos. She had always wanted a large family and Nico would make a wonderful father and they would have fun making them, she giggled to herself.

*****

"So, what's the occasion?" Ella asked as they landed at Verona airport.

"I'm not sure, just another little get-together I suppose."

"So, I take it the de Lucas' entertain quite a lot then?"

"Yes, and it's always a grand affair."

"Now you have me worried, Dante, I mean I hope my dress is all right for the occasion."

"You have excellent taste, I'm sure whatever you have brought will be just perfect, just like you." He kissed her hand.

It never ceased to amaze Ella when she noticed the chauffeur waiting for them with a big placard marked 'Signor Moretti' at arrivals. Their luggage was immediately whisked from them and placed in the waiting Mercedes.

"How far is it now?" Ella asked excitedly.

"Be patient, *Bella*, it is not very far now." Dante held her hand.

The chauffeur spoke to Dante in Italian and Dante translated everything for Ella. "Lake Garda is the largest of the Italian lakes, stretching between the Alps and the Dolomites." He paused. "I'm afraid our chauffeur used to be a travel guide and he insists I translate his every word." Smiling he cleared his throat and continued. "The scenery is diverse, ranging from low-lying countryside on its southern borders and rising to the north with perpendicular cliffs."

"It's very beautiful."

Dante laughed. "The chauffeur said, as are you."

Ella blushed as she turned her attention to the surrounding views. "Look at the bright colours of the lemon orchards."

"Lake Garda is sheltered in a natural suntrap and therefore enjoys a warm climate allowing the abundant growth of olive groves and, as you pointed out, the lemon orchards." Dante laughed at her amazement.

"It's just so stunning," she gushed.

Five minutes later and the car was pulling off the main road into secluded grounds towards a charming nineteenth century villa which was surrounded by green shrubbery so as to maintain the utmost privacy. The entire property commanded stunning views of the lake.

As the chauffeur opened the door Ella gasped as she took in the magnificence of the whole villa. She would love to own a place like this and maybe one day she would, she told herself. The entrance hall had Doric columns supporting the portico façade which the de Lucas' had lovingly extended several years prior. It was their pride and joy and the envy of many of their acquaintances.

"Do I look all right?" Ella whispered as she smoothed down her silk midnight blue, backless dress.

"I told you, you would look wonderful in anything." He kissed her on the cheek. "Come, there's Nico and Grazia." Taking her arm he led them into the main house.

"Buonasera, Dante, so good to see you," Grazia welcomed them.

After they had exchanged kisses in true Italian fashion Grazia turned her attention to the beautiful woman on Dante's arm. "Wonderful to see you again Ella, come we'll let the men catch up and we can have a gossip."

Before she knew it Ella had been whisked off for a walk around the grounds. "May I say what a charming house you have."

"Why thank you, I must say I do adore it." Grazia giggled. "We renovated it and hoped to try and keep some of it in its original glory, I think the architect did rather well."

"I was just thinking how much I would love to own a property like this."

"What's to stop you? You are a very wealthy girl after all."

"I suppose."

"And modest too. Now tell me, is it love with you and Dante?" she asked seriously.

Nothing like beating around the bush thought Ella. She was lost for words.

"I know for a fact he is totally in love with you, Nico told me," Grazia exclaimed. "Oh, how I love Italian weddings, you will be getting married in Italy of course."

Ella looked petrified.

"Oh I'm sorry, I do go on a bit you know, just ignore me. It's just I've never seen him look so happy."

"It's ok, we're really fond of each other but it's only been a couple of months."

"Tell me, do you play tennis?"

"Very occasionally," Ella told her.

"Are you any good?"

"I'm not bad."

"Then perhaps tomorrow we can have a game of doubles that will be so much fun."

"Tomorrow?"

"Yes, we are making a weekend of it, did Dante not tell you?"

"No, he didn't."

"But you brought a suitcase, yes?"

"Yes, I did."

"No matter, I've put you and Dante into our special guestroom, and I don't think Signor Mancini will be very happy, oh dear what a shame." She stifled a laugh as they stopped to view the tennis court.

"Who is Mancini?"

"Oh dear, sometimes I despair in Dante, has he told you anything? He is his uncle and also his boss, a very, very wealthy and much respected businessman," Grazia informed her, delighted that she was the one to tell her.

"Should I be worried?" Ella asked.

"Not at all, he will love you, but –" she sighed "– and you never heard this from me, but his uncle has insisted on bringing a love rival for Dante's affections."

"What?" Ella couldn't believe her ears. "Does Dante know this?"

"Yes and no. What I mean is that he knows about his uncle's wish for him to marry Concetta Ricci, but Dante doesn't know that she is coming here this evening." Grazia paused as she noticed the look of horror on Ella's face. "I'm sorry, I mean no offence, come let us take a glass of wine." She signalled to one of the waiters.

Ella sipped thoughtfully on the wine, wondering what she was going to do if Dante took up with this woman and left her to her own devices in a foreign country. She would be positively devastated.

"It is better to be prepared, don't you think?" Grazia interrupted her thoughts.

"Look, Mrs de Luca…"

"No, please call me Grazia I insist."

"Grazia, it's just rather strange for me to come here on my own and hear that there is a woman coming who has set her sights firmly on Dante." She glanced in his direction and he must have felt her gaze as he turned and blew her a kiss. Lowering her eyelids she rubbed her finger lightly around the edge of her wine glass. It was a habit that she had when she became nervous.

"You see, he adores you, there is no contest," Grazia told her. "Now, let me tell you a little secret." She linked her arm as she guided her down to the jetty. "Nico and I are going to have a baby and you are the first person I have told."

"Well, I am very honoured and congratulations for letting me into your little secret." Ella smiled, she already liked this young woman and knew that they would become firm friends. Although she was straight to the point, everything about her was genuine and the words she spoke came from the heart.

"I think you and I will become excellent friends," Grazia said as if reading her mind. "Now what do you think of the de Luca yacht?"

The forty-metre yacht was floating in the private jetty and looked every inch the millionaire playboy's toy. "Mmm, very nice indeed."

"What are you thinking?"

"Just that, you know what they say about men with big yachts?"

"Oh something to do with the size of the manhood they really yearn for? I can assure you my Nico has nothing to worry about in that department."

As both women giggled Dante appeared. "I'm afraid you're needed up at the house Grazia."

"I'll catch up with you later, I very much enjoyed our little chat."

"Yes me too," Ella told her as she watched her disappear up the small incline towards the villa.

"Having fun?" Dante said as he refilled her glass.

"Yes thanks, now about staying over the weekend," Ella began.

"Oh, did I not tell you. It's a bonding session weekend, we have them from time to time."

Ella didn't like the sound of that. "And what exactly does that entail?"

"You know, men do men things, the women do theirs," Dante shrugged.

"I hope that you haven't brought me all this way to desert me all weekend."

"As if I would leave you alone for one second, you are too valuable to me, *Bella*," he said as he kissed her hand.

Somehow Ella doubted his sincerity. She had been to these sort of bonding parties and the men always ended up in another room leaving the ladies to amuse themselves. "Well be warned, if you do a disappearing act on me then I will be inclined to do the same, perhaps by taking the next flight out of Verona back home," Ella half joked, making sure she got the message across.

"I promise that I will give you my undivided attention, now let us go and meet the rest of the guests."

Ella's heart was pounding hard. She really didn't know what to expect, but what she did know was that she wasn't looking forward to being scrutinised by Signor Mancini and this Concetta woman. Reluctantly she let Dante take her arm.

"Are you ok?" he asked in a gentle voice. "You look a little peaky."

"Do I?" Ella said as she scrambled in her bag for her lipstick and blusher. "Hold up, let me just check." Two seconds later she had recomposed herself.

"Better," Dante told her as he kissed her cheek. "You will be the most beautiful woman here tonight."

Most of the guests were on the lawn, exchanging small talk while they waited to sample the sumptuous buffet which was giving off all these aromatic smells that was driving everyone's taste buds crazy. The de Lucas were renowned for their fabulously tasty cuisine and their chef was one of the finest in this part of the country.

"Dante!" A huge fat man with a cigar hanging out of his mouth waved at him.

"This is my uncle, Enzo Mancini and his wife Rosaria, and this is Ella Reynolds," Dante formally introduced them.

Mancini waddled towards her and passing his glass to Dante he grabbed her firmly by the shoulders and kissed her quickly on both cheeks, slobbering over her for a little longer than he should have. What he wouldn't give to have her in his bed, he thought, and perhaps he would, after all he was the Mancini.

Rosaria became impatient and nudged her husband out of the way. She held Ella's hand and said something in Italian to her.

"I'm sorry but I don't understand."

"She said that she is pleased to meet you." Dante told her as he felt her uneasiness. "Now please excuse me Uncle there's someone else I want Ella to meet. I'll catch up with you later."

Mancini's bodyguard, Giancarlo, watched his boss's reaction and knew that he was not happy to be spoken to in that way. It would be interesting to see how the evening transpired, he thought as he followed closely, looking around as he did so.

"Did he upset you?" Dante asked once they were out of earshot.

"He was, well, how should I put this? He was just a little bit too familiar."

"Yes, he can be a bit overbearing when it comes to women, especially beautiful ones." He led her into the hallway.

It was decorated with rich mosaics and frescoes which had obviously been hand chosen to fit in with the whole character of the house. There was a wide sweeping staircase directly in front of them with a huge arch-shaped window just above, which let in the sunshine, which in turn lit up the entire entrance hall making it look almost magical.

Nico was chatting with a frail old gentleman who was smoking a pipe and talking loudly although, once again, Ella didn't know what the conversation was all about.

"Come and meet Nico's grandparents."

Before Ella had a chance to protest Dante put his arm around her waist and gently guided her in their direction. "Signor de Luca, allow me to introduce Ella Reynolds."

"Is that you Dante?" the old man said as he reached out to touch his face. "Such a handsome young man and who do you say this is?" he asked holding out his hand to Ella.

"It's ok, he's almost blind poor man, he just wants to touch your hand." Dante translated the words for her as he placed her hands in his.

The old man clasped Ella's hands and rubbed them. He laughed and spoke in Italian making both Nico and Dante laugh with him.

"What did he say?"

"He said that you have hands like a princess and I must keep you in the manner that you have been accustomed to!"

Nico whispered into his grandfather's ear and they both howled.

"What now?" Ella asked, feeling slightly frustrated due to the language barrier.

"I just said that Dante is a very lucky man and if he has any sense will treat you like a princess too, to which my grandfather replied, he would very much like to see that, a woman have Dante Moretti at her beck and call, that would be a first!"

Ella failed to see the funny side and once more she let her insecurities wash over her as she wondered just what kind of women Dante was used to dating.

"Dante, darling so wonderful to see you again." A tall, beautiful Italian girl with luscious cascading wavy hair seemed to just float across the room and straight into his arms.

And before Ella knew it the woman was kissing both of his cheeks in a very intimate way as she whispered into his ear. Feeling pangs of jealousy Ella tried to hide her emotions.

Dante held the woman's hands and gently pushed them away from him to try and put some distance between them. "Concetta, may I introduce you to my date Ella Reynolds?"

Concetta looked her up and down and walked straight past her and hugged the old man first, followed by a bewildered Nico who was hoping that she wasn't going to kick off and spoil the whole evening.

"It seems my friend has forgotten her manners, I am Mirella Gallo." The woman that was with her shook her hand. "So you are Dante's girlfriend?" she enquired.

"Yes, yes she is," Dante told her as he put a protective arm around Ella's waist. "Now please excuse us."

Concetta looked on in utter disgust and once they had left she pulled Nico to one side. "Why does he choose to insult me like this?" she demanded.

"Hang on a minute, Dante is a grown man and whatever he does is nothing to do with me, now if you don't mind I must find my wife." And with that Nico made his escape.

Grazia was deep in conversation with two of her friends when Nico interrupted. "You don't mind if I steal my wife away for a moment." Before Alessia and Bettina had a chance to answer he had whisked her off.

"What is it?"

"I think it was a bad idea inviting Concetta tonight. She is crazy and God knows what she will do, talk about the green-eyed monster."

"It's about time the silly girl realised that no matter what Signor Mancini says Dante does not want her!" Grazia exclaimed.

"Tell me again why we invited her."

"Because it is what Mancini wanted and it was before I knew Dante was bringing Ella. I couldn't exactly tell her that she wasn't invited anymore, could I?"

"I'm sorry my love." Nico could see that his wife was becoming exasperated by the whole thing and was worried that her blood pressure may soar.

"No matter, just try to keep an eye on her, I just want to have a quick word with Ella. Will you see how long the buffet is going to be?"

Ella was sitting with Dante near the gazebo as he chatted with the members of the band. She was beginning to feel like a fish out of water and was grateful when she saw Grazia.

"Are you ok?" she whispered.

"It's nothing I can't handle," Ella told her. The girl had merely snubbed her that was all she kept telling herself.

"Well, if it's any consolation she looks like an overstuffed meringue in that horrendous lemon creation she is wearing!"

Ella laughed. "You certainly know how to make me feel better."

"Well, it is true is it not?" Grazia stated as she looked in Concetta's direction and waved politely. "Stupid girl, she thinks I am a friend of hers."

"Are you not?"

"Of course not, it wasn't my choice to invite her."

Ella turned her attention to Dante's uncle. She had only met him briefly and had decided almost immediately that there was something not quite right about him. Apart from him being an obvious sleezeball on the exterior there appeared to be something quite darker on the inside and she definitely didn't want to find out what that was.

"Dante's uncle is very old-fashioned and desperately wants him to marry into the Ricci family, but Dante has made it clear that he is not interested in family traditions, but unfortunately Signor Mancini does not understand," Grazia told her as she noticed her husband signal her to join him. "I must go, we will talk more later."

A gong boomed and the buffet was announced open. Concetta wasted no time in linking Dante and dragging him away from Ella.

Enzo took his opportunity and took Ella's arm. "Seems like you have been abandoned, allow me." He gave her that leering look once more.

"I'm perfectly capable, I don't need an escort," Ella said as she tried to wriggle out of his grasp, but his fingers dug deep into her flesh and it hurt like hell.

"You are just a notch on his bedpost, a plaything," he whispered into her ear. "He is marrying Concetta so don't get any foolish ideas about where Dante's loyalty lies."

"I think you must escort your wife," Rosaria told him. "Please excuse us."

Ella was grateful for the interruption, she felt quite intimidated by Mancini's presence. As she helped herself to the buffet she glanced over to Dante who had managed to rid himself of the obnoxious Concetta. He was talking to Nico and a few other men.

"Ella, let me introduce you to Alessio and Emiliano, Nico's brothers."

"Oh, how do you do?"

"You have a beautiful English accent," Emiliano said.

"And you are indeed very beautiful," Alessio announced totally out of the blue, he was usually the quietest of the three brothers.

"Hands off, I saw her first," Dante told him.

"You are a very lucky man."

"Yes, so everyone keeps telling me!" Dante chortled as he tucked into the Carpacchio.

Ella picked disinterestedly at her mixed salad. With Mancini's warning branded upon her brain, she'd lost her appetite.

"Let's go and sit outside," Dante whispered.

As they sat there Ella played with the food on her plate.

"Don't you like it?" he asked.

"I'm not really hungry."

He turned to her knocking her arm as he did so.

"Ouch."

"Oh, sorry," Dante apologised as he noticed the pained expression on her face. Glancing down he saw red finger marks in her flesh. "What the fuck?" He jumped to his feet.

Giancarlo waved for him to sit back down. This was certainly not the place for a heated exchange, thankfully nobody had really picked up on the atmosphere between them.

"Dante, please." Ella pulled at his arm. "Please sit back down, don't cause a scene."

Reluctantly he did as she asked. "It was that fucker Mancini wasn't it?" he lowered his voice.

"Yes, but please don't ruin the night for Grazia and Nico, they have an important announcement to make." The words tumbled out before she could stop them.

"What announcement, what are you talking about?"

"I can't say it's supposed to be a surprise."

Surprise? Dante hated surprises and he especially hated not being privy to whatever the de Lucas' were going to spring on everyone. Was it a new business venture that he knew nothing about, that he wasn't even involved in. Had Mancini offered them something, something more than he had promised him? His mind was in turmoil.

Sensing how uptight Dante was Ella leaned towards him. "It's nothing bad."

"Bad, why would I think it was something bad!" Dante exclaimed as he knocked back the remainder of his wine and clicked his fingers at the waiter for another.

"What's got into you? I don't like how you are behaving." Ella felt slightly uneasy.

Dante looked the other direction and composed himself, putting a beaming smile on he turned back to her. "My darling, Ella, I'm sorry the last thing I want to do is upset you, I just don't like what my uncle has done to you."

"I'm fine honestly." She looked up into his eyes.

He saw that she really meant every word of what she was saying and he respected her for that. "If you're sure." As far as Dante was concerned it was just another nail in Mancini's coffin and, if he continued interfering in his life like this, then he would take great pleasure in extinguishing the fucker much sooner than he'd planned.

A gong was struck and Nico asked the guests to assemble in the garden. Everyone took their seats in readiness for the band to begin their performance.

As the band began to play softly in the background Grazia picked up the microphone. "We are so happy to see our family and close friends here tonight," she began.

Nico couldn't hold back any longer and pulled the mike from her. "We wanted you to be the first to know that my beautiful wife Grazia and I are going to have a little bambino!" he shouted in total happiness.

Everyone stood up and applauded the young couple. Dante was the first to go over and congratulate them. "So, you beat me to it you rascal." He hugged his friend to him and held his arm out to Grazia. "I thought there was something different about you." All three hugged.

The band continued to play their set. The four baritones sang harmoniously to the wonderful sounds of the mandolin, accordion, violin and piano. All of a sudden the atmosphere became totally calm and relaxed. There was an air of tranquillity about the place as the music played and congratulations were exchanged.

"Let us have a dance," Dante insisted.

"Really, I'd rather not," Ella told him.

But Dante wasn't taking no for an answer as he took her in his arms and rhythmically swayed in tempo with the music.

Concetta jealously looked on. Who was this stupid English woman who barely knew Dante and thought that she could steal him away from her? It was crazy to think she even meant anything to him and when the opportunity arose she was going to tell her a thing or two about her precious Dante, and see if she still wanted him then.

As the evening wore on and the drinks flowed Concetta could barely contain herself.

"Look, you'll get your chance, just don't make it publicly or you will spoil any future you may have with Dante." Mirella tried to stop her from doing something she may regret in the morning.

"All right," Concetta hiccupped.

"Right, that's it, let's go and get you sobered up."

Concetta nodded, one half of her brain just wanted to slap that beautiful, angelic face of this Ella woman and the other half told her to be sensible and not make a fool of herself.

Nico and Dante swapped their dance partners much to the dismay of both women.

"So, how are you enjoying the evening?" Nico asked Ella.

"It's certainly different."

"I take it that Concetta Ricci is getting to you?"

"What makes you say that?"

"It's obvious."

"Is it?" Ella said worriedly.

"I'm just teasing, pay no attention she means nothing to Dante, I can assure you."

Just then Mancini cut in. "I would like a dance with the young lady now," he ordered as he exchanged his wife Rosaria.

"What is it that you want from me, Mr Mancini?" Ella demanded.

"I could think of many things," he said as he drooled at her exposed cleavage.

Before she had time to respond Dante more or less shoved his uncle viciously out of the way nearly knocking him over. "I would like my date back now."

"I think I need a glass of water, you know, clear my head," Ella told him.

"Shall I come with you?"

Looking over his shoulder she saw Mancini glaring at her and wished she was a million miles away from this man who frightened her. "No, no, I know where the kitchen is I'll be back in a minute."

"As long as you are sure."

"I am."

Dante kissed her lightly on the lips and stroked her cheek as if to make a point. This only infuriated his uncle more.

"I don't know what you are thinking, Dante, but you must end this ridiculous affair and end it now or you will regret it!" Mancini told him as he beckoned him away from the eyes of the guests.

His bodyguard decided it was time to use the men's room and left them to it.

"Who are you to tell me what I can and can't do?" Dante demanded as they walked towards the jetty.

"I am the boss, that is who I am and you do whatever I tell you to!"

"You cannot expect me to marry that whore. She has bed-hopped her way around this island and she is not fit to be my wife," Dante protested.

"I don't care about that, it is over now, she has been told to behave like a lady."

"And why would she listen to you?"

"Why? I'll tell you why. Because the last two men she fucked ended up as shark bait, trust me she will never look at another man ever again!"

"You think that will stop her!" Dante scoffed. "You are an even bigger fool than I took you for!"

"Watch your fucking mouth, remember you have a lot to lose and if it wasn't for me..." Mancini began.

As they walked across the boardwalk Mancini lost his footing and fell over the side. Coughing and spluttering he flailed about in the water. "Help me... I... I can't swim," he gasped.

"I know," Dante whispered, laughing quietly as he waved at his uncle, good enough for the fucker he thought.

"P... please, how much do you want?" he gasped as he frantically tried to stop himself from sinking.

Dante watched as he went under and when he was sure that he wasn't coming back up he shouted at the top of his voice for help just before he jumped into the lake, fully clothed.

*****

Ella was unaware of the events unfolding outside as she asked the waiter for some iced water. As she sat down to sip it she stared into the glass as she ran her finger around the rim. What on earth was she doing here? This was not what she was used to.

"I think it is time we talked," a woman's voice said.

Looking up Ella was dismayed to find Concetta standing opposite her. "Oh, what do you want?"

"I'll tell you what I want and what I am going to get!" Concetta told her as she dismissed the kitchen staff with a quick movement of her hand. "Dante is what I want!" she hissed.

"Well, it's just a pity that he doesn't want you."

"If only you knew the real Dante."

"I know the real Dante."

"Do you?" Concetta whispered. "Do you know that he is a murderer amongst many other things?"

"You really are insane," Ella told her as she stood up. "I don't have to listen to this."

"You're right you don't, but I'm going to tell you anyway."

But before she had a chance there was a commotion outside and a woman was screaming.

Both women went to find out what on earth was going on.

"What is it?" Ella asked Grazia.

"It's Signor Mancini he has had a terrible accident down by the marina."

Flinging off her shoes Ella ran all the way down to the jetty. She saw the crowd of guests and pushed her way through, panicking that something had happened to Dante. When she finally managed to reach the front she saw Dante, soaking wet giving Mancini mouth to mouth, while his bodyguard stood by and Rosaria wailed.

Dante looked up. "I'm sorry he's gone," was all he could say as he held Rosaria in his arms.

"What happened?" she whimpered.

"It was an accident, I was just having a smoke and I heard a splash, I rushed down, but Dante was already in the lake bringing him to the shore," Giancarlo piped up.

"Oh, Dante, why?" Rosaria asked in a shaky voice.

"He seemed to slip on something and before I knew it he was in the water, I did everything I could." For effect Dante wiped a tear away. "I loved him like a father." But deep down inside he was glad to be finally rid of the fat fuck and now he was the sole heir to his vast fortune, at least until Mancini's son came of age.

Chapter Sixty-Two

After the ambulance came to take away Mancini's lifeless corpse Dante became withdrawn and quiet, he wouldn't talk to anyone.

All Ella wanted to do was go home, get as far away from this place as possible. She was sitting with Grazia in the conservatory. "I can't believe what happened tonight."

"It is very unfortunate but these things happen." Grazia tried to understand how Ella was feeling.

"I'm sorry, this was your night and now it's all spoiled."

"We can celebrate another time, but poor Signor Mancini, dying like that."

Ella's head was spinning, Dante had been the last person to see him alive and something didn't seem quite right. "Er... yes," was all she could say.

"Why don't you come up to my room and we'll talk," She glanced over to Nico who was sending everyone home. Dante was sitting inside the gazebo staring at his empty glass.

"I don't know, maybe I should just check into a hotel or something."

"Don't be silly, you and Dante are staying here tonight, I insist, no arguments please."

"Ok," Ella sighed. "I get the impression that they were close."

"Yes, yes they were, I mean Dante's father wasn't much of a father to him and well, since his sister was abducted..."

"Abducted?" Ella asked incredulously. "Why did he not tell me?"

"Please just come to my room."

It seemed there was a lot that Ella didn't know about him, perhaps there was some truth in what Concetta had been trying to tell her. "I don't understand what is going on with him, I have never seen him like this before and it scares me," Ella confessed.

When they sat down on the edge of Grazia's bed she turned to Ella. "So, why don't you tell me what happened between you and Concetta?"

"Her? She was trying to stir up trouble, make me split up with Dante, because of course she wanted him all to herself."

"That will never happen, trust me Dante only has eyes for you."

"But they used to date?"

"Yes, that's true, but unfortunately Concetta has a reputation."

"And is that the only reason Dante didn't want to be with her?"

"Why else? Would you want to be with someone who was sleeping around?"

"No, of course not." Ella remembered Mancini's words, '*You're a notch on his bedpost, he is marrying Concetta.*'

"What else is going on here?" Grazia looked into her eyes. "You must tell me."

"You will think that I'm a fool."

"No I won't, you can trust me you know."

"Mr Mancini, he… he upset me and, well Dante wasn't too happy and then they disappeared together and then, then there was some kind of accident and now he is dead!" There she had said it, got it off her chest.

"Ella, that's exactly it, it was an accident pure and simple. Dante and Signor Mancini always argued, it's a well known fact." She paused. "Don't tell me you think that Dante had something to do with his death?"

"No, of course not." Ella felt relieved, it really was all in her head, how could she even think Dante could do something so terrible.

"So, you haven't finished telling me about Concetta."

"She was just dropping all these hints that he was involved in all sorts of unsavoury things."

"All sorts, such as?"

"Murder is the one that springs to mind."

Grazia laughed. "That girl is such a case, pay no attention, she is so desperate she would do anything to get Dante back."

Ella laughed with her, it all sounded so ridiculous to her now. "Thanks for the chat."

"Any time." Grazia hugged her. "You and Dante make a very fine couple."

"I just don't think I know him very well." Ella sighed, wishing she knew what was going on in his head. "I'd better go and see how he is."

"I'll come with you."

*****

"So, what really went on?" Nico asked Dante.

"I don't know what you mean."

"Fair enough." Nico was no fool, but he decided to say nothing more, Dante was now his boss and he had to be very careful around him.

Before Dante had a chance to respond the two women appeared. "Come on it's getting late." Grazia linked her husband's arm. "Let's go to bed."

"Sure, goodnight all," Nico said. "See you in the morning."

"Let's go for a walk." Dante took Ella's hand.

"I'm sorry about your uncle," Ella said quietly.

"Don't be, I'm not."

"Don't say that."

"Well, it's true, he was a bully and a womanizer."

"No matter, he was still part of your family."

"I want you to be part of my family Ella." He suddenly stopped in his tracks and turned to her. "Will you marry me?"

"Do you really mean it?"

"Yes."

"I would be delighted to be your wife." Ella was swept up in a tide of emotion, she loved him and he loved her, how could she even contemplate saying no to him?

"You don't know how happy you have made me, let's do it tomorrow."

"What, why so soon?"

"Why wait? Nico and Grazia can be the witnesses, we can get married here."

"Oh, I… I don't know," Ella gasped.

"The way I see it, it is simple, do you love me?"

"Of course I do."

"Then why wait, what do you say?"

Ella nodded her head and that was all Dante needed, wrapping his arms around her he kissed her on the head. "I promise that you won't regret it."

Chapter Sixty-Three

Moscow, Russia

Vasiliev's private phone rang. "Yes?"
"It is Mancini, he is dead."
"How?"
"Some kind of accident, he fell into a lake and drowned."
Vasiliev put the phone down and laughed. It had to be the work of Dante Moretti, he had underestimated him. Now that he was the boss he wondered what his next move would be.
The first shipment was on route to England and if it worked out then they would all be very happy and very rich.
Pavel Junior was riding his bike through the house and it was driving Vasiliev up the wall. "Pavel, not in the house, outside," he barked at the little boy, who looked at him and started screaming. Slamming his office door shut he banged his fists on the table. He had to do something to toughen his son up, it was embarrassing, the whining he did. He was going to have to send him away, it was the only thing he could think of, either that or he would snap his neck.
He picked up his phone and rang Yakov Garshin. "You'd better keep a low profile. Moretti is now in charge of the Mancini businesses. You must never cross paths with him, if he ever finds you, make no mistake, he will kill you."
Garshin laughed. "I would like to see him try." His voice was full of bravado.
"Make no mistake, he would love to get his hands on you and if you do anything to upset me then I will turn you over to him."
"I will never do anything to upset you, you know that I am totally loyal."
"How is everything?"
"Just perfect, simple really, these stupid whores believe anything, a promise of a new life and job in England and they fall for it."

"I am glad to see that you are enjoying yourself, now is the shipment ready?"

"Yes, everything is in hand."

"Good, make no mistakes Yakov."

"I won't." Yakov slammed the phone down, the fuck, who did he think he was talking to, an amateur? He was a professional and should be treated with respect. One of these days Vasiliev would pay for treating him this way.

There was one more call Vasiliev had to make. "Dante, accept my condolences, I have just heard about your uncle." He paused. "I take it this does not change anything."

"No, nothing at all, I'll be in touch."

Vasiliev trusted Dante; he was mentally and physically strong, a bit like himself.

Just then Yelena entered the room. "You ok?"

"Yes, did the shipment go on time?"

"Of course, darling."

"Come here."

Yelena obediently went to him. "What is it?"

"You are a very attractive woman," he told her as he caressed her cheek.

Yelena cringed, Vasiliev was no oil painting. "You forget I am married to Aleksei."

"Aleksei, what use is he?"

"You insult me Pavel."

"Why do you use my first name?"

"I'm sorry I didn't mean to offend you."

"You didn't, I liked how it sounded as it came out of your pretty little mouth." He ran his finger across her lips.

"Stop." Yelena stepped away from him.

"One day Yelena I will have you, make no mistake, but I will wait until you are begging for it."

"Then you will wait a very long time, our relationship is purely professional and don't you forget that."

"Normally I wouldn't let anybody talk to me like that without punishing them."

Yelena was scared and it showed. Perhaps she had gone too far, she was forgetting who he really was.

"So, let me decide what your punishment should be." Walking towards her he laughed as she backed into the corner. "Do not worry I am not going to kill you." Vasiliev grabbed her roughly by the arms and kissed her hard on the lips.

Yelena arched her body towards him as she responded to his kiss. There was something dangerously exciting about him and she wanted him to take her right then and there.

Vasiliev roughly shoved her away from him. "I will never kiss you again until you ask me." He smiled.

"I will never ask you."

"You cannot fool me, Yelena, you enjoyed it, admit it."

"Don't kid yourself, I was scared that's all, I didn't know what else to do!"

"You can put on the act as long as you like but I know that you wanted me, if I hadn't pushed you away when I did then we would have been fucking over my desk!"

"You flatter yourself, Vasiliev." Yelena rushed out of the office slamming the door behind her.

"Call me Pavel!" Vasiliev shouted after her.

Yelena leaned against the door. She could not get involved with him, ever. It would be a complete disaster for everyone.

Chapter Sixty-Four

Lake Garda, Italy

The wedding ceremony came as a shock to both Nico and Grazia.

"Are you sure about this?" Nico had asked Dante.

"Mancini is not around anymore so I can do what I like."

"But his body is not even cold and you are marrying this woman, it is disrespectful," Nico told him. "At least wait until after the funeral, what will everyone think?"

"I don't really give a fuck what anybody thinks, this is my life and this is what I want."

"Very well, I have arranged for the jeweller to bring a selection of rings here for you to choose from, Grazia is organising everything else."

"Thank you, I appreciate it, Nico." He patted his shoulder. "I want it very low key, tell nobody, it will remain our secret for now."

"Whatever you wish."

"Good, now do you have a suit that I can borrow?"

"Of course."

"It's very short notice, so I'm afraid that we can't get a dress in time for you, why don't you look through my wardrobe?" Grazia was trying to think what she had that would be suitable for the occasion.

"That's very kind of you."

"I have plenty of dresses which I haven't worn yet and we are a similar size."

As Ella picked out several dresses she turned to Grazia. "Do you think we are crazy?"

"Crazy, what for being in love?"

Ella giggled. "I can't believe I'm doing this."

"You can still change your mind, the registrar hasn't arrived yet."

"No way." Ella picked out a short cream chiffon dress that had gold silk edging under the bust and layers of material that flowed from the waist, finished off with a bow that fastened at the back. "What do you think?"

"Excellent choice, now why don't you try it on and I'll get the gardener to gather some flowers for you."

Ella always dreamed of getting married, but she had always imagined it to be in a church filled with her family and friends and of course her father giving her away. As she slipped into the dress she wiped a tear away, she wished he was here.

"Wow, you look beautiful." Grazia smiled. "Simply stunning."

"Do you think it will do?"

"Absolutely, now have you thought how you want to have your hair?"

"A few curls would be nice."

"I'm sure I can manage that, now what about something old, something new, something borrowed, something blue?"

"Oh, I never even thought of that," Ella said as she put a well manicured hand to her head. "What am I going to do?"

"I have a pearl choker with matching earrings and a tiara you can borrow, erm... something new will be your wedding ring."

"What about the old and blue?"

"I'll tie some blue ribbon around the flowers, which just leaves the old!" Grazia was racking her brains but she didn't seem able to come up with anything.

"Do you think it will matter?"

"Of course."

Ella twisted the ring on her finger, it was eighteen carat gold encrusted with two rubies and a diamond. She started laughing uncontrollably.

"Are you all right?"

"I'm fine, I just realised my grandmother left me this ring."

"So?" Grazia was confused.

"You know something old!" she exclaimed.

"Oh!" Grazia laughed too. "Now how about a glass of wine for the nerves?"

"I'm not nervous, I'm so exited you wouldn't believe it!"

The Bellini brothers played the wedding march as Ella walked into the garden. She was stunning and Dante felt like the luckiest man in the world. As he stood there watching her he promised himself that he would cherish her and make sure that she never came to any harm.

The ceremony was all over in ten minutes. "I now pronounce you husband and wife, you may kiss your lovely bride," the registrar told Dante.

In typical Dante fashion he picked up his bride and kissed her passionately. "I love you Signora Moretti."

Nico popped the cork on the champagne as the Bellini brothers continued playing in the background.

"Not for me," Grazia told him.

"Just a little one, it's a special occasion after all."

"Ok, to Signor and Signora Moretti I hope that you will be as happy as we are." Grazia raised her glass.

Nico insisted on taking a few photographs despite Dante's protests. "I told you that we didn't want any fuss."

"It's just a few pictures, now smile please," Nico ordered. "You make a very fine couple indeed, but not as fine as me and Grazia!" he laughed.

"Nico, behave yourself." She turned to the newly married couple. "Have you thought about your honeymoon?"

"Er… no." Ella said as she looked at Dante. "Have you?"

Dante shrugged. "Do we need one?"

"Why don't you take the boat for a few days and sail around the lake. You know, get away from everything?" Grazia suggested. "Of course you can borrow our staff too, what do you say?"

"How about it, Ella?" Dante asked. "Would you like that?"

"Like it, I would positively love it!"

"Then that's settled." He kissed her. "Right now I'm starving, could you rustle something up Grazia?"

"Certainly."

"So, where are you two lovebirds going to live?" Nico asked.

"We haven't even discussed it yet." Dante wondered if Ella would come to live with him, his house needed a woman's touch.

"I quite like your house in Menaggio, maybe that should be our home." It was as if Ella was reading his mind.

"Perfect, then that's settled, now drink your champagne." Dante pulled Ella onto his knee. "We are going to be very happy together, I promise you."

Nico made an excuse and left them to it, they seemed to be very much in love, he thought, as he wondered what Concetta's father was going to do. He would not be a happy man, that was for sure.

Chapter Sixty-Five

London, England

Sandra Ennis was determined to put pressure on Petra Yanovich, she needed to know names and she was desperate to speak with her. She was annoyed that Carolyn Reid was equally determined to keep her as far away from Petra as possible. The last thing she wanted was some do-gooder interfering.

As soon as Carolyn left the centre Sandra got out of her car and lit a cigarette while she contemplated her next move. She didn't have to wait long when she spotted Petra walking in the garden. Now was her chance, she had to grab the opportunity while she could. Walking up to the fence she waved at her, trying to get her attention without anyone seeing her. "Petra… over here."

Petra looked over, she remembered that woman, she was going to take her to see her family. She ran over to her. "Where are my family, you promised me that you would take me to them?" she exclaimed.

"Shush, keep your voice down," Sandra urged. "Someone will hear you."

"What about my family?" Petra persisted.

"I've told you before give me a name and I'll see what I can do."

"How do I know that you are telling me the truth?"

"You'll just have to trust me, sweetheart."

Petra wrestled with her conscience. "But where are my family?" If they were indeed safe then perhaps she would tell her the only name she knew, but if they weren't she was risking some form of retaliation and she knew only too well what these men were capable of.

"I'll take you to them once you give me a name." Sandra smiled at her. "I want to stop them, make sure that nobody else goes through what you have."

She sounded so sincere that Petra opened her heart. "It was a Russian man, a man by the name of Yakov Garshin, that's all I can tell you, but he is one of the major players."

"Thank you." Sandra whooped with joy, now all she had to do was tell her superior and hopefully they would find him and then she would finally get her damn promotion.

"Wait, what about my family?" Petra shouted after her.

"They are all dead, shot to death!" Sandra wailed.

"No, no it's not true." Petra screamed as she gripped the mesh fence and tugged at it. "Why are you doing this to me?" *Had she not suffered enough?* she thought, as she fell to the ground.

One of the nurses came to her aid. "My dear, what on earth is wrong?"

"My family I need to call them, I have to use the phone, now!" Petra was hysterical.

"Please, come back into the building, I'll call your friend."

"If it's true I have nothing left to live for," she sobbed. "I can't bear it I have to know, help me."

"Let's get you to your room first." Once the nurse was satisfied that Petra was calmer she went to make the call. "Miss Reid, this is Nurse Peters, I need you to come to the clinic immediately."

"Why what's happened?"

"Petra knows that her family are dead and she is in shock."

"Oh my God, who told her?"

"I have no idea."

"Is anyone with her now?" Carolyn panicked.

"She's in her room, I'm waiting for the doctor coming."

"Please just go and stay with her until he arrives, I'm on my way."

Petra got out of the window and climbed up the fire escape onto the roof. Her life was worth nothing now, her whole family had been murdered and she hadn't even betrayed the men that had kidnapped, raped and beaten her. It wasn't her fault that the house they were using was raided and she was taken. She had given Garshin's name and knew either way that she was a dead woman now. But if she was going to die it wasn't going to by their hands. She would choose her own way, it would be the last decision she would ever make and on the way down she would laugh in their face.

As Carolyn pulled up to the building she saw a crowd of people gathering and staring up to the roof. Looking up, her heart skipped a beat when she saw Petra teetering on the edge.

Holding out her arms and closing her eyes Petra leaned forward and let gravity do the rest.

Her body crashed down onto the driveway and blood spattered everywhere. People were screaming hysterically as the staff tried to get them back into the clinic.

Carolyn was transfixed, distraught that she was too late to save her, the poor girl. Feeling sick she rested her hands on the car, trying to compose herself. When she turned back around one of the nurses had covered Petra's body with a sheet which was quickly turning crimson.

"Can I help you miss?"

"I'm Carolyn Reid, I am, I mean I was a friend of Petra's, what the hell happened here?"

Nurse Peters was in pieces, never, ever had she witnessed anyone take their own life. "I'm sorry, I should never have left her alone, I only left her for a few minutes just while I was talking to you."

"It's nobody's fault." Carolyn was trying to believe the words she spoke, but deep down she was kidding herself. If only she had realised how really ill Petra was from her ordeal, then perhaps she could have saved her. She was trembling and holding her head. "Oh, I feel a little faint."

The nurse quickly grabbed her arms to stop her from keeling over onto the gravel driveway. "Sit down, Miss Reid, I'll get you some water."

Carolyn nodded as she sat on the ground and leaned against her car. As she hugged her knees to her chest she relived Petra's body falling from the roof, over and over again. It was so vivid, so clear, it had been over in seconds, yet in her mind's eye she saw it all in slow motion, unable to stop it. Poor Petra, she had failed her and she would never, ever forgive herself for that.

Chapter Sixty-Six

The Riccis' holiday villa, Lake Garda, Italy

Concetta Ricci was stunned by the events of the previous evening and made no bones about how she felt. "Who was the blonde, someone serious do you think?"

Mirella shrugged. "How am I supposed to know? Anyway who cares Signor Mancini is dead!"

"I really don't give a damn about that but I do give a damn about becoming a Moretti, especially now he will inherit Mancini's fortune." She sighed as she moved her hair away from her face. "Perhaps we will move into the mansion, but of course, we would have to completely redecorate, it isn't modern enough for me, I have plenty of ideas to revamp the place."

"Concetta!" Mirella giggled. "You can't kick his widow out of the mansion, her husband isn't even cold in his grave yet!"

"What good is that lavish mansion on that silly old crow Rosaria and her two pathetic, spoilt children!"

"You really are bad, through and through, aren't you?" Mirella gasped. "What are you going to do about Dante?"

"Win him back of course, I'm going to ring the de Lucas' right now to see what's going on." Her voice was defiant. "He will not ignore me for long, he can't resist me, he loved me once and he will love me again."

But Mirella wasn't so sure, not after all her conquests. She could have at least been discreet, but she hadn't given a damn.

Concetta shouted to the maid. "Bring the telephone and make it snappy, get me connected to the de Lucas residence."

The maid went back into the house and reappeared with a telephone in her hand. She carefully walked across the patio.

"Bloody hell, woman, somebody would think that you were walking on hot coals!"

"But I don't want to trip over the wire," she protested.

"Hurry it up!" Concetta screamed.

In her haste the poor maid took a tumble and went head first into the water fountain.

Concetta shrieked with laughter. "You stupid bloody idiot, you are useless, go and find yourself a job with some other mug, but don't expect a reference from me."

One of the bodyguards looked on in total amazement, this beautiful young woman had a vicious tongue on her.

"And what are you looking at?" He was quite handsome for a bodyguard, she thought. "Perhaps you too would like to feel the wrath of my tongue?" Her voice was suggestive as she tried to get a reaction from him.

"Nothing, Signora Ricci, would you like me to help the maid?"

"If you must, but do hurry up and get her off my father's property."

Mirella passed her friend the phone. "Would you like me to dial it for you madam?" She curtsied.

"Just give me the damn phone." Concetta dialled the number. "This is Concetta Ricci. I would like to speak to Dante Moretti, I am assuming that he is still there."

"Hello, dear, this is Grazia, I'm sorry to say that he is currently indisposed." She smiled to herself, she and Nico had only waved them off twenty minutes earlier and they were anchored a few hundred metres off shore so that they would not be disturbed.

"Oh, Grazia, stop playing games and just go and get him."

"I can't do that," Grazia insisted.

"What do you mean?"

Grazia put her hand over the mouthpiece and turned to her husband. "It's Concetta, please can I tell her?" she begged.

"It's not our place, you know that," Nico told her. "But on the other hand I suppose Dante said that he didn't care who knew." He winked to give her the go ahead.

Grazia wasted no time in taking total delight in breaking the news. "I think you had better sit down for this."

"Don't be foolish, why on earth would I want to sit down!" Concetta exclaimed.

"Because Dante was married an hour ago."

"I don't believe you!" Concetta raged.

"Ah, but it is true, you see, both Nico and I were witnesses."

Concetta threw the phone down and stamped on it, screaming obscenities.

"What on earth is it?" Mirella asked, frightened of what she was going to say.

"That son of a bitch has got married."

"Who to, the blonde?"

"Of course the fucking blonde, who else? Well I'll fucking show him!" Concetta threw everything off the table, she was absolutely furious.

"Come on let's have a drink and calm down," Mirella suggested.

"Very well."

Several hours later both girls were rather tipsy. "I want that bitch dead," Concetta hiccupped.

"Oh, just forget about him, you'll find someone far richer and better looking."

"But that's just it, I fucking won't!" She jumped up off her seat nearly falling over as she did so.

"What are you doing now?"

"I'm going to ring Augusto."

"What, are you serious?" Mirella was worried now, Augusto Fierro was another one of Concetta's many conquests and also a hitman of some sort.

"Come on." Concetta grabbed her hand. "My little black book is in my bedroom, you must help me find it, his number is in there."

"Are you going to have him killed?" Mirella whispered. "What will your father say?"

"My fucking father isn't here is he?"

"I know that!"

"Well shut up then!"

Mirella wasn't sure what her friends intentions were, but she was feeling slightly freaked out by her hysteria.

As they sat on the edge of her bed, Concetta flipped through her personal phone book. "Yes, yes, here it is," she said excitedly as she phoned Augusto's number.

"Hi, Augusto, it's Concetta Ricci, do you remember me?" She paused for his response and laughed seductively. "Well if you are willing to do a favour for me not only will I pay you but

I'll also do your favourite thing again," she teased. "How about it?"

"What are you doing, are you crazy?" Mirella interrupted.

"Shush!" Concetta said as she pushed her out of the way. "No, no, not you Augusto," she purred. "It is the de Luca residence, I don't give a fuck if they get hurt, but the target is the blonde English woman, do not do any serious damage to Moretti..." she hesitated. "Oh and Augusto, let me know when it's done and I'll give you your reward."

"What if Dante finds out that you are somehow involved?" Mirella was concerned as she watched her replace the receiver.

"Why would he? He has many enemies, maybe somebody will think something sinister happened to Mancini and they wanted to take some kind of revenge, you know blame Moretti and... maybe the poor English girl just got in the way!" She giggled.

Mirella topped up their glasses. "You are a clever girl, did anyone ever tell you?"

"Yes, all the time, but usually only when I am in bed with some well-endowed hunk." Her thoughts turned to the young, fit bodyguard. Perhaps she would go and see him later that evening, once she received the phone call she would have to release all of that pent-up excitement and she could barely wait. As for stupid Fierro, well she would never allow him the pleasure of having her again, instead she would pay him handsomely. "Let's get some more wine!"

Chapter Sixty-Seven

The de Luca Residence, Lake Garda, Italy

The de Lucas were standing on their bedroom balcony looking out at the yacht.
"What do you think they're up to?" Grazia giggled.
"Probably the same thing we should be!" Nico teased. "But first I need a quick shower."
"I'm going to get some hot chocolate and a couple of headache tablets, do you want anything?"
"Only you," he told her as he kissed her lightly on the lips. "Don't be long and I'll give you a shoulder massage, ease up all those tight muscles."
As she left the room, she blew him a kiss. "I won't." She was so lucky to have such a doting husband and now they were going to be a complete family. The house was quiet as they had sent the entire staff home so they could have some quality time together. It won't be quiet once the little bambino arrived, she thought.
Augusto was accompanied by one of his gang and they were both high as a kite – just a little something to help them do the job. He wanted to impress Concetta and had bragged about so-called contract killings. She had hung on his every word and now he had to pretend he was some kind of hard man. They sneaked over the fence and stumbled around the back of the building, trying to be as quiet as possible.
Grazia didn't switch the kitchen light on; she didn't want to make her headache worse. Lighting the gas stove she emptied the milk into the pan and opened the kitchen cupboard, humming to herself as she did so. Now where on earth had the maid put the hot chocolate? She was always tidying things away and Grazia could never find them. There was a huge crash outside, making her jump with fright.
"Be still you idiot, someone's coming!" Augusto grabbed Marco and hauled him back. He held his breath as they hid just around the corner.

Grazia switched on the patio lights and looked out, the bottle bin had somehow fallen over and there were bottles strewn everywhere. Opening the doors she went to pick them up. "Is there anybody there?" Her voice trembled, she wished that Nico was there, but he was probably still in the shower. Feeling frightened she backed into the house and that's when she saw the shadows looming close by.

"Come on, she's fucking seen us, let's just grab what we can and get out of here." Suddenly feeling full of bravado Augusto dashed into the house.

Without hesitating Grazia grabbed the pan of boiling milk and threw it right at them. The boiling liquid sprayed all over Marco. As he screamed Grazia thought of her unborn baby. Racing over to the block of kitchen knives she pulled one out. "Don't come near me!"

Augusto popped a tablet and began to approach her. "I don't want to hurt you, just tell me where the blonde is!" he demanded.

Grazia didn't understand what he was talking about. "My husband is upstairs; he'll be here any second."

"There's nobody here but us, sweetheart," Augusto lunged at her as he tried to grapple the knife out of her hands.

"Let's get out of here." Marco's face was red raw. "I need the hospital man, she's disfigured me."

Grazia screamed on the top of her lungs frightening Augusto. He tried to put his hand over her mouth to shut her up; they both slipped on the spilt milk and ended up on the kitchen floor.

As Grazia dropped the knife she looked down, there was blood everywhere. "My... my..." and then she was unconscious.

They heard a man yelling from upstairs. "Grazia, Grazia!"

"Let's get out of here!" As Augusto made for the door Marco rushed back and removed Grazia's jewellery. "I didn't come here for nothing, stupid bitch!"

By the time Nico had arrived the two men had vanished and his poor wife was lying in a pool of blood on the floor. He had sent the entire staff home that evening and wondered why, what if his beloved Grazia was dead; it would be all his fault. He was

Dante's friend and with Mancini's recent death, that, quite simply made them both targets.

Feeling sick to the pit of his stomach he checked his wife's pulse, it was faint, but she was alive. "I'm going to get help; it's going to be ok," he promised as he dialled emergency services.

As he waited for the ambulance to arrive he cradled his wife in his arms. "Don't die on me, I'm nothing without you." Tears welled up in his eyes, he was in total shock.

Ella and Dante emerged from the cabin when they heard the sirens. "Where do you think they are going?" Ella asked, her voice full of concern.

Dante watched the blue lights as they got nearer to the de Luca residence. "Oh my God, we have to get back to the house, now!" He wasted no time in wakening the captain.

Chapter Sixty-Eight

By the time they got back to the house the de Lucas had gone and the police were swarming the place.

"Who are you?" the detective asked.

"We are friends of the de Lucas', now what the hell is going on here?" Dante demanded.

"It looks like somebody tried to break in."

"Where is Nico and Grazia, are they ok?" Ella asked.

"We saw the ambulance drive off," Dante explained.

"I'm afraid that Mrs de Luca has been stabbed," the detective told them.

"Is she going to be ok?" Ella thought of the baby.

"I am afraid it is quite serious."

"We better go to the hospital, if that's ok?" Dante checked with the detective.

"Yes, that's fine, but we will need to take statements from you later, what are your names?" He took out his notebook.

"Dante and Ella Moretti."

Ella was in a daze, barely registering what her husband was saying. She hoped and prayed that Grazia and the baby would be ok. Dante phoned Flavio. "I need you to take us to the hospital, now."

*****

Nico was greeted by a team of medical staff who had been alerted to the situation and were ready waiting when they arrived in the ambulance.

"She has been stabbed in the stomach and is also in her first trimester," the paramedic told the doctor as they rushed her down the corridor.

Nico held his unconscious wife's hand. "You're going to be ok."

"Mr de Luca, we must take her into surgery, please stay here, we'll be back as soon as there's any news."

"Please, doctor, don't let her die, I beg you." Nico watched helplessly as the team pushed through the automatic doors and disappeared out of sight.

"Mr de Luca, please wait in here, can I get you some water?" the nurse asked.

"No, no, no!" Was all he could say as he followed her into the relatives' room and slumped into a chair. He had his head in his hands when Dante and Ella arrived.

Fearing the worst Dante approached his friend. "Nico?"

"I don't know what happened but I'm going to kill the fucking bastard that did this to her, I swear to God!" Nico was distraught. "Someone came into our home and did this to her, why, why?"

Dante turned to Ella. "Darling, would you mind getting us some coffee?"

"Sure." Ella left the room; the poor man was verging on hysteria.

When he was sure his wife had left Dante grabbed Nico by the shoulders and shook him hard. "Pull yourself together man, what the fuck went down?"

"I don't know, I don't know!" Nico sobbed as he repeated the words. "Why, why, you've got to help me!"

Dante hugged him. "Don't worry, everything is going to be all right, you'll see." He had already set the wheels in motion; this was either a backlash for Mancini's death or revenge from the Ricci family for marrying another woman. The news had spread much faster than he had anticipated.

*****

Flavio and some of his men were watching the Ricci house while another crew watched the Mancini residence. One way or another they were going to find out who did this and, when they did, it would be payback time.

Augusto and Marco sped up the drive and Concetta came out of the house to meet them.

"What the fuck are you doing here, is she dead?"

"I... I don't know, but you better give me money, I've got to get out of here before the police catch up with us."

"The police?"

"What the fuck did you think was going to happen, nothing? I stabbed her, left her for dead and you don't think the police would be interested?"

The enormity of the situation hit Concetta like a sledgehammer. "Wait there, I'll get the money." Rushing back into the house she opened the safe and took out an envelope stuffed with money.

"What are you doing?" Mirella was very concerned.

Ignoring her Concetta ran outside and gave Augusto the money. "Here, now please go."

"If I get caught, make no mistake, I will give your name to the police," he told her as he got back into the car and sped off.

"You and you!" Flavio ordered. "Firebomb the house, I'll take care of those fuckers!"

Mirella watched as Concetta packed her suitcase. "What are you doing?" She was scared, really scared.

"Come on let's hurry."

"Why? What have you done?"

"It's all gone wrong, he was supposed to sneak in, kill her and sneak back out again, but the fucking idiot can't even do that!" she screeched.

Unbeknown to the two women the masked men entered the house and cleared out all of the servants, locking them inside the gardener's shed at the end of the lane.

When Flavio was sure that the house was clear he gave the signal. His men opened the van doors and took out the bottles of petrol. As they lit them he saw Concetta Ricci looking out of the window.

"Now!" he ordered.

His men lit the rags on the bottles and pelted the house. He had made sure that there was no way out, blocking all the entrances with dozens of petrol cans.

"The exits!" he pointed to the men he had specially chosen to finish the job.

Looking up at the window he saw Concetta's petrified face, she was banging on the window and shaking her head. He saw the money she held up and desperately pressed against the window. Removing his mask and signalling to one of his men to shine the spotlight in his face he waved at her. The look of complete horror on her face said it all. Dante wanted whoever was responsible for doing this to his friend to know that it was he who had given the order for their death.

*****

Augusto was driving like a maniac. High on coke with a wild gleam in his eyes, he felt invincible.

Marco was still shaking from the scalding burns he had received. "I gotta go to the hospital man, you have to take me."

Without thinking about it Augusto leaned over, opened the passenger door and shoved his mate out into the middle of the road. "There, go to the hospital you dumb fuck!" He looked in his rear-view mirror and laughed when he saw a truck run over him. Now he was going to get away, with Marco's injuries they would be spotted right away.

As he sped away he noticed a car following him, rubbing his eyes he cursed. "Who the fuck is this idiot?"

The car overtook him and nudged the front of his vehicle as it did so making him swerve dangerously close to the edge of the road. Tooting his horn he put his foot down and overtook the car, making obscene gestures as he did so. He was so out of it he didn't even notice the masked men, all armed waiting to make their move. "I'm king of this road, now fuck off!" he yelled winding his window down.

Carmine laughed. "So the little fucker wants to play with us, what do you say guys?" He accelerated hard and rammed into Augusto's car, shunting it into the opposite side of the road.

An oil tanker was just coming around the corner; Carmine expertly swung the car off the road and prayed.

Augusto saw his life flash before his very eyes, holding his hands over his face he screamed. He didn't stand a chance as the explosion ripped through both vehicles in an instant.

It felt like an earthquake going off. Hunks of the burnt metal were strewn for miles narrowly missing Carmine's car. They were lucky, very fucking lucky to escape with their lives, he thought. But the job was done and he could return to base.

*****

Ella returned to the family room with a tray of coffees. "Here." She passed one to Nico; his hands were shaking so badly that he nearly dropped it.

Dante gently took it from his hands. "Sit down," he ordered.

"I can't, I can't. I need to know what is happening."

Ella looked on and felt terribly for the poor man, but there was nothing that she could do. They all sat and waited, mostly in silence.

Every now and then Nico disappeared with Dante to have a cigarette leaving Ella on her own. This was supposed to be her wedding night, he thought, and now she would always remember it, but for all the wrong reasons.

Two hours later the consultant entered the room. "Mr de Luca." His voice was calm but sounded very serious; everyone knew that it was bad news.

"My wife?"

"Your wife is stable."

"Can I see her now?"

"In a little while, one of the nurses will come and get you."

Nico shook the consultant's hand. "Oh thank God, I don't know how to thank you, tell me, what can I do, how about I make a generous donation to the hospital?"

"Mr de Luca this is my job, it is what I do."

"I'm sorry. I don't mean to insult you."

Dante saw the look in the consultant's eyes, something was wrong. "What is it?"

"I would prefer to speak with Mr de Luca alone."

"No, no it's ok these are my friends," Nico told him.

The consultant hated this part of the job, he breathed in deeply. "I'm so sorry, we couldn't save the baby." He paused. "There was internal haemorrhaging and we had to do emergency surgery. It was either that or they would have both died."

Nico lunged at him barely able to understand the words that were coming out of his mouth. Before he had time to do anything Dante jumped between the two men.

"Nico, Nico, you heard him, he had to do it to save Grazia, it was the only way."

"Does she know?" Nico whispered.

The consultant was frozen with fear unable to respond.

"I said does my wife know!" he yelled making the man jump.

"No, I thought it would be better for you to break the news to her yourself." The consultant turned to leave, not having the heart to tell him that he also had to remove Signora de Luca's womb due to sudden complications. He would talk to them properly on his rounds tomorrow when there were more people around.

"One more thing." Nico grabbed his arm. "What sex was the baby?"

"A boy."

Nico let out a low howl, like an animal in pain. Dante put his arms around him to try and console him in some way. "You must think of Grazia now and be strong for her."

Nico nodded, he tried to speak but no words would come out, he was devastated to the core of his body.

"Mr de Luca, your wife is just coming around from the anaesthetic, you can see her now," the nurse told him. "Please follow me."

After he left Dante wiped a tear away from his eye. "My God, they didn't deserve that!"

"Poor, poor sweet Grazia," Ella cried, it was so sad, so very, very sad. It was only a short while ago when they were celebrating the news, the proud parents to be and now, just like that, the baby's life had been extinguished. And she didn't know how the de Lucas' were ever going to get over it.

Chapter Sixty-Nine

It had been a long night and Ella was exhausted. She desperately wanted to see Grazia but didn't know what on earth she was going to say to her. She just couldn't imagine how she was feeling right now.

"We should go and leave them to it," Dante said. "There's nothing we can do here."

Ella nodded in agreement.

"I'll just go and tell Nico, do you want to come with me?"

"Ok," Ella said in a small tight voice, she was feeling nervous, unsure of what to expect.

Holding hands they walked silently down the corridor and Dante knocked gently on the door. "Nico?"

Nico was stroking his wife's hair.

"Dante, Ella, come in," Grazia whispered. "Thank you for coming."

Dante looked at Nico, had he told her yet?

Seeing the questioning look in his eyes Grazia spoke. "I know about the baby."

"I'm so sorry Grazia." Ella went to her bedside. "Really I am, it is so awful, I can hardly believe it."

"I'm alive and I have to thank God for that," she said matter of factly.

Ella guessed that she was either suffering the effects of the morphine or she was still very much in shock.

"There'll be plenty of opportunity for bambinos," Nico told her as he kissed her hand.

The consultant appeared with a nurse and a junior doctor in tow. "I would like to speak with the de Lucas' alone."

"It's ok, we were just leaving," Dante informed him. "We'll be on the boat Nico, if you need us."

"Thanks for everything," Nico told him and shook his hand, letting him know that he understood he had taken care of the murdering scum.

The consultant kept his distance when he broke the news to Signor de Luca and his wife. Grazia never batted an eyelid; she just lay there staring into space. Nico went ballistic, smashing the place up and threatening everyone. Security had to be called and he was escorted outside the hospital until he calmed down.

Chapter Seventy

London, England

Marcus Treymayne had insisted on meeting Vitelli's associate at the docks. He wanted to see the first shipment come in and now he was stuck in a traffic jam. Picking up his mobile he dialled his number. "I'm sorry, I'm going to be late, please don't unload the cars until I get there," he insisted.

Vitelli had arranged for a meat lorry to lose its cargo, blocking all the roads. He had about twenty minutes to unload the shipment and get them out of there before Treymayne arrived. It was a race against the clock.

His men unlocked the ISO-freight container and shone in the torches. There were about thirty women of all ages huddled together at the back of the container. "Out!" he ordered.

"Quickly, quickly." One of his men had to physically grab them. "Move it!"

The women were totally disorientated, rubbing their eyes; they didn't have the faintest idea where they were.

"We gotta get a fucking move on man, you need to clear out of here right now, he'll be here any minute!"

"Don't stress man!"

The women were split up and loaded into two lorries, one was northbound, the other was to remain local.

The vehicles screamed out of the compound with seconds to spare. Vitelli's man had just enough time to lock the ISO-freight containers before Treymayne pulled up.

"Signor Treymayne, a pleasure to meet you."

"Signor Lorenzo I presume?" Marcus shook his hand. "Do you want to do the honours?"

"If you insist." Fucking imbecile, he hated these jumped-up men in suits with their fucking degrees.

He unlocked the padlock once more and stood back to watch him admire the cars being unloaded.

Marcus' eyes lit up, they were superb and would bring a small fortune. He had to hand it to Ella she had come up trumps. He would congratulate her as soon as she came home.

Chapter Seventy-One

Moscow, Russia

Aleksei had just arrived home. He couldn't wait to see his wife, it had only been a week but he had really missed her. "Yelena, where are you?" his voice echoed around the huge entrance hall.
　　Hearing his voice she called to him. "I'm in the lounge."
　　Two minutes later she was in his arms. "I've missed you."
　　"Me too," she told him. "Have you heard the news yet?"
　　"What news?"
　　"Mancini is dead, Grazia has lost her baby and Dante has married Ella Reynolds!" she exclaimed.
　　"What?"
　　"It's true."
　　"What happened?" Aleksei was shocked.
　　Yelena filled in all the details. "So, do you think we should go to Italy, personally give our condolences?"
　　"Yes, I think that is a good idea." He picked up the phone and dialled Vasiliev.
　　After a lengthy discussion he realised that Dante was now the kingpin and he had to be very, very careful around him, especially after he had learned of the recent killings courtesy of Moretti.
　　He rang Vincenzo. "Did the first shipment arrive intact?" he asked.
　　"Yes, everything ran smoothly."
　　"Did Treymayne suspect anything?"
　　"Nothing, but we had to create a diversion, he cannot be allowed to be present during the shipments."
　　"I agree, but don't do anything drastic until you speak with me."
　　"I understand."
　　Aleksei sighed, the business he was in was getting out of hand and it appeared there was no way out for him, he was up to his neck in it. He promised himself that if ever there was an opportunity to rid himself of this way of life then he would. The

murders were becoming more frequent and more vicious; it seemed that none of his allies gave a damn about human life. He knew that he had to keep up the façade to survive, it was the only way.

"The flight leaves in three hours, is that ok with you?" Yelena's voice interrupted his thoughts.

"That's fine my darling, now tell me how have you been?"

"Fabulous, darling."

"How was the Scotland trip?"

"Eventful to say the least."

"I heard the old couple had to be taken out?"

"I'm afraid so, it had to be done." Her voice was cold and unemotional.

Aleksei didn't want the details; he was finding it difficult to deal with his lovely wife killing a defenceless old couple.

"I know what you are thinking, but we had no choice if we were to rescue the boy." She sighed, tears welling in her eyes.

He held her in his arms. "I know, but we are now forever in Vasiliev's debt, both of us, do you understand?"

Yelena knew only too well, she was in this deeper than her husband could ever imagine and she was enjoying every minute. She had felt empty for years and now she had power, power over those pathetic young women who deserved every degrading thing thrown at them. "If we stick together we will be ok."

Aleksei nodded. "Yes, together we will survive anything," he told her as he kissed her.

Chapter Seventy-Two

London, England

When Sandra Ennis was called in to see her superiors she was shocked at what they had to say to her.

"So, you went to see Petra Yanovich against my strict instructions?"

"I got a result, a name; it's what we all wanted isn't it?" she protested.

"I don't know what you said to her, but soon after you left she threw herself off the top of the clinic roof." Her boss watched her face, there was no reaction, no emotion, she was cold. "Give me your badge, you're suspended and if I have my way you will be kicked out of the force for good!"

Sandra took her badge out of her pocket and threw it across the desk. "I was too good for this fucking place anyway, you're all too scared to do anything. Well I'll show you if it's the last thing I ever do!"

"Get this bitch out of my office and out of my building!" he yelled at two of his officers.

As Sandra was frogmarched through the offices her colleagues clapped. They were glad to see the back of her, she had been trouble from the offset.

"I'll have the last laugh, don't you worry!" she yelled at them.

The two officers had to forcibly drag her and chuck her onto the street.

"You'll regret this you arseholes, all of you will!" she screamed in frustration. The only way to redeem herself was to find this Yakov Garshin, bring him in and then she would be the hero of the hour.

She didn't give a rat's arse about Petra Yanovich, the likes of her didn't deserve to live in her country and she for one was glad that she had gone.

As Sandra sat in her car she flipped open her mobile and dialled a number. "I need to call in a favour."

"I'm listening," said the voice on the other end.

"I need some serious protection and a couple of flights to Russia."

"What are you up to?" Ray asked, not sure that he really wanted to help her.

"Look, if we pull this off then we will be heroes, trust me!"

"I need more details Sandra."

"I have a name, one Yakov Garshin; if we can get to him then perhaps we can get to his boss."

"Do you realise how much danger we will be in? You are talking about the Russian mafia."

"I know that, will you help me or not?"

Ray was an ex-paratrooper and also her estranged husband, together they had a volatile relationship but neither of them wanted a divorce. Still feeling drawn to her, but against his better judgement, he agreed to help.

"Let's meet up." Sandra smiled to herself, Ray was putty in her hands, he still loved her in his own way. He was one tough son of a bitch and she needed his muscle more than anything.

Chapter Seventy-Three

Ella and Dante arrived in London. She was nervous about breaking the news to her friends and family but she was especially worried about her mother's reaction. She had phoned on ahead and asked everyone to meet her at the family home. As the taxi drove up to the house, Dante squeezed her hand.

"Don't look so worried." His voice was soothing. "Everyone will be happy for you, for us."

"I wish I had your confidence."

Her mother and aunt waited patiently in the driveway wondering what the news was. "Ella, you look wonderful." Her mother hugged her. "You're not pregnant are you?" she whispered.

"Good grief no!" Ella exclaimed. "I would like you to meet Dante Moretti." She hesitated as Dante kissed her mother's hand.

"Such a gentleman." Her mother smiled, instantly liking him.

"Dante is my husband, Mum."

"Husband...? You're married, that's wonderful, just wonderful isn't it?" she said as she turned to her sister-in-law.

"It's all rather sudden if you ask me!"

"We are deeply in love, there was no point in waiting." Dante flashed her a smile and kissed her hand too. "Now, I would like to meet the guests."

Taking Ella's arm they walked through the house and into the reception room, where everyone waited patiently.

"I would like everyone to meet my husband Dante Moretti."

Her mother clapped, encouraging everyone else to do the same.

Carolyn was the first one to congratulate the happy couple. "I am so pleased for you both and I wish you every happiness." She took Ella's hand and admired her ring. "Wow, that's beautiful."

Mostly everyone was pleased for them but Ella could see a few strange looks aimed at her and a few so-called friends gossiping in the corner. "Dante, why don't you mingle while I catch up with Carolyn?"

Once they were on their own Carolyn told her everything. "So, you see that Ennis woman basically killed her!"

"That is absolutely terrible. I hope she has been severely reprimanded."

"She's been suspended while they conduct a thorough enquiry."

"What about the centre?"

"Well thanks to your generous donation plus quite a few surprising ones, I have enough to relocate. I mean, I couldn't go back there." She shuddered. "My mother and all those people were murdered there; it would just hold too many ghosts for me."

"I understand." Ella hugged her friend. "So, when is the opening day?"

"Soon, very soon, now forget about that I want to know everything."

"Oh, I'm not sure that I could tell you everything," Ella giggled.

Carolyn laughed with her. "I don't want all the details but is he a good kisser?" she teased.

"Yes, the best!" Ella told her, feeling someone staring at her she looked up. "Oh, Marcus, how are you?"

"How are you?" He tried to smile and look happy for her.

Carolyn felt sorry for him, he was definitely wounded about the wedding news and the anguish was written all over his face.

If Ella noticed she chose to ignore it. "Did the cars arrive safely?"

"Yes and I have a couple of buyers already."

"Brilliant, so do you think we should make the arrangement more permanent?"

"Absolutely. Now, are you going to introduce me to your husband?" He wanted to see the man who had stolen her away from him.

"Follow me." She took Marcus' arm and went into the reception room. Dante was sitting on one of the huge sofas surrounded by a dozen or so people. It seemed that he was an instant hit and Ella was delighted. "Dante, sorry for interrupting everyone, I would like you to meet Marcus Treymayne."

"Mr Treymayne, I have heard a lot about you." He shook his hand.

"All good I hope." Marcus had a strange feeling about this dashing young man, one that he didn't like at all.

"I hear that you have recently acquired some motors from an acquaintance of mine?"

"Oh, you are a friend of Nico de Luca?"

"Yes, we practically grew up together."

"Why don't you two get to know each other while I entertain my friends?" Ella encouraged them.

"Yes, what a good idea, why don't we go out into the garden?" Dante suggested.

Once they were outside Dante turned to him. "You don't like me very much, do you Mr Treymayne?" he stated matter-of-factly.

"I don't know what has given you that impression," Marcus said coolly.

"It's obvious you are in love with her."

"Don't be so ridiculous."

"Ridiculous?" Dante laughed. "Is it?"

His attitude antagonised Marcus and he wanted to punch him square in the jaw, knock that smug smile off his arrogant face. "I just think that this marriage was… shall we say? Rather hasty." He waited for Moretti's reaction.

"We are madly in love with each other and I make her very, very happy." He paused for effect. "Do you know what I mean? She has a body to die for and, boy once you get through that packaging it's well worth the wait."

"How dare you talk about her like she was some kind of trophy!" Marcus was seething.

Dante smiled, he had deliberately tried to get a reaction out of the man and now he was convinced Marcus was totally in love with Ella, luckily for him she didn't reciprocate his feelings.

"You boys like a drink, perhaps a whisky?" Mrs Reynolds asked as she took them both by the arm. "Ella is so lucky to have such a charming husband, don't you think?"

"Yes," Marcus said through gritted teeth, but it wouldn't last.

Chapter Seventy-Four

Moscow, Russia

It had been almost four weeks since Mancini's death and Dante was anxious to speak with Vasiliev. As he pulled up to his huge house he looked at his wedding ring. Ella was a total distraction to him and he was worried about the effect it was having on the business. His uncle had left him a vast fortune and he felt incredibly lucky to be so fortunate.

Ella was his soul mate and he adored her, but he had to be careful because, if he upset anyone, then she was a potential target. It wasn't easy keeping everybody happy but when he watched Mancini drown he knew from that moment he had to keep total control over everything.

Vasiliev was in the garden playing miniature golf with his son. "Dante, good to see you."

Dante shook his hand. "So, how are things?"

"Very good." He signalled to the nanny. "Take Pavel Junior into the house." After he left Vasiliev cursed. "I wonder if I did the right thing getting my son back."

"What do you mean?"

"He's a fucking ponce, a nancy boy, I just don't know what to do with him, he fucking hates me!"

"What makes you say that?"

"His fucking grandparents, they have poisoned him against me!" he fumed.

Dante had to bite his lip, after everything he had done to get him back and killing the old people, he would never forget it; it was something that should never have happened.

"Pavel." Yelena appeared in a skimpy dress that didn't leave much to the imagination. When she saw Vasiliev had company in the form of Dante Moretti she waved. "Oh, I thought little Pavel Junior was out here."

"He's in the house," Dante told her. He didn't know what she was playing at and he was worried about her involvement with Vasiliev.

"Yelena is working for me. She is – how do you say? – a recruitment consultant." He laughed. "And she's extremely good at it!"

"Oh, I bet she is," Dante said sarcastically.

"I'll just go into the house shall I and say hello to the little one, we can perhaps catch up later?" Yelena made a quick exit.

"Go ahead," Vasiliev told her. After she had left he turned to Dante. "There's nothing going on between us."

"It's none of my business what you get up to."

"Good, now tell me, now that you are the boss what are your plans?"

"Exactly as they were, nothing has changed."

"The shipment arrived safely but I think this Treymayne may be trouble. He seems to want to be there, you know, to oversee everything. Perhaps we need to erase him?"

"No need for that, he is just overeager, it's excitement, all those luxury motors, he can't help himself."

"Keep an eye on him and if he gets in the way, you know what to do, right?"

"Of course." Dante paused. "From now on you will be dealing with one of my men. I need to keep my distance. We do not want to be associated with each other, too much has happened, we do not know who is watching us."

"I heard about Nico's troubles, that must be very tough on him."

"Yes," was all Dante could say.

"I also heard about the revenge you exacted, it was beautiful, I hope Nico was grateful."

Nothing got past this man, thought Dante; he knew everything there was to know. "He is a close friend. There's nothing I wouldn't do for him."

"I would very much like to meet your wife, Ella." Pavel changed the subject.

"I'm afraid that's not possible."

"I am offended Dante."

"Don't be, it's not personal, now if that's all I have things to do."

"Very well, if you need to contact me you have my private number."

Dante shook his hand. "Nice doing business with you, it seems that it will be very profitable."

As Vasiliev watched him walk away he spat on the ground. Who the fuck did he think he was? He may have inherited Mancini's business but that was all, it wasn't as if he had built it from the ground upwards, unlike himself.

Yelena reappeared. "Has he gone?"

"What does it look like?" he snapped.

"You really need to unwind Pavel," she said as she rubbed his shoulders. "You are so tense these days, perhaps I could do something to help?"

"Are you fucking cock-teasing me?"

"I'm just trying to be nice to you." Yelena shrugged. "But if you'd rather I went then just say the word."

Vasiliev grabbed her by the hair and kissed her hard on the mouth. "Is that what you want, can Aleksei not get it up?"

Yelena pushed him away. "You know that I love him."

"It is a strange kind of love is it not?"

"He has a drink problem and yes, our sex life is virtually non-existent," she confessed.

"So, you are a woman with needs, I am a man of needs, it seems we could help each other out." He paused waiting for her reaction.

"Oh, you are so romantic!"

"I know nothing of romance, but I do know how to pleasure a woman, especially a woman as beautiful as you."

Yelena turned away. Despite his eye patch and raw scar there was something desirable about him, but she wasn't sure what it was. He was a brutal, unforgiving man, but deep inside she ached for him.

Vasiliev took her hand and pulled her close to him. "Feel my heart, it is racing, you excite me!" He placed her hand on his chest. "I want you."

"Oh, I don't know Pavel, if we do there is no going back, but you have to know that I will never leave Aleksei."

"I don't care about that."

Yelena wrestled with her conscience, she was seriously tempted, but somehow this was different. She had had flings in the past unaware to her oblivious husband, but they were always short-lived.

Vasiliev stroked her hair. "What do you say?"

Yelena ran her finger down his scar and nodded. "We must be careful; if Aleksei finds out he will kill me."

"Come." He took her hand and led her into the house. "I have been waiting a long time for this."

As they went upstairs they could hear Pavel Junior laughing and playing with the nanny, it seemed that he was finally settling in.

"I will look after you Yelena; you are very special to me."

The sex was wild and rough and Yelena enjoyed every moment. Vasiliev was an excellent lover, but it was only sex, she reminded herself.

Chapter Seventy-Five

London, England

Ella was missing her husband. He had only been away for a few days and she felt lonely without him. She was bored and decided to go into the office and see how Marcus was doing; she hadn't seen him since he was at her mother's house.

Marcus was surprised to see her. "You should have told me that you were coming."

"It was a spur of the moment thing, how are the new motors doing?"

"Fantastic, I have another consignment coming in three weeks. Please sit down."

Ella sat down opposite him and crossed her long legs. Marcus wished she hadn't done that, he had to stop himself from staring. "How is married life?"

"Wonderful, I've never been so happy."

"You look wonderful; he is obviously doing something right."

Ella blushed. "Is there anyone special in your life?" she asked.

"There was but now she is unattainable."

"Oh, that's a shame, I'm sure you will make a brilliant husband." She paused. "I have a few single friends, what about it?"

Marcus laughed. "I'm fine as I am but thank you for the kind offer." He tip-tapped on the desk. "And where is Mr Moretti?"

"He's away in Italy on business."

"That's a shame." He handed her the monthly returns. "You may as well have a look see how we are doing."

Ella cast her eyes over it. "Wow, are we really doing that well? I think I should give you a pay rise."

Money meant nothing to Marcus, all he truly wanted was her, but it would never happen, she had never seen him in that way and he was resigned to the fact that she never would.

Moretti had captivated her, wrapped her around his little finger and it seemed that she was totally reliant upon him. "You're the boss."

"I was going to see Carolyn in the new centre and wondered if you would like to come along, see what good our donations are doing."

"I would like that."

"Good, are you free now?"

"I can spare a couple of hours." Anything for you, he thought, any time spent with her was better than none at all.

Carolyn was delighted to see them both. "Ella, what a lovely surprise, and Mr Treymayne."

"Please call me Marcus, we're all friends here."

"I have to say that none of this would have been possible without your generous donations," Carolyn gushed. "My mother would have been very proud."

"How are you coping?" Ella asked her.

"Fine, fine, I have Valerie and Angela helping me. I have extra security, you know cameras, security guards, we are well sorted."

"Glad to hear it."

"So, how many girls do you have?" Marcus was interested in knowing exactly what Carolyn did to help them.

"We have nine at the moment, but the space we have will accommodate up to thirty. Come let me show you around the place." Carolyn was pleased with herself. She led them into the lounge and a couple of girls were watching TV. "Hi Natasha, Helena, I would like you to meet some friends of mine."

The girls were slightly nervous with a man being around.

"Don't worry he is one of the good guys," Carolyn reassured them. "It's perfectly safe."

Ella shook their hands. "I hope my friend is looking after you."

"She has been so good to us, I cannot tell you," Natasha told her.

"Natasha was smuggled into the country on a boat which unfortunately capsized and she was the sole survivor," Carolyn explained.

"Oh, my God, that's so awful," Ella gasped.

"And Helena was meeting her boyfriend here in London, but when she arrived he packed her off into a van full of other women and that was the last she saw of him."

"He did what?" Ella's voice was incredulous.

"He pretended to be in love with me, he paid for my ticket and when I got here I was taken to a house full of people like me and made to have sex with about fifty men a day."

Ella gasped at the girl's openness, she didn't know quite what to say. "I can't believe that there are such evil people in the world."

"You are very lucky to live in such a country and to have a man who loves you," Helena told her.

Ella stifled a giggle. "Oh, no, no this is my business partner, he's not my husband."

"Oh, I'm sorry you just looked like you fit, do you know what I mean?"

Marcus knew exactly what she meant; it was just a pity that Ella couldn't see it.

"It was nice to meet you and I hope that you can recover from your horrific ordeal."

"I am waiting for some test results, once I have them I will know if I can recover."

When they left the room Ella stopped Carolyn. "I can't get my head around this, it's just so awful."

"All I can do is organise medical checks for them to make sure that they are free from sexual diseases. I have several top psychologists who donate their time and hopefully, one day, some of these girls will be able to live normal lives." Her voice broke off. "Unlike poor Petra Yanovich."

"That was shocking news, what happened to that cold-hearted bitch?"

"Sandra Ennis seems to have disappeared and the police have apparently washed their hands of it, bad publicity or something."

"That woman will get her come-uppance one day, you'll see, what she did to that poor girl was unforgivable."

"I have to admire you Carolyn; you are doing a fantastic job in very difficult circumstances." Marcus was full of praise.

"It's heartbreaking at times, but I do what I can." Carolyn was determined to help these girls as much as possible, she owed it to the memory of her mother.

Chapter Seventy-Six

Vitelli had been following Ella Moretti since her husband had been away and he was intrigued when he saw her drive up to the centre. He had read about it in the paper and wondered exactly what her involvement was. It was strange, considering the business Dante was in, perhaps he would tell her everything, ruin the fucker's marriage. But he had second thoughts about that. If he spilled the beans then that would mean they would all have a massive financial setback and he didn't want that. The money he was getting was setting him up for life, it was far more than he had ever expected.

There was no point in disposing of Ella Moretti just yet, but he was desperate to take some kind of revenge for Esposito's murder. As Dante had no family as such there was no one he could get close to. But then he had a brainwave. Sitting opposite the Reynolds' residence he watched as Moretti's wife hugged her mother; it seemed she was quite close to her.

Determined to find out everything he could about her he searched the Internet and discovered that she was a struggling alcoholic since Mr Reynolds' death. Perhaps he could turn this to his advantage; if her death destroyed Ella then it would seriously get to Dante. He laughed, it would be fun coming up with something, but it would have to look like a suicide. Rubbing his hands at how clever he was, he drove off. He would have to stake out the house at a later date, somehow get in and tamper with her gin bottle. But one thing was for sure, he needed to do it quickly and most definitely before Moretti returned from his latest trip.

*****

Helen Reynolds was in one of her manic depressive moods again and she had sent the housekeeper home. She just wanted to be left alone with her gin, as she took the lid off the phone rang. Tutting to herself she went into the lounge, who the hell was it?

"Hi Mum, I was going to come over, if you're not doing anything?"

"Ella, I'm just about to have a long soak and an early night."

"Tomorrow then?"

"Of course dear, goodnight love."

"Goodnight Mum, love you."

"Love you too darling and give that gorgeous husband of yours a kiss from me when he returns from his business travels."

"Will do."

Helen replaced the receiver and returned to the kitchen, she opened the gin and poured herself a large one.

"Hello Mrs Reynolds," said a strange voice behind her, making her jump and drop her glass.

"Who are you, what do you want, how on earth did you get in here?"

"Just sit down," Vitelli ordered pointing a gun at her.

"Do you want money?" she asked noticing he was wearing gloves.

"Just shut that fucking hole in your face!" He picked up the gin bottle. "Here!"

Helen was shaking. "Go on, have one, it will steady your nerves." He thrust the bottle into her trembling hands.

"I... I don't understand, I don't want a drink!"

"Don't be fucking ridiculous, you're practically an alcoholic, it says so in the paper!"

Her hand was shaking so much she could barely pour it into a glass. "Please... what do you want?"

"Just fucking drink it!" he ordered.

Helen gulped it back, but no amount of alcohol was a comfort to her right now, she didn't know if this man intended to rob her, rape her, or both.

Vitelli picked up the bottles of medication. "Antidepressants, very interesting indeed, here!" He threw them at her. "Take them."

"But they are very dangerous."

"Take them or I'll fucking shove them right down your throat you fucking old witch!"

Helen starting taking the tablets one by one as she silently cried.

"Shut up fucking bleating or I'll put a bullet in you head!"

"Why? Why do you want me dead at least tell me that?" she said quietly, frightened that her voice would make him do something even worse.

"I'll tell you when I'm sure you ain't coming back!"

Helen's head throbbed. "I... I can't take any more it's making me ill."

He walked towards her making her shrink down into her chair.

"Ok." There was no point in resisting; he would only force her to take them.

Vitelli threw a notebook and pen onto the table.

"What's that for?" Helen's voice sounded slurry and her eyes were hazy.

"Your suicide note, you do want to leave a note for Ella don't you?"

"Ella...? Ella, you know my daughter? W – why are... you doing this?"

"Just say your fucking farewells lady before it's too late!"

Helen picked up the pen and then dropped it. "I... jush... can't... she... it."

Vitelli put the pen in her hand. "You must do this, it is the last thing you will ever do."

With every ounce of her energy Helen mustered up enough strength to scrawl the words, 'Ella, I love you, be happy, I am going to be with your father.'

Vitelli grabbed the notepad and read it. "Oh, how touching, how very touching."

Helen grabbed her chest, she had the most awful stabbing pain, she couldn't breathe and fell onto the floor convulsing.

Vitelli sat and watched, it was all over within seconds and he felt like justice had been served, at least for now, but there was plenty more hate inside him still to be released. That Dante prick should have disposed of him while he had the chance.

He found the security tapes and erased the CCTV footage. He had to be very careful indeed, the last thing he wanted was to leave any trace of his presence. He left the house in darkness as he sneaked out of the property, all in all a good night's work.

Chapter Seventy-Seven

Maria set off at seven thirty a.m. as usual, it was just another normal day and she loved working for Mrs Reynolds. The pay was good and she liked to keep a special eye on her ever since Mr Reynolds died, she felt she owed it to her. The job had never been a chore to her and she looked forward to going into work five times a week. Sometimes she would work extra hours if the Reynolds were holding a special party and she missed that. Seeing all the people dressed up and admiring each other always gave her a giggle, but one thing about the family was that they were always down to earth, they liked to have nice things but they were definitely not snobs. Some of her friends were housekeepers for rich families too but the difference was that Maria was treated with respect, and she appreciated that.

She pressed the intercom button. "Mrs Reynolds, it's me, Maria." That was unusual, she thought, she was always up bright and early, unless of course she had hit the bottle again. Sighing she punched in the security code and waited patiently for the gates to open.

Taking her keys out of her purse she opened the front door. "Yoo-hoo, Mrs Reynolds it's only me, where are you?" There was no response.

Maria hung her coat up in the hallway and got the hoover out of the cupboard, perhaps the noise would wake her up. As she busied herself she switched on her MP3 player and listened to Il Divo, it always made her smile and occupied her while she cleaned the house. She started off in the lounge, she hoovered every day and polished three times a week, Mrs Reynolds loved the house to be immaculate.

Humming away to herself and with the noise of the hoover she never heard the telephone ringing.

"Mum, if you're there pick up please, it's almost eight and as I've been awake for an hour I thought I would come on over, perhaps we could go shopping, I've seen some fabulous shoes and they are just you. Ok then, see you soon."

Maria had worked up a sweat and was in desperate need of an ice-cold drink of water, but what she was about to discover was going to scar her for life. As she swung open the door to the kitchen she was greeted by her boss lying on the floor, her face was blue and her lips black. Screaming she ran to her. "Oh, Mrs Reynolds, Mrs Reynolds, please wake up!"

As she touched her cold lifeless body she realised that the poor woman had obviously lain there all night. She jumped when she heard the intercom.

"Where is everyone?"

Oh my God, it was Ella, she couldn't let her see her poor mother like this, but she didn't know what else to do.

She ran into the hallway and picked up the phone. "I need an ambulance please."

"Is it for yourself?" the operator asked.

"No, it's for my boss, she's dead!" Maria exclaimed.

"Give me some more details and the address and I'll get someone to you as quickly as possible."

Maria had told her everything she could and had just finished relaying the address when the front door opened.

The look on Maria's face instantly told Ella that something was dreadfully wrong. "What is it, is it Mum?" Ella dropped her handbag on the floor. "Where is she?"

All Maria could do was point towards the kitchen. "But, I beg you please don't go in!"

Ella's instinct was to see if her mother was all right, but Maria barred her way.

"I'm sorry, Ella, but she is dead and I'm afraid it is not a pretty sight, please, please don't go in!"

But her words fell on deaf ears as Ella pushed past her. When she saw her mother lying still on the floor she took a step back and leaned against the door. She was totally horrified and felt sick to the pit of her stomach. As she looked at her mother's face she couldn't hold back any longer and ran to the sink.

"I've phoned an ambulance and they are sending the police, just as a precaution," Maria told her.

"Ambulance? Police, I don't understand." Ella's head was spinning.

"Apparently it is normal in these circumstances."

"I think we should cover her up," Ella told her as she picked up a towel from the laundry basket.

"Ella, there is something I must tell you about Mrs Reynolds."

"What?"

"I think she may have done this to herself." There, the words had come tumbling out; somebody had to tell her, somebody should have told her a long time ago.

"How dare you! My mother was fully recovered, she was starting to enjoy life again!" Ella could hardly believe what their long-established housekeeper was saying.

"Talk to your aunt, she knows the truth, this isn't the first time she's tried to take her own life."

"No, no, it can't be true, she was so happy for me, she wanted to be a grandparent, she would never do this!" Ella protested, but really what did she know about her mother's mental state? She had barely seen her over the past few months.

Maria pointed to the table. "Look, the pills are almost gone." And the bottle of gin was almost empty, too.

Ella picked up the pills, it was true, the bottle was virtually empty, then she spotted the note: *Ella, I love you, be happy, I am going to be with your father.* She handed it to Maria. "It looks like you were right."

The last thing Ella remembered were the sirens before she fainted.

When she came to she was just in time to see the paramedics carrying her dead mother away on a stretcher. "I just can't believe she would do this to me, not now, I thought that she was fine, how could I have been so wrong?" Ella gasped as she fell into Maria's arms.

"Don't blame yourself child, it's hardly your fault, if anyone is to blame it is me, I should have done something more."

"What could you have done?"

"I really don't know but I will never forgive myself," Maria told her. "She was a good friend to me and I'll never forget that."

"What happens now?" Ella asked the policeman.

"We'll take the bottle and the pills for examination and the Coroner will do an autopsy. When we are satisfied that there was no foul play we'll release her body." He paused. "I'm sorry Mrs Moretti, but it's standard procedure."

"Ok."

"In the meantime please provide your home address and we will contact you as soon as possible. Do you have someone we can call, your husband perhaps?"

"I'm afraid he's out of the country," Maria informed him.

"I told you I'll be all right," Ella insisted as she blew her nose.

"Would you prefer us to contact someone else in the family?" the officer enquired, feeling that they ought to do something to help.

"No, no, it will be better coming from me."

Chapter Seventy-Eight

Moscow, Russia

Sandra Ennis and her ex-husband were shacked up in a shabby, backstreet hotel wondering what their next move should be.

"So, do you have any contacts?" Ray asked her.

"While you were having a shower I made contact with a Russian detective, he's meeting us in a small bar, here I've written down the directions." She passed him a piece of paper.

"Are you fucking serious? You may as well have announced our arrival to the criminal element, we better get the fuck out of here."

"Don't be stupid, he knows fuck all, just that I am trying to trace someone and I'm willing to pay him well for doing that."

"Did you tell him that you were staying here?" he demanded.

"Did anyone ever tell you that you are paranoid?" Sandra laughed.

"What is this really about?" Ray asked as he passed her the illegal firearm he'd managed to acquire, courtesy of the hotel manager who told him he could get them whatever they wanted, for a small price of course.

"I've been thinking, perhaps we can make ourselves some money out of all this." She loaded the gun and put it in the holster.

"I don't know where you are coming from and I don't like it, not one fucking little bit!"

"I meant that since I never had a chance to mention Garshin's name to the police –"

"You fucking what? You mean to tell me that no fucker else knows that we are here or that this guy even exists?" She was a fucking idiot after all, Ray thought, how could he have trusted her in the first place?

"You know what Ray, you worry too much, no wonder we separated!" she snapped. "Are you coming with me or not?"

"Of course." It didn't look like he had much choice in the matter; he was in it for the long haul, whatever that was.

Detective Ivanov was intrigued by the mystery phone call but was very interested in the amount of money that was mentioned. He waited patiently for twenty minutes before a tall, gangly woman entered the café and nodded at him. He clocked the big gorilla she had close behind her, which was obviously her protection. Pity she didn't know that he owned the café and they were being watched from all angles in case this was some sort of set up.

"Hello, Ivanov?" Sandra shook his hand.

"Please sit." He glanced over to the bar and saw the bulky man order a coffee. "How can I help you?"

"I'm looking for someone and I am prepared to offer the amount we discussed."

"I'm listening."

She leaned across the table. "A man named Garshin, Yakov Garshin."

Ivanov didn't flinch. This woman couldn't be serious, he thought, she must be off her fucking head to think that he would offer him up just like that. "The price has just tripled," he said matter-of-factly.

"What, but we agreed!" she protested, trying to keep her voice as low as possible.

"That is up to you." Ivanov stood up and scraped his chair back.

Ray jumped out of his seat and went to reach for his gun, before he had time to do anything two men grabbed him from behind and quickly had him on the floor with a gun to his temple. "Don't fucking move," one of the Russians ordered.

"Who the fuck is this performing monkey?" Ivanov spat.

"He... he is my husband." Sandra was scared. She felt seriously out of her depth.

Ivanov signalled to his men who hauled Ray to his feet and shoved him towards their table. "Sit!"

Ray looked like he was ready to explode at any moment and Sandra had to try to diffuse the situation before one or both of them ended up dead. She nodded at him. "Just do as he says."

Despite his better judgement Ray sat down. All he really wanted to do was grab the gun out of the fuckers' hands and shoot them all down, but thinking better about it he did as he was told.

"Look, can you help us or not?" Sandra asked calmly.

"Triple your offer and anything is possible."

"Very well."

"Let's say half now and half when I locate him."

"How do I know that I can trust you?"

"You don't," Ivanov said simply. "So, what is your decision?"

Sandra reached into her inside pocket. All of a sudden all guns were aimed in her direction. "It's the money that's all," she told him.

Ivanov reached over the table and pulled her by the jacket; it was all Ray could do to keep calm. If they hurt her in any way they would all be fucking dead, he visualised it in his head. All he needed to do was stay focused and when the opportunity arose launch himself at this so-called detective pull out his hidden knife and press it to the fucker's jugular. Sandra would instinctively elbow one of the fuckers in the balls, grab the gun and kill them. A few years ago he wouldn't have hesitated but now he didn't know if he could react that quickly, so reluctantly he let the insane moment pass.

When the money was safely in Ivanov's hands he smiled. "Nice doing business with you, I'll be in touch." And he made to leave.

"Wait, how do you know how to contact us?"

Ivanov laughed hard. "Did you hear that?" He turned to his men. "I fucking knew you were here before you did." He threw some change onto the table. "Get him a stiff drink; it looks like he's pissed his pants!" All of his associates laughed.

Sandra watched Ray's neck, the veins looked like they were going to pop out and his hands were clenched in tight fists, ready to attack at any moment. "Fine, I said that's fine isn't it?" She touched Ray's hand.

"Fine," Ray said through clenched teeth, barely able to get the word out.

Ivanov and his two hard men left the café.

"Well fucking done, that's the last we'll fucking see of that, what a wasted trip."

The waitress came over with a bottle of vodka and put two shot glasses on the table. "Sir?"

"You got any money left?"

"This is on the house sir, compliments of Mr Ivanov." She filled both glasses and left the bottle on the table.

"Join me?" Ray asked as he looked at the glass in front of him.

"Just like the old days," Sandra said as she picked it up and knocked it straight back. "That's good shit!"

Ray agreed as he went to pour another. Sandra put her hand over his glass. "Not in here, let's go back to the hotel."

Putting the lid back on the bottle he stood up. "Ok."

Once they were outside Sandra laughed hysterically.

"What the fuck are you laughing at?" Ray asked. "Are you fucking insane? We have no fucking money left and we still don't know where this Garshin bloke is."

"Ah, but I do," a voice in the shadows spoke out.

"Who's there?" Ray demanded reaching for his knife.

"I wouldn't do that if I was you!" The man behind them boomed. "Drop it!"

"Fuck me; we've been set up, Sandra." It was the first time that Ray had felt so scared in all his life and he hated not being in control, he had definitely lost his edge. There had been times when he would have expected something like this and would have been totally prepared. They were on a wild goose chase and it looked like they were finally going to meet their maker.

They were gagged and blindfolded. "It is better that you do not know where we are taking you, it's for your own good."

It seemed like hours before they arrived at their destination. The road they travelled was rough and uneven as they were physically jolted around the van.

They were dragged from the van and taken into a building where they were forced into chairs.

"Remove their blindfolds and untie them," Vasiliev ordered.

Both of them blinked as a spotlight was shone right into their eyes.

"So, Mr and Mrs Ennis, what can I do for you?"

"You are Garshin?" Sandra gasped as she focused on the man's eye patch and red scar.

"No!"

"Then what the fuck are we doing here?" Ray demanded.

One of Vasiliev's men slammed the butt of his gun into his shoulder sending him flying across the floor. As he lay there gasping Vasiliev lit a cigarette. "So, I repeat, what the fuck do you want?"

"We are looking for a man that's all, we don't want any trouble!" Sandra exclaimed.

"I'm afraid it's too late for that!" His voice was dark and menacing.

"Please, just let us go!"

"You really don't fucking know what you are getting into, do you?"

One of Vasiliev's men grabbed Ray by the hair and dragged him by it as he kicked and writhed trying to get out of his vice-like grip.

"Please, stop, stop!" Sandra pleaded. "Yakov Garshin," she yelled.

Vasiliev put his hand up. "Now we are fucking getting somewhere." He sat down and put his legs up on the table crossing them in front of him. "Please continue," he said as he blew smoke rings into the air and waited, when there was no response he nodded.

A glinting blade flashed before Sandra's eyes and, before she knew it, her face had been slashed open, slicing her right down to the bone. The blade was razor sharp and her flesh was hanging down her cheek. Moaning in agony she tried to feel the damage but couldn't bear to touch it.

"You're just some fucking jumped-up disgraced ex-copper, who nobody gives a fuck about!"

"You're wrong!" Ray yelled his voice full of bravado.

Vasiliev walked over to him and as his men held him down he put his cigarette out on his face. As he screamed in pain, Vasiliev kicked him in the head, rendering him unconscious. "What the fuck do you know, a loner, a discharged soldier, a fucking disgrace to the army!" he spat on him. "Clean up this fucking mess!" He barked at his men as he stepped over Ray's body.

"Our things... in the hotel," Sandra gasped, trying one last-ditch attempt to save their lives, but it was all in vain.

"Disposed of already!" Vasiliev flicked back his long leather jacket and looked straight into her eyes.

The scar on his face was long and deep and it was the last thing she saw before she felt the knife going into her chest.

Before Ray could react one of Vasiliev's henchmen got his neck in a vice-like grip and in a split second snapped it.

Ivanov appeared from the shadows.

"Pay him!" Vasiliev ordered as he left the warehouse.

Chapter Seventy-Nine

Twelve months later
London, England

Ella could hardly believe that it was coming up to a year since her mother's death; she still couldn't get over her aunt and Dr Shaw hiding the truth from her and had been unable to speak to either of them since. As she laid flowers and wiped the headstone, she looked at the inscription. *Beloved mother and doting wife of the late Philip Reynolds, resting together, forever in eternal peace.*

Dante put his arm around his wife's waist. "Ready to go?" he asked gently.

Ella nodded her head. "Yes."

"What time are you meeting Carolyn?"

"Around one."

"I'll give you a lift and meet you back at the apartment, say at five?"

"How long do you think we will need to catch up?" Ella managed a small laugh.

"I know how you girls like to gossip," he teased. "Besides I have to talk through a business plan with a potential client." He yawned.

"Fine."

He hated seeing her like this and had always regretted the day he wasn't there for her. While she was beside herself with grief and being comforted by Marcus Treymayne, he'd been arranging a few large handouts as pay-offs for the demise of the scum who had destroyed Nico's family. Ever since that day he had treated her like a princess and swore that he always would She was his world and he wanted to protect her from anything life threw at them.

He pulled up to the restaurant. "Are you sure you will be all right, I can cancel if you want?"

"No, honestly it's fine; just make sure you get the deal."

"I will, *ciao Bella*." He leaned over and opened the car door.

As she walked away she could feel his eyes on her, so she turned and blew him a kiss, he pretended to catch it. It always made her smile when he did that, it was a little thing that they had to show how much they missed each other when they were apart, whether it be hours or days.

Carolyn was sitting in the window and grinned to herself when she saw the exchange, she was happy that they were obviously still so much in love.

"Hi." Ella hugged her friend. "It's so good to see you."

"And you, my God you look absolutely fabulous darling."

"You don't look too bad yourself and is that an engagement ring, let me see!" Ella exclaimed.

Carolyn extended her hand. "Do you like it?" She beamed with happiness.

"Like it? I love it!"

"Andrew wants us to get married straight away."

"So, why not?"

"We've only been dating seven months!"

"Are you in love?"

"Of course."

"So, what's the problem?"

"I keep thinking about my mum not being here for the wedding." She stopped in mid-sentence. "Damn it, I could eat my words sometimes!"

"It's no big deal, I chose not to invite anyone to my wedding remember?"

Carolyn felt bad. "I still shouldn't have said that."

"Seriously, it doesn't matter; now tell me how he proposed!" Ella had never met Andrew Falconer in person, but she had heard from Carolyn about the great things he had done for the girls in her care and the day-to-day running of the centre. He was a solicitor and was responsible for presenting cases before the courts and obtaining special permits and visas to allow the girls to stay in the country.

"Oh, he took me for a meal and beckoned a lone violinist over to serenade us and when he was finished I was presented with a little black velvet box…"

"And?" Ella interrupted.

"Well, if you give me a chance woman, I'll tell you!"

"Hurry up then!" Ella laughed loudly, which made the other customers look in their direction.

"Shh, you'll get us thrown out for causing a scene."

"Carolyn!"

"Ok, then he very romantically got down on one knee and well, as they say the rest is history."

"Yuck." Ella stuck her finger down her throat pretending to be sick. "Just kidding."

"You idiot!"

"What other news?"

"Valerie is my right hand and I am so thankful to have her, she has been a rock to say the least, I don't think that I could have managed without her."

Ella felt a little pang of jealousy, once the two of them used to be so close and now it was Valerie this, Valerie that. "I'm glad that you have such a good friend."

"Thanks, but she's not you Ella." Carolyn touched her hand as if trying to comfort her. "I would have loved for you to help me but our lives have taken very different paths."

"True." Ella's mind turned to Grazia de Luca. She had spent a lot of time with her since the death of her baby and it had taken its toll on Grazia's tiny frame.

"You look deep in thought," Carolyn commented.

"Just thinking about poor Grazia."

"How is she coping now?"

"She has an eating disorder and the doctors reckon that she always will, it's very sad. Her husband Nico wanted them to either find a suitable surrogate or go for adoption, but Grazia was having none of it."

"Jesus that's terrible, it's a wonder they are still together."

Ella nodded. "Thankfully Nico adores her, but God knows he has had a lot to endure, everyone seems to have forgotten the effect it must have had on him too."

"Unfortunately it's not unusual for the father to be forgotten in these sorts of circumstances."

Ella half laughed. "How did we get to be so goddamn sensible?"

"God knows, it beats me!" Carolyn laughed. "Now enough sad talk, let's talk about my wedding."

"I thought it was all too quick for you!" Ella teased.

"Well, it seems to have worked out for you, so why not for me?"

"I'll drink to that." Ella sipped happily on the chilled house wine, completely ignorant of her husband's secret life and the impending consequences of his forthcoming actions, which were about to rip through her whole life.

Chapter Eighty

Dante had been hearing a few rumours about someone on the take and he was not having anyone taking the piss out of him. Now he was married, it was as if he were an easy target and he wanted to nip it in the bud and fast, before he looked weak and vulnerable to attack. Flavio and Carmine had gone on ahead to make sure they were completely alone and that the place wasn't bugged. Dante had chosen the venue; he had booked the conference room under a false name and was ready for the meet.

He was slightly surprised to see Vitelli sitting with Vincenzo, pretending to be his right-hand man. He was dressed up like a fucking Christmas turkey, no dress sense at all, the suit was a cheaper version of the one he was wearing.

"Signor Moretti, it isn't often we are graced with your presence these days." Vincenzo stood up to greet him.

After they embraced Dante sat opposite him. "What the fuck is he doing here?"

"Vitelli, you mean? He plays a major part in the business and I couldn't do it without him."

"Whatever, now I'll get straight to the point shall I?" Nobody spoke. "The takings have dropped and I want to know why, are we not paying you enough?"

"It's not as simple as that," Vincenzo protested, shooting a dark look at Vitelli, who had promised him nothing would go wrong as long as he was in charge. "The fact of the matter is that it's becoming more and more difficult to move these girls, we are having to pay much more than we ever have. You see, people aren't prepared to take the risk unless we give them something more substantial."

"I want fucking names and I want them now!"

"You know who we deal with Moretti!" This came from Vitelli's mouth before he could stop himself, immediately regretting it.

"Are you going to allow this disrespect?" Dante spoke to Vincenzo.

"I do apologise, sometimes he lets his tongue run away with him."

"Then perhaps you should shut him up." He paused for effect. "Permanently."

"Are you fucking threatening me? Me, who has been keeping this business afloat for a jumped-up fucking tosser who doesn't give a fuck about the major risks our families are taking!"

Flavio shoved him back down into his chair.

"I want the list of names now you fuck, anyone that wants to negotiate a pay increase must come through me, I am the fucking boss, not you!" Dante was livid.

"Boss," Carmine whispered in his ear. "We don't want to draw attention to this room." Pointing to the case he added, "It's supposed to be a wine conference, remember."

Dante composed himself. "Never, ever do you agree to anything without my say so, or I will cut you out of the business, just like that!" He clicked his fingers.

"So, what do you want us to do?"

"I want you to be fucking professional, if we get rumbled because these fuckers are getting too greedy then we all go down."

Vitelli curled his lip in disgust. "We are professionals," he insisted.

"Obviously not professional enough."

"What are you going to do?" Vincenzo asked worriedly. He was onto a good earner and prayed that it wasn't all about to go down the pan because of the dumb fuck next to him creaming off more than he should.

"I'm bringing some of my men in."

"There is no need for that, give me another chance to sort this mess." Vincenzo tried his best to convince him.

"Give me one good reason why I should?"

"It's one of the Russians he's got some of his men putting the thumbscrews on us." Vitelli offered him the information, trying to throw him off the trail. It was true that they had muscled in and taken more and that's why Dante had noticed the amounts increasing.

"If this is true, then I need a name."

"Will it get us off the hook?" Vincenzo asked.

"Yes!" Dante slammed his fists onto the table.

"It's someone called Garshin," Vitelli told him.

"What did you say?" Dante's hands went white as he gripped the table.

"Yakov Garshin."

So, Garshin was still alive and well it seemed, he could scarcely believe it. "This meeting is over, give the details to Carmine." And with that he made a quick exit. Once he was outside the door he leaned onto it, trying to steady his nerves. His heart was beating so fast he thought it was going to explode. Now, after all these years, he was finally going to meet the scum who took his sister.

He had planned what he was going to do to him, imagined slicing the fucker into small pieces and feeding him to the fish, but that was too good for the sick fuck. Whatever he did was never going to bring Rosa back, she was gone for good.

For years he had desperately tried to find him, but it was like he had fallen off the face of the planet, nobody seemed to know the name. He immediately thought of Vasiliev, he must have known all along, there was nothing that man didn't know especially about a fellow countryman, one that was in the same line of business as himself. Dante cursed, he had found Pavel Junior, killed for him and this is the respect he had shown him.

Consumed with rage he sat in his car, contemplating his next move. Just then his mobile began to ring, looking at it he saw Ella's name flash up. Taking a deep breath he answered. "I am missing you already, darling." His voice was full of warmth and love but, deep down inside, he wanted to scream at the top of his lungs.

Chapter Eighty-One

Moretti Residence, Menaggio, Italy

"It seems that we have visitors," Ella remarked, noticing a car in the driveway.

"Are we expecting anyone?" Dante asked, wondering who it was.

Ella shrugged. "I don't think so, I mean we don't usually get visitors out here, I guess it must be important."

When they entered the house they were greeted by the Petrovs. "Dante, good to see you."

There was an awkward silence. "Well, aren't you going to introduce us?" Ella asked.

"Sorry, darling, this is Aleksei and Yelena Petrov, old friends of mine."

"I've heard so much about you and now finally we get to meet," Yelena drawled. "You are much more beautiful than I expected."

Dante was livid. He didn't like this not one little bit, there was something not quite right about the Petrovs turning up just like that, totally out of the blue.

"My, dear, you must be exhausted," Yelena continued.

"Not really, it's only a short flight."

"Anyway, I took the liberty of asking the chef to prepare us all a nice meal. You know, so that we can get to know each other, especially now that you are coming to Moscow." She glanced at Dante, waiting for his reaction.

Dante bit his lip. "Err... I don't think we can make it, you know how business is."

"I'm sure Ella wouldn't mind, would you?" Yelena was very persuasive. "You will adore my country, it is so full of character, don't you think Dante?"

"I have some meetings that I just couldn't possibly cancel."

"All taken care of," Aleksei told him as he handed him a glass of wine. "Now why don't you two ladies get acquainted, while Dante and I catch up?"

"Oh, yes, I would so love to see your wedding pictures."

"Well, I must warn you that there aren't many."

"That's right, you crazy kids got married on the spur of the moment, how very, very romantic, I suppose that is Italian men for you," she purred.

"True, he swept me off my feet all right."

Yelena took her arm. "Come, show me." As they walked away Yelena looked over her shoulder and winked at Dante.

As soon as they were out of sight Dante grabbed Aleksei by the throat and shoved him out into the garden. "What the fuck are you doing here, are you out of your mind?"

"Orders from above man, that's all." Aleksei tried to wriggle out of his grip.

Slowly letting go Dante glared at him. "Whose fucking orders?"

"Vasiliev of course, who else!"

"What has Ella got to do with this?"

"Just a little insurance in case!"

"In case of what?" Dante didn't like to be threatened and especially not by Petrov, he thought he was a better man than that. "Sit!" he barked as went back into the kitchen and reappeared with two glasses of wine. "Here."

"I'd rather have a vodka," Aleksei smiled.

"What the fuck are you smiling at? This is no fucking joke!"

"Calm down, Dante, everything is going to be all right."

"I'm not bringing Ella and that's final!"

"Then you will not have your revenge on Yakov Garshin," Aleksei said simply.

"So, you are blackmailing me into bringing my wife along." Dante knocked his drink back. "You're right, I need a vodka."

After he had placed the bottle on the table he tried to understand what was going down, it all seemed a bit of an odd way to do things. "Explain exactly what is going to happen if I bring Ella."

"Yelena will entertain her, while we go and attend to some overdue business, it's all set."

"And Vasiliev, he knew about Garshin all this time?"

"Yes, he has been working for him for many years, quite an expert in the field, one that is very valuable to him." He paused to gulp down his vodka. "But you are far more important to him."

"But why, why now?"

"He knew that you had found out about him, so he took matters into his own hands. You see, he respects what you did when you found Pavel Junior."

"What a fucking joke, he stood in front of me thanking me for what I had done and not once did he mention Yakov fucking Garshin." His voice was dangerously loud.

"Quiet, do you want the lovely Ella to hear?" Aleksei reminded him.

"So, how is this going to work?"

"I'm sorry, not even I know the details."

Dante studied his face and knew that he was telling the truth. "Should I be worried for my life?"

"No, Vasiliev has made it clear that he has chosen you over Garshin. He was becoming too much of a liability and this is his way of cleaning up his mess without getting involved himself. So, are you in?"

"It doesn't look like I have much choice in the matter does it? But I warn you right here and now if so much of a hair on my wife's head is harmed there will be a fucking war like you've never seen before."

Aleksei laughed. "I wouldn't expect any thing less from you Signor Moretti."

"Are you boys having fun?" Yelena asked as she walked over to Aleksei and sat on his knee. "Look what I have, their wedding album, how long has it been now?"

"Almost fourteen months." Ella smiled.

"Early days then. Remember when we were first married, darling?"

"How could I forget?" Aleksei stroked her cheek. "Nearly seven years for us."

"Yes, we were childhood sweethearts." Yelena looked into her husband's eyes. "Together forever."

"I'll drink to that." Aleksei topped up his glass and swallowed the liquid in one go.

"Hey, slow down I don't want you getting drunk tonight!"

"I can hold my alcohol Yelena; it is you who can't, remember!" he teased her.

"So, getting back to Moscow, I have spoken to Ella and she is so excited and you wouldn't want to let your wife down, now would you Dante?"

He could feel her outstretched leg digging into his knee. "If that's what Ella wants, then that's fine by me." That fucking evil bitch, she was up to her neck in it with Vasiliev and after the Babichenko murders she was capable of just about anything. He looked at Aleksei. If only he knew about their little set up, he perhaps would be killing her right now. She was trouble with a big capital T and he, for one, wanted nothing to do with her.

"To Moscow then!"

Chapter Eighty-Two

Moscow, Russia

As soon as the two couples were outside the airport they were greeted by a chauffeur driving a white stretch limousine.

"Ooh, you must be very important," Ella giggled.

"No, not important darling, just very, very rich." Yelena opened the fridge. "I think we should perhaps open the champagne, it is nicely chilled, what do you say?"

"What are we celebrating?" Dante glared at her.

"Let's say a belated wedding anniversary?"

"You are almost two months late." Dante sighed, sick of the sound of her voice.

"No, matter, what did he get you Ella?"

She showed her the eternity ring, Dante had matching ones especially made for them.

Yelena held her hand as she looked at it. "It is truly magnificent." She whistled. "Oh, and I see your darling husband has an identical one, how very sweet."

"Yes, I am a very lucky woman."

"Very." Yelena smiled as she popped the cork on the champagne bottle, spilling the liquid everywhere, but mainly over Ella. "Oh, darling, I am so sorry, here let me try and wipe it for you."

"No, no!" Ella protested.

"That dress is unique and was handmade especially for my wife, there is no other like it in Europe."

"Oh, my God, the first thing we should do is have my designer come to the house; we could have a private fashion show," she said excitedly. "Choose whatever you want and of course I will foot the bill, it will be my pleasure."

"Oh, don't be silly!" Ella exclaimed. "I couldn't possibly accept."

"No, I insist, call it a belated wedding present and anyway the men will be talking business all night and I for one find it all very tiresome." She put her hand over her mouth and feigned a yawn.

At this point Dante didn't know if he was about to have Garshin handed to him on a plate or if he was about to be taken out himself. At least if it was the latter, Ella wouldn't be far behind him and that gave him a little comfort. He looked at her, she was so happy it was written all over her flawless face.

Yelena noticed the way he looked at her, he absolutely adored her. She used to think that he was incapable of loving anyone and it amused her that he had proved her wrong. But this woman was going to be his downfall, once she found out what he was all about it would be over in a flash and she hoped to be there when it happened.

*****

Once they had eaten Dante and Aleksei excused themselves. "Just going to catch up with some old pals," Dante told his wife. "Take good care of her."

"Of course I will, darling," Yelena laughed. "What else would I do?"

The underlying tones in her voice was getting under Dante's skin. All he wanted to do was get this fucker Garshin out of the way and get back to Italy and the sooner the better, he still had serious reservations about the Petrovs' real motives.

"You coming?" Aleksei patted his arm. "Or can you not bear to be parted from your beautiful wife?"

Dante took Ella in his arms and kissed her passionately not caring what the Petrovs were thinking. If he was going to die on this night he wanted to remember the warmth of his wife's body next to his and the sweet taste of her lips.

"Anybody would think that he wasn't coming back!" Yelena laughed loudly.

"Don't wait up; it could be a long one!" Aleksei told the women.

When the two men finally left Yelena telephoned her designer friend. "Just throw in whatever you have available, darling, it's a private showing with a dear friend of mine so nothing outrageous!"

"You needn't go to all this trouble for me," Ella told her.

"It's no trouble, darling, now tell me how have you been managing in Menaggio, is it all you thought it would be?"

"I don't know, sometimes I miss home very much."

"But you travel back and forth, yes?"

"Not so much now, we spend most of our time between Menaggio and Milan."

"Oh, yes you are friends with Grazia and Nico de Luca, it's such a shame what happened to them." She paused. "That was the evening of the day you married Dante, yes?"

"Yes, yes it was, the poor things."

Yelena was taking in all the information; it seemed that Mancini's sudden death perhaps played a part in what happened to the de Lucas'. "So, you and Dante were on the boat, weren't Grazia and Nico supposed to be on it? I mean, they were on it most weekends."

"What do you mean?" Ella was trying hard to understand what she was getting at.

"Nothing, darling, just me being silly."

Just then the maid appeared. "Vadim Rachek has arrived."

"Oh, wonderful, tell him to set up in the dining room, have the staff remove the table, give the girls room to model the clothes," Yelena ordered.

Ella smiled to herself, she was so glad not to be like Yelena Petrov bossing everyone around and shouting in Russian. She could tell that she was annoyed by her high-pitched voice. She had never met anyone quite like her and had a feeling it was going to be quite an entertaining evening.

*****

The rendezvous with Vasiliev was at the warehouse and Dante was feeling a little edgy.

"You, ok?" Aleksei cast him a sideways glance.

"Never felt better," Dante lied. He felt sick with anticipation, he had waited a long time for this and now that it was here he wasn't sure how to feel about it.

As they got out of the car Vasiliev's men greeted them. "He's inside."

With trepidation Dante walked steadily into the warehouse, it was cold and dark and he wasn't sure what to expect. Putting his hand on his gun he checked out the room. There was no escape exit, if he was going to die then so be it, but he would take Vasiliev with him. Just then the spotlight came on blinding him.

"What the fuck!"

He was grabbed from behind and dragged to the waiting chair and forcibly shoved into it. So they were going to kill him after all, he couldn't quite believe it. One day he knew that his lifestyle would catch up with him, but never like this.

"Dante." Vasiliev appeared. "How are you?"

"What the fuck is all this about?"

"You wanted to find Yakov, didn't you?"

"Yes!" He was raging inside and just wanted to tear the fuckers head off.

"Good, I'm glad that I have your attention." He pulled a chair up and sat opposite him. "What is Yakov worth to you?"

"How do you mean?"

"What would you do to repay me if I handed him to you on a plate?"

"Whatever you wanted," Dante told him, not knowing where the conversation was going.

"I am disappointed in you, it is a sign of weakness dropping everything and coming here like this!"

"I didn't have much of a choice," Dante reminded him.

"There's always a choice Dante, you would do well to remember that."

"I'm not one of your fucking employees Vasiliev and you do well to remember that!" His voice was full of bravado.

"Yes, that may be true but I am not the one sitting in the fucking chair with a gun pointed at my head."

"And the point is?"

"This is a lesson and I hope that you will never be this stupid again!"

"I've came all this way for nothing!" Dante spat the words out. "Are you fucking serious?"

"Deadly."

"You forget one thing."

"What is that?"

"If anything happens to me, my men have instructions to bring you all down!" Dante was thinking of the disk that was steadily increasing with names, dates and times of Vasiliev and his business associates.

"Is that some kind of threat?" Vasiliev laughed in his face.

Without warning Dante punched the man next to him in the crotch, totally taking him by surprise, making him drop his weapon. A split second later he was pointing the gun at Vasiliev's head. "Now call your fucking monkeys off!" His voice was dangerously quiet.

Vasiliev signalled to his men to lower their weapons and then he calmly took a slow puff on his cigarette as he waited for Dante's next move. "So, now you have my attention, what do you intend to do with it?"

Dante laughed. "You fucking idiot, why all of this?" He put the gun down on the chair.

"So, you would have taken me out?"

"I would have taken most of you in this room out before you killed me."

"Bravo." Vasiliev clapped his hands. "Now, I have a present for you."

Dante turned when he heard footsteps behind him. Yakov Garshin was smiling one minute and the next his face dropped.

"What the fuck is he doing here?" he demanded.

"So, we finally meet." Dante's voice was surprisingly calm.

"I spit on you and your fucking whore sister!"

Dante looked at Vasiliev and waited for the go-ahead.

"I believe Dante has a score to settle with you."

"What?" Yakov was trembling now; he was used to bullying and preying on the weak and vulnerable and always had protection around him. But this was a different ball game now and he was no fighter, that was for sure.

Vasiliev stood up and brushed down his leather jacket. "I do not get involved in these personal issues, so may the best man win." He shook both men's hands. "My men will lock the door from the outside, when it is over bang on the door." He pointed to a wooden crate on the table. "You will find some items to help you in there, but there are no guns, I don't want this to be easy for you." But he was no fool either. He had a camcorder secretly planted in the room, he didn't want to miss a second of this.

Once they were alone both men looked at each other and then at the box, wondering who was going to make it first. As they raced towards the table Dante launched himself at him and they both fell heavily onto the concrete floor.

Yakov head butted Dante as he tried to free himself from his grip. This only enraged Dante and he grabbed his legs as he tried to reach for the table. "Not so fast you little fucker!"

As Yakov fell backwards he cursed. "Get your fucking... hands off me!" he panted.

Dante was like a madman as he wrestled him to the ground with ease.

Yakov put his hand inside his boot and pulled out a flick knife which he desperately tried to use on the mad bastard.

The blade flashed past Dante's eye. Frantically he gripped Yakov's hand by the wrist, trying to stop him from shoving it into his neck.

"Now, who is in control?" Yakov smiled. "Pathetic, just like your big sister!"

His words only hastened Dante's anger and suddenly with all his might he snapped his wrist. As Yakov dropped the knife and yelped in pain Dante made a dash for the crate.

Looking inside he found two items, a metal chain and a machete. Yanking the chain from the box he wrapped it around his hands and went to finish it. Yakov was on his stomach, crawling in the opposite direction. Before he knew it the chain was around his neck and Dante tightened it, dragging his victim back towards him.

"Not so fucking cocky now, eh, Garshin?" Dante spat. His eyes were wild and his face contorted in sheer anger.

Yakov was desperately trying to loosen the chain but to no avail, he was slowly choking. *But she is still alive*! he wanted to scream it at him in the hope that he would let him live, but no words came out.

Dante released the chain and kicked him full in the guts. He stood and watched as Yakov's eyes rolled back into his head and then, suddenly, he coughed up blood.

Putting his hand to his mouth he looked at it, he'd never seen his own blood before and it scared the hell out of him.

Dante went back to the table and opened the bottle of vodka which Vasiliev had left for the victor. He wanted to take the edge of what he was about to do.

Yakov made a last-ditch attempt to retrieve the knife as Dante listened to his movements, still with his back to him. He would give him another couple of seconds just for the fun of it. Calmly picking up the machete he somehow became detached from his normal brain function. Turning, he walked slowly towards him.

"Dip, dip, which one will it be?" Raising the machete he hacked off Garshin's left leg just below the knee. As he screamed in agony he continued to try and get to the knife. The blood was like a fountain and spurted up into Dante's face. As he wiped it from his eyes he raised the machete again, this time concentrating on his right leg.

Suddenly the warehouse doors were opened and Vasiliev stood in the doorway. "Well, what are you waiting for, finish it!"

Without hesitation Dante raised the machete one last time and made several attempts to sever Garshin's head from his body. Dropping the axe he spat on the twitching corpse in front of him.

Vasiliev ordered his men in to remove the body. Dante watched in silence as they wrapped his remains up in plastic sheets and taped it up.

"We had better get you cleaned up, go with Aleksei," he ordered.

Aleksei had been watching on a laptop outside and would never have believed that Dante could be capable of what he had just witnessed. Taking his arm he led him out into the yard. "Strip."

Dante did as he was told. Once the ice-cold water hit him he came to his senses. "I hope you've brought me some clean clothes, Aleksei," he laughed. "I'm fucking freezing my bollocks off here!"

Vasiliev threw him a towel. "Enjoy the rest of your stay, Dante." He grinned at him; if anyone crossed him in any way then he had no doubt that there would be serious consequences, not unlike the events of that very night.

Aleksei unwrapped the suit from its packaging. "Here, this should fit you!" He noticed the bruising on his body slowly coming out, he would be almost certainly black and blue in the morning and he wondered how he was going to explain it to Ella.

As Vasiliev drove away he patted the camcorder on the seat next to him, it was his insurance. If Dante ever got out of line then he would use it to remind him just who he was dealing with.

"I can't go back yet," Dante told him. "Let's go for a drink."

*****

Several hours later and much worse for wear with the amount of alcohol they had consumed between them, the two men arrived at the Petrov house.

Yelena and Ella were in the lounge still discussing their designer purchases when they were startled by the noisy entrance.

"Is that you, Aleksei?"

The two men stumbled into the room. "Of course... who else!" Aleksei hiccupped.

Ella was stunned to see Dante in such a state; she had never seen him drunk like this before and didn't know how to handle it.

"W – where... where... is my... *Bella* Ella!" he giggled. "Ella ... *Bella*, Ella!"

"I think we had better get these husbands of ours to bed before they drop on the spot!" Yelena shook her head as she took Aleksei by the hand.

"No... no... I want... another drink!"

"I think you've had quite enough, don't you?" she tutted.

Aleksei grabbed her by the waist and they both toppled onto the sofa nearly turning the whole thing upside down.

"*Bella*, Ella." Dante sang. "Let's go... to... bed!" he slurred the words.

Disgusted she pulled him by the arm. "What on earth's gotten into you?"

"You... you have... you are... you are in... here." He placed her hand on his chest. "Feel... it beats... only... for you." He sighed.

"Come on." She shoved him out of the room. "See you in the morning, Yelena."

Yelena laughed, her husband was unconscious and snoring his head off. "I think I'll leave him here, I'll just go and get him a blanket."

As Ella struggled to get Dante up the stairs Yelena took his other arm. "I'll help you; it will be quicker that way."

"Oh, thanks."

As they dropped him unceremoniously onto the bed he grabbed one of the pillows and snuggled into it. "Ella..." He smiled as he shut his eyes.

"I'm so sorry. I've never seen him like this before," Ella apologised.

"Don't be, I guess they had a lot of catching up to do."

"I suppose."

Yelena quietly shut the door behind her. She was going to check on Aleksei and then she was going to ring Vasiliev for all the gory details.

Chapter Eighty-Three

Ella was up bright and early and was looking forward to visiting the Red Square. She'd only ever seen it on the television and was intrigued to know more about the place. She looked at Dante who was still asleep and shook her head; he had been so drunk when he and Aleksei eventually stumbled into the house. No doubt they would probably have hangovers from hell and not much memory of what they had been up to the previous evening. Just then, Dante's eyes flickered open.

"Good morning," he said as he stretched. "Oh man, I must have been wasted." He laughed as he noticed that he was fully dressed. "How did I get here?"

"Yelena and I practically carried you up the stairs!" Ella was not amused.

"You're not mad with me are you?"

"I will be if you don't get a move on, you promised to take me sightseeing before we go home, remember?"

"As if I could forget, whatever you want to do is fine with me."

"Here." Ella tossed a bottle of headache pills at him. "I thought you may need these."

"Thanks, you're very considerate."

"Pity you're not."

"Oh come on, *Bella*, don't be like that." He got up and walked towards her. "It was a one-off that's all, old friends catching up." Pulling her into his arms he kissed her.

"Oh, Dante, go and have a shower, you smell like a brewery!" she tutted.

"You love me really."

"Well somebody has to!" she joked as she gently pushed him towards the bathroom. "Don't be long."

As Dante undressed he caught sight of himself in the mirror: he was covered in bruises. Shit, how was he going to explain this to Ella? He switched on the shower and stood in a trance under the hot spray remembering what he had done. He jumped when Ella knocked on the door.

"I'm going downstairs, can I get you anything?" she shouted.

"Just stick some coffee on; I'll be down in a few minutes." Pushing the image of Garshin's mutilated body to the back of his mind he took a deep breath and started whistling to himself. That part of his life was over now and he had to forget about it and move on if he was to keep his sanity. Finally he had justice for Rosa.

"Good morning." Yelena smiled as she saw Ella enter the kitchen. "Coffee?"

"Yes please."

"How is Dante?"

"A little hungover, and Aleksei?"

"He's fine."

"I hope I didn't get him in trouble," Aleksei said as he poured himself a glass of water.

"Not really," Ella said, but deep down she was annoyed that this man had taken Dante out and had gotten him paralytically drunk.

"Please accept my apologies for leading him astray."

"Apology accepted." Ella couldn't be bothered yelling at him, which is what she really felt like doing. But she didn't like confrontation so decided to say nothing.

Thirty minutes later they were on the road. Dante seemed distant and Ella put it down to the alcohol. "Cheer up," she told him.

"Sorry, *Bella*, still got a bit of a sore head." He squeezed her hand. "I'm still happy to do whatever you want to though."

"We're here." Aleksei pulled into a parking bay.

"Wow, it's a lot bigger than I expected." The place was huge and milling with visitors. "What's that building over there, it looks like it's straight out of a fairytale!" Ella pointed at the exuberant colours, gasping at its splendour.

"That's St Basil's Cathedral," Yelena told her.

"Can we go there first, take some pictures?" Ella was excited.

Yelena shrugged. "Ok." But really she couldn't be bothered; all she could think about was seeing that video. Looking at Dante she could hardly believe he was capable of doing such a wicked thing and it amazed her how he was acting like nothing had happened.

"Dante, will you take a photo from here first? I want to make sure that we get all the domes and spires in the picture, isn't it amazing?"

"It was built in the mid-fifteen hundreds to commemorate Ivan the Terrible's capture of the Mongol stronghold of Kazan," Aleksei informed her, he had always had a fascination about his country's colourful history.

"Oh, Ivan the Terrible, but he was evil wasn't he?" Ella tried to remember when she was at school; the name definitely rang a bell.

Aleksei chortled. "I suppose that's a matter of opinion."

Once Dante had finished taking the photos, Ella grabbed his hand. "Come on, I want to get close up and look at the design."

Yelena looked at her husband.

"Come on, dear," Alexsei insisted.

Reluctantly she tagged along, her feet were killing her already and she wished she'd never decided to wear her stilettos.

"Wow, just look at the detail."

"You know it took over two hundred years to decorate it," Aleksei said seriously.

"Really!"

"It's amazing to see this building intact after surviving numerous fires and enemy invasions over four hundred years," he continued.

"You are so clever, darling." Yelena kissed him. "Such a mind of information, it reminds me of why I married you!"

"You flatter me, darling wife."

"Should we go inside?"

"It's not very impressive."

"I think you're joking, if this is the outside then the inside must be just as wonderful."

As they entered the building Ella's face dropped, it was very plain and boring and the place seemed very small and cramped. "Oh, dear." The disappointment in her voice was apparent to everyone. "It's just that the outside has such a vast array of colours, I thought the inside would be just the same."

"Never mind, it is a fascinating place though isn't it?" Dante put his arm around her.

"Yes, definitely." She turned to Aleksei. "So is the naming of the Red Square to do with Communism?"

"Not at all, most people seem to think this, but actually the name comes from the Russian *krasniy* meaning beautiful."

"And it is." Ella was pleased to be back out in the fresh air.

"Why don't we go and have a look at Lenin's Mausoleum?" Aleksei suggested.

"I'm afraid I don't know much about him," she admitted.

"He was the founder of the Soviet state and because of his revolutionary activities had this museum dedicated to him. There are over twelve thousand exhibits of his memorabilia including some of his personal belongings, photographs and gifts that he received from people during his life."

"And when did he die?"

"In nineteen twenty-four."

"Fancy having something like this dedicated to his memory, he must have been a great leader."

Yelena was bored, she was becoming exasperated with all this history talk and all she really wanted to do was go shopping, it was what she did best.

"You all right, darling?" Aleksei asked, sensing his wife's feelings.

"It's just that my feet are killing me, I'll wait here, you go on ahead."

"No, I'll stay with you."

"Just go darling, I'll be ok and anyway Ella won't understand anything unless you explain it to her." She paused. "No disrespect meant Ella."

"That's ok, none taken." She smiled.

Yelena couldn't stand her, she was far too nice. Surely she must have another side to her sweet nature, everyone did, didn't they? But she doubted Ella had.

Once she was alone she rang Vasiliev. "It's me, when do I get to see the video?"

"Jesus, you really are a sick fuck after all, a woman after my own heart!"

"I'm just curious. If you hadn't told me then I wouldn't be so desperate to see it, was it really gruesome?"

Vasiliev laughed. "In parts."

"So, when can I see it?" she persisted.

"I have to send Aleksei to Yugoslavia to fill the void Garshin left; he will be gone for several weeks."

"When is he going?"

"Soon, just be patient." Vasiliev hung up, that woman was hungry to see what Dante had done, but he was going to make her wait, just because he knew that he could.

Ella gasped when she saw Lenin's corpse lying in a glass casket, he looked like a wax model. "Is that really him?"

"Yes, that is the embalmed body of Vladimir Lenin."

"My God, it's horrible."

Dante laughed. "Do you want to leave?"

"Just a little browse around first and then I want to see the Kremlin wall."

Almost forty minutes after Ella had satisfied her curiosity about this man she was ready to go. "Oh, Aleksei I totally forgot about Yelena, I hope she's not cross."

"It's ok, I'm here." Yelena's voiced echoed in the vast hall, she took Ella's arm. "Are you having a good time?"

"It's so fascinating; I can't begin to tell you!" Ella gushed.

The Kremlin wall was situated behind the mausoleum. It had an eerie feel to it and Ella shivered. "I don't like this place."

"Not many people do. You see, it contains a mass grave of the Bolsheviks who died during the battle for Moscow in nineteen seventeen."

"No wonder I don't like it!"

"You know it also contains the ashes of Yuri Gagarin, the first man in space."

"Really?" Ella stared at the tall walls and tried to imagine what was inside it.

As they walked along Aleksei pointed out another grave site. "This has the ashes of six unidentified soldiers from six different cities who died in the Second World War."

Ella looked at the six urns and shuddered. "That is so sad."

"And the flame constantly burns as a reminder for all of those unfortunate souls who perished during the war."

Ella had a tear in her eye. "It makes me realise how lucky we all are."

"Yes, quite." Yelena was sick of hearing the simpering bitch. It was many years ago, the men were long dead, who gave a shit?

"I'm starving," Dante announced rubbing his rumbling stomach.

"Me too," Aleksei agreed. "I know this nice restaurant, the Kachanov; it's in Teatralnaya Square, very close by."

"What are we waiting for let's go!" Dante ordered.

The restaurant was typically Russian, decorated with ornaments and frescoes, with huge oak tables and carved chairs. It was quite dark after being out in the bright sunshine and Ella was glad when they were shown to their table and the waiter lit all the candles surrounding it.

"I recommend the sevruga caviar for the appetizers." Yelena was in her element, she was an expert when it came to exceptional food and she wanted to show off. After all, her husband had been the centre of attention all day and now it was her turn.

"Very well," Dante replied.

"I'm not sure, I've never had caviar before, I hear that it is an acquired taste."

"Oh, just try a little," Yelena tried to persuade Ella. "It is extremely good for the complexion you know."

"Oh, all right then." Ella smiled politely, but secretly she didn't want to embarrass herself by spitting it out in public.

When it came Ella smiled with relief, the French baguette was lightly toasted accompanied by a hard-boiled egg, shallots, *crème fraiche*, a pot of caviar and a chilled bottle of vodka.

"It's a bit early to drink, don't you think?"

"Ella, relax, Aleksei is driving, just enjoy your last few hours in Russia." Yelena opened the bottle and poured the shots. "To the Morettis!"

"Oh thank you so much for your hospitality, I know it was a short stay but I truly enjoyed it," Ella told her.

"I'm so glad, now drink."

"I think we should order beef stroganoff for our main course followed by a traditional Russian dessert." Yelena took charge of the orders.

"What is the dessert?" Ella asked.

"It's wonderful, a cream cheese concoction, flavoured with chopped almonds and dark chocolate, you'll love it trust me."

"Mmm, sounds divine."

"How's the caviar?" Dante asked her.

"Not really for me I'm afraid, sorry everyone."

"Don't apologise darling, we're not all connoisseurs," Yelena laughed, the sooner the goddamn meal was over the sooner Aleksei could get them to Domodedovo International airport and finally get Ella out of her hair.

Chapter Eighty-Four

*Six months later
London, England*

The Reynolds' house wasn't the same since her parents had died and Ella was still thinking about selling it.

"But what about when we decide to have a family?" Dante asked her. "This place would be ideal to bring up children."

"I wasn't planning on having any in the near future," Ella laughed.

"Well, one day then, whenever you are ready my love." He pulled her into his arms and kissed her. "I adore you and I always will."

"And I adore you; you are the best thing that has ever happened to me."

"Then we will have a wonderful life together, you and I."

"I know." She sighed. "So, should we move in then?"

"Absolutely."

"Carolyn will be thrilled to finally have the apartment all to herself, not that she spends much time in it herself these days."

"I'm sure she'll miss having your bright, sparkling personality around the place."

"And I'll miss her too," Ella admitted. "We've had some good times there."

"It's not the end of the world you know."

"I guess, but it was nice having her around."

"She'll still be your friend."

Ella smiled. "I know that, silly, anyway right now all I want is a hot bath to try and unwind."

"Would you like some company?"

"Only if you give me one of your special massages."

"What are we waiting for?" Before she had time to respond Dante scooped her into his arms and carried her up the stairs.

"Do you think that it will always be like this?" Ella sighed as he stroked her hair.

"Of course it will." Dante reassured her. "I love you and I always will."

Ella snuggled up to him. "I love you too." She yawned. "Boy, I'm tired."

"I hope you are not too tired."

"My God you are insatiable!" Ella giggled.

"You wouldn't have me any other way!"

"True." Her whole being glowed with happiness and she felt so lucky to have found him; he certainly was one in a million.

*****

"What's the plan for today?" Dante looked at the clock; it was eight in the morning.

"Probably look in on Marcus and see Carolyn; I'll have to get the rest of my things."

"Do you need some help?"

"No thanks darling, you just relax for the day."

"I'll probably use your father's office if that's ok, do some work."

"That's fine, now what do you want for breakfast?"

"Just you!" he teased.

"I think that you may becoming obsessed!" she joked.

"You'd better believe it."

"I'll see what's in the fridge; Maria should have refilled it for me." Ella made an attempt to get out of the bed but Dante pulled her back towards him.

"Not yet, darling," he pleaded.

"You know when you use that little boy voice I can't resist you!" She turned to him and kissed him. "I just melt into your arms."

It was an hour later when Ella finally got dressed and went down into the kitchen to rustle something up. Looking in the fridge she saw some bacon and eggs – good old Maria, she really did look after her well. As she busied herself with grilling the bacon and frying the eggs she smiled to herself, she had never felt so blissfully happy. Hearing footsteps behind her she turned around.

"Something smells good," Dante commented.
"It's nearly ready. Do you want tea or coffee?"
"A nice big pot of tea."
"Coming right up."
"I'll stop off and see Marcus first," Ella told him.
"Is it wise to see him on your own?"
"Pardon?"
"Well he does have a thing for you."
"Don't be silly," she laughed.
"I'm being serious, maybe I should come with you?" he offered.
"I'm a big girl now Dante, I don't need a chaperone!"
"Ok, ok, but he does fancy you!" he insisted.
"Well, even if that was true I only have eyes for you."
"Glad to hear it."
"Now, eat up." Ella placed the food on the table.
"Do you know that you have a bit of a bossy side?"
"Me, bossy?" she giggled. "Not as bossy as you are in the bedroom."
"Fair point!" he laughed with her. "Now, come and sit and have some breakfast with me."
"Yes sir!" She saluted him. "I always obey orders!"
"Yes, but only mine."
"That's very true." Ella took a bite of his toast. "See you later."

*****

Marcus was pleasantly surprised when Ella walked into his office totally unannounced. "Ella, how long are you back for this time?"
"I'm not sure yet, how's things?"
"Couldn't be better."
"That's good."
"Nico told me about what happened to his wife, what a terrible shame."
"I know, it's so sad for them, now they will never have a family of their own," she said pensively.
"And what about you?"

"Me!" Ella exclaimed. "I'm having too much of a good time to start thinking about having babies!"
"I see."
"Why the interest?"
"Sorry, I didn't mean to pry."
"Anyway, why don't you take me down to the showroom, I'm dying to see the consignment!" Just then her mobile rang. "Hold that thought." She held her hand up. "Carolyn, I was just coming to see you."
"There have been some exciting developments."
"Oh, tell me more?"
"Well, it turns out that two of the girls at the centre know each other, or should I say they came across each other while in the process of being trafficked." She paused. "Ella, do you know what this means?"
"No, tell me."
"One name, two witnesses and they are prepared to talk!"
"I'll be right over." She turned to Marcus. "Sorry the cars will have to wait!"
"What's happened?"
"Looks like one of the major sex traffickers are about to get their comeuppance, at long last!"
"That certainly is wonderful news."
"I'll catch up with you before I leave. I guess there are the accounts to look at?"
"Only if you want to, if you don't have time I'll courier them to you."
"You are very meticulous, Marcus, did anyone ever tell you?" she laughed.
"As a matter of fact, no."
"Ok, bye then, got to dash!" And with that she disappeared from the room.
Marcus sighed, it just wasn't fair that she was married to Dante Moretti; he certainly didn't deserve her love.

Chapter Eighty-Five

Carolyn rushed over and hugged her friend when she saw her arrive. "Great to see you, you look absolutely gorgeous!"

"Thank you and so do you," Ella returned the compliment. "Now, tell me everything."

"Do you remember the girl called Natasha, she was the soul survivor on the boat?"

"Yes, yes."

"Well, she came across another girl called Zeta and she was left behind in some kind of seedy strip joint-cum-brothel." She looked around. "Look, you'd better come into my office."

"I don't understand," Ella said trying to keep up with what her friend was trying to say.

"Sit, sit!" she ordered as she shut the door.

"So?"

"After I spoke to Zeta about what happened to Petra Yanovich and the other girls who were brutally shot dead, along with my dear mother, bless her soul, she managed to persuade Natasha to give a statement!"

"What happens now?"

"They've been whisked off to a safe house and are going through photofits as we speak, although I don't think Petra ever met the man in person."

"But Natasha did?"

"Yes, she did."

"And then what?"

"I guess then they try and locate him. Once they do I suppose Interpol will send in some kind of elite team to bring him back to the UK, so that he can stand trial, but then again you know how long these things take."

Valerie's heart pounded as she listened outside the door. That man's name once again, it was going to continue to haunt her for the rest of her life, she was sure of it.

"What do you think the chances are of actually finding this man?"

"Very good, the girls even remember the name of the bar they were taken to but not exactly where it was, but it was definitely in Moscow!"

"Wow, I don't know what to say, but I sure hope that these women get some kind of justice."

"Me too, now I've said enough, the more we know the more risky it could be for us, so don't speak to anyone, not even your husband," she warned.

"Don't worry; I won't breathe a word, although I do hate keeping secrets from him."

"It's for the girls' protection more than anything, now tell me how you've been?"

"Just wonderful, and I have some news too!"

"Oh, you're not pregnant are you?"

"What is it with everyone? First Marcus was asking me and now you!" Ella exclaimed.

"Marcus, is he still hung up on you!"

"Listen Carolyn, I'm not pregnant and Marcus isn't hung up on me!" She laughed loudly. "The biological clock isn't exactly desperate yet!"

"Ok, ok, I give in. What's your news?"

"We're going to move into my parents' house and make that more of our base, so not so much travelling anymore."

"Will you miss it?"

"Yes and no I suppose, but my heart always belonged in England." She sighed.

"You're definitely an English girl at heart," Carolyn agreed.

There was a knock on the door interrupting their conversation. "Yes?"

"I've brought you some tea," Valerie announced as she opened the door. "Thought you might like a brew."

"Oh, thanks you are a darling."

Valerie smiled. "You know it's my evening off don't you?" she reminded her.

"Sure, you out with Giorgino tonight?"

"Yes, I am."

"It's so wonderful that you are dating."

"It's very early days and he knows nothing of what happened to me, so he's just a very good friend." She sighed,

Giorgino Vitelli treated her like a princess and she was enjoying every minute. He hadn't pressured her to move their relationship on even though they had been dating for several months. He merely thought she worked in the centre, which is the way she wanted to keep it.

After she left Carolyn shrugged. "The doctors have told her that she is still able to enjoy a normal sex life even though she is HIV positive, but I really don't think she is interested."

"I didn't realise, was she trafficked too!" Ella gasped.

"Yes, but she only recently confided in me, there was only my mother that knew."

Vitelli was listening in and couldn't wait to turn the information over to Vasiliev. He was definitely moving up in the world now he would show that fucker Moretti, he was much more powerful than he ever thought possible. Poor pathetic Valerie Cooper, he wined her and dined her and showered her with gifts and the silver pen complete with listening device was one of his better ideas. It appeared that she was so fond of it she took it everywhere with her, hence his knowledge of the impending events. Thankfully she had no idea that she was simply part of his elaborate plan to keep one step ahead, and as far as he was concerned this was just the beginning.

Chapter Eighty-Six

Moscow, Russia

"What are you doing, calling on my private line?" Vasiliev spat, totally enraged at the audacity of the little fucker.

"It's all right Esposito gave me it, I have some very important information for you," Vitelli told him.

"Spit it out then."

Yelena was kissing his neck which enraged him even further as he shoved her away. "What did I do?" She shrugged.

"I'm listening."

"It's Moretti's missus she's somehow involved in a sting to take out Garshin and the Blue bar." He waited for his response. "Are you still there, Mr Vasiliev?"

"Of course I'm still fucking here, now you've got my attention, tell me more."

"I don't really want to say too much over the phone, just trust me."

"And if I do as you say?"

"Then Interpol will be none the wiser, it will give you time to do a clean-up job on the place."

"And when is this about to take place?"

"On that I'm not sure yet, it could be as early as next week or perhaps a month's time."

"And what the fuck am I to do in the meantime, tell me that?"

"Transport more merchandise through the Reynolds' business, that way if anything does go wrong I can tip off the police and – hey presto – Ella Reynolds or should I say Ella Moretti is actually in the frame, could also implicate her husband. He does a lot of travelling after all."

"I get the impression that you have something against Dante." Vasiliev laughed, it was a good plan though he had to admit, he looked after number one and nobody else, if it came to the crunch he would hand Moretti over in a flash if it saved his own skin.

"I have a vested interest in the business, it is making me a rich man and that is all I care about."

"If you say so."

Yelena was listening in on the other line. If the place was to be raided then they would all be in the frame, potentially this Ella bitch could inadvertently bring them all down.

"Keep me informed of any developments, it will take me time to set up a new halfway house." Vasiliev replaced the receiver. "Well what do you think?"

"I think this Ella Moretti could become very dangerous to us, why don't we just have her extinguished?" She clicked her fingers. "It could be arranged just like that."

"Impossible! It would bring too much attention and then where would that leave us?"

Yelena was bitterly disappointed and it showed. "It was only a suggestion, I thought you trusted my instincts. She will be the death of us all if we don't do something now!"

"You overreact. She is nothing, a nobody, you think she is dangerous? You need your head looking at!"

"Mark my words, Pavel," she said coldly.

"You know, I would very much like to meet this woman that intimidates you so much!" He laughed loudly. "She must really be something!"

"Have it your way then." She took a cigarette out of her purse and lit it.

Vasiliev watched her with interest and wondered what she was thinking, because she was always thinking about something and that's what he admired about her.

As she flicked the ash onto the floor her eyes lit up. "I've got it. Why don't we break the Morettis up? That way there will be absolutely no connection between any of us ever again, it's foolproof!"

"What did you have in mind?"

"The tape is what I have in mind darling!" she said triumphantly.

"You can't be serious, what if it fell into the wrong hands?"

"So what if it did? Moretti murdering Yakov Garshin, the very man who killed his own sister!" she exclaimed. "He would be arrested and then that would be the end of the search for Garshin!"

"And you think he wouldn't talk?"

"He definitely wouldn't talk; he never talks about her to anyone!"

"Then how do you know about her?"

"Something he once said to Nico and then in turn Nico told Aleksei and then of course he told me."

"You have a very powerful imagination to come up with such an elaborate plan."

"So, what are we going to do?"

"We, darling, are not going to do anything, whereas I on the other hand am going to suss out a new venue and wait for the word from Vitelli before I make a final decision."

"Do you think waiting is wise? I think we should do it now!" She picked up the ashtray and slammed it hard on the table, nearly shattering it.

"I do like your little habits; it's such a turn on!"

"Do this one thing, do it for me, we need to be safe, you know it makes perfect sense." Her voice softened as she stood up and rubbed his shoulders. "I'll personally send her the video, it will be my pleasure. I will go to Yugoslavia and send it from there."

"But Aleksei is on his way home."

"Then entertain him until I return, I will go under one of my false passports, you know, wear a wig, it will be fun. Then if Dante sees where the package was posted from he will automatically assume one of Garshin's associates secretly took the video and sent it to his wife." She paused. "Probably hoping that the police would intercept it, either way it is a win-win situation."

"Yes, I see where you are coming from now. Then Dante will be so hurt and devastated at losing his beautiful wife he will come to me for help and I will point him towards the scum Garshin left in Yugoslavia. He can dispose of my little problem without me getting my hands dirty!"

"I told you that I was a clever girl!"

"Come sit here." He patted his knee. "I have something for you."

"You know that I would do anything for you Pavel, but how much longer must I stay with my husband?"

"But I thought that you would never leave him," he said as he pushed her head towards his groin in anticipation.

"That was before I had all this power," she said as she obliged him.

"Patience Yelena I am not finished with him yet!" he moaned, enjoying her fleshy mouth pleasuring him.

"Then, it's agreed." She stopped for a second.

"Yes, yes, don't stop!" he said gruffly as he gyrated his hips towards her. She was good, he thought, no amazing and he was beginning to realize the power she had over him now.

"Oh, thank you, Pavel, you won't regret this." She looked up into his eyes as she watched the excitement on his face until finally he was finished.

"Now, go and do it before I change my mind!" He unlocked the safe and tossed her the disk.

As she left the room she turned and looked at him. "You really are fantastic!"

"Don't flatter me too much, Yelena, there's still time to stop you from leaving."

Knowing when to shut up she hurriedly left the room, hugging the tape to her heaving bosom she laughed quietly. What a fucking idiot! It was she who held all the cards, not him. One day, when she disposed of him and took over the business, he would finally realise that.

Chapter Eighty-Seven

Several weeks later
London, England

Dante was up early; he had a few errands to run and didn't want to disturb his wife.

As Ella turned over and reached for her husband all she found was an empty space. She sat up and rubbed her eyes it was eight thirty. "Dante...? Dante where are you?"

Tutting to herself she slipped into her slippers and pulled on her dressing gown. He had sneaked off somewhere and hadn't bothered to tell her, which usually meant she was in store for a present of some kind. Sweeping her hair up she heard movements downstairs, it was probably Maria.

Ten minutes later she could smell the aroma of freshly ground coffee wafting up the stairs, yes it was definitely the housekeeper, she smiled.

Maria was busy tidying up the kitchen when Ella finally came down. "Good morning, how are you?"

"I'm fine, Ella, thank you for asking. Shall I make you some breakfast?"

"No, it's ok, I'll just have a bowl of cereal and some of your lovely coffee thanks." She paused as she picked a brown padded envelope up from the table. "Oh, when did this come?"

"I bumped into the postman on the way in."

Ella shook it lightly, wondering what it was.

"It is addressed to you." Maria laughed. "You can open it."

"You know how I love to guess what's inside, it feels like a DVD or CD or something similar." Noting the postmark she was baffled: Yugoslavia. But she didn't know anyone in Yugoslavia.

"So, have you decided what you are doing this summer?" Maria enquired thinking about her own plans.

"Funny you should mention it. I suspect my darling husband is booking somewhere suitably romantic for the next four weeks!"

"You lucky young thing, is there any room for a little one?" Maria joked.

"Somehow I think it would cramp Dante's style," she laughed.

"That's a shame. So tell me, where do you think he is taking you?"

"Somewhere in the Caribbean I hope, I've been dropping enough hints, so hopefully he will have got the message."

Maria sat down next to her. "So, do you think it would be all right if I went to stay with my sister in the Lake District for a few weeks while you are away? I'll have my niece Loretta keep an eye on the house and of course George will be around every day, you know how he likes to keep the grounds maintained."

"Of course I don't mind, you've got a life too and you should enjoy a nice relaxing holiday from time to time just like everyone else."

"Oh thank you, I knew you would say that."

Maria stood up and headed for the laundry room. "Enjoy your breakfast; I'll catch up with you later."

Ella nodded as she ate her cereal but she couldn't take her gaze off the brown envelope. Putting down her spoon curiosity got the better of her. She picked it up and went back to her bedroom. Ripping it open she tipped it onto the bed and a silver disk fell out. Peering into the envelope and short of ripping it apart she could find no note.

As she popped the disk into the DVD player she was just about to press play when the telephone rang. "Hello, this is Ella Moretti."

"Are you dressed yet?" Dante asked.

"No, not yet, why?"

"I have something for you and I think you will want to show me your gratitude."

"Oh yes, it had better be good then!" Ella teased him, wondering which exotic location he had decided on.

"Just stay where you are, I'll be about twenty minutes."

"Yes, Signor Moretti."

"See you soon, *Bella*."

"Very soon, darling."

"And, Ella?"

"Yes?"

"I love you."

"And I love you too."

After he had hung up she lay on her stomach and leaned her head into her hands ready to watch the mystery DVD. But nothing could have ever prepared her for what she was about to see.

It was Dante and he was having some kind of fight with a man she didn't recognise. There were bits that she couldn't quite make out, but she could tell that the fight had intensified and it looked almost as if it was a fight to the death.

She watched as the two men struggled with a knife and Dante managed to escape. As he neared the table she could see his wild eyes. He looked almost possessed and it frightened the life out of her. It must be some kind of play-acting surely, it had to be. She turned the volume up but all she got was a load of fuzz. Putting her hands over her eyes she slowly peeped through the gap she had made. She saw the chain being tightened around the other man's neck as Dante dragged him with such force he was nearly choking to death, his eyes bulging as if about to burst out of his face.

What the hell was this? It had to be some kind of sick joke, because it definitely was the sickest thing she had ever seen. She heard Maria on the landing and quickly knocked it off.

"Shall I come back later?"

"No, leave up here until tomorrow," Ella told her.

"Are you ok, dear? You look a little peaky to me, can I get you anything?"

"Please stop fussing around me like some silly old mother hen and just go!" Ella's tone was sharp and abrupt. "Oh, sorry Maria, I'm just starting with a migraine and I can't bear any noise right now."

"Oh, you should have said dear, better take some tablets and rest up," she advised.

"Thanks." When she heard Maria's retreating footsteps she flicked the disk back on. The grisly sight before her eyes made her literally want to scream; quickly she pressed her hand to her mouth and bit down hard on her lip, so hard that she could taste her own blood. The man she loved took a machete and without any warning like a wild animal attacked the man while he lay defenceless on the floor, crawling away from him, fighting for his very life. No, this couldn't be happening, it wasn't real, it couldn't be…

She gasped as she caught sight of the last clip. It was a date, and it meant something to her. She cast her mind back and realised it was the very date that they were in Moscow together. It was the night Dante had acted all weird and came back to the Petrovs' house absolutely off his head. She had never ever seen him like that and there hadn't been a flicker of that man from that night ever since. To her it explained his bizarre behaviour that night and now she began to understand why he went missing for the best part of the evening, off with Aleksei on some kind of boozed-up night out. My God, he must be in on this too, she thought, it was beyond all comprehension to her. It was vicious, ruthless and needless torture of another human being. The man she loved, somehow she just couldn't get her head around it, the tears welled up in her eyes. Pausing the disk she wondered what to do about it. Should she discard it and forget about it forever, be with the man she adored or should she confront him with the dark brutal truth? How would he explain it, could he even explain it? She just didn't know. As she lay there wretched on the bed she heard voices in the hallway. Oh no, it was Dante, he was back.

When he came into the room Ella was still sitting on the bed in a trance-like state with the remote control in her hand and the picture of him with the machete on freeze frame.

Dante immediately went downstairs and asked Maria to leave.

"But why? I'm not finished yet," she protested.

"Please do as I ask, I need to speak with Ella alone," he stressed.

"But I am busy, I won't hear a thing!" Maria laughed thinking that he wanted to be alone with his lovely wife to celebrate the gift he had just purchased.

"No, please," he insisted.

"Ok, I'll see you tomorrow as usual then."

"I'll call you, now please leave." He pushed her unceremoniously out of the door.

"Well, I know you want to be alone with her, Mr Moretti, but I don't think being forced out of the house is quite necessary, do you?"

"I do apologise." And with that Dante slammed the door shut and he leant his back onto it. Jesus Christ, some fucker had stitched him up good and proper and he had no idea how he was going to come out of this unscathed.

When he returned to the bedroom Ella was throwing all of his things out of the closet into a heap in the middle of the room. She couldn't think about what she had seen, she didn't want to remember what she had just seen. Now she was on autopilot, she had to erase every trace of this murderer from her life and quickly. Her thoughts turned to the callous murder of her own father, a murder that to this day was still unsolved and probably always would be. The person who did it was a monster and in her eyes Dante, her own husband, was no better.

"Ella, I can explain, please!" he begged her.

"You've ruined everything, all the love and the trust I had for you gone in a split second, just like that!" She clicked her fingers.

"No, my darling, it isn't what you think; I promise you, let me explain," he begged her.

"Explain? How can you possibly explain what you did to that man, it was... so, so... absolutely shocking... barbaric in fact!"

Dante looked on helplessly as she continued to pile up his belongings.

"*Bella*, please." He touched her arm and she jumped. "I would never hurt you. Never, ever doubt how I feel about you, it can't end like this, it just can't!"

"It already has, Dante, I want you out of my life." Her voice was tight and quiet.

"You don't mean that."

"I know what I am saying, Dante, I may be in shock, but I have been here before remember?"

"Your father?"

"Yes, my father, of course my father, what else!" Her voice was verging on hysteria. "How could you do this to me, after all

I have endured. Don't you know what you have done? It's like all the love we had together meant nothing to you!"

Dante grabbed her gently by the arms. "My darling, Ella, I love you, let me talk to you about this, it's the least you owe me."

"Make no mistake, Dante, I owe you nothing and never will!"

"No, the last couple of years have been the best of my life, you are my everything."

"Really? Then why would you do such an evil thing, it is beyond my comprehension! It's like I have been living with a complete stranger all this time."

"Ella...?"

"It's over, Dante, I mean it. This was some kind of whirlwind romance that should never have happened." She paused. "No, we should never have happened, all I want to do is erase the years we have spent together and go back to the start."

"But we can start again, I'm not that man anymore, it's over..."

"Damn right, it's over. Now get your things and get out of my house, I never want to see you ever again."

"You don't mean it, *Bella*."

"Oh, I mean it, now fuck off and never darken my door again!"

Dante was shocked to hear his wife using such an obscenity. All the time they had been together she had never once uttered a profanity and that was part of the initial attraction. "I'll do as you ask, but I will be back in the morning to sort this out."

"And your fucking belongings will be outside in black bin bags!"

"You don't mean it."

"I fucking do, now just go, you disgust me, I can't bear to look at you, you are pure evil!" she screamed at him. "Get out I said, get out!" She threw everything in sight at him, until finally he leaned over and ejected the disk and left.

Collapsing in a crumbling heap on the floor she sobbed her heart out. It was over, there was no going back now. There was no way she could condone murder, it just wasn't acceptable in any shape or form, no matter what the reasons.

Chapter Eighty-Eight

The de Luca Residence, Milan, Italy

"Dante's on the telephone, he sounds really angry, it's something to do with Ella." Grazia passed her husband the handset and shrugged.

"What is it?" Nico asked, his voice full of concern for his friend.

"What went down in Moscow, Ella knows!"

"I don't understand, how could she possibly know?"

"Some bastard taped it and mailed it to her, she saw everything..." His voice was breaking up, the emotion overwhelming him. "It... it's over... she threw me out and that's it!"

"No, she loves you, surely if you told her about Rosa...?"

"No, I can never tell her about that!"

"But, Dante, you must, then at least she will understand why you did what you did," Nico tried to reason with him.

"Nothing I do or say will change her mind, I just know it, I've never seen her like this, she truly doesn't want me back." He stopped for breath. "What am I going to do?"

"Where are you?"

"In London."

"Get the next flight back and I'll pick you up at the airport, and Dante, try not to worry, we'll sort this out, I promise you." Nico was trying to think who would stitch him up like this, ruin his life just like that.

"Ok." Dante slammed his mobile shut and looked back at the Reynolds' house. He had blown it and he knew deep in his heart Ella would never forgive him, no matter what explanation he came up with. Right now all he wanted to do was smash the disk into a million pieces and erase that terrible night.

*****

"What is it?" Grazia asked.

"Dante and Ella, they have had one hell of a row and it seems like it is over."

"Over?" she repeated. "But it can't be, they were so happy, I don't get it!"

"Who knows what goes on inside anyone's marriage?"

"Oh my God, has he had an affair?" It wouldn't be the first time Dante had two-timed a woman, no matter how much he appeared to be in love with her. He was well known for being unfaithful and, given his track record, she was surprised the relationship had lasted this long. "I'm going to call her." She picked up the telephone and was just about to dial her number when her husband gently touched her hand.

"No, don't, not yet, let's give it a few days, see if they can sort this thing out."

"The poor thing, she must be in bits." Grazia shook her head. "What a shame, they seemed so perfect together, so happy." The tears welled up in her eyes, she really liked Ella.

"I've told him to come and stay with us for a few days until everything calms down, I hope you don't mind."

"Mind, why should I mind?"

Nothing seemed to matter much to Grazia these days, Nico thought. His beautiful wife still looked the same on the outside but deep inside her she was a shell of her former self, her personality crushed from within. "Why don't I invite my brother and his wife over with the kids?" he suggested.

"Whatever." Grazia looked at him blankly, he really had no inkling of what she was going through. It was all right for him he could still have children if he wanted, but she never would, she thought bitterly.

"Darling, we could always adopt?"

"Nico, we've been through this, it wouldn't be the same, you know that as well as I do."

"I thought maybe one day you would change your mind," Nico said softly.

"I have my dogs and my horses, they are like my babies." Grazia smiled.

"You know that I would do anything for you, don't you my darling?" He took her in his arms and kissed her.

"I know, I'm lucky to have you." She sighed as she tried to hold back the tears.

"No, that's where you are wrong, I am the lucky one." He held her tightly. "You are all I need in this life, remember that."

Chapter Eighty-Nine

Moscow, Russia

"It's me, Nico."

Aleksei was a little surprised to hear from him. "Yes?"

"It's Dante; someone has sent his wife a disk with damning evidence on it!"

"What's on it?"

"Garshin," Nico said quietly. "Do you know what I am saying?"

"Yes, but who would do such a thing?"

"It must have been one of Vasiliev's men, it's the only explanation."

"Do you know what you are saying?"

"I know exactly what I am saying and when Dante comes to his senses he will come to the same conclusion and then all hell will break loose."

"So, what do you want me to do?" Aleksei bit his lip, he didn't like the sound of this one little bit.

"You need to speak with your boss and tell him what has happened!"

"Me, why me? Wouldn't it sound better coming from you?" Aleksei sat bolt upright in his chair. It was more than his life was worth to accuse Vasiliev of somehow being involved in taping the murder.

"He will appreciate it if you discuss this with him, or would you prefer Dante to come in with all guns blazing so to speak?"

"I'm not sure."

"Well, you better be sure, because if you don't find the person responsible for doing this, then mark my words Dante will, one way or another." Nico slammed the phone down, Petrov was a quivering wreck, how he lasted in this business he would never know.

Yelena was just coming into the house from one of her many shopping trips and noticed her husband's face. "Dear God, Aleksei, you look like someone has just died!"

"Someone just might!" His voice was totally serious. "It's the disk of Moretti and Yakov, it was sent to his wife!"

"Really darling, is that all?" Yelena sat opposite him on the huge leather sofa and crossed her legs seductively.

"Don't be an idiot, if he finds out that we were privy to the taping of it then we will all be dead!" he exclaimed.

"Calm down darling, everything will be alright." She went over to him and sat on the floor next to him. "You do trust me, darling, don't you?" She looked into his eyes and smiled.

"Oh, Yelena, maybe we should just move away, far away from here. It is just getting too dangerous!"

"Don't be silly, darling, look around you, look at all this you have worked for, how could you leave this behind?" She waved her arms around the room.

"It's only a building!" Aleksei persisted.

"Yes, bricks and mortar it may be, but it is our home and I for one am not leaving it!"

"De Luca wants me to speak with Vasiliev to see who could have sent it to Moretti's wife!"

"So, Ella has seen it then?" Yelena's ears pricked up. "What did she do?"

"What do you think she did?"

"Is she going to the police then?"

"No, Nico would have told me if she intended to do that."

"Oh dear, so poor Dante has been rumbled by his pretty little wife," she gloated. "It's all a bit of a mess isn't it?"

"You could say that."

"So are you going to speak with Vasiliev?"

"I don't think that I have much choice in the matter, do you?" Aleksei was dreading the thought of it, he hated confrontation and even more so with a man like his boss.

"Why don't you let me talk to him. I am a woman and I can be more subtle if you know what I mean," she said swinging her leg.

"You would do that for me?" Just for a moment Aleksei was tempted to offer his wife to his boss because he would be lucky if he lived after he told him what Dante suspected. Quickly he jolted himself back to reality. "No, no, I can't let you do that!"

"Darling, I wouldn't have to do anything for him, I would just turn on the charm, tell him what you told me," she suggested. "You know while we discuss business."

"I don't think that's a good idea, it should really come from me."

"I do work for him now and he trusts me, I wouldn't even mention that you told me if it helps, I'll say that I overheard you talking with Dante on the telephone?"

"No, don't lie to Vasiliev, it's the worst thing you could do, believe me, he hates liars and you don't want to end up like the ones he has dealt with of late."

"So?"

"I better see him myself. I am only the messenger after all," he reassured her.

"True, but perhaps I should still come with you?"

Aleksei gazed into her eyes, she was such a wonderful wife, he wondered what he had ever done without her. "Don't you worry your pretty little head about it, this is up to me to sort out, not you, now tell me what delights you have purchased today." He was putting on a brave face and hoped that she bought it, but either way he knew she wouldn't say another word.

Chapter Ninety

The shit was well and truly hitting the fan and Vasiliev had less than three hours to clear the club before Interpol arrived to raid it. Thanks to Vitelli's tip-off he had managed to bring in the trucks and remove any trace of the girls ever being there. He had arranged for a little present to be left for the team in command of the operation and watched from a safe distance. Any time now, he thought, laughing to himself: nobody fucked with him and his organisation. Just then his mobile rang, cursing he answered it. "Yelena, I'm fucking busy this had better be good!"

"It's the tape, Ella Moretti has seen it and threw Dante out, it's over between them!"

"Good, then she can no longer be in any way connected to us." Vasiliev shut his phone, it was only a matter of time before Dante's wife found out the real nature of his business interests and, when she did, it would have brought them all down. The connection between her company and the de Lucas' would be exposed and he couldn't take any chances, not now that it had become so lucrative. Ella Moretti would then put two and two together and speak with this Reid woman and they would realise what had really been going on. It was better getting rid of her this way than permanently taking her out: one, it would only draw attention to her business and have the police crawling all over it, and two, Dante would be interrogated.

His thoughts were interrupted by a loud explosion. He watched as the building collapsed. There was no way any of those fuckers would survive that, he thought laughing out loud as he lit a cigar. And once they cleared the debris away they would find Yakov Garshin's corpse, investigation over. Smiling once more his thoughts turned to Moretti. He would tell him that Yakov's men must have secretly taped what happened in the warehouse and he would arrange for a few killings to take place just to convince him. Then not only would Moretti be indebted to him he would also take out some of the irritating scum who were planning some kind of takeover. All in all it worked out to his advantage.

As he made the drive back to his residence he rang Aleksei. "Get over to mine and make it quick!

When Aleksei finally arrived he sat in his car and looked at the house, popped a couple of pills and prayed that he would make it out alive. Vasiliev's men nodded at him as he passed them and he nodded back. Taking a deep breath, he knocked on the office door and waited.

"Come in!"

Aleksei nervously opened the door and walked slowly into the room, ready to make a break for it if need be.

"You took your fucking time! Now, what's all this shit about Moretti thinking I have something to do with sending this fucking tape to his wife?" he demanded.

Aleksei was taken by surprise. "B – but how do you know that?"

"I know every fucking thing there is to know, now sit!" he barked, pointing to the chair in front of him.

Obediently Aleksei did as he was told and waited for his boss to tell him what he had to do.

Vasiliev enjoyed watching him squirm and as he calmly lit a cigarette he spoke. "Dante must never know that I made that tape."

"Of course," Aleksei agreed. If he told Dante the truth then he would be incriminating himself as he, too, watched as the action took place.

"Good I am glad that we understand one another."

"So, what are you going to tell him?"

"Me, I am going to tell him nothing, this is all down to you my friend." He smiled through gritted teeth, waiting for his reaction.

"What… what will I tell him?" he stammered.

"The truth of course!"

"The truth, but I don't understand." Aleksei was totally confused.

"Here." Vasiliev suddenly got out of his chair making Aleksei jump. "Calm down my friend, I am not going to hurt you. You are my ally of course."

Aleksei looked at the list containing six names. "What does this mean?"

"You are to take complete responsibility for removing these enemies of Dante, the ones who made the tape and sent it to his wife."

The names were of people who had challenged Vasiliev and were in fact his enemies and not Dante's. "What about the details?"

"I don't really give a fuck how you dispose of them." He paused. "The deadline is forty-eight hours so you had better get on with it!"

"What do I tell Dante?"

"I told you, tell him whatever the fuck you want. It doesn't matter how you found out about these conspirators, the point is you asked for my backing and as I am a friend of Dante's and he was personally hurt we took evasive action."

"Very well."

"Now fuck off out of my sight and let me know when the job is complete." He dismissed Aleksei as if he were a little boy.

Once he had left he rang Yelena. "He will be gone for the next couple of days, so why don't you pack an overnight case and come on over?"

"Do you promise to tell me what happened?"

"Depends what you can do for me!"

"I'm open to offers, Pavel; you know that, anything to please you."

Chapter Ninety-One

London, England

Ella was confused about everything that had happened and she didn't know what she should do about it, her head was spinning. As she poured a drink of water she looked at the answer machine: nothing. He didn't even have the decency to ring her, that's how much he really cared about her. She felt totally alone, how could she ever tell anybody about what she had discovered without sentencing her husband to life in prison? Even Dante didn't deserve that. The man he had murdered must have deserved it, he just must have, she told herself.

She rang Tara in France. "Hey, it's me."

"Ella, oh it's so nice to hear from you, when are you coming over?"

"I was thinking tonight?"

"Tonight? It's a little short notice but I think I can handle it."

"Good, then can you meet me at the airport?"

"Of course, just ring me later and confirm you flight details and I'll arrange it."

"Fabulous." Ella needed to get away, to think about her future and she couldn't do that here, especially if Dante did turn up.

"I'll look forward to seeing you both."

"Dante's not coming," Ella said simply.

"Oh, is everything ok?"

"Fine, he's away on a business trip and it could be some time before he returns," Ella told her, hoping she wouldn't ask any more questions as she was just about to break down again.

"Ok, I'll look forward to seeing you later."

Ella put the phone down and went to pack a small suitcase but a photograph caught her eye. "You son of a bitch," she whispered, "why did you have to go and ruin everything?" Turning the photo face down she turned the music up loud and busied herself getting ready for her trip.

She was oblivious to the front doorbell continually ringing.

"Ella, please let me in, I don't want it to end like this," Dante pleaded. "I can only ask that you forgive me if not now then in time, what we have is special; you and I both know that." He realised that his words were falling on deaf ears, his wife just didn't want to know and he couldn't really blame her for that. "So be it."

The only thing he could do was ring her in a few days' time and beg her forgiveness all over again. Their love was strong and he believed that it would see them through anything.

Reluctantly he phoned a taxi and jumped in. "Gatwick airport please." His heart sank as they drove away, things would never be the same again and his Ella was lost to him now.

Ella threw herself on the bed and sobbed into her pillow. It wasn't fair, her life had been almost perfect and now it was all crashing down around her. The shrill ring of the telephone startled her, maybe it was Dante trying to make amends, quickly she picked up the receiver. "Whatever you say means nothing to me, it's too late!" Her voice was verging on hysteria.

"What...? It's me Marcus, is everything ok?"

Hearing a familiar voice Ella broke down once more. "No, no it's not, oh, Marcus!" she wailed.

"Is there anything I can do, should I come over?" His voice was full of concern.

"I wish there was something, but you can't help me, no one can."

"I'm coming over." Marcus put down the phone, that bastard husband of hers had done something terrible to her. If he was still there when he arrived he would have strong words for him. Nobody hurt her like that, least of all that man who apparently adored her.

When he arrived Ella didn't want to let him in, she didn't want him to see her in such a state and she certainly didn't want to explain why she was so upset.

"What has he done to you?"

"It's nothing, I'm fine," Ella insisted.

"You're far from fine, come on let me make you a strong cup of tea and you can tell me what's going on." Marcus took her by the elbow and guided her into the conservatory.

Ella's hands trembled as she tried to sip the scalding liquid.

"Do you want to talk about it?"

"There's nothing to talk about, it's over between me and Dante." Her voice was firm.

"Tell me, what he did to you that is so bad you can't fix it?"

"It doesn't matter."

"Of course it matters, look at you, you are in pieces."

"Thanks for the concern but this is something that I have to deal with by myself." She placed the cup on the table.

"Are you going somewhere?" Marcus noticed the suitcase.

"Yes, I'm going to stay with a friend in France for a while, I need some space."

"Is there anything I can do?"

"You can give me a lift to the airport and perhaps contact Maria to look after the house while I am away."

"No problem, how long will you be gone for?"

"I'm not sure." Ella sighed, as long as it took to get over him, she thought.

All the way to the airport she was quiet and subdued and Marcus was concerned for her. "Are you sure this is what you want to do?" He glanced over to her as he pulled into departures.

"Yes."

Dante had just checked in, he couldn't leave Ella like this it just didn't feel right. Perhaps if he did tell her the truth as Nico had suggested she could find a way of forgiving him? Flipping open his mobile phone he rang the house. "It's me, I have to talk to you, my flight leaves in two hours." He paused. "If you don't ring me then I know it's over and I promise I will never contact you again and Ella, remember that I will always love you and if ever you need me –" his voice broke off. "Well, you know where I am." He closed the phone and put his head in his hands, he had really messed up and now he was paying the price.

Marcus waited until Ella had her boarding pass. "Keep in touch."

"I will." And with that she disappeared through the doors.

He stood there for a minute pondering what he should do, but he realised that this was none of his business and Ella had to work it out for herself. He hated seeing her so distressed, whatever Dante had done must have been unforgivable. It was probably some sordid affair, he thought, what else could have torn them apart. If ever he saw him again he would have it out with him, one way or another force the truth from him.

Ella's flight was called and she made her way to the departure gate. Just as she handed her boarding pass in she heard an announcement.

"Last call for Mr Dante Moretti…"

Ella froze, *Oh my god he must have followed me*!

"Mr Dante Moretti can you please make your way to departure gate 22A."

Ella scanned the departure board for flight 22A. She gasped, he was going to Milan. She put her hand to her chest, he felt so little for her he was leaving the country!

"Are you all right miss?" the woman at the check in desk asked.

"I will be," she muttered as she took the ticket stub from her. The son of a bitch didn't even have the decency to stick around, try and salvage what was left of their marriage. As she fastened her seat belt the cabin crew came around with refreshments.

"Anything from the trolley?"

"A vodka and coke please, no, make that a double." Ella sank back into her chair and gulped the drink down in one. She couldn't believe Dante had abandoned her just like that.

Dante checked his mobile; there was nothing, no message, no call from his wife.

"I'm sorry, sir, I must ask you to switch that off now," the air stewardess told him.

Reluctantly he turned it off, that was it, she didn't give a damn, it was over. He felt sick to the pit of his stomach. It was a feeling that he had only ever experienced when he had found out about his sister Rosa. Somebody was going to pay for sending that tape to Ella and he clenched his fists as he thought about what he was going to do to them.

Chapter Ninety-Two

Milan, Italy

"So, what did Vasiliev have to say?" Dante demanded, he was livid.

"It was nothing to do with him," Nico told him.

"Do you seriously expect me to believe that?" Dante banged his fists on the table.

"Calm down, you can't go on like this!"

"It's not your fucking wife they sent the tape to is it?" he raged. "She was everything to me, the love of my life and now it looks like it's all over."

"No, it's only over if you let it be." Nico put his hand on his shoulder. "Ella loves you; she will forgive you, in time."

"I want an explanation and I won't settle for anything less than hearing it from the horse's mouth!"

"Aleksei assures me that it was all down to Garshin's followers."

"And what do you think?"

"It's possible I suppose."

"Possible, isn't good enough, that fucker Vasiliev has done this and I for one want to know why!"

"Ok, I'll arrange a meeting." Nico shook his head; he had a feeling that this was all going to end in disaster. "In the meantime I suggest you get your head together, think seriously about what you intend to do, there's a lot to think about."

"I don't give a fuck about the business anymore it means nothing without Ella." Dante's voice was distant as he thought about her.

"Just be aware if you take him out there will be repercussions, and your wife will be in the line of fire."

Dante sat down, it was a no-win situation, Nico was right. He would have to bide his time and strike when the moment was right, when Ella was finally out of the picture. He realised that the only way to keep her out of this and to be able exact his revenge on Vasiliev was to divorce her, let the dust settle, wait until she moved on and then make his move. "Yes, you're right my friend."

"I'm glad that you are finally seeing sense, there is a time and a place for everything and this is not the time or the place. We have too much to lose, all of us do." Nico thought about his wife, his parents and his brothers, if Dante so much as lifted a finger they would all be snuffed out.

"Very well, but I still wish to speak with Vasiliev, listen to what he has to say, see if his story adds up."

"And then?"

"Then it's business as usual, for now at least." He rubbed his chin, there was a mad look in his eyes, deep down he knew that Yakov Garshin only did what his boss told him to and that meant he too knew of his sister's disappearance and he wanted to get to the bottom of it, if it was the last thing he ever did.

Chapter Ninety-Three

London, England
Two months later

Carolyn picked Ella up from the airport. "You look very well, the French weather must have agreed with you."

"Tara was really great, she kept me busy slaving away in the bed and breakfast," she laughed.

"And Dante?" Carolyn enquired.

"Who?"

"What are you going to do about him?"

"I'm going to divorce him."

"You can't be serious."

"I'm perfectly serious. It's about time we both moved on, you see there is no me and him anymore."

"Have you spoken to him?"

"No and I don't want to!" Ella snapped as she felt her emotions surging to the surface.

"Don't be hasty, that's all I ask," Carolyn said softly as she drove up to the Reynolds' house.

"It's ok, really," she insisted. "I know exactly what I am doing."

But Carolyn had her doubts. "Are you ever going to tell me what he did?"

"Maybe someday when I'm over the whole sorry saga, but not now, I can't bear to talk about it."

"Then I'll respect your decision." She parked the car. "Do you want me to come in with you?"

"No, I'll get unpacked and speak to you tomorrow."

"Make sure you do, I don't like you being all alone in such a vast house."

"Don't be silly, I grew up in that house!" Ella laughed. "Now open the boot and let me get my luggage out."

She waved to her friend as she drove off. As she opened the door and punched in the code for the alarm she shuddered. It did feel strange being all alone in the house and she wondered if it was a good idea after all.

Maria had left her a note: *Welcome home, I have stocked the fridge and placed your mail on the kitchen table, love Maria.'*

Ella left her case in the hallway and headed for the kitchen. She quickly flicked through the letters and stopped when she saw one from Italy. Her hear pounded as she ripped it open. *My Bella Ella, I didn't want it to end the way it did and I'm so sorry for hurting you.* She looked at the postage date; it was dated a few days after she had left for France. *Please contact me so that I can explain it* continued. *If I don't hear from you in a week then I can only assume that it's over, but I beg you to reconsider, give me one more chance, give us one more chance.*

The tears started flowing and Ella was a quivering wreck. Wiping her eyes she read the rest of the letter. *If you want a divorce I will not contest it and I will make sure you are well compensated, it is the least I can do.* A divorce, her heart sank, the word 'divorce' hit her like a sledgehammer. She had left it too late and now she had to accept that it was well and truly over.

Pressing playback on her answer machine she heard Dante's voice. "It's me, I have to talk to you, my flight leaves in two hours. If you don't ring me then I know it's over and I promise I will never contact you again, and Ella remember that I will always love you and if ever you need me… well, you know where I am."

His voice sent shivers down her spine; he just had that effect on her. Picking up the phone she rang his number.

"Yes?" A woman's voice answered.

Ella immediately replaced the receiver, so much for always loving her, he had moved a woman into their house and she couldn't bear it. Ripping the phone out of its socket she threw it hard against the wall. It was going to be a miracle if she ever moved on from the break-up, but she had to for her own sanity.

Chapter Ninety-Four

Six months later

"I've got my decree nisi," Ella told Carolyn. "That's it, the whole thing is over, done, gone!" She threw the envelope onto the table. "What say we celebrate?"

"Are you sure you want to?"

"Damn right."

Just then the door opened and Valerie appeared. "Oh, sorry have I come at a bad time?"

"It's all right, Ella's just telling me that her divorce has come through and she wants me to help her celebrate."

"Celebrate, but I don't understand?"

"It doesn't matter, that chapter of my life is gone, dead and buried and now finally I can move on." Ella was dying inside but put on a brave face to the outside world.

"I just came to tell you my news."

"Oh, what news?"

"Giorgino has asked me to marry him and I've accepted." She smiled. "Who would have thought anyone would want me? I can hardly believe it."

"Oh, Valerie I am so pleased for you." Carolyn hugged her. "That's fantastic news, isn't it Ella?" She turned to her friend.

"Yes it is, congratulations, I hope you have better luck than I did!" she said bitterly.

Valerie looked a little stunned. "I'm sorry, I didn't mean to upset you."

"It's all right, it's not your fault I married a ruthless bastard!"

"What about that celebratory drink?" Carolyn tried to calm her down.

"It doesn't matter, I don't much feel like celebrating anymore." She grabbed her handbag.

"Where are you going?"

"For a long walk, weigh up my life and decide what I want to do with the rest of it!"

"You won't do anything silly, will you?"

"You mean top myself? I'm not my mother you know." And with that she stormed out of the centre.

"Your friend is very upset, what did her husband do to her?" Valerie asked.

"Whatever it was she won't tell anyone, not even me and I'm her closest friend." Carolyn sighed, swiftly changing the subject. "Now, I want to know all the details."

"We are getting married in the registry office in three weeks, will you come?"

"As if I would miss it."

"Giorgino wants us to have a normal sex life."

"Oh, what about your illness?"

"I've told him and he says that he doesn't care about that, he just wants us to be complete, a normal couple, or at least as normal as possible."

"So, I take it you have changed your mind about being celibate?"

"Yes, yes I have, but we will wait until our wedding night." She sighed. "I'm so happy; it's incredible I never ever thought I could be happy again."

"Do you plan on contacting your family?"

"I can't it is too dangerous."

"Why have you never talked about them?"

"If nobody knows who they are then no one can do them any harm, it's a sacrifice I chose to make to keep them safe."

"But Yakov Garshin is dead. Surely you can contact them now?"

"No, he may be gone but there is always someone else to pick up where he left off."

"I know what you are saying, but if you change your mind you know that I will help you in any way I can."

"Thank you, I am so glad that we met, I really don't know what I would have done without you."

"I hope that you are not planning on leaving us once you are married."

"Of course not, Giorgino wants me to stay on."

"Thank goodness for that." Carolyn hugged her once more. "And we could always do with an extra hand."

"You are offering a job to Gio?"

"Yes, why not? There's always plenty to do around here."

"Oh, I'm so excited, wait until I tell him." Valerie was thrilled; it would make him extremely happy.

"Why don't you use the office phone to tell him?" she offered.

Valerie punched in his number. "Gio, it's me, I've just told Carolyn the news and guess what?"

"What my love?" Vitelli waited for her answer.

"She's offered you a job, how about that!" she exclaimed.

"Wonderful, tell her I accept."

"He accepts!"

"Tell him to come and see me sometime this week and we'll sort out the details."

Carolyn left the office and rang Ella's mobile but she didn't answer. "I'm worried about you. Please call me when you get this message."

Chapter Ninety-Five

Three weeks later

"I'm so glad that you decided to come, it means a lot to me and of course to Valerie," Carolyn told her.

Ella smiled. "I'm going to be ok, you know that, I've moved on."

Carolyn looked at her friend, she could hear the words but she still wasn't sure that Ella really meant it.

She glanced over her shoulder. "Is Marcus just dropping you off then?"

"Hell no, he's my date for the day," Ella chuckled.

"Oh, I see."

"Don't act so surprised. You know that there's always been an attraction between us, you can't deny it."

"You are playing with his emotions, Ella; you know how deeply he cares for you," Carolyn warned her.

"And I care about him, he is everything Dante wasn't."

"It's early days, Ella, just take your time, all I'm saying is please don't rush into something you may regret."

"Oh, don't worry. I'm not on the rebound if that's what you think!" she laughed.

"I'm not saying that, I just want you to take it slowly."

"Why?" She waved over to Marcus as he got out of the car. "I could do worse, in fact I did do worse!" She laughed at her own wit. "He is an open book, no hidden depths to him, what you see is what you get."

"It's your life I suppose."

"Yes, it is."

Marcus walked towards them. "So, where is the bride?"

"Oh, she's in the toilet re-applying her lipstick, speaking of which –" Carolyn pulled her lipstick out of her bag "– I'll go check and see if she's all right, keep an eye out for Giorgino."

"But I don't know what he looks like!" Ella shouted after her.

"It's ok, we should be able to spot him, he's arriving with Andrew." Marcus put his arm around her. "Did I tell you how beautiful you look?"

It was a gorgeous summer's day and Ella was wearing a cream short-sleeve dress which clung to her perfect body like a second skin. "Why thank you, you don't look too bad yourself."

"Nico and Grazia will be arriving at the end of the week," he told her.

"So, why are you telling me?"

"I just wanted you to know in case you bump into them at the office."

"It's no big deal. Oh, look! There's Andrew." Carolyn had done well for herself, her fiancé was a handsome-looking man, tall blond and bronzed. "He looks nothing like a big shot lawyer does he, more like a male model!" Ella giggled.

"Yes, I suppose so."

"I can just imagine him modelling some speedos!" she giggled once more. "Oh dear, I'd better get that image out of my head!"

"Yes, you better." Marcus gently stroked her back.

Andrew introduced the groom. "This is Giorgino Vitelli. I would like to introduce you to Marcus Treymayne and Ella Moretti."

"Er... no, Ella Reynolds," she corrected him.

"I'm so sorry, Ella, I can't believe I just said that." Andrew put his hand over his mouth and went crimson.

"So nice to meet you." Marcus shook Vitelli's hand.

"You are friends of Valerie?" the young man asked as he stared at Ella's flawless complexion. Wow, she really was stunning close up, he thought, no wonder Dante had fallen for her.

"I'm afraid I haven't had the pleasure of meeting her yet," Marcus admitted.

"He's my date for the day," Ella explained. "Valerie is a lovely woman, you are very lucky."

"Yes, I am very lucky indeed," Vitelli admitted. He hadn't meant to fall in love with her not with her past history, but she had such a sweet nature that he couldn't help himself.

Ella smiled at him. "So, you were born here in London?"

"Yes, a London-born Italian," he laughed.

"You better hadn't keep the bride waiting," Andrew told him.

"Very well." Vitelli smoothed down his suit and combed his jet black curly hair. "Will I do?"

"Yes very handsome," Ella told him. "Now let's go."

The ceremony only lasted ten minutes and Ella couldn't help but wipe a tear away as they sealed their marriage with a kiss.

"Are you all right?" Marcus whispered into her ear.

"I always cry at weddings," she admitted.

Thank goodness for that, he thought she was having some kind of flashback.

Ella had taken it upon herself to hire a stretch limousine to take them all to the wedding reception. It was the least she could do and together with Carolyn they had booked a surprise week-long break in the Lake District for the happy couple.

Carolyn was busy being the photographer for the day, despite Valerie's protests. "I don't like to have my pictures taken, you know that."

"Darling, it's your wedding day, just let me take a few and I promise I will not take anymore."

Gio held his wife's hands. "Just a few."

"Ok, you win."

They posed beside a rose bush in full bloom which delighted Carolyn. "Oh, that looks wonderful, I think this one should be your main wedding picture, it will look perfect mounted in a gilded frame, just perfect," she gushed.

"I want to throw the bouquet now," Valerie told her.

"But don't you want to do that at the reception?"

"No, it will be better here." Secretly Valerie hoped that Carolyn would catch it and there was every chance as there was only Ella, Natasha and Zeta. She would close her eyes and aim it in her direction.

"Come on ladies, let's move back," Carolyn told them.

"Count me out," Ella laughed.

"Oh, please, Ella, it's just a bit of fun." Carolyn winked at her.

"Go on," Marcus encouraged her,

Tutting Ella went to take her place in the line.

"Ok, after three, one, two, three." Valerie threw the bouquet up into the air.

The women all made a dash for it and Ella just stood in a trance and was amazed when they landed directly into her arms. "Oh, you've got to be kidding me, here." She passed them to Carolyn.

Marcus laughed. "Don't tar all men with the same brush, Ella, we're not all bad."

"I know that!"

Valerie clapped her hands when she saw the white stretch limousine. "Oh my God, is that for us!"

"Of course," Carolyn told her. "And I have something else for you, from me and Ella."

"Oh, what is it?" She ripped open the envelope. "Oh, thank you, look." She gave Vitelli the paper.

"It's a trip to Windermere in the Lake District for a week, how wonderful." He kissed Valerie. "Well Mrs Vitelli, what a wonderful present."

"Yes, yes it is we can't thank you enough, it was so thoughtful of you." Valerie hugged Carolyn and then Ella. "You are both so kind."

Esposito's successor Franco Gianelli was sitting in the car park totally stunned. Surely it couldn't be her, could it? He grabbed his binoculars from the glove box and focused on her face. When he saw the distinctive mole just above her lip he dropped them in shock. Jesus Christ, it was her, Dante Moretti's sister! Vitelli had just unwittingly married his arch enemy's sister, Rosa.

Chapter Ninety-Six

Milan, Italy
The Moretti Residence

Dante cast his mind back to the meeting with Vasiliev; he had sworn that he had nothing to do with capturing him on video. He was an impossible man to read and he couldn't tell if he was lying or not. Deep down he knew that he must have ordered the taping of the last minutes of Garshin's life and he couldn't help but wonder if there were other copies. Vasiliev had promised him that he and Petrov had taken out Garshin's associates along with the original recording of the murder.

He still missed Ella, but Luciana was a distraction for him, every time he made love to her he pretended that it was his ex-wife. Against his will he had forced himself to cut off all ties with her. It was for her own protection, he told himself, one day she would realise that.

"Darling, dinner is ready." Luciana stuck her head around the door.

Glancing up Dante smiled. "I'll be with you shortly, sweetheart." She was very pretty, he thought, with her long cascading dark hair and her big brown eyes and olive skin, but she wasn't in the same league as Ella and it pained him to think of her taking up with Marcus Treymayne.

"Are you all right?"

"Yes, fine, just finishing off, five minutes." Nico had told him all about the visit to England; it was nearly a month ago now and he still couldn't get the vision of them together out of his head. He had demanded to know every detail. Grazia had said how wonderful Ella looked and how Marcus doted on her. Dante pretended to be happy that she had moved on, but no matter how much he tried to push her to the back of his mind, she still kept reappearing.

He shook the thoughts from his mind and concentrated on the disk in front of him, Vasiliev was on the top of the hit list and now he had hard evidence to back it up. His own name was second on the list, along with Aleksei Petrov and Nico de Luca. He wasn't quite sure what he was going to do with it, but if he sent it anonymously to the police then he, too, would be arrested with the rest of them. Shaking his head he couldn't believe the type of people that were mixed up in the trafficking business, men and women of all ranks, politicians, actors, socialites, the list was endless.

The knock on the door made him jump. "Yes," he said as he ejected the disk and hurriedly locked it in the safe.

Luciana wondered what he was up to. Vasiliev was paying her good money to keep a close eye on him and if he was planning something then she had to find out what it was. He carried the key with him at all times and it was virtually impossible to take it without him finding out, but somehow she had to find a way.

"I told you I'm coming!" Dante snapped.

"All right, keep your hair on," she tutted at him. "I went to a lot of trouble preparing this meal for you."

"I know, sweetheart, and I appreciate it," he said softly. "You are an excellent cook, nearly as good as my chef."

"Oh, that's sweet of you to say so, darling."

"I'm off to London tomorrow, so let's make it an early night."

"Oh, that's sudden."

"Yes, there's been another incident; Gianelli is up to his neck in it."

"Just be careful darling, that's all I ask."

"I'm always careful," Dante laughed. Gianelli was on his way out; he had been fucking around with the cargo and had passed some of the girls on to his own business associates. He was drawing unnecessary attention and it couldn't go on any longer, the fucker must have thought he had gone soft or something.

He tucked into the plate of pasta. "Perfect."

"Yes, you need to keep your strength up," Luciana giggled. "Your body is mine tonight!"

Dante smiled at her, but he really couldn't be bothered with her she was over him like a rash. His mind turned to the possibility of seeing Ella again.

Chapter Ninety-Seven

London, England

Franco Gianelli was surprised that Moretti hadn't even made a move against him, maybe he was losing his touch after all, he thought. No matter, he would continue helping himself until he did.

Dante had brought two sidekicks, Flavio and Carmine, who knew how to watch his back.

Franco was busy in his restaurant making his speciality, spicy Italian meatballs in his secret sauce that his customers loved so much. He was startled when Dante burst through the kitchen door and lunged right at him. Getting him in a head lock he shoved his head towards the huge pan, allowing the steam to sear his face.

"Stop, stop!" he shrieked.

Dante punched him in the guts and Franco dropped to the floor gasping for breath. "So, why are you ripping us off?" he demanded as he kicked him in the head.

"R… Rosa."

"Don't you dare mention my sister's name!" he grabbed the kitchen knife off the table. "I'm going to gut you like a fish, you fucker!"

Franco held his hands up to protect his face. "It's true… Rosa is alive… I've seen her."

Dante dropped the knife, which narrowly missed Franco's head; he leaned back onto the kitchen unit. "What…? Why the fuck would you say something like that?" his voice was incredulous.

"I'm telling you the truth." Franco tried to get to his feet, but Dante was too quick for him and held him down by shoving his foot into his throat and pressing it so hard that his eyes were rolling back into his head.

Carmine had to physically pull his boss away from Gianelli who was struggling for breath. "Dante, if he's telling the truth…"

"All right." Dante glared at him. "I'm waiting!"

"I... want to... to... cut a... deal... first," Gianelli gasped.

"Deal? A deal with a fucker like you? Tell me where she is and then if it checks out, perhaps we will cut a deal."

"She... works in the Reid centre."

"The Reid Centre." He racked his brains. Shit, it was Carolyn Reid's place, Ella's best friend.

"There... there's something... something else."

"Spit it out." Dante's voice was hard and emotionless, he couldn't grasp what this meant, all this time he thought that Rosa was dead and she had virtually been under his nose.

"She's married... to... Vitelli."

"Vitelli? Are you fucking joking me or what!"

"It... it's true."

Dante completely flipped out and lifted the pan of sauce off the cooker; he poured the scorching liquid onto the helpless Franco. He screamed like a stuffed pig as the sauce burnt through his flesh.

Carmine was baulking, the smell was disgusting and the noise coming from Gianelli sent shivers down his spine.

"Finish it!" he barked to him.

Carmine picked up the kitchen knife and rammed it into his chest, but the fucker still wouldn't die. His arms and legs were flailing wildly as he made a last ditch attempt to grab Dante's feet.

"If I want something done right I guess I have to do it myself!" He picked up the rolling pin and bashed him over the head, cracking his skull. "Be still you fucker, don't fight it anymore, it's over."

Several seconds passed. "Check his pulse!" Dante ordered.

Flavio was keeping watch at the door. "We better go out the back, now, his men are coming."

Carmine grabbed Gianelli's wrist, there was nothing. "He's dead all right."

"Thank fuck for that, now let's get out of here, I need to get this stench off me."

Chapter Ninety-Eight

Dante sat outside the centre just staring at the building. He had no idea what he was going to do, he wanted to see if it was true. He caught his breath when he saw Ella pull up, but his heart sank when he saw that she was with Marcus Treymayne. It didn't take him long to muscle in, he thought, and it certainly hadn't taken Ella long to forget about him. For a split second all he wanted to do was rush over, punch Treymayne in the guts and take Ella back to Menaggio with him, but right now that wasn't an option.

When he saw Ella stroke his face he nearly lost it, clenching the steering wheel until his knuckles went white he reminded himself why he was here: it was for Rosa, not Ella. He looked at his watch, there was no sign of his sister and his flight was due to leave. Gianelli had been taken care of and hopefully the business would now be back on track. Cursing he turned the ignition, he would leave Flavio to find out where his sister was living and then he would take the appropriate action to bring her home. As for Vitelli, it pained him that Rosa had married him, but there was not a lot he could do about that right now.

He flipped open his mobile. "Carmine meet me at the airport, put Flavio on the line."

"Yes?"

"You are to stay here and watch the centre. When you see Rosa follow her, find out everything you can about her, and Flavio?"

"Yes boss?"

"If Vitelli rumbles you, kill him." He put the car into gear and sped off.

*****

"Valerie, Giorgino, how was your trip to the Lake District?" Ella smiled.

"Oh, wonderful. It was so peaceful and relaxing, it was like being in another world, all that unspoilt countryside, it was totally mesmerizing," Valerie enthused.

"The only thing that spoilt it was all the tourists!" Gio joked.

"I wanted to ask you something." Ella's voice was serious. "Why don't you stay at my house until you get your deposit together?"

"Oh, that's far too generous," Valerie told her. "We'd be happy anywhere, wouldn't we, Gio?"

"Of course we would, darling." He kissed her on the cheek.

"It would be my pleasure, I mean it's sitting there all empty, you would be doing me a favour," Ella persisted.

"Oh, I don't know, we may cramp your style."

"Gio, the house is huge, you will have one wing of the house and I will have the other, we will barely see each other."

"What do you think, Valerie?" Gio took her hand. "It's a good offer until we get the money together for our own little love nest."

"Why not? Thank you so much Ella, it is really kind of you."

"Not at all, here –" she passed them the key and a piece of paper with the code number for the alarm "– just memorise it and eat it."

"What?"

"I'm just kidding," Ella laughed.

"So, when can we move in?" Gio asked.

"Whenever you like, I've told Maria, my housekeeper, she'll be expecting you, I've asked her to cook you a romantic meal tonight, so why don't you pick up what you need and get the rest tomorrow."

"Sounds like a plan." Gio shook her hand. "We'll never forget your generosity." If only she knew what he had made her mother do, and now he was returning to the scene of his own crime.

"That's settled then." Ella took Marcus' arm. "Got room for one tonight?" She looked up into his handsome face.

"Er… you want to stay with me?" He blushed.

"Is that a refusal?" She winked at Valerie and Gio.

"Are you serious?"

"Perfectly serious."

Marcus beamed from ear to ear. He couldn't believe his luck, after all this time, she was finally going to be his, he was nervous and excited at the same time.

When they got outside of the building Ella threw the car keys at him. "Here, you drive."

"Are you sure about this? I mean, I wouldn't want you to regret it tomorrow," Marcus told her.

"Shush, don't say a word." She leaned over and rubbed his thigh. "You have great muscle definition."

Marcus was shocked at her forwardness and swerved the car. "Whoa, I'm driving remember, we don't want to have an accident."

"You're so sensible, Marcus, that's what I adore about you."

Adore, he smiled, so finally she adored him, that was a turn up for the books. He knew that she would never love him like she loved Moretti, but adore was certainly a good start. He accelerated hard.

"What's the rush?"

"I just want to get you back to my house before you change your mind."

"Oh, I won't change my mind, Marcus, you see, I need you."

"You know how long I have waited to hear you say that?"

"No, do you want to tell me?" she laughed as he sped up the driveway and came to a sudden halt.

He leaned over to her. "I think I have always loved you, ever since I first set eyes on you."

"Really?"

"Absolutely." He kissed her and she responded eagerly.

"What are we waiting for Marcus?" she whispered as she put his hand on her breast.

"My God, Ella, behave, the neighbours will see." But he was enjoying every second; the feel of her perfectly formed body was driving him crazy with desire. Without warning he jumped out of the car and dashed around to open the door for her.

"My, you are keen." Ella giggled as she grabbed him by the lapels and passionately kissed him. "You are a wonderful kisser."

"That's the best compliment I have ever had."

"Really? Then I must compliment you more often." She held his hand as he opened the front door.

Slamming it shut behind them Ella kissed him once more as she unfastened her dress and slid out of it.

"My God you are incredibly beautiful."

She started to unfasten his shirt and playfully kissed his smooth chest as she did so. "Take me to your boudoir, Mr Treymayne."

"It will be my pleasure, I can assure you." Marcus took her hand and led her into his bedroom. "Last chance to change your mind," he whispered into her ear as he unfastened her bra.

"Just make love to me, Marcus," she sighed, as he obliged.

It felt strange being with someone else after Dante, she didn't feel the same passion, the same excitement. She felt Marcus' breath on her and looked up at him.

"Are you ok?" he said gently, noticing a tear in her eye.

"After that, are you kidding?" But all Ella could think about was Dante. Marcus was a kind and gentle man and she was happy to settle for second best.

"Ella, we've known each other quite a while now, how would you feel about becoming Mrs Treymayne?" His heart thudded in his chest; he couldn't believe the words had just came out of his mouth.

"Why not?" she replied, feeling safe in the warmth of his arms. She didn't want to be alone anymore and Marcus doted on her.

"Really?"

"Really, Now, how about we order a takeaway I'm starving." She patted her rumbling stomach.

"Sure." Marcus pulled on his trousers and went down stairs for a menu. Did that really happen? he thought, as he pinched himself? Ella Reynolds had just agreed to be his wife and he should be the happiest man in the world. The only thing that bothered him was Dante Moretti; he could never live up to him and hoped that he would be enough to keep Ella.

Just then she appeared wearing only his white shirt which was way too big for her. "Did you mean that, that you really want to marry me?"

"Yes I did, why? Have you decided to turn me down?"

"No, I would be happy and delighted to become your wife," she told him as she stood on her tiptoes to kiss him.

"There's just one thing I need to ask you, Ella."

"I'm listening."

"Are you still in love with Dante Moretti?" There he had asked it.

"No, I admit it took me a while to get over him, but I can assure you he is in the past and definitely staying there."

"Glad to hear it. Now what will it be, Chinese, Indian, Mexican?"

"How about a nice Englishman?" She grabbed his hand and dragged him back upstairs.

"What about the food?" he laughed.

"The food can wait, but I can't!"

"Then I will be happy to oblige."

Chapter Ninety-Nine

Milan, Italy

Dante burst into the de Lucas' house. "Nico, Nico, where are you?" he shouted.

"What's all the commotion about?" Grazia was standing at the foot of the stairs.

"Where's Nico?"

"He's just getting out of the shower. Come, I will make you some coffee while you wait," she offered.

"Thanks." Dante followed her into the huge kitchen.

"So, did you see Ella?"

"Yes, I did."

"And?"

"And nothing." Dante was miles away; he was staring out of the window taking in the landscape. It was like being in a different world and, right now, he wished he was.

"I don't understand." Grazia passed him a mug of coffee.

"She's taken up with Marcus Treymayne," he admitted. "It was too late to do anything."

"I'm sorry about that Dante, but you know you should never have let her go in the first place." She regretted saying the words as soon as they came out of her mouth.

"You're right, but she looked happy and I couldn't bring myself to interfere with that. I've done enough to her, she deserves better."

"Never mind, you have Luciana now."

"Yes, I have Luciana." He laughed as he sipped his coffee.

"Dante, you're back earlier than I expected." Nico walked over to greet him. "How was the trip?"

"I think I'll leave you boys to it, I'm off to get my hair done." She kissed her husband as she left the room.

Nico poured a coffee. "So, did you find out why Gianelli was taking the piss?"

"He's not a problem to us anymore and good fucking riddance!"

"You weren't supposed to kill him."

"There were no witnesses, we were in and out." Dante looked at him, wondering whether to confide in him.

"There's something else on your mind, what is it, Ella?"

"Partly."

"Look, sit down and explain because I can tell that you are holding something back."

Dante sat down opposite him. "It's my sister, Rosa."

"What about her?"

"She isn't dead," he said seriously.

"How do you know, have you seen her?" Nico was gobsmacked. "I thought that she was dead," he whispered.

"I always assumed that she was, until Gianelli told me otherwise."

"I'm sorry; I'm a little confused by what you are trying to say."

"Rosa is alive and well, living in London."

"That's fantastic news! Why didn't you bring her back with you?"

"I wish it were that simple. You see, not only does she work in a centre for trafficked women, she is also married to Giorgino Vitelli!"

"Good God." Nico dropped his cup. "Fuck!" Jumping up he pulled off his trousers. "Damn it!"

"You want to get some ice on that," Dante laughed at him.

Nico nodded as he got some ice out of the freezer and wrapped it up in a towel. He sat back down and held it on his burnt thigh. "Shit that stings!"

"It's only a little red mark Nico, don't be so fucking dramatic!"

"So, have you spoken to her?"

"No."

"Have you seen her then?"

"No."

"Well, not being funny man, how the fuck do you know that Gianelli wasn't just winding you up?"

"Maybe, but if he was telling the truth I will find out soon enough."

"Dare I ask if you saw Ella?"

"Yes I fucking saw her with Treymayne and he was all over her!" He slammed his fist on the table. "Just couldn't fucking wait to move in on my woman."

"You divorced her, remember," Nico reminded him.

"I didn't have much choice, remember?" Dante said sarcastically. "And one day some fucker will pay for it!"

"Whoa, calm down; let's just focus on the business in hand."

Dante composed himself. "Yes, you're right."

Chapter One Hundred

London, England

"Let's not tell anyone Marcus, you know how judgmental Carolyn is. Let's just take off to Gretna Green and get married over the anvil. It will be just you and I and a couple of witnesses, which we can drag in off the street, what do you say?" Ella chattered.

"Are you serious?"

"Totally, why don't we just pack a bag, say we're going away for a week and come back as Mr and Mrs Treymayne?"

"I'm not sure, Ella, don't you want to wait for a while, to make sure it's what you really want?"

"Are you backing out on me?" she laughed.

"Definitely not, I can't wait for you to become my wife."

"So, let's go tomorrow then, we can pick up some outfits on the way!"

"My God, slow down, what's the rush?"

"There's no rush I suppose," she sulked.

"Are you sulking?"

"What do you think?"

He leaned over and kissed her. "If that's what you want then that's what we'll do."

"Oh, fantastic, I knew you would see it my way." She clapped her hands excitedly.

"Now how about one more time as single people?" He reached for her but she was too quick for him.

"Sorry Marcus but you will have to wait until that ring is on my finger, speaking of which we'd better go shopping."

"Ella… come back to bed," he groaned. "You can't tease me like this."

"You only have to wait a day or so."

"Only?" He picked up the pillow and threw it at her. "Get some clothes on before I take drastic action and ravage you!" he chuckled.

"I'm going for a shower and I suggest you do the same."

"Is that some kind of invitation?"

"Definitely not, use your guestroom facilities!" She tossed back her blonde hair and blew him a kiss. "It will be even better once we're wed, trust me!"

"Just get out of here!" He threw another pillow at her as she vanished into the en suite. She was going to be his wife, he couldn't believe his luck. He would treat her with the respect she deserved. Dante's loss was definitely his gain.

His thoughts were interrupted by the bedside telephone. "Hello?"

"Marcus, how are you?"

"I'm very well thanks, what can I do for you?"

"Grazia and I would like to invite you over for the weekend."

"Oh, that's very kind of you, but I have plans."

"That's a shame, Grazia was so looking forward to seeing you, and Ella of course."

"Ella?"

"Yes, you are an item aren't you?"

"How do you know?"

"I'm not a fool, I've seen the way you look at her, the way you talk to her, you will look after her won't you?"

"Why all the concern about Ella?" Marcus couldn't understand where Nico was coming from.

"I like her very much and after Dante I wanted to make sure that she is going to be ok."

"What business is it of yours?" Marcus was incensed, how dare he question him like this? "Moretti was bad news, you know it, I know it and, most of all, Ella knew it, that's why she is no longer with him!"

"I'm sorry. I didn't mean to offend you."

"It's all right, I know Grazia cares about her, but tell her we'll come over in a couple of weeks."

"I will." Nico replaced the receiver and looked at Dante. "Well you heard what the man said, she's ok, you have to move on, she obviously has."

Dante clenched and unclenched his fists, Treymayne wasn't right for her and now there was no going back. "Ok."

"You all right?"

"Fine, I'll let you get on." Dante was just about to leave when his mobile went off, it was Flavio. "Yes?"

"I've seen her, Rosa; she's staying at the Reynolds' house," he told him.

Dante nearly dropped the phone. "You what, she's staying with Ella?"

"No, it looks like Ella has taken a trip with Treymayne."

"Ok, don't approach her, I'll be over tomorrow and then we'll decide how best to handle it."

"Who was that?" Nico asked him.

"Flavio, he's seen Rosa."

"Do you want me to come with you?"

"No, this is something I have to do on my own."

"Just be gentle with her, she must have been through hell, the poor girl."

"Don't worry, she's the last of my family and I won't do anything to jeopardize that," Dante reassured him. "I'm bringing her home."

"And Vitelli?"

"I'll just have to wait and see how it all plays out, but one thing is for sure, he has got no future with my sister!"

Nico watched him as he jumped into his Maserati Spyder and sped off. He couldn't help but think that it was all going to end in disaster.

Chapter One Hundred and One

Gretna Green, Scotland

"I booked separate rooms for us tonight," Ella told him.

"Really?" Marcus groaned.

"I told you that we weren't going to be together again until our wedding night!"

"You're a hard woman!"

"You better believe it, just be hard for me tomorrow night!"

"Ella...! Sometimes you completely take me by surprise," he gasped.

"As long as I can keep you on your toes, that's good enough for me."

"I can't wait until after the wedding!" he admitted. "And I can't believe that you are going to be my wife, I keep thinking I am dreaming!"

"I can assure you, it is not a dream." She pinched his bum as he got out of the car.

"Right, now we must be sensible and go and sort the paperwork out with the registrar, make sure everything is in place for tomorrow," Marcus reminded her.

"I promise you that I will be a good wife."

"I know you will." He put his arm around her as she snuggled into his chest. "What about your dress?"

"Hopefully it should be hanging up in my room."

They checked into The Blacksmith's Cottage. It was warm and inviting and the wedding coordinator was at hand to discuss the final details.

"Look Marcus." Ella pointed to the plaque.

"Named after John Linton, Gretna Hall's famous wedding blacksmith of the 1800s."

"By signing our marriage document at his table we will become part of 200 years of history, tradition and romance. How romantic is that?" Ella looked up into his eyes and stroked his face.

"I'm Mrs McDougall," a stout middle-aged woman introduced herself. Beckoning she added, "Please follow me to the office. Thank you so much for choosing us for your special day, you will love the venue I promise you. How many guests do you have?"

"We hoped that we could pull in two witnesses off the street so to speak," Marcus announced.

"I'm sorry dear, but it doesn't work that way."

Marcus' heart sank. "Are you telling me that we came all this way and we can't get married?"

"Not at all, dear, we have professional witnesses; I'll make a few calls," she reassured him. "Now I must talk to your future wife in private."

"Ella?"

"Go and have a pint or something, I'll see you really soon."

"All right."

"He's seems very charming and I must say you make a lovely couple," Mrs McDougall told her with complete sincerity.

"Yes, he is a wonderful man," Ella agreed.

"I'll sort out the witnesses, that's no problem. What about the cake, the reception, the music?"

"I quite like the idea of the piper, that would be quite lovely."

"That is an excellent choice."

"We want it simple, you know, no fuss, a cake and reception are not necessary."

"What about a nice bottle of champagne and chocolates in the honeymoon suite?"

"Yes, please, is there anything else?"

"Just a meeting ten minutes prior to the reception."

"Shall I pay you now?"

"It's ok lassie Mr Treymayne has already asked for everything to be billed to him." She winked. "He is totally besotted with you."

"Have you ever seen *Pride and Prejudice*?" Ella almost giggled as she had an insane vision of Dante coming to stop the wedding.

"Of course lassie, doesn't it have that famous scene in it, the one where the furious father races after his daughter to stop her marrying and of course arrives after the event," she chortled.

"Yes, that's the one, funny isn't it how things stick in your mind?" But it won't be my father who rescues me, she thought.

"Yes it is, now is there anything else I can do for you?"

"Tell me more about marrying over the anvil."

"Well, the anvil is the lasting symbol of Gretna Green weddings and in times gone by the local blacksmiths were known as 'anvil priests'. As a forger the blacksmith marries hot metal to metal over the anvil to signify the union between man and woman," she explained.

"It's so quaint, I mean it's almost like stepping back in time, the history of this place is quite fascinating."

"And of course we are one of the most popular wedding venues in the world, in fact we have many foreigners coming over year after year to tie the knot, that's how special this place is."

"Just one last question."

"What is it lassie?" Mrs McDougall peered down her half-rimmed glasses.

"How old is this place?"

"It's been around since the early seventeenth century."

"Wow." Ella stood up and shook her hand. "Thank you for your assistance I, or should I say we, both appreciate it."

"Anything to help, now enjoy your last night of freedom."

Ella forced a smile, if only she knew that this was her second marriage and that her first husband was a cold-blooded murderer. She stifled a laugh as she left the room, all this was insane, leaning against the door she toyed with the idea of doing a runner, but it was too late now, she had committed herself to Marcus and now she had to make the best of it for both their sakes. Yet Dante would always be in her thoughts and she would always have a place in her heart for him. Pulling herself together, she marched into the bar.

"All sorted?" Marcus beamed at her.

"Everything is under control."

"Glass of wine?"

"Dry white would be nice, thank you."

Marcus passed the glass to her. "Here's to us."

Ella raised her glass and hoped that she wasn't making a terrible mistake. "To us."

The pub started filling up with loved-up couples and Ella couldn't stop thinking about Dante, the more she drank the more she wanted to call him. "I think I'm going to have an early night." She kissed Marcus on the cheek.

"Ok, my darling, I will see you at eleven, and don't be late."

"I won't." Ella was relieved to be alone in her room; she opened a bottle of wine and slowly sipped it. The more she drank the more she was tempted to pick up the phone and dial his number. She looked out of the window and saw the bright northern star. *I wish I may I wish I might have the first wish of the night*, she thought, *I wish Dante would tell me that he wanted me back.*

She picked up the phone and rang reception. "I want to make a long-distance call to Menaggio, Italy please," she told the operator.

"Certainly."

She waited patiently as the telephone rang. Jesus, if he answered what would she say? Slamming down the phone she decided to run a bath, try to relax, this foolishness would have to stop before she ruined everything.

Putting on MTV she turned it up as loud as she dared and sank into the foam-filled bath, it felt good, she closed her eyes. Marrying Marcus wasn't so bad, he was a lovely genuine man, she told herself.

Dante checked his missed calls and didn't recognise the last number, intrigued he dialled ring back.

"Good evening, The Blacksmith's Cottage, can I help you?"

"Er… somebody just placed a call to me."

"Where to and I can check which room number it was?"

"Menaggio, Italy."

"Oh, yes that was Miss Reynolds, would you like me to try and put you through sir?"

"Yes." Dante's heart pounded. She'd rang him! Actually rang him.

"I'm sorry sir there's no answer, can I take a message."

"Where is this place?"

"This is Gretna Green in Scotland."

"Is she attending someone's wedding?"

"No, I believe she is getting married in the morning sir, do you want to leave a message?"

"No, it doesn't matter." He put the phone down. Devastated wasn't the word for how he felt. No doubt Treymayne was the lucky man. Pushing it to the back of his mind he thought of Rosa, she was the only thing that he had left now and he had to make sure she came home, no matter what.

The following morning Marcus went to pay the bill, his heart nearly stopped when he saw the long-distance call. "What is this?" he asked the receptionist.

"Oh, there's no charge sir, Miss Reynolds never got connected." After paying the bill he went outside and banged his fist into the wall. What the hell was Ella doing to him? If she still loved Moretti then what was she doing with him, how could she be so cruel? He tossed the truth around in his head – did she want an escape route? Is that why she rang Moretti or was she waiting for him to come and rescue her? Maybe he should have it out with her once and for all, or maybe he should say nothing? All he knew was that he loved her, wanted her more than anything in the world and nothing was going to come between them, least of all Dante Moretti.

Chapter One Hundred and Two

London, England

Flavio watched as Rosa Moretti entered the centre. Finally, he thought. He'd been sitting waiting for days and he was bored rigid. Now all he had to do was wait until she left, somehow get her on her own, tell her about her brother.

Several hours later he tailed her to the Reynolds' house. He dialled Dante's number. "It's me, your sister has just arrived at the house, what do you want me to do?"

"Is she alone?"

"Yes, Vitelli's just left."

"Right, this is what I want you to do," Dante explained.

"Very well boss."

Flavio rang the bell on the gate and waited patiently.

"Who is it?" Valerie asked not recognising the tall, slim man.

"Is that Rosa Moretti?"

Valerie let go of the intercom button. Jesus Christ somebody had come for her, she had to get out of there and fast. Putting a hand to her chest she reached for her inhaler.

"Rosa, I'm not here to harm you, Dante sent me."

"How do I know that you are telling the truth?"

"He said that you would say that, wait a minute I'll get him on the mobile." Quickly he punched in Dante's number and pressed it to the intercom.

"Rosa!" Dante yelled as loud as he could. "It's me Rosa, let Flavio in, can you hear me?"

All she could hear was loud, screeching static.

"I don't think she can hear you, just hang on, let me try again." He left the phone line open. "I swear your brother sent me, he just wants to talk to you."

But Rosa was scared, how could she trust this stranger? He could be anyone, someone from the past come back to kill her. "Please just leave."

Flavio relayed her response down the mobile.

"Fuck it, tell her I know that her favourite colour is blue, her first boyfriend was called Stefano and she named the little black stray cat Brios because of her love for croissants."

Flavio repeated exactly what he was told.

Rosa gasped, it must be her brother – it was the cat that clinched it, nobody knew it existed only her and Dante. "Nobody is supposed to know where I am, I have a new identity, a husband." She panicked.

"I've got her attention now boss, shall I ring you back, when she let's me in?"

"No, keep the line open." Dante paced up and down his office, he had to speak to her. Until he did then he would not quite believe it.

Luciana held her breath as she listened outside the door, she knew Dante was agitated with all the thudding around he was doing and the mention of Rosa Moretti made her ears prick up. She knew that he had a sister who disappeared although he had never discussed it with her, perhaps this news would be of interest to Vasiliev?

Rosa let Flavio into the house. "You should not be here; you are putting me and everyone around me in great danger."

Flavio passed his mobile to her.

She stood and stared at it. What was she going to say to him after all these years? She wasn't that slip of a girl anymore and she was frightened of his reaction. She put the phone to her ear. "Hello?"

"Rosa, is that you? You sound remarkably English."

"I had years of intense lessons to pull this off, so that no one would suspect my true identity."

"Rosa, you must come home, you belong here."

"Dante, if only you knew what happened to me, you would not want to know me."

"You are my sister, my flesh and blood, just come home, I promise you that you will be safe."

"I can't do that, my life is here now, I want no part of my past, I'm sorry, Dante." She flatly refused to change her mind.

"Rosa, I remember you were stubborn but not this stubborn."

"I have a husband now and friends, they know nothing of you, nothing of my real name, I cannot risk losing them."

"But I am your family."

"I have no family anymore." Her voice was hard and unemotional.

"But father sent me off to Sicily; I didn't know anything about your kidnap until a couple of years later when I finally got it out of the old bastard!"

"It doesn't matter, nothing will change what happened."

"I tried everything to find you, I promise you."

Rosa passed the phone back to Flavio. "Please I want you to leave now before my husband comes home."

Flavio stood there. "Boss, she's asking me to leave."

"Tell her not to do this; I am her family not Vitelli!" he yelled.

"He asks you to reconsider."

"Leave now and never come back here." Rosa pointed to the door. "I mean it. Tell my brother he is dead to me."

"I'm sorry Boss, I did my best," Flavio told him as he sat on the car bonnet. "What else can I do? She was adamant."

"She takes after me, very stubborn." There was nothing for it, he would have to personally fly over, see her in person, persuade her to come home and, if that failed, he would have to kidnap her himself.

Rosa was shaking from head to toe, Giorgino would be home any minute and she would not be able to lie to him. Perhaps now was the time to sit him down and tell him the truth. She poured a strong cup of tea and sat in the chair waiting for her husband. Dante would not let this lie, he would come for her, of that she was totally sure, so it was better to tell Gio now.

"Valerie, I'm home, where are you?"

"I'm in the conservatory." Her heart felt like it was going to explode out of her chest. The only person she had fully confided the truth in was Sheila Reid and she was long dead. Gio loved her, he would understand, she told herself, and together they would decide what to do for the best.

"Some house this isn't it?" Gio kissed her. "You look serious, is something wrong?"

"You'd better sit down. I think it's time I told you all about who I really am."

"I told you, I don't care about any of it, it's all in the past just let it go." He gently rubbed her arm.

"Gio, please sit down, something's happened."

Sensing the urgency in her voice he obediently sat down and clasped his hands. "What is it?"

"It's someone from my past, they know where I am."

Gio jumped to his feet in a rage. "Who the fuck is it? Tell me, I won't have anyone putting the frighteners on my wife!"

Rosa felt intimidated by his sudden outburst, this was the first time she had ever seen him like this.

"I'm sorry my love, I didn't mean to scare you." Realising he had to calm down he took a sharp intake of breath and sat back down. "Go on."

"My brother sent someone here, to this house, he wants to see me."

"Why is it so bad?"

"I haven't seen him for years. I can't bear the thought of him looking at with me with disgust, because I just know that he will."

"Why would your brother judge you? It wasn't your fault what happened to you, I thought you stopped blaming yourself and anyway what possible harm can it do?" Gio didn't understand.

"The shame I brought on him, the family, it was better them all thinking I was dead. Do you really think I want to explain to everyone where I have been all this time? It would be like re-living it all over again."

"Whatever you decide to do will be fine with me, just don't regret your decision, think long and hard, this may be the only opportunity you'll ever get to make your peace."

"You do talk sense at times."

"Yes, just some times!" he joked. "So are you going to tell me who you really are now?"

"I thought you didn't care about that." Rosa wasn't sure, yes he was her husband, but he was of Italian descent and she didn't really know who he was.

"Then I'll say no more about it."

"I think I'll take a long hot soak in the tub."

"Ok, darling, I'll make us some dinner," he told her as he watched her leave the room. Intrigued he went into the surveillance room and checked the video tape. He wound it back and paused it: fucking hell, it was one of Moretti's sidekicks. What the fuck did that mean? Her brother sent someone, but who the fuck was her brother? He jumped out of his seat. My God, why had he not seen it before? Valerie had the exact same eyes as Dante – Jesus, he was her brother! He bent over double and laughed a rip-roaring laugh, which thankfully Valerie, or rather Rosa Moretti, wouldn't hear on the other side of the house. How fucking ironic. He rubbed his hands together. Now he finally he had his revenge on the bastard, wait until he found out who his lovely sister was married to. It was fucking bizarre and hilarious at the same time! He would encourage her to invite him over, meet him together. Just to see the look on the fucker's face when he saw them, ha! That would be a fucking picture he would never forget. He could just imagine his reaction and then his lovely sister would really see his true colours and, once his temper got the better of him Valerie would want nothing to do with him. Then Dante would really lose his sister for good. Gio rubbed his hands together. It would be easy to persuade her, he would just turn on the old charm, simple. He leaned back in the swivel chair and spun around on it. He maybe wasn't man enough to physically smash Moretti to a pulp but a least this would be forever imprinted on the fucker's brain, that he, Giorgino Vitelli, meant more to his sister than he ever would. He set about erasing the tape – no need for anyone to see that. Then he suddenly realised whose house he was in, it got fucking better, he couldn't contain his glee and burst out laughing. Yeah, the reconciliation would take place here, he thought; make sure that Ella Reynolds was here, that would enrage Moretti even more. When Moretti flipped, as he surely would, they would both see they were right to get him out of their lives.

He saw Ella letting herself in through the electronic gates, accompanied by Marcus. Quickly he dashed into the kitchen and threw some minced beef into the frying pan and added a jar of sauce as he whistled to himself.

"Hi, Giorgino." Ella smiled. "Sorry I should have rang on ahead but my battery died!"

"So did mine," Marcus admitted. "And there was nowhere to charge it."

"You making something nice?"

"Do you want some, there's enough to go around?"

"No, it's fine, I just wanted to pick up a few things. I will be staying with Marcus for a while, at least until you guys get your own place and then we'll probably move into here."

"Oh?" Valerie walked into the kitchen. "So, you two are finally going to make a go of it?"

"Seems like we have to now." Marcus smiled as he put his arm around Ella's tiny waist and hugged her close to him.

"Should we tell them or not?" Ella looked at her husband.

"I suppose we better had."

"Well, put us out of our misery then."

Ella flashed her wedding ring at them.

"Congratulations." Valerie was the first one to congratulate them. "Isn't that wonderful news?" she asked Gio.

"Bloody marvellous." He could barely contain his excitement, now he wanted them both to be here when Moretti arrived.

"Why thank you for the enthusiasm, Giorgino, I hope Carolyn will see it that way!"

"Carolyn will understand," Valerie told her.

"I hope so, but remember don't breathe a word to her, she will be hurt if she knows that I told you first."

"Don't worry your secret is safe with us," Gio told her as he tossed the onions and peppers into the pan.

"Good, now I'll just nip upstairs, you coming Marcus?"

"Sure."

"Good luck to them," Gio mumbled as he beamed from ear to ear; he looked like the cat that had got the cream, or was just about to.

Chapter One Hundred and Three

Milan, Italy
One week later

Nico met Dante at the airport. "Ok, so what's the plan?"

"Flavio rang Rosa again and she has agreed to see me, but is still set on staying in England with her so-called husband!"

"It's so bizarre to think that that little shit is with her, do you think he knows about her?" He paused. "About you?"

Dante shrugged. "I have no idea whatsoever, that's why I need you for back-up, to help me try and persuade my sister to come back with us."

"What are the chances of that, now she is happily married to Vitelli?" Nico asked.

"That's where you come in, you used to have a soft spot for her, remember? She might listen to you."

"We were just kids Dante, a lot has happened since then."

"I know, but I'm relying on you, I don't know what else to do." He sighed. "And anyway she isn't even legally married to Giorgino Vitelli and that will horrify her."

"Dante, I hate to tell you man but she won't be the same girl we remembered. You can't go in heavy handed, you've got to be gentle or else you could blow it forever."

"I know, I keep telling myself I have to remain calm and I will."

"No matter what she says?"

"No matter what she says, I'll honour it." But Dante knew that he would never accept it, she had to come back to Menaggio with him and that was it, Nico didn't need to know the details.

"You ok?"

Dante went white, in his haste to leave the house he'd left the safe key in his jacket pocket which was hung over his chair in his office. "Bollocks, I've left something."

"We'll miss the flight if you go back for it now," Nico warned.

"So? We'll get the next one, come on."

*****

Luciana was using the office telephone. "He's going over to England, should be boarding any minute now," she told Vasiliev as she rocked back and forth on the chair. "And it's something to do with his sister Rosa."

"What do you mean?"

"I'm not sure what it means, but she is definitely alive and well."

"That can't be, Garshin convinced me that she was dead!" he snapped. She would be able to identify him if ever she set eyes on him and then there would be a full-scale war, he had to think of something and act fast. "Where is she staying at, for fuck's sake? What the hell am I paying you for?" he ranted at her.

"God, give me a second to speak and I'll tell you."

"Well?"

"Ella's."

Vasiliev put his hand to his head in frustration – fucking Ella Reynolds, that's all he needed! Things were definitely heating up and he had to put a stop to it. Banging the phone down on Luciana he started shaking with rage, he was totally infuriated.

"Anything I can help with?" Yelena interrupted his thoughts.

"No!" he screamed at her.

"Are you sure?" she put on her sweetest voice.

"Just fuck off out of my sight, I have business to take care of!"

"Charming, I'm sure." Yelena slammed the door behind her; one minute he was all over her like a rash and the next he treated her worse than a dog. She punched in Luciana's cell phone. "It's me. Fill me in on what the hell is going on."

*****

Dante was just pulling up on to the drive when he saw the light on in his office, which was strange, he didn't leave it on.

Reaching across Nico, he took the gun out of the glove compartment.

"What is it?" Nico looked a little surprised.

"Someone's in my office."

"Who?"

"How the fuck do I know? Come on, let's find out!"

Nico followed behind him as Dante peered in through the window. "It's all right, it's Luciana." He was just about to put the gun away when he saw her search his jacket pocket and take out the key.

"Let's go in then."

"Shush, she's up to something." Dante put his finger to his lips and pointed.

They both watched as she opened the safe and rifled through it, pulling out the disk she put it into the disk drive and clicked it open.

"You stay here," he ordered Nico.

When Dante barged in and pointed the gun at her she nearly fell backwards out of the chair in a state of shock and total surprise.

"What the fuck are you doing and more to the point, who the fuck are you spying for?"

"Please don't shoot me!" Luciana put her hands up.

"I'll ask you one more time, who the fuck are you working for?"

"I can't tell you, he'll kill me, please don't make me!" she begged.

"Not good enough, I allow you into my home, I trust you, I give you anything and everything you want and this is how you repay me."

Luciana was trembling. "P... please don't kill me," she winced.

Just for a second Dante was seriously going to put a bullet in her head – but no, he had a better idea. He would let her go, have Carmine follow her, see who she ran to. "Just get the fuck out of my house and think yourself lucky that I am allowing you to live, don't make me regret it!"

"What about my things?" she said in a quiet voice.

"Your fucking things?" He laughed. "I own all of your fucking things you stupid bitch, even that dress you are standing up in!"

Luciana slowly got to her feet.

"No, stop!"

"W... what?"

"Take it off!" he ordered.

"But I have no bra on."

"That's not my problem, if you want to live take it off and do it now!" His voice was menacing.

Obediently she did what he said and stood with her hands covering her breasts.

"Now get out before I change my mind."

Luciana made a dash for the door and Dante grabbed her arm and pressed the gun hard into her temple. "Make no mistake. If I ever see you again I'll use this!"

She started sobbing. "I... I'm... so... sorry."

Dante let go and laughed as she grabbed her car keys and ran outside, nearly knocking Nico over in the process.

Being the gentleman he was Nico took his jacket off and gave it to her. "Here."

Grateful she snatched it off him and quickly pulled it on.

"Was that really necessary?" he asked Dante as he entered the office.

"You soft prick, where's your fucking jacket?"

"I couldn't let her go like that man, it's inhumane."

"She shouldn't be messing with things that don't belong to her!"

"What the fuck is so important to you that would make you do something like that?" Nico pushed past him and stared at the computer screen. "What is this?"

Dante pointed the gun at him. "A little insurance policy, that's all, a confidential insurance policy that only I know about, do you understand what I mean?"

"Fuck me, are you trying to get yourself bumped off man? And for fuck's sake stop pointing that gun at me!"

"Can I trust you implicitly, Nico?" Dante asked still pointing the gun at him.

"I can't believe that you are even asking me that."

Dante put the safety catch on and laughed. "Just checking."

"Shit, all these names." Nico scratched his chin. "What are you planning on doing with this – and why the fuck is my name on it?"

"So's mine!"

"I don't get it."

"You don't have to get it!"

"Well now that I know about it, perhaps you had better enlighten me." Nico sat down and studied the list.

"Don't get me wrong, I don't plan on using it."

"If this fell into the wrong hands…" his voice broke off when he saw, Petrov and Vasiliev's names. "Jesus, you can't be serious, this Russian fucker would have you removed in an instant if he knew this existed."

"But it doesn't exist does it Nico?"

"This can only bring destruction, to us, to our families, our friends. Don't you understand what you have here, you need to destroy it and do it now. Wherever Luciana is running to, whoever she is running to she is bound to spill her guts."

"I suppose." Dante ejected it. "Here." He passed it to him.

"I don't fucking want it, Jesus, it must have taken years to compile this list."

"I was given it by Mancini; part of the deal was to keep it up to date."

"But don't you see how reckless this is?" Nico couldn't help but think that he was completely insane. "I can't believe you are updating it."

"Do you think I am crazy?"

"I can sort of understand why Mancini would have something like this, but not you, unless you are planning something, something big, some major operation."

"I have contemplated it, sure, who wouldn't? But the time is not right," he admitted.

"Is this about Vasiliev?"

"He's a dangerous fucker and look at his allies. Yet with him out of the way, we could control his share of the business and all of those influential high-ranking bureaucrats."

"He's very powerful." Nico shook his head. "No, it's not up for discussion."

"Very well, then the disk is for you to do what you want with."

"Let's destroy it then, before somebody comes back and turns this place upside down."

Dante had been thinking about a major takeover, but now that his sister had turned up he would have to put it on hold. "Follow me."

He led him into the lounge where there was a rip-roaring fire. "It's up to you."

"Even if I burn it, what's to say you haven't got it all up here." He pointed to his head. "Or even another copy somewhere?"

"You'll have to trust me on that one."

Nico threw it into the fire. "We must never tell anyone about this and we must never discuss it again, do you agree?" He turned to his friend.

"What's the big deal? It would have been fun turning them against each other, we could have had everything, the whole fucking empire."

"Don't you get it Dante?"

"Get what?"

"We're both in it, up to our necks as it is, if you started some kind of game, it wouldn't be long until you were rumbled."

"Maybe, but we'll never know now, will we?"

Dante's mobile went off. "Excuse me for a minute. Yes? Ok, no don't follow her I'll have someone take over from you in Moscow, just get back here."

"I take it that was an update on Luciana?"

"How did you guess?"

"So, you think she works for Vasiliev?"

"Of course, and I also think all the little things that have befallen us my friend have all been instigated by him!"

"What things?"

"Think about it, my friend. We did not have much trouble until we took up with him."

Nico cast his mind back, what Dante said had an element of truth about it. "Perhaps, but then perhaps we are just experiencing a run of bad luck."

"Maybe we will never know, but I wish that I had never gotten mixed up with the psychotic bastard!"

"What are you going to do about Luciana?"

"What do you think we should do?"

"Me?"

"Yes, you always wanted some responsibility and now you have it!"

"You can't be serious, why would you give control to me?"

"I'm going to take my sister away, so I won't be around for a while," he told him.

"Where to?"

"Maybe Sicily, we have family and friends there and she will be perfectly safe... then."

"Then what?"

Then, once Dante confirmed Vasiliev was involved in his sister's abduction, he would murder the fucker. "Then, I will be back to take the reins my friend, now let's get back to the airport." He smiled to himself, a copy of the disk was hidden at Ella's house and once he got there he would retrieve it. The plan was to make Vasiliev squirm as he saw his empire disintegrate before his eyes and then, when he was at his lowest ebb, he would finally eradicate him.

Chapter One Hundred and Four

London, England

"So, how are you feeling?" Gio rubbed Rosa's shoulders. "I can sure feel the tension in there."

"Nervous, I can't believe you talked me into this." She sighed, not sure if she was doing the right thing.

"Don't forget Carolyn will be here too for moral support."

"What exactly did you tell her?"

"Just that your long-lost brother has traced you and wants to see you, other than that nothing, I didn't think that was my place. What you tell her is entirely up to you."

"It's better that she knows nothing."

"Whatever you decide is fine by me." He continued to massage her shoulders. "There, how's that?"

"Much better thanks, but I think I need a stiff drink."

"Just a little one then, you must keep a clear head."

The doorbell rang. "That must be Carolyn; I'll go and let her in." Gio smiled as he passed her a small brandy.

Rosa's head was spinning. Her life had drastically improved, why was she letting the past get in the way of any future happiness she had with Gio?

Carolyn walked into the lounge and shook her head. "Oh, Valerie, I can't believe you have a brother, I didn't realise. I mean, obviously you had a life before your abduction but it didn't even enter my head that somebody would actually come and look for you," she chattered. "Oops, sorry! I can see that you are nervous enough without me blabbering on like a stupid idiot."

"It's ok, please sit down." She patted the sofa. "Can Gio get you anything, a coffee perhaps?"

"Yes, that would be lovely, thanks Gio." She turned and nodded to him. "So, when did all this happen, I mean how did it all come about?"

"I'm sorry, Carolyn, I really don't want to tell you any of the details right now."

"It's ok." She leaned over and squeezed her hand. "I'll be in the other room if you need me."

"I'm very grateful."

"Think nothing of it," Carolyn assured her. "You know me, anything to help."

Gio rang Ella Treymayne. "It's me Giorgino." His voice was slightly panicky.

"Oh, is something wrong?" Ella heard the tremble in his voice.

"It's Valerie, she's expecting her brother any minute now and, well, quite frankly it's been such a long time I really don't know how she will react."

"It's ok, calm down, what do you need me to do?" Her voice was full of concern.

"You must not let on that I told you anything, she would go mad with me if she knew I was talking to you about this."

"Go on."

"Just turn up unexpectedly, pretend you have come to pick up your mail, it wouldn't exactly be a lie as you do have some waiting for you."

"Have you spoken to Carolyn?"

"I can't get hold of her," he lied. "What Valerie needs right now is a friendly face and after Carolyn you seemed the most obvious person."

"Do you want me to come now?"

"No, I'll text you… oh and it would be wise to bring Marcus with you," he told her.

"Why, her brother isn't dangerous is he?" Ella put her hand on her chest.

"Not as far as I am aware."

"Very well, I'll wait until you contact me." Ella placed her mobile on the table.

"Something I should know about?" Marcus asked noting the concern on her face.

"We need to go over to my house later."

"Oh yes?"

"Mmm, seems like Valerie has a brother."

"She does?"

"Yes and she's meeting him at the house tonight."

"Is that something we should be worried about?"

"Obviously she hasn't seem him for some years so it's going to be a little awkward, so Gio has asked if we wouldn't mind just turning up, you know in case Valerie gets upset and has no way of getting rid of him," she tried to explain to him.

"Isn't that Carolyn's job?"

"Yes, yes it is but Gio can't get hold of her."

"I see, so I take it Valerie doesn't know we've been summoned to be the protection team?" He laughed. "Don't look so worried, it's her brother, he must have gone to great lengths to find her."

"I guess so, I hope it goes all right for her, the poor thing, she certainly doesn't need any more upset in her life. She has endured more than most people could bear and is still suffering for it now."

"I know, I can't imagine what it must have been like being bought and sold like that, she must still have nightmares."

"No, I meant her being HIV positive, and please Marcus you must not repeat that to anyone, Carolyn told me in complete confidence."

"My God, she seems so well! You wouldn't even know."

"She's on various forms of medication which she will have to take for the rest of her life. Thankfully this new batch of medication she is on has slowed down her symptoms, so she is very optimistic about having a good many years yet; it's amazing what these specialists can do nowadays."

"Yes, absolutely amazing," Marcus agreed. "She is one hell of a woman, isn't she?"

"Absolutely."

*****

Dante and Nico drove up to the wrought-iron gates, closely followed by Flavio and Carmine who were keeping a safe distance.

"Are you ok?" Nico asked as he glanced at his friend.

"Fine."

"Doesn't it feel strange to be going to meet your sister at Ella's house?"

"Of course it fucking does, but she's not here is she!" he snapped.

"Hey, I'm just showing some concern, that's all."

"Sorry, man." Dante pressed the intercom button and waited to be let into the grounds.

That was the first time Dante had ever apologised to anyone. *That was a first*, thought Nico. *He must be feeling a bit apprehensive about the meeting. Hell, even I'm feeling a little jittery.*

"The code is Sheila0156," he told Flavio. "Only come in if absolutely necessary." He flipped his mobile shut.

"I didn't realise you knew the code."

"Well, I'm hoping it's still the same, put it that way."

As they got out of the car Dante straightened his tie and brushed back his hair. "Do I look all right?"

"No offence man, but you would think that this was some kind of business meeting."

"Well, I suppose it is in a way." He pressed the doorbell.

"Remember, we are only in the kitchen if you need us," Gio told her.

"I'll be ok, don't worry." Slowly she opened the door and gasped when she saw her handsome brother. "Dante." She stood there with her mouth wide open with her inhaler in her hand.

"Aren't you going to invite me in then?" He never knew that his sister had asthma.

"I'm sorry please excuse my manners, please do come in." Opening the door fully she was shocked to see Nico de Luca; she blushed remembering their hasty fumblings as young teenagers.

"Rosa," Nico nodded, not knowing what to say in case he somehow offended her.

"Follow me." She led them into the lounge. "Please, have a seat."

"Shall I wait in the car?" Nico asked.

"Yes, I think that is a good idea," Rosa told him. "No offence but I must speak with my brother alone."

"As you wish." She looked wonderful, blossomed into a beautiful woman, but that was no surprise, she always stood out from the rest of her girlfriends and that, unfortunately, was probably why she was targeted.

"So, how have you been?" Dante went to hug her, but she took a step back.

"Just because you are my brother does not mean to say that we have to pretend we like each other."

"Rosa, we rowed as children, what siblings don't? It's all part of growing up," he said gently.

"You have no idea what my life has been like," she said bitterly. "The things they made me do, I nearly went insane until I was finally rescued from that shameful existence."

"I've spent all my life trying to find you."

"Have you?"

"Yes, it's true."

"Why?"

"You and I are the only family we have left now."

"Mama and papa, they are dead then?"

"I'm afraid so, papa had a heart attack a few years after you disappeared and mama died of a broken heart. All she ever wanted was her baby back."

"Nobody did enough to find me. Perhaps if anybody had cared my life would have been very different."

"I have found you now. Your life can be very different if that is what you want."

"I told your friend I am happily married, my life is here now, I don't belong in Italy anymore."

"I have a nice villa in Mennagio, where nobody will know what happened to you, it is very quiet and picturesque, you would love it."

Ella and Marcus pulled up to the wrought-iron gates and spotted Nico's car sitting outside the property.

"What is he doing here?" Marcus asked.

"I haven't got a clue; maybe he's looking for you," Ella told him as she punched in the code.

"I'm not expecting him."

Ella knocked on his window. "Nico?"

"Oh, er, hello Ella, Marcus." He was dumbfounded; the last thing he had expected was seeing these two.

"Can I help you?"

"I'm just waiting for Dante," he admitted.

"Dante? But I don't understand." Ella couldn't make any sense of it.

"Just go in, then you will." Nico wound his window back up.

Ella knocked on it again but Nico ignored her.

"What the hell is going on here?" Marcus could feel his anger rising to the surface. "The fucking audacity of that man."

Ella opened the front door. "Hello?" she shouted.

Hearing her voice Dante jumped. "I thought we were meeting alone."

"It's Ella's house, she comes and goes as she pleases, why is it a problem?"

"You really don't know?"

"Know what?"

"She's my ex-wife."

Just then Ella appeared in the doorway. "Valerie?"

"No, this is Rosa, Rosa Moretti, my sister."

"W... what?" Ella gasped. "Is this true Valerie?"

"Yes, it is."

"Are you all right?" Marcus asked her. "Would you like him to leave?"

"No, I'm ok, we were just catching up."

"I'm just collecting a few things and then we'll be out of your hair."

"Why don't you stick around for a while? Gio and Carolyn are in the kitchen."

After they left the room Dante turned to her. "You're so afraid of your own brother you've got a fucking house full of people?" His voice was incredulous.

"Why should I feel safe with you after what you did to Ella?"

"What do you know about it?"

"That you'd barely been married when you took up with another woman and broke her heart into little pieces."

"Oh." Dante was relieved that she didn't know the truth, if she did then there definitely would be no way they would ever be able to be a family again.

"Is that all you can say? You have so little respect for her, she was in a right state after what you did to her, you should be ashamed."

"I am ashamed, I loved her, no I still love her and I will always regret what I did to her."

Rosa was surprised to hear the sincerity in his voice. "You really mean that don't you?"

"Yes, but it's too late for me and Ella, but not too late for us to make a fresh start."

Rosa's heart softened towards him and she was tempted to throw her arms around him and sob like she had never sobbed before.

"You know that family is important to me, even more so now, at least think about coming out to Menaggio for a couple of weeks, no pressure, the offer is there."

Rosa sat down, she hadn't realised how much she missed her Italian roots. "I don't know, I will have to talk to Gio, see what he thinks."

"I understand." Dante turned the other way: that fucker Vitelli, if he fucked things up he was a dead man. Biting his lip he regained his composure. Turning back around he smiled at her. "Just think about it that's all I ask."

Carolyn was both surprised and happy to see Ella and Marcus. "What are you guys doing here?"

"We could ask you the same question."

"Sorry, it was me; I was just concerned about Valerie that's all."

"It's all right, we don't mind, do we Marcus?" Ella squeezed his hand.

"No problem, we'll stick around until he leaves." He looked at his wife; he couldn't help but notice that her eyes had lit up when she had seen Moretti. He kept reminding himself that she was his wife now and that's all that mattered, who was he kidding? he thought. The love between them was still there, even now, he wondered if given the chance they would resume their relationship. That was it, he would try to encourage Valerie to return to Italy, that way at least Dante wouldn't be turning up here every five minutes.

"I'll put the kettle on," Gio broke into his thoughts. "Don't worry, she'll soon let us know if she needs anything." Secretly Vitelli was loving it. He looked at his watch, any time now Valerie would bring him into the kitchen and introduce him. He poured the drinks and sat down with the others, trying to look like they were all the best of friends just to piss Moretti off even more. The clock chimed seven and he glanced at the door.

"Everything ok?" Carolyn asked, noticing his anguished look.

"Yes, yes." He sipped his tea.

"He must be leaving," Marcus commented hearing the footsteps in the hallway.

"Sounds like they are heading this way." Gio smiled, finally the moment had arrived.

Valerie appeared in the doorway. "I know some of you already know my brother, but Gio I would like you to meet Dante Moretti, Dante this is my husband Giorgino Vitelli."

Dante kept a blank expression on his face and reached for his hand. "Pleased to meet you." He held Vitelli's hand in a vice-like grip trying to get the message through to him, *hurt Rosa and you will answer to me* he willed the words to him.

"Likewise." Vitelli was courteous but all he wanted to do was yank his hand away.

"And this is my boss, Carolyn Reid."

Dante loosened his grip and gently shook her hand. "Hello again." He smiled. "Rosa has told me a lot about you, it is very admirable what you have done for her and other women in the same situation."

"So, how have you two got on, if you don't mind me asking?" she asked.

"Good, better than I thought," Rosa admitted. "Dante has invited us to Menaggio for a few weeks to see if we can build on our relationship, what do you think Gio?"

Before he had time to answer Marcus butted in. "Personally, I think it is a wonderful idea."

"You do?" Ella was surprised by his reaction; she thought he would have been dead set against it. "Gio?"

"Whatever Valerie, I mean, whatever Rosa wants, it's such a beautiful name isn't it?" He smiled sweetly at his wife. "It really suits you." He could see the colour rise in Moretti's face and knew he was about to kick off any second, then everyone would see him for what he was really like.

Forcing a smile Dante spoke up. "I agree Gio. Do you mind if I call you Gio? After all, we are family now."

Nico was still sitting in the car outside wondering what the hell was taking so long. He couldn't wait any longer as he desperately needed the toilet. He got out and stretched his legs, as he yawned he rang the doorbell.

"I'll go," Ella told them.

"I'll just go and check on Nico." Dante followed her out of the kitchen and shut the door behind them.

"What the hell are you doing?" Ella gasped. "My husband is in there."

"I'm well aware of that." He touched her arm and she jumped.

"Don't do that," she exclaimed.

"Why, does my touch still excite you, *Bella* Ella?" he whispered as he stroked her cheek. "You look even more beautiful than the last time I saw you."

"Dante, please don't, I have a new life now with a man who is completely honourable."

"Honourable?" he laughed. "Yet so predictable, face it Ella he isn't exciting enough for you and never will be."

"And you are?"

"You know this already," he told her as he stood between her and the door.

"You really are an arrogant son of a bitch; now get out of my way!" She tried to push him away with little success.

"Not until you promise to meet me." He paused. "You know that you want to." He pulled her to him and lightly brushed his lips against hers.

For a second Ella forgot about what he had done and leaned her head against his chest, all the emotions came flooding back and she realised how much she still loved him. The doorbell rang once more which startled them. "Let me go," she whispered.

"Only if you agree to meet me," Dante persisted.

"Ok, where?"

Dante pressed a piece of paper into her hand. "Ring me."

Ella was just opening the front door when Marcus came rushing down the corridor. "Are you all right, what has he been saying?" he demanded pointing at Dante.

"Everything's ok, it's just Nico."

"Hurry up; I need to use the bathroom."

"Down there and turn right," Ella and Dante said in unison.

Marcus was furious. "I think it's about time we were leaving."

"Ok, honey, let's go and say goodbye first."

"Very well." Reluctantly Marcus followed her; he glared at Dante letting him know that he was not happy with him.

*****

Wearing balaclavas and armed with silencers Vasiliev's men stood outside the house ready to go on their boss's signal.

"The target is Rosa Moretti."

"Very well."

"But if anybody else is there, take them out too. You can't leave any witnesses, do you understand?" he told Rachek.

"Understood." He turned to the other two men. "Now, go, go, go!"

*****

Carolyn's mobile rang. "Hi Andrew."

"Hi, I just got in, it's been a long crazy day, I'm just going to take a shower, how long will you be?"

Before Carolyn had a chance to answer, there was a loud crash, which startled her and she dropped her phone onto the floor.

The three masked men were in and out and it was all over in seconds.

Carolyn retrieved the phone. "Hello, are you still there?" she gasped. "Andrew...? Andrew, answer me!" She hit end call and re-dialled his number, but the line was busy.

Marcus took the phone off her. "What is it?" He put the phone to his ear.

"Something's wrong, I can just feel it, I better get over there." Carolyn's voice was shaking, she was seriously worried.

"Ella and I will come with you," Marcus told her. "Come on."

Rosa look confused. "You don't think this has something to do with me, do you?"

"What makes you say that?"

"I don't know, just a nagging feeling inside."

"I'll stay here with Rosa, call me, let me know what is happening," Dante called after them as they rushed out of the front door.

"Anything I can do?" Nico asked.

"Not sure yet." He glanced at Vitelli. "You stay here. I need to pick up the rest of my things."

"But we haven't asked Ella," Rosa protested.

"It's all right I know what I am looking for and I know this house like the back of my hand."

Before she had a chance to stop him he was taking the stairs two at a time. He went straight into the walk-in closet and removed the air vent. Putting his hand in, he felt around and smiled when he pulled out the disk, thank fuck it was still there.

Hearing fast-approaching footsteps he shoved the vent back into place and quickly stowed the disk in Ella's jacket.

"What are you doing?" Vitelli questioned him. "What are you after?" he demanded.

"I told you, I'm collecting some of my things." He pointed to the designer suits and Italian leather shoes. "Is that ok with you?"

"Just get downstairs where I can see what you are doing!" Vitelli barked at him.

"So, now you think you are the big man, just because you are married to Rosa, hiding behind a woman's skirt."

"That woman's skirt happens to be your sister and don't you forget it."

"No, don't you forget it." Dante gripped him by the lapels and pulled him so close to him that Vitelli could feel his breath on his face. "Fucking hurt her in any way and you are a dead man!"

"Dante, Dante, we've got to get out of here right now man!" Nico yelled up the stairs.

"You'll keep." Dante let go and patted his shoulders. "For now, Rosa is our priority, got it?"

Vitelli nodded.

"Good, now let's go."

*****

Carolyn rang the police. "It's my fiancé…" She broke down.

Marcus took charge. "There has been a shooting at…" He walked into the bedroom, out of earshot.

Ella gently put a blanket over Andrew Falkoner's bloodied body; the amount of blood spattered all over the apartment shocked the hell out of her. She tried to pull Carolyn to her feet, but she sat there frozen to the spot, her dress soaked in blood. Silently she cried, rubbing her face she smeared Andrew's blood across her cheeks, making her look almost demonic. "Why, why?"

Getting to her feet Ella rang her house and Nico answered. "Listen," she whispered, "you must get Rosa out of there, Carolyn's fiancé has been shot dead not long ago."

"Ok, thanks for the warning, Ella."

"And Nico."

"Yes?"

"Tell, Dante to get her out of the country and I will be in touch when I can." Quickly she snapped the phone shut.

"The police and ambulance are on the way," Marcus told her. "They'll want to interview Rosa, just in case this is anything to do with her."

"No, no you can't do that," Ella pleaded.

"Why not?"

"This is serious Marcus. Any one of us could be on the hit list if we mention the others."

"We have to tell them."

"No, we tell them nothing." Carolyn looked up. "Ella is right, let Dante get Rosa and Gio out of the country where they will be safe."

"Are you sure about this Carolyn? You're in shock."

"Very sure, I haven't helped to keep Rosa safe for all this time for her to be questioned like some kind of criminal."

Marcus understood where she was coming from, but quite frankly he was unsure of Ella's true motive. Was it really for Rosa or did it all come back to Dante frigging Moretti? "Then I'll say you were with us when you called him and we rushed over here when you realised something was wrong."

Carolyn nodded. "Yes, yes, it's for the best."

But Marcus couldn't help but think this was all down to Moretti, not Rosa. He just prayed that finally he had seen the last of him, for all of their sakes.

Chapter One Hundred and Five

Three months later

"Marcus, will you take my jacket to the dry cleaners?"
"Which one?"
"The cream short one."
"Ella, you have so many jackets, I'm not sure which one you mean."
"Look, I have to go, Carolyn is putting the food out, I'll call you later."
"Ok, see you later."
Marcus trawled through the walk-in wardrobe and finally found the right jacket; he checked the pockets and found a disk. Wondering what it was he made his way down to the office. Curiosity got the better of him and he loaded it into the disk drive. It was a list of names, not understanding what it all meant he paged down, Moretti, Vitelli, Vasiliev, Petrov and de Luca were all there. What was Ella doing with this and, more to the point, what did it all mean? Scratching his head he rang his wife.
"Ella, what does this disk mean?"
"What disk?"
"The one I found in your jacket."
"Honey, I really don't have the foggiest idea what you are talking about."
"Ok, we'll talk about it later. What time do you want me to pick you up?"
"A couple of hours?"
"No problem."
"Has Nico arrived yet?"
"No, he's making his own way from the airport." Marcus hung up, the disk was strange and, as he mulled it around in his brain, he realised that somehow all these people were connected. It was something to do with Dante, of that he was absolutely certain. Picking up the telephone he dialled his number.
"Yes?"

He recognised Valerie's voice. "Hey, it's Marcus here, how are you doing?"

"Oh, Marcus, it's so nice to hear your voice, I'm great thanks, how are you and Ella?"

"We're just fine, is Dante there?"

"Dante?" Rosa was slightly confused; why the hell did he want to talk to his wife's ex-husband it just didn't make sense to her.

"Is he?" Marcus persisted.

"Hang on, I'll just get him."

Marcus waited, not sure of what he was going to say to the man he despised so much.

"This is Dante, is Ella all right?"

"Ella, what concern of yours is she?" Marcus was annoyed. "I'm ringing about something else."

"What?" Dante was intrigued. What could he possibly want with him?

"Something has come into my possession, which may belong to you."

"Oh?"

"A disk."

Dante's heart nearly stopped. "What disk?"

"The disk you left in my wife's jacket."

"I don't know what you are talking about."

"Look, I don't like you and you don't like me, whatever this means I want no part of it."

"I told you I have no idea what you are talking about."

"Stop with the bullshitting, I've seen the names."

"Fine just mail it to me, Ella doesn't need to know about this."

"Ok." Marcus cursed as he put the phone down, whatever it was Moretti was acting too cool, it was obviously important to him.

Dante rang Nico. "It's me, where are you?"

"I've just got off the plane, why?"

"You know that disk I showed you?"

Nico remembered it all too well. "Yes."

"Well Marcus Treymayne has a copy."

"Are you fucking joking me or what?"

"I wish I was."

"So, what do you want me to do?"

"Retrieve the disk and dispose of Treymayne."

Nico gripped the phone not believing what he was hearing. "Run that past me again."

"Get the disk and eliminate him." He paused. "It's the only way."

"How?"

"I don't really give a damn, just remember, you are there and I am here and it has our names on it!" he exclaimed.

"I fucking told you to destroy it." Nico was furious. "I can't believe you have put me in this impossible situation."

Dante's phone was tapped and Vasiliev heard everything. It was time he made a move and, if that meant taking them all out, that was what he intended to do.

*****

Marcus was in a flap. He was unsure of what he should do, so burnt another disk, just in case he told himself – in case this was the end of him. He had told Moretti in anger and now he hoped that he wouldn't live to regret it. Placing the disk in his wife's Gucci handbag he went back downstairs to open the door to Nico.

"Hi, how long are you here for?"

"Just a day or so, I need to get back home to Grazia, we have been thinking about a surrogate mother."

"Really?"

"Yes, it's taken me a long time to persuade her, but now I think she finally agrees."

"I hope it all works out for you."

"Thanks, you seem a bit edgy. Is everything ok with you and Ella?"

"Of course, never better, she is the best thing in my life."

Nico tried to detract himself from the situation, he liked Treymayne, but now that he knew about the disk, he had to dispose of him.

"Do you fancy a drink before we discuss the next delivery?"

"Sure, make mine a Jack Daniel's." Nico knew that he would have to have a few before he killed him.

Marcus was completely oblivious to the danger he was in. He opened the drinks cabinet and slowly poured them out. "There you go."

"Thanks." Nico didn't know what to say as he downed it in one.

"Another?"

"Why not, are you not joining me?"

"No, I'm driving later, picking Ella up from Carolyn's."

"How is she?"

"Still in a pretty bad way, what happened to Andrew is still a mystery." Marcus suddenly realised that everything all added up and he was afraid, afraid of what Nico might do to him, he had to get out of there and do it now. "Why don't you come with me to pick Ella up? She will be happy to catch up?"

"No, I don't think so."

Marcus looked up. He was shocked to see the gun pointed at him. "What is going on Nico?"

"I'm sorry," Nico said. "You discovered something that you shouldn't have, something that could bring us all down and I couldn't let that happen."

"For the love of God at least tell me what it was that I discovered."

"A sex-trafficking ring with major players, trust me I don't really want to do this, you are my friend."

"Friend? You know fuck all of friendship." He paused. "Tell my wife how much I love her." The last thing he saw was the gun pointing at him.

Marcus' body slumped to the ground. Nico wiped a tear from his eye, poor Ella she had definitely had a raw deal out of all this, and it was all down to Dante.

He went into the other room and deleted the security footage; no one would ever know that he had been there. On his way out he would leave the gates open and it would look like some punk had taken a risk and trashed the house, Marcus would have stumbled across them and paid the ultimate price with his life.

Picking up the disk he put it in his jacket pocket. "It's done."

Dante was relieved to hear the words. "And the disk?"

"I've got it."

"Then get rid of it!"

"Fine." Nico shut his mobile phone and broke the disk in two. His attention turned to Marcus' body, he felt so terrible about killing him like that. It wasn't as if he hadn't killed before, but somehow it all felt wrong, very wrong. Flipping open his mobile he rang Grazia.

"Nico, when are you coming home?"

"I'm getting the next flight back, so I'll be back in the early hours."

"I'm glad that you talked me round," she said nonchalantly.

"Me too, I love you," he said as he ended the call.

He was just about to leave when two masked men rushed into the house and pinned him down.

"Where is the disk?"

The Russian accent whirred in his head, so Vasiliev now knew about it. "Destroyed."

"Get on your fucking knees, now!" One of the men ordered.

Nico did as he was told. So this was it, this was how he was going to die, without a fighting chance and without saying goodbye to his beloved wife. He supposed that it was his just desserts for all the bad things he had ever done. He put his hands behind his head, waiting for his fate.

Chapter One Hundred and Six

Ella was becoming very concerned about her husband, usually he was so prompt, you could set your watch by him. "I can't get through to him; perhaps I should just get a taxi or something."

"I have to say that I am worried, it is so unlike him," Carolyn voiced her concerns.

"I better go, find out what is happening."

"Do you want me to come with you?"

"Would you mind?"

"No, you're my friend, I'll call a cab." Carolyn dialled the number.

It felt like an age before the taxi finally arrived. As they pulled up to the house Ella's heart sank when she saw that the gates were wide open. They never left them open, ever, and now she knew that something awful had happened. She squeezed Carolyn's hand. "Wait here and keep the meter running," she told the cab driver.

Carolyn opened the car door and was just about to get out when Ella stopped her. "No, please just wait here, I won't be long, if I'm not back in five minutes call the police."

Slowly she put the key in the front door and punched in the security code. "Marcus?" she called out his name and as her voice echoed in the hallway there was an eerie silence. Panicking she switched on all the lights and shouted again, but still there was no response. "Marcus, please where are you?"

The hitmen were still in the office unbeknown to Ella, both hiding on either side of the door. Gently she pushed it open. She saw two bodies and they were obviously dead, one was her husband and the other was Nico de Luca. Giving out a small cry she ran to her husband. "Oh God, oh God, Marcus!" She stroked his face.

As she knelt over him she heard a noise behind her. Before she had a chance to react she felt a heavy object smash down onto her back rendering her unconscious.

Carolyn looked at her watch. "Call the police," she told the cab driver. "There's something very wrong here."

She entered the house and shouted her friend's name, there was no answer. Picking up the brass candlestick she braced herself: if this was some kind of nightmare she wished that she would wake up right now, she was so unsure of what to expect. Checking the lounge she found nothing, she headed down the hallway and saw that the office door was ajar. She gripped the candlestick and got ready for whatever was waiting for her. As she tried to shove the door wide open she glanced through the gap. Ella was face down on the floor. With all the strength she could muster she gave the door one final heave and finally burst through it. "Ella, Ella, please, please wake up! It's me, Carolyn."

Putting her hand over her mouth she was shocked at what she saw. Marcus was obviously dead, holding her stomach she felt like she was just about to vomit. As she looked the other way she saw Nico de Luca.

Ella was just coming to when the sirens wailed in the background. "Marcus...?"

"Oh, my poor Ella, I'm afraid he has gone."

"Gone," she whispered. "What do you mean gone?" Looking over her shoulder she saw him. "Oh no, no, no, is he... is he?"

"I'm sorry."

Ella screamed, a high-pitched scream. "No, no, it can't be true! Tell me that I am dreaming."

She flung her arms around Carolyn. "It's a dream, isn't it?"

"No, darling, I'm sorry."

"And Nico." She pointed to his body.

"Dead," was all Carolyn could say.

The policeman burst through the door. "Nobody move, stay perfectly still." He noted the two dead bodies and the guns next to each of them. In his book it looked like they had both tried to kill each other and that's what he would say when he wrote out his report.

Chapter One Hundred and Seven

Mennagio, Italy

Dante received a call from Grazia and what she told him blew him away. "Dead, but he can't be!" he exclaimed.

"It's true, Ella called me, Nico and Marcus are both dead," she cried.

"I'm coming over, just stay where you are." Dante was beside himself with grief for his best friend. They had grown up together and had always looked out for each other, only this time he hadn't been there for him. It was supposed to have been a simple job, kill Treymayne and retrieve the disk. His head was spinning as he got into his Maserati.

"What's going on?" Vitelli asked him.

"Just look after Rosa, I'll be back tonight." His voice was serious.

Giorgino was worried, over the last few months he had actually grown to like him which had totally taken him by surprise. "Should I be worried?"

"Look Vitelli, I know there is no love lost between us, but promise me you will look out for my sister, it is of the utmost importance," he stressed.

Gio watched as he drove away, something was happening and he felt very afraid, afraid for himself and for Rosa. If anything happened to Dante that would be the end of them all, of that he was certain.

Rosa came out of the villa. "Where's Dante gone?"

"I'm not sure, something to do with business, he'll be back later."

"Come on then, let's make the most of it, while he's away." She got hold of his hand. "Let's have a dip." Stepping out of her dressing gown and exposing a teeny bikini she smiled at him. "What are you waiting for?"

"Ok, I'll race you!" Gio legged it around the back of the house and stripping off, jumped into the pool.

Rosa was hot on his heels and dived in after him. "I'm glad that we came to live here." She flung her arms around his neck.

"Yes, me too." He caressed her face. "I do love you."

"You sound so serious."

"But I am serious, seriously in love with you." He held her close and kissed her.

The young couple were watched from close by. "There's no sign of Dante," the Russian hitman told Vasiliev.

"Just don't kill the girl, we need her alive," he warned.

The armed men crept slowly around the back of the house. "Don't harm the girl, she is important to Vasiliev," he told them.

Rosa was floating on her back, staring up at the blue sky. It was so peaceful and so relaxing here and she was the happiest she had ever been. She was startled by a loud bang, looking around she saw Gio face down in the pool, surrounded by crimson water. Screaming she swam towards him. "Gio, Gio…!" But there was no response.

"He's dead. Now get out of the pool!" the man barked at her.

Rosa put her hand over her eyes. "You murdering scum!" she screamed at him as she gasped for breath. "Why did you do that, what has he ever done to deserve this?" She held him in her arms.

"He was married to a Moretti, that's what he did." The man pointed the gun at her. "Now get out!"

Rosa let go of Gio and swam towards the steps, this couldn't be happening, not now. These men were Russian and she remembered all too well what they were capable of. Her past had finally caught her up and her poor husband had paid for it with his life.

The man threw a towel at her. "Get dried off!"

"Can I at least get some clothes on?"

"I'm not a complete monster, but be warned if you try anything I will kill you, make no mistake."

Rosa pulled the towel around herself and tried to think how she could escape, there was no way she was going back to that life no matter what. As she went into the bathroom she was closely followed. "Do you mind?"

"I've seen it all before love." The man stood there and leered at her. "Are you getting changed or what?"

Rosa bit down on her lip, if he tried anything she would cut his fucking bollocks off. Pulling on her top she undid her bikini. The man immediately pulled her to him and groped her breasts.

"You feel really good." He pinned her to the wall and tugged at her bikini bottoms.

His rancid breath made her want to puke, desperately she tried to wriggle out of his grasp but he was too strong for her. He flung her to the ground and ripped her underwear off. As he forced his erection into her she let out a small scream. He grabbed her by the hair and laughed in her face. "I can tell you like this, don't you bitch!"

His comrade was standing outside of the bathroom, Vasiliev would not like this one little bit, they were told not to hurt her in any way. Turning his back on them he tried to block the noise out, the woman was obviously in distress and he couldn't watch it any longer.

Rosa summoned up all of her strength and bit the man's neck as hard as she could making him reel with pain. He smacked her hard across her face splitting her lip wide open.

"You stupid fucking bitch!"

Rosa laughed. "I'm not the one who just fucked someone with AIDS, you dumb fuck!"

The man got hold of her head and bashed it hard on the ceramic tiled floor. "You've given me AIDS you dirty fucking bitch!"

"Stop it, stop it!" the other man yelled. "Don't kill her."

Rosa was unconscious, barely breathing. "For fuck's sake, clean this place up, I'll take her to the van, Moretti must not know that she has been harmed in any way otherwise we are screwed!" Picking up her limp body he opened the doors and lay her in the corner.

He rang Vasiliev. "On our way now."

Vasiliev rang Dante. "Do you want to see your sister again?"

"What the fuck? You better hadn't hurt her or I'll fucking kill you, I swear to God!"

"I want the disk, then you can have her back."

Dante slammed on his brakes. "I don't know what you are talking about."

"Fine then your sister is dead." Vasiliev hung up.

Panicking Dante immediately rang him back. "Ok, I'll get it to you."

"Meet me at the warehouse, tomorrow at seven, bring the disk and I'll exchange your sister for it. What do you say, is it a deal?"

"It's a deal." Dante banged his fists on the steering wheel, they were both dead now and if he was going to die then it would be under his terms and not that Russian prick's.

He rang his house number but there was no answer, quickly he turned the car around and headed back towards the villa. As he pulled up he cursed Vitelli, he was supposed to look after Rosa and he couldn't even do that and now, because of him, she was going to die. Racing into the house armed with a pistol he shouted his name. "Gio? Gio, where are you?" But the house was deathly quiet, so quiet that you would be able to hear a pin drop. Noticing the back door was open he slowly edged out of it. His eyes rested on the swimming pool – there was a body floating. Dashing over he realised that it was Vitelli, taking off his jacket and shoes he jumped in and dragged him back to the steps. "Gio... Gio?" He checked his pulse, there was nothing, he was dead.

"Jesus Christ, what the hell did that bastard do!" He pulled the towel off the sun lounger and placed it over Vitelli's lifeless body. His sister had loved this man and he would have to avenge his death. But there was a problem, the disk had probably been destroyed by now and he would have to think on his feet. He couldn't be sure if Nico had managed to dispose of the disk before he was assassinated. If he hadn't and it fell into the wrong hands, he dreaded to think what the consequences were.

"Mr Moretti... Dante Moretti?"

Dante jumped. "Who the fuck are you?"

"We're from Interpol and we would like to talk to you."

"What about?"

"We've been watching your sister for some time and finally we have an opportunity to bring down Vasiliev. She, or rather, you, will lead us to him."

"What?"

"Let's talk inside," the head of operations told him.

Dante went into the lounge. "What are you talking about?"

"Do you want Vasiliev to get away with what he did to your sister and her husband? You always suspected he had something to do with her abduction."

"What do you mean?" Dante demanded.

"Look Mr Moretti, we know that you are up to your neck in this, but if you help us get Vasiliev perhaps we could make some sort of a deal."

"What kind of a deal?"

"A lighter sentence."

"And what do you expect me to do, Vasiliev's reputation is notorious and he will not surrender easily."

"He has Rosa, what does he intend to do with her?"

Dante had to think fast. "He wants to exchange her for me."

"You must be a serious threat to him and his business."

"Really!" Dante laughed. "Believe me, nobody is a threat to him."

"We need you to wear this."

"No way, I'm not wearing a fucking wire and that is final."

"Then how will we know when to come and rescue you and Rosa?"

"Leave that to me!"

"When and where is the exchange due to take place?"

"A warehouse in Moscow."

"Right, we will make the flight arrangements and David Pearce will accompany you."

David shook Moretti's hand. "Don't worry I will blend into the background, you won't even know that I am there."

"I better fucking hadn't or else we are both dead." He smiled at him through gritted teeth.

"I am the soul of discretion, now let us get started."

Chapter One Hundred and Eight

Moscow, Russia

"You must go to Grazia de Luca."

"What for?" Yelena was busy filing her nails. To get her attention, Vasiliev threw the cup at her, narrowly missed her head.

"Do you mind?"

"Do you? You silly fucking bitch."

"There's no need for that, Pavel."

"Just do as I say. With Nico dead, I need to find out what Grazia knows."

"Poor Nico, what a shame. He was a lovely looking man."

"Will you get a fucking grip?" He grabbed her by the shoulders and shook her hard.

"Ok, ok, I'll go."

"You must go now."

"Jesus, Pavel, what's the urgency?"

"If she knows anything at all, you must kill her."

"Very well." Yelena put her nail file away. "Anything else?"

"A quick shag would be good."

"Ooh, I love it when you talk dirty to me."

*****

Grazia was in deep conversation with Ella Treymayne. "I can barely believe it, what happened?"

"Someone made it look like our husbands shot each other!"

"But that's totally insane."

"I know." Ella's voice was quiet and controlled; the last thing she wanted was to appear hysterical.

"I think that we need to meet," Grazia told her. "To talk, see if we can figure out what really happened."

"What do you think it was all about?"

"Ella, I need to talk to you in person, I can't do this over the phone."

"Ok, I'll get on the next available flight." Ella sat on the stairs and sobbed, her husband was dead, they had had very little time together and now he was gone. She got to her feet and went upstairs to pack an overnight case. Throwing some things into her case she grabbed her Gucci handbag. Marcus bought her that on their first wedding anniversary, she hugged it to herself. Why was her husband dead, what had he ever done to anyone and what did Grazia de Luca know about all of this? Whatever it was, she was about to find out.

*****

It didn't take long for the news to reach Aleksei Petrov, he was a worried man. If Nico had been killed and now it was Dante's turn then surely he would almost certainly be next. The three of them had been allies for many years and now they were all being disposed of. Vasiliev had become greedy and wanted it all for himself. He had to disappear, make his boss think that he was dead.

"Yelena."

"What is it Aleksei?"

"There's some serious shit going down and I need to ask you a favour."

"Of course darling, what is it?"

"I need you to be a witness to my death."

"What?"

"It's either that or die for real."

"I don't understand."

"De Luca is dead, Moretti is next and you can guarantee that I will be the third."

"But why, you are not them!"

"True, but I have been associated with them for many years and whatever they have been up to will also fall at my door."

"So, what are we going to do about it?"

"Fake my own death."

"What, are you crazy?"

"I'm perfectly serious, once the heat dies down you can come and meet me, we'll get away from this life once and for all." Finally he had found a way out, it wasn't quite the way he had imagined but, still, it was happening and that's all that mattered to him.

"How are we going to do it?" Yelena loved her life and there was no way she was leaving it no matter what her husband said.

"One of the boats, some kind of explosion."

"What about the body?"

"I was thinking about that guy who is homeless, you know Nikolai."

"Yes, I think it might work."

"All you have to do Yelena is give him a bottle of wine, one filled with sedatives, once he is out of it, we'll get him onto the boat. I'll steer it out onto the lake and set a bomb, once I'm far enough away I'll trigger it."

"Where will you go?"

"My darling, don't worry I will not be far away, here." He passed her a mobile phone.

"What's this for?"

"So we can keep in touch with each other, we don't want anyone to rumble me, now can you do it?"

"Of course."

"Good, that's settled then."

Chapter One Hundred and Nine

Rosa woke up in a dark room, her head was throbbing. As she touched her head she winced, that man had nearly killed her. She scanned the room, looking for an escape route, but there were no windows. Suddenly the lights were switched on and she hugged her knees to her chest not knowing what was about to happen.

As her eyes adjusted to the light she gasped in fright. "You…" Her voice broke off. She would never forget what that sadistic man had done to her.

"Yes, it is me, how have you been, Rosa?" Vasiliev smiled, one of his cruel little smiles which sent shivers down her spine.

"I spit on you." Rosa spat onto the floor.

"Now, now that is no way to speak."

"Do your worst you pig."

"I am offended." He walked towards her and laughed when she cowered in the corner. "I have no intention of harming you in any way." As he got nearer he noticed her bloodied face. He reached over and touched the blood. "What is this?"

"Your men rough handling me, fucking scum!" Her voice was full of venom.

"It won't be long now."

"What won't be?"

"Dante, as soon as he gets here I will let you go."

Rosa was gasping for breath. "What has my brother got to do with this?"

"Don't you know?" He smirked. "He is in the same business as me." He threw the inhaler at her. "Looks like you may need this."

"No, I don't believe you, you're lying." Rosa sucked deeply on the inhaler, terrified of what he was going to do.

"Believe what you like."

"No, he would never hurt women, he isn't like that!"

"What can I say? He went to Sicily and came back a changed man, he is just as bad as me."

"Nobody could be as bad as you."

Vasiliev banged on the door. "Bring it in."

Rosa watched in silence as a television and DVD player were brought into the room.

"I will show you what Dante is capable of." He played the DVD.

Rosa put her hand to her mouth and gasped. It was Yakov Garshin and her brother, they were fighting, she turned her head the other way.

Vasiliev got hold of her face and made her watch until the end. "See what he did for you?"

Suddenly she felt sick, as she started to gag Vasiliev pushed her away from him. Unable to hold back any longer she threw up in the corner.

"Christ you have a weak stomach!" He threw a cloth at her. "Get yourself cleaned up." And with that he turned on his heel and left her alone.

Dante had murdered Garshin in revenge, that was all she told herself. But the scary thing was that her brother actually looked like he enjoyed every minute of it. Holding her stomach she felt the bile rise once more, as she spewed her guts up the tears flowed. Her brother was somehow involved in the trafficking of women – how could he, especially after he knew what had happened to his own sister?

Chapter One Hundred and Ten

Lake Garda, Italy

"I'm so glad that you came." Grazia embraced Ella. "We have both lost loved ones."

Ella went into the house. "There's something very wrong here, I want to know what they were involved in."

"I don't know what you mean."

"Please don't treat me like a complete idiot."

"I know that Nico was involved in a few dodgy dealings but I don't know any of the details."

"Oh, please." Ella was exasperated. "Surely you must have talked about it."

"No, the truth is I didn't want to know and he respected me for that."

The women were interrupted by the loud ring of the telephone. "Hello."

"It's me, Aleksei is dead."

"Oh, my God, what happened?"

"Some kind of boating accident." She paused. "I don't know who to trust and I afraid that something will happen to me too," Yelena cried.

"Why don't you get the next flight over? Ella is here too. It seems that we have all lost our husbands."

Yelena looked at Vasiliev and he nodded at her. "Very well, I'll make the arrangements."

"What is it?" Ella asked her.

"Yelena's husband has died in some kind of boating accident, but I don't believe that for one minute, he was an excellent seaman."

Ella closed her eyes and hoped that when she opened them again everything would be as it should be.

"I think we should get some rest and talk tomorrow when Yelena arrives," Grazia told her. "Come on."

Ella followed her to the guest room, her mind flashed back to the last time she was here with Dante. Suddenly and without warning her emotions overwhelmed her and she sobbed uncontrollably.

"My dear, dear, Ella." Grazia hugged her as the tears welled up in her eyes. "I know exactly how you feel."

Grazia decided to have a nightcap, she went to the bedside cabinet and took out a bottle of whisky, behind it she found an envelope with her name on it.

If you find this then I am almost certainly dead. Go to the office and in the safe is my diary, it will tell you everything you need to know. I will always love you, just try to be happy, one day we will meet again my love,
 ciao,
 Nico x.

She poured the whisky with a shaking hand, nearly spilling it everywhere. Gulping it down she read the note one more time. So he had been murdered, yet the police said both Nico and Marcus had killed each other. The one thing that connected them was the car business and the office in Milan was the key to finding the answer.

Tomorrow she would go and find out exactly what was in her husband's diary and then and only then would she be able to rest. The truth was of the utmost importance to her, no matter how terrible it was.

Chapter One Hundred and Eleven

Present Day

Yelena started up the engine. "So, what exactly is the plan?"

Ella stared into space out across the crystal-blue waters wishing she could turn back time, back to when everything was so simple. Poor Grazia had been shot to death and she couldn't get the image of her bloodied body out of her head.

"Ella?"

"What did you say?"

"Where to?"

"I don't know, just get out of here, anywhere as long as it's as far away from the villa as possible."

Yelena put the boat into gear and gently steered out onto the lake. She needed to know what Ella was up to, who this person was that was going to help them. Was she supposed to wait until it was too late to do anything? If so, then perhaps she would end up dead too.

"You seem to handle it pretty well, for a novice," Ella noted.

"I forgot to say I have been taking lessons for a while now," Yelena snapped at her.

"I see." Ella badly wanted to ring Dante, tell him to hurry up before it was too late. Her stomach was in knots and she had a gut feeling something terrible was about to happen.

Yelena glanced at her. "So, are you going to tell me who you called?"

"I'm sorry I can't do that, it's better that you don't know." Ella wondered why she was so suspicious.

"This is my life too you are talking about."

"Yes I know." Ella was still reeling from Grazia's brutal murder.

"So, these people that want this disk, what do you think is on it?"

"I have no idea, but one thing I do know is that it connects all of us in some way, and we have to think hard what that is if we're to have any chance of coming out of this unscathed."

Yelena looked at her and nodded her head in agreement. "I'm going to see what supplies we have on board." Ella disappeared into the galley.

Once Yelena was sure she was out of the way she got on her mobile phone. "It's me."

"Thank God you are safe my darling it won't be long now, did you get it?"

"No, not yet, I'm not even sure if Grazia got it, we didn't find anything in her bag."

"Yelena, time is of the essence. We must find it first."

"Who else is after it?"

"Vasiliev and Moretti, but honey this is our ticket out of here, it's our safety net."

Yelena's heart skipped a beat. The reputation of those two men frightened her, she knew what they were both capable of. She just hoped that if they caught up with her first then it would be a quick death just like Grazia's. But she knew too much and if they knew Aleksei had faked his own death and was still alive they would almost certainly torture her. "What do you want me to do?"

"Get rid of Ella, if she contacted Moretti he could be coming for her. Do it now Yelena."

Yelena shut the phone as she nodded to herself, what was she going to do? She didn't have a weapon of any sort and she was becoming frantic. She spotted the fire extinguisher. Turning off the engine, she reached for it and made towards the lower deck.

Ella sat at the table and proceeded to empty Grazia's bag, there had to be something here, why else kill her? Slowly she sifted through the items: nothing, absolutely nothing. Rubbing her eyes she picked up Grazia's compact and opened it; a piece of paper fell out. Her heart was pounding as she opened it up, inside was a carefully folded piece of paper. Holding it up to the light she tried to read the scrawled writing, she couldn't quite make it out. She strained her eyes: *Dante will help you; he knows the importance of the names contained on the disk, that's if it still exists.* What the hell did that mean? Her head was spinning, what was going on? Was her husband somehow mixed up in it and is that why he was murdered? What about the others, what was the connection between the men, the motor business it had to be, but what was it that they deserved to be murdered for? Before she had time to make sense of it she felt a sharp blow to the back of her head and fell to the ground.

Yelena was picked up by another boat, one that had her husband on it. She threw herself into his arms. "Oh Aleksei, I have missed you so much." Touching his face she tenderly kissed him.

"Did you get it?"

Opening her bag Yelena produced the piece of paper. "Yes, look," she said as she passed the note to him. "Dante must have it, and he is sending someone for Ella, all we have to do is wait," she said triumphantly as she reached for the gun in his holster.

He lifted her off the ground and swung her around. "You are the best, Yelena." As he put his arms around her he felt something cold and hard on his chest.

"Move back, Aleksei."

Aleksei took a step back. "Is this some kind of fucking joke?" he asked incredulously. "You said it yourself, we get to Dante and get the disk then we will have all the power, Yelena tell me your not serious, you love me."

Yelena shook her head. "I am afraid that I am totally serious, you should have just stayed dead."

"What, has someone threatened you, offered you money, tell me, what?"

Yelena laughed. "No, nothing like that, I am in love with Vasiliev."

"This is some kind of sick joke, you are fucking kidding right, tell me this is not true!" Aleksei could hardly breathe. "I love you."

"I am sorry really I am," Yelena said as she shot him in the chest.

Aleksei's expression was one of total disbelief as he dropped to the ground, it was over in seconds. Yelena signalled to one of the minders. "Dispose of the body, wrap it in a blanket or something and use some weights to make it sink to the bottom of this goddamn lake." She had been in Vasiliev's pay for some time and poor, dumb Aleksei had no idea, faking his death had been a godsend. Now she was going to get to the disk first and screw Vasiliev – he was just a means to an end, that was all. She was going to be rich beyond her wildest dreams; all she had to do was get to Dante and retrieve it. Nobody else knew where it was and once she got her hands on it she could use it anywhere in the world, somewhere safe. It was time to put all her planning into action and with her other lover on board it would be easy. He was her bodyguard and would do anything for her and, now he was about to prove exactly how loyal he was.

Ella was unconscious in a pool of blood when Flavio found her. "Boss, Yelena Petrov has gone."

"And Ella?"

"She has taken a nasty blow to the head."

"Will she be ok?" Dante demanded. He didn't want to lose her, not now, not ever again.

"Yes, she will be fine."

"Bring her to me."

"Very well."

Dante's life was on the line and if he didn't get to the disk before Vasiliev then he had no bargaining chips. Just for a split second he wanted to take Ella and flee the country, go somewhere far away where they would never be found. But too many people were tightening the screws and it was only a matter of time before they caught up with him. Whatever he did now wasn't to save his own skin, it was for Rosa and it was for Ella, the only two people in the entire world that he ever cared for. So, if his time was up then all he could ask for was justice to be finally done and for his beautiful Ella to be left alone to live the rest of her life happy and free. Right now he had to focus on saving his sister, and the only way to do that was to find the disk and do the exchange.

Ella came round and was frightened when she saw the man towering over her. "Don't worry *Bella* Ella, I am Flavio. I work for Dante, are you alright?"

"What happened?"

"Yelena Petrov is what happened. Now we must get out of here." He helped her to her feet.

Ella felt sick, her head was throbbing. "I don't understand."

"It's a long story, Dante will explain everything." He paused. "Do you know where the disk is?"

"What is on this disk that everybody wants so badly?"

"Names."

Ella's legs were shaking. "Oh, I don't feel very well."

Flavio caught her. "It's going to be ok, come on." He steered the boat into the jetty and half carried her off the boat.

Yelena smiled. "Good, they're going to Dante." She had to make sure that she was the one to get the disk, no matter what.

Flavio drove up to the house and helped Ella out of the car. "Come, he's waiting for you."

As Ella walked into the house her heart skipped a beat when she saw her ex-husband.

"Oh my God, what did that bitch do to you?" He put his arm around her and guided her into the lounge.

"Dante, what is going on?"

"My sister has been kidnapped and Giorgino is dead, if I do not give them the disk then they will kill her."

"Rosa, who's got her?"

"A Russian man by the name of Pavel Vasiliev, but everything is going to be all right now, I promise you."

Flavio passed the handbag to her, as she reached for it she missed it and all the contents spilled out all over the carpet.

"Here, allow me." Dante knelt down and started picking everything up. As he shoved them back into the bag something caught his eye. Pulling back the inside zip, he pulled out the disk. "Jesus, you had it all the time." He kissed her on the cheek.

"But, I've never seen it before in my life."

"Perhaps Marcus put it there."

"Marcus, so he knew about it too?"

"That's probably why he was killed."

"Let me see it!" she demanded. "If my husband was murdered for this I want to know what's on it."

Dante ignored her and put it into his laptop. Quickly he deleted his name and Nico's.

"What are you doing?"

"Nothing, just checking it."

"I think we should call the police, this is evidence," she told him.

"No, no police, Rosa will die if I involve them. Right now I have to go to Russia."

"Then I'm coming with you," Ella insisted.

"I can't allow that, it is better and safer if you stay here."

"You forget how many people have died because of this. I have to see this through to the very end and I'm not taking no for an answer."

"Very well, now I suggest you get some sleep, the flights are early tomorrow morning."

Ella got to her feet. "So, if you give this man the disk he will let Rosa go?"

"Yes." But Dante knew that there was no chance of that, once Vasiliev got the disk they would both be history.

"Give me the disk."

Dante hesitated.

"It was entrusted to me after all." She held out her hand.

He ejected it and passed it to her. "I trust you."

"It's a shame that I don't trust you!" she snapped.

Dante shrugged. "I'm sorry you feel like that."

Ella left the room and picked one of the guest rooms to stay in. After a long soak in the bath she dried her hair and slipped in between the bed covers. She carefully placed the disk under the pillow and closed her eyes.

Yelena waited patiently until she saw Dante's bedroom light go out. She crept around the back of the building and ordered her sidekick to prise the conservatory door open.

Suddenly all the lights came on. "Fuck it," Yelena gasped as she saw the gun pointing at her.

"Both of you get your hands up!" Flavio ordered.

"Wait, we can do a deal can't we?" Yelena batted her eyelids.

"That doesn't work on me love. I wouldn't touch you with a barge pole!"

"How fucking dare you!" she shrieked.

They were startled by Ella, who had come downstairs for a glass of water. "What's going on?"

The Russian man lunged at Flavio and the gun went off straight into his chest. Ella screamed, wakening Dante. Jumping to his feet he grabbed his gun and raced down the stairs. He was greeted by Yelena holding a gun to Ella's head.

"I want the disk," she ordered. "Or I'll kill Ella."

"Perhaps we can do a deal?"

"With you, you must be fucking kidding right?" Yelena laughed. "As I see it, I am the one holding all the cards." She pressed the gun hard into Ella's head.

"Please, Dante, just give her it." Ella was trembling.

"Yes, Dante, listen to Ella."

Dante lowered the gun. "Where is it?"

"Under my pillow."

Yelena laughed. "Do you think that I am fucking stupid? You go with him," she told the Russian.

"Leave the gun here!"

Dante walked slowly up the stairs and into the guest room; pulling back the covers he found the disk. Turning around he head-butted the man which sent him reeling across the room. He grabbed the gun and bashed it over his head until he was sure that he was dead. Now all he had to do was dispose of Yelena Petrov.

Climbing out of the window he made his way around the back of the house.

"So, you think you know Dante?" Yelena laughed. "He is just like me, a cold-blooded killer and he loves it!"

"I don't believe you."

"Oh, the things he has done. That man that he murdered when you were staying at my house," she mocked. "The look in his eyes, was one of pure lust. You see, he gets off on making people suffer."

Ella put her hands over her ears. "I'm not listening to any of your poison."

Yelena shoved her into the chair. "You know what; you are one pathetic sad fucking bitch!"

"Thank God I am not you, how could you pretend to be someone that you are not, I feel sorry for your husband!"

"Oh, don't feel sorry for my husband, darling," Yelena purred as she held the gun to her temple.

Ella didn't like the tone of her voice. "What do you mean?"

Yelena turned to the opposite direction. "Stupid, stupid, Aleksei, you see love never meant anything to me and probably never will."

Taking the opportunity Dante fired a bullet into her head.

Ella screamed as she landed on her, covering her in blood. "Get her off me!"

Dante pulled Yelena's body off her and threw her to the ground. "Are you alright?" He looked into Ella's eyes.

But Ella was so traumatised that she couldn't speak.

"Ella." Dante roughly shook her by her shoulders.

"W... what?"

"Come on, you need to get cleaned up." He rang Carmine to dispose of the bodies.

Chapter One Hundred and Twelve

Moscow, Russia

Vasiliev unlocked the padlock and pulled back the wrought-iron bolt, allowing daylight to flood the warehouse.

Rosa rubbed her eyes. The bastard had left her locked up all night, in this freezing ice block with no food and no blanket, he was a fucking sadist.

"Good morning." He laughed as he looked at her dishevelled appearance. "Not so pretty this morning, eh?"

Rosa ignored him; she wasn't going to give him the satisfaction of humiliating her anymore. Glancing around the room she looked for some kind of weapon.

"I hoped you enjoyed the video."

"I'm glad Garshin's dead if that's what you mean!"

"My, my, so you are a Moretti after all, like brother like sister," he mocked her.

"What do you want?"

"Now, now, that is no way to talk to your captor you should be nice to me."

"I thought Dante was coming."

"Patience, he will be here soon enough, in the meantime you are coming with me."

"I think I would rather wait here!"

"You must be cleaned up; you wouldn't want your brother to see you like this surely?"

"I don't really give a damn what I look like you murdering fuck!"

"Still full of bravado I see." He waved to the two men behind him. "Put her in the van, and boys, do be gentle with her."

Rosa knew that if she went with them she was a dead woman and she didn't want to die just yet. The thing uppermost in her mind was to finally destroy Vasiliev and his bunch of goddamn evil sidekicks. As they bundled her into the van she struggled to break free.

"There is nowhere to run," one of the men told her.

Reluctantly Rosa did as she was told; he got into the back with her and played with his Kalashnikov. "This can do an awful lot of damage, especially at close range." He aimed it at her. "Just one pull of the trigger and your brains will be splattered everywhere."

"Vasiliev told you not to harm me."

"I can do what ever I like." He licked his lips. "You see, I too am very powerful." He pushed the barrel of the gun towards her and brushed her hair from her face. Slowly he ran cold metal down the side of her body and settled on her breast. "Very nice."

"Hey what the fuck are you doing?" the other Russian shouted from the front of the van. "Get off her."

"Oh come on, she's damaged goods anyway, what harm will it do. Why don't you pull over and we can have a bit of fun?" He laughed.

"What about Vasiliev?"

"Do you want to fuck Moretti's sister or not?"

"Wait until I find somewhere quieter."

But he couldn't wait any longer and yanked Rosa off the seat. Yanking down his trousers he frantically tried to force her down onto him.

"Wait... what is the hurry? Don't you want to do this properly?" She asked in the most gentle voice he had ever heard.

"Now, you understand."

"Why don't you unfasten my hands?" She smiled sweetly.

Without hesitation he pulled the knife out of his inside pocket and cut the rope.

"What the fuck are you doing?"

But he ignored his comrade and continued to become aroused; he couldn't wait to feel her warm, sensuous mouth around his hard member.

As Rosa bent down her head she looked up and smiled at him, and suddenly without warning she sank her teeth into his erect penis and bit down on it as hard as she could. The man screamed and fell back onto the floor.

"What the fuck?" The driver swerved across the road.

Rosa picked up the Kalashnikov. "You know just one pull of this trigger and your brains will be splattered everywhere."

She released the safety catch and closed her eyes. The force of the shot sent her reeling towards the back of the van.

The sound had practically deafened her. When she opened her eyes, blood and gore were spattered everywhere and she was covered in the remains of the fucker's face, which no longer existed.

Picking up the gun she pointed it at the driver. "Fucking pull over right now!"

"Ok, ok!" He looked through the rear-view mirror, Rosa Moretti looked like a mad woman, like something off a horror movie. She almost looked demented and had a wild look in her eyes. He had seen that look before, and realised that it was Dante, when he had disposed of Yakov Garshin. "Look... look I don't want no trouble; I'll do whatever you ask."

"Do you have a mobile?"

"Yes, yes."

"Give me it."

He leaned over the seat and passed it to her.

"Now pull over, turn down that dirt track road," she ordered as she flipped open the phone and rang Dante, but it went straight onto the answer machine. She kept the gun aimed at the driver and glanced back and forth as she began to speak into the phone.

"It's me, don't go to the warehouse it's a trap, and whatever you do, do not hand over the disk." Quickly she snapped the phone shut. "Get out of the van and put your hands on your head... and do it slowly."

Climbing over the seat she kept the gun aimed at him. "Get that filth out of the back!" she yelled.

As he walked in front of her he decided evasive action was the only answer. In a split second he turned around and made a lunge for her. But Rosa reacted like lightning and shot him dead. "Fucking Russians!" She spat on him.

She opened the van door. It looked like she had to do this on her own. Grabbing his legs she dragged the headless corpse out of the back. He was much heavier than she expected and it took all of her strength to pull him out. Feeling a little dizzy she sat on the edge of the van and took a deep breath to steady herself. When she had regained her composure she slammed the doors shut. Walking past the dead men she shuddered, barely able to believe that she was capable of doing something so horrendous.

As she got into the driver's seat she looked in the glove box, there was a bottle of water and a cloth. Pouring the water onto it she looked in the mirror and quickly scrubbed the blood off her face.

She felt good, the best she had felt for years and it shocked her that she could kill two men so easily. Starting up the engine she turned the van around and headed back towards the warehouse. She would wait until it was dark and then kill Vasiliev. If it was to be the last thing she ever did on this earth, it would be worth it.

*****

It was six thirty and Dante was ready to meet his fate, whatever that would be. "If I'm not back in two hours there is a flight to London at ten thirty, be on it!" he told Ella.

"But this is insane."

"Carmine will stay with you."

Carmine nodded. "Don't worry she will be safe with me."

"You're not going alone?"

"I never go anywhere alone," he reassured her.

Ella flung her arms around him. "You will come back to me, won't you?"

"Of course I will, you know my heart and soul belongs to you, they always have and always will," he told her as he gently stroked her cheek.

Without thinking about it Ella kissed him. "I still love you," she whispered in his ear.

A tear came into Dante's eye. *Now she tells him just when he had accepted he would not be returning but now he had something to live for!*

They were interrupted by Dante's phone bleeping. "It's a message." He played back the answer machine, it was Rosa, she was still alive. Checking the time she rang, it was over an hour ago, he wasn't sure if that was a good sign or a bad one.

He pressed ring back. "Rosa?" He held his breath and felt totally relieved when he heard his sister's voice. "Thank God, where are you?"

"I am very close to the warehouse, where are you?"

"I'm on my way, don't do anything until I get there, promise me!"

"I promise!" But Rosa did the sign of the cross, if she got the opportunity to kill Vasiliev then that was what she intended to do.

"Good, now stay put, I have some of my men in the area."

Dante got into his hire car and rang his contact in Interpol. "The meeting is set for ten thirty tonight." He flipped his phone shut, that should give them enough time to be in and out and on the flight to London.

Rosa jumped when the mobile phone rang, picking it up she pressed it to her ear and waited for someone to speak.

"Very clever, very clever indeed," Vasiliev laughed. "Perhaps you would like to come and work for me as an assassin?"

"Fuck you!" Rosa screamed as she threw the phone down. She grabbed her inhaler but it was empty.

Within minutes she was surrounded by armed men. "Get out of the van."

Her heart skipped a beat and she reached for the gun.

"Throw the gun out in front of you and come out with your hands up."

She slipped the mobile into her jeans pocket and slowly opened the door. Gently she dropped the gun onto the ground. There was no way she was letting these Russian animals near her. Ramming the vehicle into reverse she slammed into the men behind her. "Eat shit, you fuckers," she gasped.

As she careered down the hill she spun the van around and headed full speed towards the warehouse.

The shots rang out as they aimed for the wheels and Rosa lost control. Putting her hands to her face she screamed as the van hurtled towards the compound.

Vasiliev cursed, he didn't have time to do anything to stop the impending collision. Damn it he had wanted her alive. Now he had nothing to bargain with, that was until he heard that Ella

Treymayne was in the country. No matter, that was even better. He peered through the binoculars as he watched the huge explosion, which took out at least a dozen of his men and set fire to the warehouse. "Move out!" he spoke into the walkie-talkie. "There's nothing left for us to do here."

*****

Ella was pacing the floor, beside herself with worry.

"Can you stop doing that?" Flavio asked. "No offence but you are doing my nut in!"

"Sorry, I'm just worried sick."

Just then the door to the hotel room flung open. "Get your fucking hands up, now!" Vasiliev barked.

Ella was frozen to the spot.

"Do as he says," Flavio told her.

"Yes, do as Flavio says!"

Ella put her hands up. "Who are you?" She cringed at the man with the eyepatch and distinctive neck scar.

"I am Pavel Vasiliev and you, Ella Reynolds, I finally get to meet, at long last. A pity it isn't under better circumstances."

"What have you done with Dante?" She demanded.

Vasiliev smirked. "You really are hung up on him and I do not understand why!"

"What about Rosa?" Flavio asked.

"I'm afraid that she is dead, poor, poor Rosa, it is such a shame, but she made her choice. Get them out of here!" he barked to his men.

"You can't do this!" Ella yelled. "Help, somebody please help!"

Vasiliev laughed. "Shout as much as you like, nobody is coming, I own everybody in Moscow, amongst many other places." He grabbed her by the arm. "Come."

They were handcuffed, blindfolded and shoved into the back of some kind of vehicle. Ella's heart was pounding, she had never felt so scared in all her life and Rosa, God bless her, was dead. The journey seemed to take forever and nobody spoke a word, the eerie silence chilled her to the very core of her being.

As the vehicle came to a halt they were bundled out and shoved into a room.

Vasiliev watched as the blindfolds were removed. "Welcome."

He walked towards Flavio. "Now, I would like you to make a call to Moretti."

*****

Dante saw the fireball from the hilltop and cursed, they were too late. He rang one of his men. "Where the fuck are you?"

"I'm sorry Dante but by the time we got here it was all over, and Vasiliev has gone."

"And Rosa?"

"Nowhere to be seen."

"Fucking drive down and obliterate anybody still left standing, I'll be there in a couple of minutes."

Dante's men proceeded to shoot on sight.

"Wait, wait." One of the Russians dropped to his knees and put his hands up. "I surrender, let me speak to Moretti, I have information."

"Stop!" Dante barked the order. "What information?"

"I am afraid to say that your sister is dead, she was in that van." He nodded at the burning vehicle.

"You're lying, you fucker!" Dante turned his back to him and put his hand to his face, after all this and she was dead! He turned back around. "Are you sure?"

"Yes."

Dante turned to one of his men. "Kill the fucker and let's get out of here!"

As he walked away his mobile rang. "Ella?"

"Yes, it's me."

She sounded so scared he thought. "Where are you?"

Vasiliev pulled the phone from her ear. "With me."

"You bastard, you better hadn't hurt her or I swear I'll fucking kill you!"

"It's such a shame about Rosa!" he tutted. "So headstrong, so very much like you," he taunted.

"Just tell me where the fuck you are!"

"At my house, do come over." He paused. "And Dante...? Bring the disk and the exchange will still go ahead." He threw the phone onto the ground and stamped on it. "Don't even think about trying anything Flavio, the house is well protected and you won't get very far, I can assure you."

After they were left alone Flavio turned to Ella. "Don't worry if anyone can get us out of here, Dante can."

"I still can't get my head around this, it's like some kind of a nightmare, I didn't think men like that really existed," she whispered, shuddering as she visualised his scarred face.

*****

The first thing Dante did was to destroy the disk, there was no way he was even contemplating handing it over to that fucking animal, not now, not ever.

Once more his mobile started to ring. "Yes!" he barked down the phone.

"What's going on Moretti? I hope you aren't thinking of leaving us out of the picture, we've just been to the warehouse and there's a lot of carnage down here, where are you?"

Dante didn't need this; he got his mobile and hurled it as far away as he could. He summoned his men and gave the orders.

"Ok, this is the plan," he began.

*****

Vasiliev was sitting in his warm office smoking a cigar when he saw Moretti pull into the driveway. At fucking last, he was fed up with all this messing around, finally the disk was his. He put out his cigarette and got to his feet to go and welcome him for one last time.

The boot of Dante's car was full of grenades and all he had to do was drive it as close to the house as possible and his men would shoot at it. Bracing himself he got out and allowed himself to be searched by one of Vasiliev's men.

"Finally." Vasiliev stood in the doorway and smiled at him. "Do come in, I have been waiting some time and you know that I do not like to be kept waiting!"

Dante walked towards him and held out his hand.

"What is this?"

"For old time's sake."

Vasiliev was a little surprised by his offer of a handshake. Just before they touched hands Dante's men started lobbing grenades and Vasiliev fell backwards into the house. The car was taken out in seconds causing a huge explosion which rocked the entire building.

*****

"What the hell is going on?" Ella trembled. "It feels like some kind of earthquake."

"It's Dante." Flavio smiled. "I knew he would come."

Just then the door burst open. "Get on your feet!"

Both of them obeyed, petrified that they were going to be shot there and then. "I work for Interpol, I don't have much time." He pulled the key out of his pocket and began to take off Flavio's handcuffs. "Here." He passed the key to him. "Get out of here if you can, because all hell has broken loose!"

"What about Dante?" Ella asked her voice full of concern.

"I'm not sure."

"We can't leave without him," Ella told Flavio. "Please, don't leave him with that madman!"

"Very well." Flavio was loyal to his boss and he would do all he could to ensure he survived this. "Let's go."

"Here," the man passed Flavio a gun.

*****

Vasiliev was pinned down by Dante with such force that he could barely breathe. Reaching into his pocket he pulled out a small blade and shoved it deep into his side. Dante gasped and rolled off him.

"You can't take me out you stupid fucker!" Vasiliev raged.

Dante mustered up all his strength. "Remember this!" He pulled the knuckleduster out of a hidden pocket and put it on.

Vasiliev roared with laughter. "Come on then give it your fucking best shot."

Both men were completely oblivious to the gun shots and screams all around them as they faced off to each other.

Dante lunged towards him and Vasiliev easily moved out of the way.

"You're dying you dumb fuck just give it up!"

Scrambling back to his feet Dante ran at him again, only this time Vasiliev fell backwards onto a glass table. Grabbing him by the lapels Dante pulled him up. "Fight me like a fucking man!" he raged.

Vasliev was stunned and unsteady on his feet, the glass had pierced the back of his neck and the blood was spurting everywhere. Dante immediately let go of him and threw the knuckleduster next to him.

He watched as Vasiliev put his hand on his neck and looked at the blood, he laughed a blood-curdling laugh. "It will take more than that to kill me!"

There was a single shot and in an instant Vasiliev dropped to the floor.

"Dante, Dante." Ella ran to him as he collapsed. "Oh, my God you have lost a lot of blood, Flavio we need to get him to a hospital and fast."

"No, no, no hospital!" Dante point-blank refused. "Is there another way out of here?"

"I don't think so," Flavio told him.

"Don't worry Interpol are here," Ella whispered as she cradled him in her arms, slowly feeling his life's blood slipping away. "Please don't die on me Dante, I need you."

Dante put his hand up to her face. "My, *Bella* Ella..." he gasped as he took his last breath.

"No, no, no, Dante... Dante!" she wailed.

Flavio check his pulse. "I'm sorry Ella, but he is dead."

"This is Interpol, the place is surrounded. Everybody drop your weapons, there is nowhere for you to run."

Nick Beaumont, the head of operations headed straight towards them. "Is he dead?"

Ella nodded as the tears streamed down her face.

"Come on, let's get you out of here." He gently moved Dante's body and wrapped a blanket around Ella Reynolds. "He helped us bring down an international sex-trafficking gang and without him we would never have been able to do that. He died saving thousands of women, you should be proud of him," he tried to comfort her.

But no words would be a comfort to her ever again.